Kathy Priddis is a writer who is
strongly influenced by her work as an
internationally-known portrait painter
and as a practising potter.

In each *genre* she seeks the story --
in portraiture, the story behind the face;
in pottery, the geological story of
the Herefordshire countryside where
she lives, and in her writing, the stories
created by the interaction of the central
characters with the world they inhabit.

Daughter of a German-Jewish refugee,
Kathy Priddis is married to a bishop in
the Church of England.
They have three children.

The Necklace is Kathy's second novel.
Her first novel, *Night Fires*, is a love story
set amidst the religious conflict of Nigeria,
and was published in 2009

*For images of her work see her
website* www.kathypriddis.co.uk

The Necklace

Kathy Priddis

 New Generation Publishing

To my mother, Maria Rotenberg

1912 – 1994

Had they deceived us
Or deceived themselves, the quiet-voiced elders,
Bequeathing us merely a receipt for deceit?
The serenity only a deliberate hebetude,
The wisdom only the knowledge of dead secrets
Useless in the darkness into which they peered
Or from which they turned their eyes.

There is, it seems to us,
At best, only a limited value
In the knowledge derived from experience.
The knowledge imposes a pattern, and falsifies,
For the pattern is new in every moment
And every moment is a new and shocking
Valuation of all we have been.

TS Eliot Four Quartets -- East Coker

PART 1

primary colours

Home is where one starts from...
old stones that cannot be deciphered.

TS Eliot Four Quartets -- East Coker

1

In later years Cat thought of her tenth birthday as the day her mother started to love her. As a small child she had leaned into the circle of her arms, felt the caress of her long, auburn hair on her face, and smelt the scent of her *eau de Cologne*. She remembered it clearly. It was a vivid, extremely sensual memory, so it must have been habitual, this reclining against Rute's body. But, even then, associated with it was a sense of unease; Rute's face, above her, was remote, as if she was thinking of something else. Or someone else. Maybe, once upon a time, there'd been a sister or brother for whom Rute was grieving, but whose death couldn't be mentioned and whose names she sometimes called her in her more absent minded moments, 'Leebling' or 'Leebchen'; foreign-sounding names which Cat had never encountered in school. But although Rute never laughed out loud Cat could remember how she looked when she smiled, how her face seemed to lighten as if from within, and she'd planted an apple tree in the garden so that Cat could have a swing.

These days Rute was awkward with her and undemonstrative; she rarely smiled, she rarely spoke and she rarely left the house. She would brush Cat away with a dismissive wave of her bony hand, like a pestering fly that had trespassed into her kitchen. 'Caterina, some of us do have work to do, you know! Oh, go up to your bedroom; read a book or something.' Something, *anything*, so long as Cat got out of the way. Her bedroom bookended her days; there she could be herself, and her mother rarely darkened the threshold.

Time might have levelled her accent, as sand is dragged smooth between two waves of the sea, but 'leave' was always 'leef', 'have' was always 'haf', 'work' always 'verk', and her speech was littered with German phrases. 'You *nervos machen* me,' was in regular use, as was *Gott willens*, usually when she doubted He would.

Their evening meal was the time when they might have shared the happenings of the day, but instead Rute presided over the table with monosyllabic indifference, broken only by her tired, inconsequential demands. 'Fetch down your washing if you have any'. Or 'Have you tidied your room this week?' Or 'Caterina, how many times I tell you, *don't* leave hairs in the basin!' Sometimes Cat would deliberately answer back. 'I'll do it later. And the hairs were probably yours.' Just to elicit a response, some emotional reaction. Yet when it came, when she saw the expression on her mother's face, she always regretted provoking her.

'You don't know how lucky you are, to...' but then Rute would break off, stifling the words with a weary throwaway gesture of her hands, as though nothing could possibly matter enough to argue about it. Especially, thought Cat, if it meant having a conversation.

'You always say that. So, how am I lucky?'

Rute had a necklace which she habitually wore, a long string of gold and silvers bars punctuated by delicately-moulded silver rosettes, and when she was distressed she'd reach for it, twisting it round and round her fingers, and looping it over her hands.

'Oh Caterina, please don't be rude to me.'

Yet she was a good mother, thought Cat; her clothes were always washed and ironed for her, her meals – concoctions of the cheapest ingredients from the corner shop, augmented by spices – cooked for her, the house kept clean. Unlike some of the other mothers she'd seen at the school gate, who she couldn't imagine doing anything of the sort. Why should she complain, when her own mother did everything necessary for her? She'd somehow stopped loving her; that's all.

So what had she done wrong? Why was she being punished in this way? What could she possibly have said or done to offend Rute so much that she seemed to actively dislike her? She searched her mind, but she knew it was nothing she had said or done. Her mother had no feelings, she thought angrily, either for her or anyone else. It wasn't asking much, was it – a bit of affection, to speak a gentle word here or there? It wasn't as if anything might be taken away from her if she did! She never hugged her or called her 'darling', as Cat had heard other mothers call their children – even those slatternly ones at the school gate called their kids 'dearie'. It was what Cat wanted, almost more than anything else, to be called 'darling', even in exasperation. 'Darling, I did ask you, fetch down your washing, would you?' That would do. Or, 'Darling, you said you'd tidy your room today, didn't you?' Which would also do. Then she could respond, call her 'darling' back – oh, how she would love her! How, knowing she was loved, she would make her mother feel loved! She could ask her, then. 'Ma, darling...' she would say – and then all her questions could come pouring out; they'd sit close together again, Rute's long auburn hair gentling her face, and she'd lay out the answers for her as someone might arrange food on a plate for her delectation.

She couldn't initiate it, 'darling' not being within her vocabulary; it had to come from Rute in order to be given back. Else, how false it would sound. 'OK, so what do you want now?' her mother might say with a dry laugh. Cat had heard that, too, in the street.

She had a whole list of things lined up to ask, if truth be told and if Rute had cared enough to answer her, such as why they lived the way they did, with no wider family or friends calling round, or why, when they went to the park or to the shops, they were always alone. Or why she had no father – which was the other thing she desperately wanted to happen, to be told where or why not. To have a father might be rather disconcerting – a man's presence in the bathroom, his socks, his crumpled newspaper, his smell; but not to have a father was equally disturbing; an unknown, father-shaped space, a father-shaped gap at Parent's Evenings. To love, and be beloved.

At the turn of the century High Wycombe had spread westwards along the main road, spawning innumerable rows of small, redbrick houses with roofs of grey slate, tucked into the valley, each terrace with its own central alleyway that led into the back garden. Years of coal fires had blackened the chimneys but on Monday mornings the women still strode out along their cinder paths to hang out their washing between the now dilapidated wooden fences, where it hung limp and lifeless, spotted with smuts of ash. It often came in as damp as it went out.

Nine year old Cat and her mother had an end of terrace house in Green Street next to a derelict plot of land. It was hardly more than a confusion of nettles and brambles surrounded by dilapidated chain-link fencing, but from Cat's bedroom window it gave the illusion of space and privacy. Their immediate neighbours were an extended Bangladeshi family whose shrill, guttural squabbling was clearly audible through the thin walls – unlike their own house, which Cat often thought might have been empty for all the noise they made, as though no one had ever lived there and never would. Such was the silence that she and her mother made together.

It was such a vivid picture that she sometimes dreamt of it, might even have painted it, a vision of empty rooms slowly growing old all by themselves with nobody to see. In school they were reading *Great Expectations,* but she could hardly compare her obsessively clean mother with Miss Haversham, that garrulous, dusty old women who so tormented Pip, although the sense of unanswered questions was like. In place of Miss Haversham's cobwebs and that musty smell of age and decrepitude which hung around her, was Rute's sparkling kitchen and the pervasive aroma of her newly baked bread. Yet Miss Haversham and Pip *talked* to each other; it was their conversations that sustained them while, in the still, quiet atmosphere of Cat's home, uncontaminated by discourse, she sometimes struggled hard to find any indication of her own existence. It wasn't until the eve of her tenth birthday that she finally plucked up the courage to face her mother with it.

For once Rute had accepted her help in the kitchen and as they cleared up the meal her expression seemed softer, less remote. She was paler than usual, but occasionally Cat was conscious of her eyes on her, that sometimes her mouth opened as if to speak. She felt her whole being come alert. Her mother was going to say something to her; she was about to tell her really significant things; perhaps, at last, she was going to answer, in one fell swoop, the questions which had been piling up inside her since she was small. Cat felt her eyes widening with expectation, and put an encouraging smile on her lips.

'You want to say something, Ma?' Quickly she looked away, simulating indifference, and then glanced back again. 'What were you going to say to me?'

Rute arched her eyebrows, and her mouth twisted. 'Say? What could I possibly want to say?' She picked up the dirty plates, piled them in the stone sink and left the room.

Cat sat very still over the crumbs; she had that familiar resigned, leaden feeling in her stomach which usually came after disappointment. Always that dismissive wave of the hand, and the turning away! But then she rebelled; it was too much; she would face her with it now. She scraped back her chair on the lino and followed her mother out of the room.

Rute had switched on her desk lamp and was picking up her sewing.

'Ma, you *were* going to say something, weren't you?'

Rute sighed. 'Oh, Caterina, was I? Perhaps, though I can't think what it was now. Did you finish the washing up?'

Cat looked at her mulishly, and then she took the opposite chair and sat down. She sat on the very edge of it, so that if her mother moved she might spring up and stop her. Rute's face, as she bent over her sewing, was screened by her hair, its warm auburn lit to bronze by the harsh light from the lamp. Her fingers were busily threading her needle.

Cat let the silence fall, then she said, 'Ma, why don't we ever go out? I mean, other people have family, people they go and see... Why don't we? They just get on a bus or a train or something. I've never been on a train. Couldn't we do that, sometime?'

So that I don't get teased all the time for not knowing things, she thought, and before I'm too old to enjoy it. She hated herself, whining about journeys when it was the other things she needed to know, but it was too oblique an approach and Rute reacted sharply. Her mouth dropped open and her eyes flashed with anger and incredulity.

'How can you say that? Why, only last weekend...'

'Yes, we went to the park. Again. That's all we've ever done and it's *boring*. And it's not as if you've ever play with me when we get there! You've never played with me. Other people's mothers do. We never do anything together.' Tears of frustration pricked her eyes. 'We're just stuck at home all the time. I'm fed up with it!'

Rute pursed her lips. 'Anything else on your little list?'

'Well, like chatting together. Telling me things. You

16

never tell me anything. I'm nearly ten, Ma. I'm not a child anymore. I see what other kids do. I see them with their... fathers.'

Rute's face paled and she turned from her. 'Caterina, you can be very hurtful sometimes.' Deliberately, she wrapped up her sewing in its linen dustcover and stabbed the needle into it to seal it. Then she rose to her feet. 'Ach, Caterina, you *nervos machen* me; I am going from here.'

The door closed behind her and Cat heard her leaden tread on the stairs.

Cat had no recourse to another language, even that of rage. Her mother's mind was closed to her, as surely as the blank, uncommunicative door through which she went.

That night Cat dreamt that Rute started talking to her, really talking, and her ears yawned open to hear what she would say. But her words were as indecipherable as falling rain, a rain that suddenly became so thunderous that the rooms overflowed with it; sentences, whole speeches, a veritable deluge of explanations that dripped down the walls, leaked under the back door and then flowed milkily away down the garden path to splash against the back fence and form enormous muddy puddles of print, blurred and spiky. Like the spider she'd once seen caught up in the ice, which one day disappeared, as if it had formed the letters together and read 'thaw'. And no one any the wiser, least of all her.

It was a recurring dream, and sometimes, when she woke, the sheet under her was wet.

2

It was a pity that her birthday fell on a school day. Nevertheless, lying in bed Cat felt a frisson of excitement at the thought that maybe, just maybe, there was a present waiting for her downstairs. On the other hand Rute might react as she did last year and give an exasperated sigh and say she couldn't afford anything. But surely something could be saved for birthdays.

Through the window she could see her mother hanging out the washing, wrestling the damp sheets on to the line which bounced with their weight. Her old swing was there, hanging crookedly from the apple tree, and below was a patch of bare soil where her feet had scuffed the grass.

Cat dressed quickly. She covered her bed, trusting that the damp patch would be dry by nightfall, and went downstairs. The morning was already warm, the back door wide open, and she could hear the mutter of next door's radio. As usual the house smelt of the ash of the coal fire which Rute damped down each evening to save the embers, but there was also a smell of yeast, and she saw that on the side was a large steen of rising dough covered in a tea towel. She waited as long as she dared, watching the clock, then she fetched her packed lunch from the larder, picked up her satchel and trailed miserably down the narrow hallway to the front door.

Rute came after her just as she was leaving. 'You've got your lunch? Come straight home today, Caterina. Don't play around after school.' She made no mention of Cat's birthday.

'Ma, I always come straight home.'

She had no alternative; the others never invited her to skip with them, play handstands or hopscotch, or kick a ball around with them, or to huddle with them in playground cliques, mocking the dinner ladies behind their hands. Occasionally she put herself forward and joined in with their *Piggy in the Middle*, but they always threw the ball well beyond her reach and she was left dodging helplessly from side to side, smiling fatuously, as if she didn't mind. Or their spiteful arm-pinching, face-slapping form of tag, or their malicious hide and seek, when, facing some wall or other, she ended up shouting out 'ninety-nine-one *hundred*!' to an empty street. The trouble was, she didn't know how to behave with them, how to speak to them. She didn't know what was normal, though she craved it with all of her being.

She left for school feeling hurt and resentful. Other children walked the same route, up the hill to the Victorian buildings of the school. Few people had cars and, apart from an occasional Austin or a battered Ford Popular, there was little traffic. On one side of the road were the St Vincentians kids, heavy limbed and giggling, blouses already un-tucked; on the other side the slim, secretive Bangladeshi girls, their brothers walking behind, sternly protective. Cat walked in the gutter, head down to the broken kerbstones, kicking at the litter and scuffing her lace-up shoes against the pavement. The few white children who lived on her side of town ignored her and she made no attempt to catch up with them.

Somehow she got through the day. At playtime she hid in the toilets, a brick building at the edge of the playground, shady, now, and cool, and she returned there at lunchtime to eat her packed lunch. It was only corn beef, but her mother's homemade bread was solid and comforting. At close of school she made her way down the hill through the tangle of dirty streets towards their house in Green Street. The whole day was ruined and it was her mother's fault; to have forgotten her birthday seemed the last straw. But what was she to do with this straw except fly it in the wind, along with all the other stupid straws she'd thrown against the wind?

When she got home Rute was in the back room, and since the only predictable thing about her was her silence, Cat slid quietly up to her bedroom, took off her uniform and threw herself down on the bed. She woke clammy with sweat. It was half past six, time for supper.

Outside, she could hear children playing, although she wasn't sure whether the sound came from the street or from the playground beyond the houses. Their voices seemed louder in the evening, more raucous, as though they dreaded the loss of freedom that night would bring. She opened the window a crack and peeped out.

'Caterina, it's freezing in here. It's not healthy for you.' Rute was standing in the doorway, hugging her cardigan around her. Winter and summer she was always cold.

'Is it supper time?'

'Not yet. Put something on and come downstairs. It's warmer there. I've lit a fire.'

'Ma, it *is* July, for heaven's sake. And I haven't worn my blazer all day.'

'Caterina, don't argue with me, please. Just do as I say, and come down. Wash your hands first. And don't touch the walls — I am always wiping your finger marks. And close that window.' Her 'w's' transposed.

Perhaps she hadn't forgotten, after all, and with some anticipation Cat put a tee shirt over her panties and followed her mother down the narrow staircase. The back room was oppressively hot, the open door causing the smoke from the fire to waft inwards, blue and pungent. Rute had been sewing again, decorating cushion covers with a delicate pattern of unidentifiable flowers, and on the arm of her battered chair were small packets of silks like coloured water.

'Why've you drawn the curtains, Ma? It's still light

20

outside...'

'I have something to say to you...'

'I thought you had! Last night, I *said*...'

'Have you washed your hands?' Rute's lips tightened and her face took on the air of someone totally ground down by hardship. 'Caterina, why do you always ignore what I tell you? Oh, do it in the kitchen. And shut that door! The smoke...'

There was no sign of a meal being prepared, so Cat cut a thick slice of new bread and buttered it. She munched it, gazing around at the kitchen. Everything was clean and tidy, as though put away for the day. She thought, 'It's my birthday; I keep forgetting it's my birthday.' Her bread finished, she hurried back to her mother. Her resentment had evaporated. At last Rute was going to tell her things. She had been longing for this moment all her childhood, and now, when she least expected it, it had come.

Rute pushed her sewing aside and sat with her head bowed in thought, her face glowing rose in the firelight. Cat squatted on the carpet, watching her, and waiting for what she would say, but when Rute raised her head it was to speak, not of Cat or her birthday, but of herself.

She took a deep breath. 'I have to tell you some things. Things about me, about my life.'

She looked up, as if for approval, and Cat nodded.

'So, to start. I was born in 1926, in a small town in East Germany called Zwickau. My father was a Rabbi. His father was a Russian refugee from Vladivostok. My mother was a Polish refugee from... where, I never knew. I have this from her.' She patted her necklace. 'I am Jewish, Caterina. As you are, through the female line.'

Cat nodded again; the necklace was familiar, 'the female line' incomprehensible, but in school the next day 'Vladivostok' and 'Zwickau' rolled round her tongue with such relish that she was given a detention for swearing.

'My twin brother, Reuben, is your uncle. Hannah, my older sister, is your aunt.'

Cat's eyes lit up. We *do* have family! Where?'

Rute waved a dismissive hand. 'Israel, America, it doesn't matter. They are living; that's what matters. Don't interrupt.' Again she paused, her eyes inward, attentive to her memories. 'My father... my father was a man of generosity and wisdom.' This made him sound aloof, but no – 'He was greatly loved. They loved him for his care of them, and for the way he conducted the festivals. His favourite was *Simchat Torah* which comes after *Sukkot*....'

The unfamiliar terms rose in Cat's mind like rocks. 'Simkat..?'

Her mother made a guttural sound in her throat. 'Sim-*ch*at, Caterina, *Simchat Torah*.' She sighed. 'OK, I'll explain. It's a festival that celebrates the giving of the Law. My father, he takes out the scrolls from the Ark and then over all the heads they pass and everyone dances. A strange dance, with slow, shuffling steps, like this.' She walked her hands in the air, one in front of the other, her face radiant with memory. 'Imagine it, Caterina, a great crowd of men in gabardine coats and homburg hats sliding across the floor in waves. You can *feel* the joy – even in the gallery you feel it.' She frowned and passed her hand over her mouth. 'Not *Yom Kippur*. *Yom Kippur* comes earlier in the month and it's, how do you say? Melancholy. There's no food served, or even water. You cover your head and wail and you sing the *Kol Nidre*. That's a hymn; it asks to be forgiven all the careless promises you've made during the past year. To God, I mean. But *Pesach* – the smell of roasting lamb – that was something, I can tell you!'

It was a long speech, the longest Cat had ever heard her mother make, and she was surprised and gratified, but at this talk of food she shifted impatiently.

'Ma, are we eating tonight?'

'You had a bite, already. There are crumbs on your tee shirt. Oh, I'll make us a sandwich later.'

She carried on speaking as if there had been no interruption. She described Reuben's *bar mitzvah* when their mother wore a new red wig and a long-sleeved dress and she hinted at the envy she felt on his first day at *yeshiva*, about his new *yarmulke* and *tefillin*.

'That's when my piano lessons started. For English I had a governess but for piano my father sent me to Artur Schnabel.' She spoke the name with pride and a sideways, self-deprecating smile. 'He was staying in Zwickau and he was famous, even then. My father bought me a baby grand.' She smiled at Cat's bewilderment, but didn't elucidate. 'We were rich. We had servants for everything, cooking, cleaning, polishing... We had a tall townhouse with lofty rooms and huge mahogany furniture, curtains of damask, and astrakhan rugs...'

'Astrakhan?' Cat might have said 'damask' but she needed to hear her own voice.

'Lamb's wool.' Cat glanced down at their worn carpet. 'No, this is just cheap stuff. Lamb's wool is the warmest.'

Cat felt no envy; her home was the only one she knew and the carpet, though rough under her bare knees, was warm enough.

'Ma, why're you telling me all this... tonight?'

Rute pulled a face. 'I *have* to tell you. I've waited... You *have* to know.' She began to finger her necklace, looping it over her fingers, but at that moment a coal fell from the fire on to the rug, sparks flying, and Cat made a grab for it.

'*Don't,* Caterina!' Rute licked her fingers, threw the coal back into the fire and brushed the smouldering ash from the carpet. 'You could have burned yourself, *liebling*! Show me – have you burnt your hand?'

Cat almost wanted to have been burned, to prolong the moment, but she said, 'Ma, I'm fine. And I've got spit, too.'

'Well, you should have used it.'

Rute sat back in her chair. 'Ah, coal. How I hate the smell of it! I can't tell you the associations it has for me. You think we are poor, but at least we have coal!' Cat had no idea they were poor, but nodded dutifully, her smile still on her lips. 'At home we were *really* poor. No coal, no wood, no nothing.' She mused for a moment, her mood once again sombre. 'After Hitler came to power, everyone was poor – if they were Jewish, that is. He gave their jobs to Aryans. It was a propaganda device – no appeal, no argument, that was *it*.' She slapped her knee. 'Even domestic servants, if they worked for non-Jews. Ach, what harm could they have done? None.'

Rute wiped her eyes with her apron and continued her story. How they were forbidden to use the buses; about the arguments at home about who could travel where and how; about her father's shame at the imposition of the yellow star – 'Which should *not* have been shame to us; it was the *Magen David*, the Star of David – you know, like that plastic one in the downstairs lav? Then Yiddish was outlawed, then concerts halls, theatres and libraries.' Punctuating each word with a wave of her hand. 'So people came to our house instead, to read, study Talmud and make music – we'd sit on the stairs, listening.' She raised her head as if breathing fresh air. 'Ach, such lovely music, and how loud it was, the sound of the fiddle in the room with the shutters closed! But then we'd hear footsteps in the street and everyone would suddenly stop playing. Then, one night, my father came home, head down, filthy. "The synagogue is gone – burned – what are we to do? These cursed *Sturmableilung* – they're everywhere!" I never saw him weep before but he wept then. That was only the start. In 1938, after

24

Kristalnacht, all the synagogues were burned, but we'd gone by then.'

The names piled up in Cat's mind, as they had piled up on the meal table in the Zwickau nights. The rabbi's voice hoarse with bewilderment, his plate untouched, and how angry his wife was at the waste of food, and how he shouted, "I'm not hungry!" gesticulating outside — "Give it to *them,* they're the ones who are hungry!"

There were other sounds, of shouts and screams at night, of breaking glass. Their local bookshop, ransacked and burnt; how, afterwards, people came in a great silent rush and parcelled up the tattered books and took them away; how loose, blackened pages fell about the blackened street and on to the blackened snow and were even found caught up in the branches of the blackened plane trees. How they were suddenly strangers in their own town, wary even of those they had known as friends; because 'They were so angry with us! So offended by our Jewishness!' and how utterly impossible it was to resist that anger or to reason with it.

All of which Rute soaked up from her father's throat at the meal table and now, twenty years later, regurgitated to Cat in the little house in High Wycombe. How her brother's *yeshiva* was closed; how, afterwards, a not very able tutor came secretly to the house to teach him Talmud, how scathing Reuben was of him and rebellious — 'Why can't my father teach me Talmud — he's a rabbi, isn't he?' But his father the Rabbi was always out, 'lending' their meagre resources, a piece of meat here, a loaf of bread there, and bits of coinage, until their mother screamed at him, "Food from your own children's mouths!" At which Cat hugged her stomach, and said nothing. "'Always, always, Mattheus, you forgive the debt — why do you always forgive the debt?'" and how, with the flat of his hand, he pushed down air. "*Enough,* already!'"

It was now well past Cat's bedtime but her hunger was forgotten in her absorption in her mother's story. It seemed as if her dream had come to life; that the room in which they were closeted was saturated with pictures of that time. They ebbed and flowed around her, some benign, others malevolent, yet others totally incomprehensible. How could her mother expect her to understand what she was telling her, let alone what it meant? Yet this was what she'd been waiting for; she was ten years old and she could learn. If Rute went on like this she'd have to learn. She'd ask her, later, and she could read books about it. She had no idea that Rute was skirting the edges and that the heart of her story was still to come.

3

In Zwickau people were selling furniture, clothes, books, jewellery, anything that could fund a ticket to the States, among them Rute's older sister, Hannah, a recalcitrant, flighty girl of eighteen. Reb Feugler was afraid for her. Somehow he got the money together to pay the fare and put her under the protection of another family with relatives in New York. Her mother was shattered but she was powerless to resist her husband and she respected his wisdom.

'Hannah stayed with them just long enough to find someone to marry,' said Rute. 'A silk merchant with a big house in Brooklyn. He didn't tell her he'd already lost his money in the 1926 slump – oh no, he was far too grand for that! For a while they were destitute, but I think he recovered later. I know that much but no more. Hannah and I were never close and after... Well, just say, we lost touch.'

In Zwickau people began to starve and there were brief, furtive meetings in the street, the covert exchange of liquor and bottled fruits for bread. Rute's mother became ill with anxiety and malnutrition and, with Hannah gone, the management of the house fell to Rute who soon became weighed down by the responsibility. Her one high spot of the week was her music lesson with Artur Schnabel. She had been due to make her début at the Dresden Symphony Hall under his baton and she deluded herself that it still might happen.

One evening, when she emerged from Schnabel's house, the streets were ominously quiet and black with rain. Her journey home should have been a simple bus ride of two stops, but this, as a Jew, she was forbidden to take.

Rute's green eyes were liquid, incredulous. 'I was just walking along the street, hanging on to my precious music case. It was dark, but not so much to frighten me. Then, from an alleyway, I hear a scream; it's a terrible scream, Caterina, when a man's screams. Then I am frightened. I do not know what to do, what to think. I peer round the corner, and there is an old man against the wall, and soldiers beating him. He has his arms right over his head. He is Jewish – I see his *yarmulke* on his head. They beat him, Caterina, and he falls to the ground.'

Eyes staring at her staring eyes, Cat asked, in equal whisper, 'What did you do?'

'What could I do, a young girl on my own? I wanted to shout, "Stop! What do you think you are doing?" But the words stay frozen in my throat. So I creep away, Caterina. I cross the road – *ja*, I cross the road.' Her voice rasping, her face shrouded by her hair, Rute averted her eyes. 'I just... walked away.'

'Of course you walked away,' said ten year old Cat, conversant with evasive action. 'They'd have beaten you up, too.'

'I could have waited till they'd gone. I just wanted to get home. I wanted to tell my mother how ashamed I was... to have just walked away.'

'I can imagine.' Seeing with her mother's mind, would she not want her mother, too? But Rute was oblivious.

At home the house was already in uproar, and there was no comfort from her mother. Reb Feugler had been arrested and Reuben, after telephoning Schnabel's house and discovering that Rute had already left, had flung out of the house in search of her.

Cat glanced at the clock, incredulous at the way the hands jerked around its blind moon-face. It seemed not to matter that she was late to bed. By now she was famished but she wasn't sleepy. Her eyes felt stretched with what she was hearing.

'Suddenly there was a knock at the door. Loud,

insistent, jarring. No one except *them* knocked on doors at night, and we huddled together, terrified. But, *Gott danken*, it was only Schnabel. He was holding Reuben by the scruff of the neck. He'd met him in the street.' Her lips twisted. 'Imagine it, Caterina. 'Foolhardy', 'dangerous', 'stupid' – the words flew round the house. Reuben, screaming at Schnabel in fury: "*Dummkopf Greis! Dummkopf!*" Stupid old man, he called him. And Schnabel screaming back: "*Dummer schruke Schläger! Dumme kleine Fledermaus!*" – a thug, a silly little bat.'

Against the backdrop of awfulness these picturesque syllables came as a welcome relief, and Cat chuckled. Rute reproved her with a look.

'Caterina, there is nothing about this to smile. Reuben was frantic with worry, imagining me, alone on the streets, but what he'd done was dangerous. It was very, very dangerous, to leave the house like that. Anything might have happened...' She pulled a wry face. 'Well, it did happen, later. Everything happened, later.' Her voice broke, and in spite of the fire she began to shiver. 'Ach, I am so cold! Don't you find the house cold, Caterina?'

Cat was also cold. She had been sitting rigid, ashamed of her levity, and now she was chilled to the bone. She scrambled out of her chair and ran upstairs to fetch her mother's cardigan. Outside the sky was dark and the street lamp lit her mother's bedroom to a pale orange. She could see cars lining the road, and there were few lights on in the houses. It was very late.

On the landing she stopped, dismayed. Her mother's voice, a faint, mewling sound, like a kitten.

'Oh, Papa! Oh, my beloved *fater*...'

At that moment Cat felt what she was missing. To have a father and to adore him as her mother had adored *her* father; to be praised and cherished. To feel his warm, fatherly hand on hers, whenever was appropriate. A fleeting thought, only.

She hurried to her room and flung on a pair of trousers, then rushed downstairs and draped the cardigan round her mother's shoulders. Rute's fingers scrabbled in the wool, plucked at her necklace, winding it round her fingers and letting it drop again.

'Don't go on, Ma, not if it's...'

'Oy, oy... Well, I will finish... Schnabel said they wouldn't hold my father – he wasn't an enemy of the State, he said, just a rabbi, going about his business. And he did come back, but he wouldn't speak to us. He wouldn't even look at us. He just disappeared into his study with Schnabel. It was hours before they came out, hours.'

Rute turned her head and gazed at the curtains, her face desolate at the images beyond them, and she began to make small snuffling sounds, like a child bereft. Cat had frequently heard her mother weeping – was this why, then? – but to *see* her weeping completely overwhelmed her and, for a moment, she felt faint.

Rute seemed not to notice. She wiped her eyes on her apron and took a deep, sobbing breath.

'All night... we sat up waiting for them all night. Schnabel said, for him it was the end. He'd return to Berlin, collected his things and leave. For Italy, I think. I don't know how he managed. Forged papers, perhaps... He told my father to get the rest of us out of Germany... while the going was good.' She gave a cynical laugh. 'Ach, the going was never to be good.

And so the family was broken. Not immediately, for their father was resourceful and he fought tooth and nail to protect them. In defiance of daily announcements bayed through loudspeakers on street corners that Jews must register for transportation, he found hiding places where they could be together. One small suitcase each. For a while they lived in darkened rooms with dubiously loyal neighbours, but at night, after their father left for the ruined synagogue, they slipped their mother's leash and prowled the streets for scraps of food and gossip. At first they roamed in groups, feral and defiant, but as they saw their companions picked up, saw their shadowy figures bundled into the backs of military trucks in the full glare of spotlights, heard their howls of rage and disbelief, they became afraid. Inevitably, they were caught, and it happened inauspiciously, in the rain, with no dispute or protest but almost a sense of resignation.

Her father was out that day, caring for the frail remnant of his people, and there was no leave-taking, however anguished. He took refuge in a friend's attic bedroom until he was denounced and sent to Auschwitz, along with their cousins on their mother's side, other more distant relatives, and innumerable close friends.

'They perished. They were... ash.'

Cat could connect, albeit dimly, with hiding, loss and heartache, but ash? She had no conception of what it meant. The image entered her soul, garish and over-blown, utterly removed from everything she knew. Except in the storybook on every child's shelf, the far-fetched tales of Hoffman's *Strewwelpeter*.

So she was burned with all her clothes
And arms and hands and eyes and nose
Till she had nothing more to lose
Except her little scarlet shoes
And nothing else but these was found
Among her ashes on the ground.

But even Hoffman at his most rabid would not haunt her as much as the brief but chilling description of how Rute's mother, at the very last moment, came rushing from the house, how she gathered her twins in her frail arms and turned to run, and how she was stopped in her tracks. Guns were raised at her; there was pushing and shoving, the deafening sound of horns, squealing tyres and screamed commands, and she became disorientated. Powerless to resist, they were herded into the trucks and sent to join the others in the ghetto.

'What's a ghetto, Ma?'

Rute's eyes widened in shock, as if she had only just realised that Cat was listening, but she recovered quickly.

'It's... it's a sort of small village. Not a place to make a home. Four years we were there.' She ran a hand over her face. 'Four years.'

'You grew up there? How did you...?'

Rute's eyes blazed. 'Don't *ask* me about it, Caterina. Just... don't ask. I'll never, never tell you. Never!'

'But what about your piano lessons?'

'Cate*rina*!' Rute raised her hand as if to slap her, and Cat flinched. They looked at each other, horrified, and then Cat got to her feet. 'I am going from here,' she thought, but her legs were stiff and cramped and she stumbled.

Rute put out a hand to steady her. 'Oh *mein Gott,* what have I done? Oh my darling Caterina, don't be angry with me. But please, please don't ask me about that time. I just need you to... listen.'

'I *have* been listening to you! I've done nothing *but* listen to you, for half the night!' She glanced at the clock. 'Look, it's nearly four o'clock in the morning!'

But secretly she was hugging herself. At last her mother had called her 'darling'.

'Is it really that late? I'm sorry, you must be tired. I'd no idea...' She stood up and folded Cat in her arms. Surprised, Cat stood immobile, and then put her own arms round her mother's thin body. She could feel her spine beneath her hands.

'Go to bed, child. Take a sandwich upstairs with you and go to bed. I'm too exhausted to do anything tonight.'

But the stairs were dark and Cat was afraid to go to bed.

It had been a complex tale; a tale, not for the blithe, radiant evenings of summer, but for a winter manufactured from closed doors and drawn curtains. Cat hugged the pillow, frozen, wide-eyed and hollow; brimful with nightmarish images of darkened streets and saddened faces, of cold snow, of black sludge. It made her inexpressibly sad to think that Rute had kept all this pent up inside her for so long, and that she might have spoken sooner, had she chosen. But something hinted that she'd been told too much – and yet, five hours of the telling and nothing at all about her father, not a single word! Tossing and turning in her bed, she puzzled over why her mother had chosen her birthday to tell her these things. What had triggered it, a chance encounter in the street, a news item? She did listen to the radio a lot. Or was it because she was ten? Perhaps she'd thought: *She's old enough, now; she's ten.* She might have thought: *I was ten when it all started.* Somebody's mother at school had had a breakdown, whatever that meant. There was a garage by the school which advertised 'Breakdown & Recovery Services', so perhaps Rute was having one. Cat was in two minds about that. On the one hand she hoped she would recover quickly, otherwise what would become of them? On the other hand it might be worth it for a little bit of loving and a few hugs. But something inside her, some deep, grave intuition, told her that surely, if children couldn't be protected from the events, at least they should be protected from hearing about them. And yet, were people ever old enough to hear such things? Her last thought before she finally drifted off to sleep was that her mother should have known better.

The next morning she woke to an unaccustomed

weight on the bed. For the first time for years Rute had come into her room and was sitting beside her. When she saw that Cat was awake, she took her hand. Her skin felt dry, water-worn, but oh, the softness of her touch!

'I've been up for simply hours,' she smiled tenderly. 'Baked you an *apfelkuchen*. A belated birthday present. Best eaten warm, *liebchen*.'

'Ma, what's it mean, 'Leebchen'? You call me that a lot. *And* Leebling.'

'Oh, that's just my way. They're German for 'darling' or 'dear', that's all.'

4

Rute Feugler was a diminutive woman with distinctive green eyes that showed every emotion, especially fear. She arrived in England afraid, and she stayed afraid; afraid of showing her feelings, afraid of going out, of meeting strangers. 'I was terrified of being lifted up by the scruff of her neck and taken back.'

'Even now, after all this time?' asked Cat. 'But who'll know? One small woman in one small house in one small street in a very small town?' Smiling at her mother with all the sophistication of her eleventh year. And with deep affection.

'You forget. I was born in a small town. People have short memories – it's only twenty years since...' It was a few years more, but Cat knew what she meant.

Telling her story had released something inside her and she became more motherly, if cooking Cat's favourite foods and avidly watching her eat was motherly. It was a clinging sort of love, almost cloying; she wanted to know where Cat was, every given moment. On her return from school each day Cat would find her waiting at the window, squeezing her lips between finger and thumb, tweaking shut the net curtain when anyone went by. At bedtime she hovered, tidying Cat's clothes, folding them and patting them flat on the chair before reluctantly leaving the room. Eventually, in defiance of her agoraphobia, she started meeting Cat at the school gate. White-faced, she would grab Cat's hand as she came out and rush her away, as if from contamination.

She became interested in the other women, and would stand on the very edge of the group, backed against the railing, observing their dress and the patient shifting of their slippered feet on the hard pavement, how they folded and unfolded their arms. She eavesdropped blatantly, eyes down, ear cocked for cadences, trawling their conversations for useful English idioms. On the way home she would criticise them, the way they chucked their butts into the gutter or their habit of coming out in curlers and aprons which were never quite clean. She had always taken in washing to make ends meet and now she did the ironing with the radio propped on the kitchen windowsill. Cat would find her bent over her notebook, crumpled shirts abandoned.

Her text books were second hand magazines, children's books and Cat her co-conspirator, her resident language consultant. In the evenings after her chores were done she would perch on Cat's bed.– 'Right, now is English-time! Score me out of ten, Caterina...' From Enid Blyton she had *"Ripping! Super! Jolly!"* – and from *Peter Pan,* in simulated Teutonic tones: *"Vy can't you fly now, Mozzer?" "Because ven peoples are grown up zey forget ze vay."* Or from magazine articles – *"Dior's clothes, like zose of ozer fashion hauses, haf brought new glamour to ze scene."* Ach, I should be so lucky! How did I do?'

She was still anxious about going out alone, afraid of betraying her origins by saying or doing the wrong thing, and one day, while rummaging through piles of tattered books in the charity shop, she found a dictionary of surnames and instantly decided to change their own.

'But why worry?' said Cat. 'There're all sorts of surnames in class; Patel, Singh, Alleyne, Silver – '

'But that's a Jewish name!' her mother said.

'Well, there you are.'

'No, but Feugler's so obviously... And I don't want you growing up with a Jewish name!'

'But it's who I am, aren't I? Remember what you said, the female line? I might even marry a Jew.'

'There's no compulsion.'

Reluctantly, Cat agreed at least to look, and after supper that evening they huddled over the grubby book, tasting the names on their tongues.

'*Hah,* see this?' said Rute, stabbing at the page with her finger – '*Fake*'. I never heard such a thing... Do we qualify, you think? Oh no, it's German... but, look, it says *a falcon or hawk; daring or enterprising* – are *we* daring and enterprising?' She examined the flyleaf of the book. 'Ach, this is American. I wonder who it belonged to.' She began to giggle, and under the curtain of her dark hair her green eyes sparkled with enjoyment and mischief. 'What appalling names some people have... Can these really exist? *Fausette, French...* That's one step nearer, but I thought that was a tap... *falsehood, cheat, forgery* – oh... well... yes...' She slammed the book shut and tossed it aside. 'Oh well, Feugler it is; it's who we are; it'll have to do. But what a waste of a sixpence!'

The image of the ghetto was planted it in Cat's mind, and it took root. If her mother had not been so angry with her when she questioned her about it, her first description of it as 'a small village', or her dismissive 'not a place to make a home' might have been less significant. But it sounded more sinister than that; it was more like a black hole into which Rute had tumbled; not a single fall from which she had recovered – otherwise, why her anger? – but a prolonged, destructive, four year gap in her mother's life of which Cat knew nothing, the years of her youth. Rute had told her the rest, saturated her with the rest – why not those four years? Intuition told her it was an important omission, but she had no way of knowing for sure. Nor could she tell whether her mother's refusal to elucidate merely illustrated her immense capacity to dissemble, or whether it masked something deeper. Or both; a continual battling of her mind and spirit.

The tortuously convoluted narrative of Cat's tenth birthday was only the beginning, although they never again stayed up so late. A curious, unspoken bargain was struck between them; that if some memory surfaced, Rute would find a ready audience in her daughter. It could happen anywhere and she would suddenly launch into speech and tears.

At first Cat revelled in her attention; she even found herself colluding, an unconscious participant in the stories, correcting words or finishing Rute's sentences for her. At other times she thought that if she was a better daughter she could make them stop. The images haunted and oppressed her, but she feared the return of the old silence. She felt that to listen was her only route to her mother's love and that outweighed any objections she might have voiced. In fact the stories had a peculiar fascination for her; they concerned her mother's secret life and she learned them by heart as she might learn arithmetical tables.

But although they were Rute's memories, in Cat's dreams she remembered them as hers.

One dream finds her leaning from an open casement, looking down on to a cobbled street. Below is a great crowd of gabardine men, their shapes splintered by the charred branches of plane trees, their faces white with anger, their words muffled by their long beards. Her nightdress, also white, flaps in the breeze; tendrils of hair obscure her vision, damp from blown rain. Her teeth are clenched.

Now she stands on wet cobbles, tram doors trapped sharp on her fingers, the passengers looking at her with guilt or contempt; yet others with indifference. Now she's on a train, not in a carriage, but crammed in with forty others in a windowless truck designed for cattle. Someone's hair tickles her face and she cannot breathe. And always before her is the dark, bottomless pit into which she falls, panic stricken, with no one to rescue her, a yawning hole of deep, black silence broken by a roaring sound inside her head, like a plane droning overhead, to which she wakes. She has no idea whether she has invented the plane or whether the roaring was part of the dream. Neither does she know where the images come from; she does not understand what her mother has been telling her.

One night Cat woke to the scent of *eau de Cologne,* her mother's necklace trailing against her face like gossamer web. Rute's body was quivering and she was gripping Cat so tightly that she wrestled away from her. She could see the hurt in her face.

'You were dreaming, Caterina.' She stroked Cat's forehead with the wash-board, sand-paper palm of her hand. 'You were calling out.'

Cat wanted to scream at her, to yell into her ear with the loudest voice she could muster. 'It's the *stories*, Ma. It's all the *stories* you tell me. They give me *nightmares.*' But instead she said, 'It's nothing. I heard something roaring, like a plane. A big plane, high up in the sky. It gave me a bad dream, that's all. Oh Ma, leave me alone!'

She felt impatient that her mother assumed that she could comfort her during the night when, during the day, it always fell to *her* to be the source of comfort. But her momentary rejection of her mother had broken their fragile bargain. The next time Cat found her weeping and went to her and put her arms around her and said, 'Don't cry, Ma. What's the matter, Ma?' Rute merely repeated her own words back to her. 'Nothing. It's... nothing.' And once more she became morose and uncommunicative, as if feeling more keenly her friendless isolation.

Watching her, Cat felt guilty, heavy-hearted. She wanted her mother to take control of their lives again. She hated this distance between them. Once, and only once did she try and break the pattern, go to her and say, 'Don't you love me anymore, Ma?' but, in spite of hugs and cloying closeness, it would be over forty years before what should have been a simple, automatic response would reach her from her mother's lips.

Rute was wary of strangers and found it hard to accept kindness. Aware of their circumstances, the butcher and the milkman frequently slipped her a cheap cut or an extra third of milk, but because, on one occasion, a piece of meat was stale, or the milk sour, henceforth all the meat was stale, all the milk sour. And when the son of the new people next door accidentally cracked the back room window with his football, she feuded with them over the fence, amid talk of 'trespass' and 'compensation'.

The window stayed cracked, less as a conscious reproof to the neighbours, but also because Rute was incapable of mending anything. If Cat found something broken her mother was like a child caught out in misdemeanour, full of airy excuses. 'Oh, that broke a while ago.' Or when the bath plug disappeared and she stopped up the hole with tissue paper; 'I wonder how that got there. Ach, perhaps it just fell out of my sleeve.' Her account of how she attempted to sew up the frayed cotton sheath on the flex of a table lamp was told with disarming candour. '*Mein Gott,* Caterina, I shot right across the room!'

Typical of this was her attitude to shopping, done on a Saturday when she could be sure of Cat by her side. Until one day when Cat, intent on a drawing, made excuses not to go. Thwarted, her mother looked from side to side and then she wrung her hands. Cat had heard of this action but never seen it, and it pierced her heart. She jumped up and put her arms around her.

'Ma, I didn't say I wouldn't go,' she said gently. 'I just said, not *now.*'

'No. Well. Right, I'll go on my own, then.' With a martyred look Rute stuffed her string bag into her pocket and slammed out of the house. She hated crowds – she knew what crowds might signify – but she had chosen the busiest time of day when the streets were full of people and the bus home had been packed with shoppers.

Cat came into the kitchen as she was unloading her carrier bags, her face still white with tension.

'Let me help with that.'

'I don't need your help.' And she remained tight-lipped until the next Saturday, when Cat accompanied her and realised, for the first time, the magnitude of her mother's phobia and how much it cost her to go out. Timidly, she suggested a diversion, and they made their way to Rute's favourite charity shop. There, for the first time, watching her mother joke with the volunteers and seeing her visibly relax, she recognised what a solace the place was to her, and how naturally attuned she was to the detritus of other people's loss; the undemanding, unremarkable, infinitely redeemable, second hand clothes.

5

At fourteen Cat's genuine interest in her mother's family revived. She was particularly interested in Rute's twin, but her questions were dismissed with a shake of Rute's head, as if Reuben was a secondary character in a two-bit novel.

'I'll tell you more about my father, if you want. I thought you were tired of it all.'

'No, I'm not tired of it all.' It was a lie, but Cat thought that, with a little encouragement, she might lead the conversation to the subject of her own father, for whom she still yearned.

They were walking across Wycombe Marsh in the sunshine, and ahead was a stream than ran through the park. Rute nodded towards it. 'In Zwickau there was a huge river called the *Zwickauer Mulde* where my father took us sailing. I remember his hand holding mine, so warm! He loved all of us equally, but I think he loved me best. After things got bad – but you don't want to know about that.'

'No, but you'll tell me anyway.'

Rute gave her a sour look. 'Well, after things got *bad* he agreed to teach us Talmud privately, both of us together in his reading room. That was quite rare for a daughter.' Her expression, as she said this, was complacent, almost vain. 'I was bright, I suppose, and of course we were twins...'

Cat, unable to stop herself, interrupted, 'I'd have liked that when I was little.'

Rute laughed. 'What, Talmud?'

'No. To be read to.' Greatly daring, she repeated the accusation of her tenth birthday, 'We never did anything together.'

Her mother's eyes flashed. 'You've accused me of that before, Caterina, and it's just not true! We did all sorts of... We picnicked here when you were small, for one thing. I had an old coach-built pram for you and piled all the shopping on top. Trudging these hills with that, what a weight! But all through the fifties we had poor summers and we hardly went anywhere. Floods everywhere and such storms – don't you remember those gales? You hated it, the wind banging against the windows.' She looked away. 'And I *did* read to you. All those cardboard books? No, I forget; I gave them away when you grew out of them. '

I remember you read to me later, thought Cat, when you practiced your English on me, but cardboard books as a toddler? She had no recollection of them, nor could she recall a single occasion when they'd picnicked by the river. Why was her mother making things up?

'Sorry,' she said. 'Go on with what you were saying. About your father reading to you.'

'It was *study*. Real study, Caterina, not children's books.'

Their father would question them in the same rhetorical style he used in the synagogue, with a tiny gesture here or a whispered hint there, to help them understand and to which he expected them to respond. Dark-haired Reuben, with his nascent beard and large, avid eyes, stood proudly behind the Rabbi's lectern while Rute snuggled against her father, watching his lips move and occasionally picking off the long auburn hairs that strayed on to his black caftan.

'He had a long stick with a pointing finger to show the text he was reading from. Called a *Yad Torah*. Boxwood, worn almost to silver. His side locks used to tickle my neck.' She chuckled at the memory. 'His hands were very white, and he always kept his nails very short.' With a gesture characteristic of her, she pulled off the elastic band from her hair, stroked it back with her fingers, and fastened it up again. 'I may not have learned much from my father but I have never forgotten the touch of his hands.'

Cat had to stop her mouth and remember that at least she hadn't lost her mother as Rute's parents had been lost.

'What about *my* father, Ma? You've never said anything about him.'

The words were out before she knew it. They could not be taken back, and she was horrified at herself. All those years of repressing her questions, and here she was, blatantly infiltrating her mother's story with her own!

'No, that's enough for now.' Rute bent and tightened the strap of her shoe. 'Come on, let's go home.'

Cat stood immobile, looking after her. She was stunned. She found it incredible that her mother had never intuited that she might have been curious about her father or whether, for example, she was a wanted child. Was that asking too much? Bleakly, she got to her feet and followed her mother up the path.

'I would like to know sometime, Ma. I think I deserve to know. But tell me what you want, or nothing at all. It's your choice.'

'There's nothing *to* tell.' Rute's face had paled and, although the path was not steep, she was breathing heavily. 'But since you insist, I met him in the kibbutz. He was a construction worker and he came into the office. I was working as a secretary then, but later we moved to Tel Aviv. His name was Aaron, Aaron Rosensweig. He was... he was very good to me. He was a dear friend, but, well, I just didn't want to make my life with him, that's all.'

She opened the park gate and they crossed the road together, dodging traffic.

'Anyway,' she added, as they reached the pavement, 'we couldn't have married. He was a Jewish Christian. How could I marry a Christian, already, after what had happened in Germany?'

44

After a pause Cat asked, her voice thin in her throat. 'Am I like him, Ma?'

Rute glanced at her, her face inscrutable. 'You couldn't be,' she said, but her voice was gentle. 'You're like me.'

'I could have been a twin. You and Uncle Reuben are twins.'

Rute's green eyes flashed with exasperation. 'Oh, Caterina, *enough,* already! At least you're British. Just be thankful it wasn't a virgin birth!'

Over succeeding months Rute became distant again, not aloof as she had been in the past, but preoccupied. Books appeared on the kitchen table, dusty, second hand editions of Schiller, Goethe and some Thomas Mann, with yellowed, parchment covers and thin canvas spines. One day, when her mother was out of the room Cat opened one of them, running her fingers over the dark German-Gothic script, and wondering what new fad this was of her mother's. Yet although she never saw Rute with one in her hand, and she never seemed to open them, they seemed to have a life of their own, their own perambulations, as if they were following Rute around the house. She would lift them to wipe the table underneath, or she might move them to the window sill while they ate, but the next morning they were back on the table. They'd be in the living room, tucked into the lid of her mother's sewing box, later, at the foot of the stairs. Their presence in the house seemed to make Rute fretful, as though she was apprehensive about opening them.

One evening after their meal, she suddenly pushed back her chair and announced that she would read out loud from Schiller. She marched out of the room with her brisk, bird-like step, and returned with a couple of books in her hand.

'Now, Caterina, listen to this,' she said, sitting down again and flicking through the pages. 'This is *Nanie,* a classic. Brahms wrote music for it, four voices and orchestra.' She began to recite the poem, but stopped immediately, repelled by the opening lines.

'*Auch das Schöne muß sterben*... But that's terrible! "Even beauty must die"?' She scanned the yellowed page, muttering under her breath. '*Um eine Klage auf den Lippen des Geliebten zu ist herrlich*... What? "To be a lament on the lips of the loved one is *glorious*"?' She slammed the book shut, and dust rose in the air. 'Hah! So much he knew, already! Oh, but I don't remember it like this... My father must have... No, I can't read such romantic nonsense!'

She opened Thomas Mann's *Der Junge Joseph* and flipped through the pages.

'We had one of the first editions of this when I was young,' she said. 'It's the story of Joseph in the Bible – but everyone knows this story, Caterina.' Again she turned the pages. 'Here we are, *Joseph und seine Brüder*.' Again she began to read, but when she got to the words *Sie fallen allesamt über ihn her und verprügeln ihn*... she leaned back and put a hand to her mouth. 'Ach, it says they fell on him and beat him! Well, of course I knew that. I did know that, but I don't remember... it didn't make such an impression on me before.' She put the book down and covered her face. 'I don't know *what* I think I am doing,' she mourned. 'I can't even hear his voice!'

Cat knew instinctively what her mother had been trying to do. She had been trying to resurrect her own childhood and to recreate, in their little house in High Wycombe, something of that intimate embrace of presence, of particularity and of word which she had known with her father. She didn't know what to do, what to say to comfort her. She watched her retrieve her sewing box from its alcove, take out a skein of silk, divide it into thinner fronds, and snip it short with her tiny embroidery scissors. At that moment she caught Cat's eye, and gave a sad, whimsical smile of

46

resignation. 'Those *dummerblitzen* books! I got them from the charity shop so I won't even get a refund.'

The unidentifiable flower motif of Cat's tenth birthday proliferated; it appeared on pillow cases, on a charity shop tablecloth, on pillowcases, on old sheets cut up for napkins and even on the corners of towels, their hooks recycled from pyjama cords. Rute had no other design. Craving company, she would take her sewing box to Cat's bedroom, to the upright chair and, while Cat crouched over her essays, trying to block her ears, she would sew and fuss and tut, and inbetween the sewing and fussing and tutting she would exercise her rememberances and once more speak of turmoil, separation and grief until it was time for sleep. But neither slept well; both had nightmares; Rute, because she was re-living her stories through Cat; Cat, because she was living them for the first time.

6

In spite of Cat's craving for the stories to be finished Rute seemed unable to contain herself, but now she focussed less on the events than on their effect on her. Her dominant theme was the loss of trust, which she said was the main reason, apart from the violence, why the break up of her family was so traumatic. The purge of the Jews, she said, was like the pages of a book being ripped out and the book binned – a book such as the Bible, relied on in times of need, trusted for its authority, and then discarded, as the Jews were. Another theme was hatred. She found it utterly inexplicable that people they had known intimately as friends, met at concerts and theatres, travelled with or worked with, could detest them so much.

Her experience of these things at such a young age both challenged and sustained her identity but her temper was mercurial. She would rehearse her grudges out loud to the kitchen sink, hands flying amid the soap suds, and some second hand china was broken. Once she broke the leg of a bedside table, shoving it had against the wall in her anger. Both the china and the bedside table she mended with black insulating tape, but the sight of them were a constant reminder of her bitterness, and one day she hauled all her breakages outside and dumped them on the wasteland beside the house.

To utterly forget was impossible; she carried deep wounds at the heart of her being. It did not take much to trigger the hurt – once, a broadcast of a Beethoven piano concerto. Cat arrived home to find her in tears, shaking uncontrollably, gesticulating at the radio. 'My piece... that piece... my concert debut in Dresden.' Cat leapt for the switch and in the silence led her mother into the back garden, where the only tunes were birdsong and the distant sound of lorries thumping down the main road.

Whatever her mother's characteristics, inherited or acquired, Cat accepted them unquestioningly. She wanted to comfort her and, if she could, to protect her, yet, at the same time, she was wearied by her constant allusions to the Holocaust and felt she could no longer respond with the appropriate emotion. One day she said that she was tired of hearing about it.

'Ma, I'm sorry, but it wasn't my war, was it? I don't know anyone else who talks about it, let alone *thinks* about it. Look,' she added, 'you know what we get taught in History? We get taught the *Romans*, Ma; later on the *Tudors*. And you wonder why I'm not interested in history! Most people my age can't even *imagine* some of the things you tell me. And look what's happened since. It's been *years*, now,' she pleaded. 'Can't you just...let it go?'

This raised her mother's protest, her voice pleading, poetic, sibilant. 'You're wrong, Caterina. What you call history is people's memory, *my* memory. It's like... like a taste on the tongue that won't go away. Like... I don't know, those traces you get under a ploughed field.' She was whispering, now. 'Old footprints, Caterina, old villages. How do you learn about them if you're not taught, or if you don't ask?' Her voice rose and became vehement. 'You're the younger generation, Caterina, and it's your *responsibility* to ask. So, *ask*! Even land has a memory, so *ask* why nothing grows there; *ask,* where the people have gone; *ask,* why their communities were broken! How can they *be* remembered, except by memory?'

'It's your memory, not mine,' Cat muttered.

Rute got up to leave the room.

'Caterina, you *nervös machen* me − I'll take my tears elsewhere! *You* don't cry for me, do you?'

At the door she turned with a parting shot, her thin finger, arthritic from laundering, wagging in Cat's face. 'But let me tell you this!' she said. 'Never again! Never again will we be led like lambs to the slaughter! Never again will they try and push us into the sea!'

Never again, never again – a mantra for the angry, a vow for the desperate, spoken without faith, without confidence, from tight lips. For Rute it was an empty vow to an absent God. Against her better judgement Cat pursued the subject, only to encounter more stories, this time about Palestine, the primitiveness of the kibbutz, the hostility of Arab neighbours, and a vague reference to how utterly chaotic 'things' were. Then a quick, evasive jump to an 'escape'; hints about a train, a coal barge, about dirt and cold and of a long voyage on the sea, hints made worthless by her perpetual refusal to be specific.

Escape from where? The kibbutz? What voyage? Where on *earth*, in all this, was the chronology?

It was all in the past, anyway, thought Cat, feeling in the dark for answers, and surely not enough to cause such fearfulness in her mother *now*, in High Wycombe, or such appalling distress at night. There must be something Rute was hiding. Was it grief, the lingering darkness of the camps; was it the innumerable ghosts of the lost, or was it... *Yes,* guilt – guilt at having survived, added to that former guilt of not having intervened in the matter of the elderly Jew in the street. Was that it?

When Cat used the word, Rute flushed. They were clearing up after supper, Cat at the sink and her mother drying the saucepans. Rute stared at her, the tea towel suspended. 'What do you mean, guilt?' She gave Cat a suspicious look, as though a secret had been fathomed. '*No*! I just wanted a new life, away from all that... that....' She pursed her lips and clattered the saucepan into the drawer.

Reuben had married by then. 'Suffering makes strange bedfellows,' Rute said later that evening, although again she didn't elucidate. 'But at least Amit was an old friend. That's when I left Israel – and here we are,' she exclaimed guilelessly, 'all tucked up safe in our darling little house in High Wycombe!'

Cat frowned. 'Darling little house, Ma?'

'Ach, it was in this magazine I picked up...'

'But why England, Ma? Why not America, where your sister was?'

'Ah, but England won the war and I already spoke the language.' An absurd sort of reasoning, thought Cat, and typical of her. 'Why Wycombe? Who knows? A lottery. The Embassy helped. Oh, but Caterina,' she said, a whimsical, sideways look on her face. 'I'd never learned to cook or bake, though I could make a reasonable sauerkraut. On the kibbutz I made yoghurt; I cooked *gefilte* fish; I could bake *matzos*...' Stressing the words, laughing, self-deprecating. 'But I had no idea how to cook *sausages,* or handle an English *butcher,* or even what was kosher. In the end I thought' – she threw up a hand, spread-fingered – 'why bother? I was no longer a true believer; I put all that behind me.'

'Ma... was there no joy in your life?' Cat's voice was quiet.

'Joy? *Joy?* What joy there was went with my father. I told you.'

7

At school, Cat's teachers were frustrated by her lack of progress. Apart from Art and English, in which she excelled, her work was mediocre. At sixteen, she was still diminutive, like her mother, and like her, she grew her hair long. Socially she was awkward; she perceived herself of little significance. What few invitations she received, she refused, conscious that they would have to be returned, but she balked at the idea of subjecting her mother to adolescent eyes and herself to more adolescent teasing. She inhabited two worlds; her mother's, where, for the most part, she could be herself, and school, where she was self-conscious and reticent.

Deep within her she craved a more normal life, which meant having what others had and doing what they did; it meant light-hearted chatting; it meant going to the flicks; it meant family, visitors; it meant styling her hair instead of tying it back with an elastic band; it meant *television*. People who had fathers had television; somehow the two things were connected, and Cat loved television. In spite of the grey monochrome of the faces, she delighted in examining bone structure, speculating about complexions. Her A level course included portraiture and the previous week her art teacher, whom she revered, had instructed her pupils to bring to the next lesson a newspaper cutting of a face to paint over with flesh tones. Cat chose the Chancellor of the Exchequer with his red briefcase, and brought it to the art lesson.

In the cutting, his face was lowered towards the briefcase as though rehearsing in his mind its contents, and Cat imagined how the red would resonate upwards into his features. All the downward facing planes she painted a bright scarlet; all the upward facing planes she painted a complementary green. The background and his suit, she left a monotone grey.

But, 'What's *this*? I said *flesh tones*. What makes *you* think you can...? Who do you think you *are*?' and 'And where do you think you're going?' – for Cat, disheartened by her teachers crass incomprehension, had closed her eyes and walked away. The second detention of her life, and, except for her marriage, the last.

Cat was taking her exams. She worked deep into the night and her sleep was dreamless. Rute no longer waited for her at the school gate, but on *Shabbat* Eve she would meet her off the bus and buy her a treat at the small café where she'd taught them how to make her lemon tea. They would scramble for a seat in the window, giggling like schoolgirls, nibbling their chocolate truffles to make them last, scooping the crumbs with a wet finger. Rute would peer out down the road, her eyes gleaming with anticipation. An over-hanging belly, a builder's bottom, a bald head – anyone, so long as it was male – and she would nudge Cat with her bony elbow and wink maliciously. 'Here comes a fine figure off a man! *Mein Gott*, what an awful vorning!'

She had a gutsy, pertinent humour that compelled Cat to see the world though her eyes, although at the back of her mind were many moments of doubt or confusion, which, out of loyalty, she hastily stifled. Doubts, not about the veracity of Rute's story, but about the chronology she had suppressed.

'These truffles, they're not a patch on the truffles in Berlin.'

'When were you in Berlin? You never mentioned Berlin...'

'Didn't I?' Rute's green eyes slanted away, her fingers playing with her necklace. 'I was there once,' she muttered. 'A concert with my music teacher.'

'Schnabel? You said he lived in Zwickau.'

'He was *staying* in Zwickau. He *lived* in Dresden. Oh, just don't ask, OK?'

Cat studied her mulishly and Rute's eyes flashed. 'You think I make this up! Why should I make things up, already? I had truffles in Berlin, OK? Don't keep *on* about it, Caterina!'

'You went to Palestine as well, didn't you?'

'What of it? I told you, by coal barge.'

'Where from, Ma? I mean, from which docks? And why not on a proper ship? Why don't you tell me, Ma? You don't trust me? You trusted me before, and I was only ten...'

'Hah! *Only* ten, she says! I waited half my *life* to tell you! Half my *life*! *And* I had to explain everything twice!' Her face softened and she gave a shy, enigmatic smile. 'Ah Caterina, leave me my seventh veil.'

At home again, Cat pored over her European atlas, but the scale was so vast and the sheer mass of unfathomable place names so dense, she could make nothing of it.

Zwickau, born there. Ghetto, if there was one, where? Warsaw? It was just a name. Where *were* those ghettos? She was possessed by ignorance yet forbidden to ask.

She had been kneeling on the floor, the atlas at her feet, and at this *impasse* she sat back, and gazed out of the window. At that moment a bird flew by, and after it, quick as a flash, a sparrow hawk. It struck, and Cat jumped up, her hands to her mouth, and burst into tears. Nature, red in tooth and claw.

There was nothing in the school library about the Holocaust, so the following day she skipped afternoon school, went into town and found the Library. Rejecting anything with Hitler's face on the cover, or a swastika, she chose a couple of more sober-looking hardbacks and settled down on the floor with them. She was afraid of being seen but she soon became too engrossed to care.

What she read was a revelation. It seemed that all over Europe the earth had churned up its own surface, a great groundswell of people passing through, either in flight from German Occupation or on Jewish transportations. She whispered to herself the place names, the innumerable railway stations of Germany, Poland, Czechoslovakia and France – Bobigny, Drancy, Metz, Perpignan, Grenoble, Andelys, the Quay d'Orsay.

The centre of one book was filled with photographs. Nazi parades; Hitler, with his irritable face and grotesque moustache; Goering, the flying ace with the deadpan look of a solicitor; fat jowled Himmler, battery chicken farmer and mastermind of concentration camps. Photographs of book burnings, the arrival of inmates at Birkenau, of the sign above the gateway at Auschwitz, *Arbeit Macht Frei*, of camp chimneys belching smoke, of walls filled with last messages and prayers, of *menorah* and the *Magen David* scratched in the plaster by desperate fingernails. Of skeletal women, of gaunt, hairless men and emaciated children, of piles of shoes, skulls, watches, gold teeth, of graves stacked with the naked dead. Everything was there in black and white. No need to dream up colours to coat them with; they were Hitler's colours; red and black, the colours of blood and darkness.

She felt cold to the soul. Her legs felt numb, and when it was time to leave she had to make herself move, to get up, to return the books and go and meet her mother. Her mother, who might have been caught up in it all. Her poor mother!

Outside, she walked into a world of delicate, watery colour and clear skies, of noise, traffic and chatter; the normal hustle and bustle of an everyday English town in mid afternoon. The contrast was appalling to her. She felt deeply sad that she'd been left to discover all this on her own. She felt sick. She had been too quiescent, too trusting, accepting her mother's stories like mother's milk, and had been made to wait for meat until she was nearly grown. Her mother's question – 'If you're not taught, how can you know?' had shamed her, but now she thought, Oh Ma, *you* could have told me! She repeated the words out loud. 'You could have told me, sometime over the last seven years!' All those interminable stories about the past! All that eccentricity and underhandedness! All those evasions! Leading where? To this moment, to this... this *nausea.* She had been trusted to listen, but not trusted enough; not enough to be told everything, to understand.

It was at that moment that Cat felt the first stirrings of rebellion. She would have to break free. With each step the words pulsed like a mantra in her head. I have to break free. I have to break free. But as soon as she caught sight of the slight, wan, defenceless figure of her mother, standing anxiously by the bus stop, her mood changed. It was futile to be angry; she had never been able to articulate it, and it would always pale into insignificance beside her utter comprehension of *who Rute was* – a volatile, quixotic, but immensely vulnerable woman who was, after all, her mother. Her mother, whom she loved. Her mother, with her seventh veil.

When she confessed where she had been, Rute gave a wintry smile, but said nothing. As soon as they got home she took a book off the shelf and handed it to her.

'You want to know what happened, read this. *Then* you will understand.'

Night, by Elie Wiesel; a signed copy, dated 1987.

Cat looked at her, bemused. 'You met the author? Where?'

'It was a book-signing, OK?'

'But where, Ma? In London?'

'Of course not! I do read, you know!' Preening, in her inimitable way: 'Elie and I, we have a lot in common.'

Cat dropped the book on the table. 'Oh, Ma, why do you always make a mystery of things you can't bear to talk about?'

'Mystery? What mystery?' Rute flushed. 'I don't know what you mean.'

Cat hesitated, not wanting to upset her. 'Those four years, for instance. Ma, what *happened* to you? You've never told me...'

'No, and I've no intention of doing so!' Her eyes sparked with anger and distress. 'I told you once and I don't expect to have to repeat it! All these years – you've no idea how hard it was for me!'

Cat studied her. 'Yes, what a burden round your neck I must have been.'

Rute took a breath and her anger dissipated. She looked watchful, almost wary.

'Sometimes, perhaps, when you were small. But we coped, didn't we? And I've answered all your questions, haven't I? Told you what you want?'

Cat gaped at her. Her rebellion was still incipient, and if Rute had hugged her with a mother's hug, stroked her hair, told her she was beautiful, said, 'Of course you're not a burden – you're a blessing!' it might have appeased her. But Rute had neither sensed her need for affirmation, nor considered the effect of unsatisfied need upon her peace of mind. She had never shown any awareness that her stories might have been unsuitable for a child's ears, let alone those of her own daughter, or how they might become an insufferable burden. She had never known how lonely Cat had felt as a child, and still felt; how she had hidden her feelings, pretended tranquillity in her play and braved the nightmares. Protective to extremes, sometimes, when it came to her life's chronicle Rute had failed, and Cat felt it in her innermost being.

Over the years they had reached a kind of equilibrium and the stories had stopped; but now the discussion of the stories also had to stop, and with the calculated arrogance of youth, Cat chose the one question which she intuitively knew would either seal her mother's lips forever or break open the floodgates. That one yowled question for which no prophet nor politician nor theologian nor theorist had ever reached conclusion, the meaning of suffering, that malevolent demon that stood forever on Rute's shoulder.

'Why did you survive, and not the others?'

Always her oblique sub-text; always the same, unanswered plea. Why was I born? Have I made no difference to you at all? But ah, her frail and fragile mother! The question paled her face. Her eyes grieving, she said, 'Caterina, there are no answers to these things. Oh, why disturb yourself about it? What's the *purpose* of all this... *discussion*?'

Cat looked at her blankly, and then she went up to her room. Given that she was studying Eliot in school her mother's words had resonated strongly. *To what purpose, disturbing the dust on a bowl of rose-leaves...*

She wrenched at the clasp on the window, opened it and leaned out. *Purpose?* she thought, her teeth clenched. Ma, I'm a child of a Survivor, and I *love* you! I want to *understand*, else how will I ever learn to grow? I've never needed what you told me; all I needed was what you've never told me.

It seemed to her something of an achievement to have reached adulthood without ever saying the words out loud. Poetry had helped, in particular R.S. Thomas and Eliot. In them she rested; they gave her permission to feel what she was feeling and the words to express it. Eliot's *Four Quartets* was on her bedside table and, tucked into the flyleaf, Thomas's *Bright Field*, cut out of an examination paper – *I have seen the sun break through to light up a small field... Discuss.* But, in the end, her painting had taken supremacy; it was where the poetry led; it became her 'bright field', the one place in her life lit to magic. She loved the phrase for the way that the poet, with characteristic insight, had realised that he might have missed the brightness had he not stepped aside to look, or if the rest of the landscape had not been monochrome, featureless and dull.

As her life with Rute had been. As must be all life, without truth in it. Much as her mother loved her – for Cat, in her wiser moments, knew she did – she would never tell her more. She would never break her word. She might confide in someone else but, as her daughter, the truth was barred to her. So she would go; she would leave her mother to her memories, to her silly, stupid *blundering about* in this dirty, poverty-stricken town and she would make a new life for herself somewhere else.

Without discussing her plans with anyone, she applied for a place at a teacher training college to study Art and was accepted.

PART 2

tonal values

Dawn points, and another day
Prepares for heat and silence.
Out at sea the dawn wind
Wrinkles and slides. I am here
Or there, or elsewhere. In my beginning.

TS Eliot Four Quartets 11 East Coker

1

At the age of forty two Catherine Adamson, *née* Feugler, left her husband and fled up the motorway to Rute. She drove the way she'd lived, her half-blind eye on the road ahead, the good one on the rear view mirror. Only when she could be sure that Bill's dark Audi wasn't looming up behind her, she would relax, but right now she had that familiar, tense knot of fear in her stomach and her knuckles were white on the wheel. On the hard shoulder were two cars, hazard lights flashing, and as she passed she heard the sound of shouting – 'road rage', they called it these days, but mere bickering compared to Bill's, if he caught up with her. On the other side of the motorway the traffic was queuing up at the junction, forming a bottleneck behind, their lights a crystal haze over the road. Cat marvelled that each morning, while she'd been battling away at home, thousands of people all over the country were sitting on motorways in the dark with nothing to worry about except being late for work. But how did anyone know what took place behind the closed doors of their homes, what misery and heartache they might have left behind them?

The road was swinging round to the north and ahead was the sign for Bicester; she was well away, now, and she eased back on the wheel. It was getting light; below the dark bar of clouds the sky was a limpid cerulean blue and away to the east the sun was rising. It was going to be a fine day.

She felt stunned by what she had done; finally, she had walked out; finally, she had left him. She was going to her mother; she was going to Rute.

But would Rute have her? She'd not have forgotten the time of Cat's denial; she, herself, had never forgotten her mother's white-faced shock or her averted eyes. She drove on auto-pilot, oblivious of the rising hills or the beauty of the sunrise, conscious only of her memories. Images from the past reared up in front of her on the windscreen like a film show, as disjointed and unsynchronised as she was.

College, and her unassuaged hunger for friendship, the isolation, the humiliation of weekly tutorials, the hatefulness of the rowdy, undisciplined children in overcrowded countryside schools, her inability to break the link with home and the endless telephone calls to Rute, just to have someone to speak to, someone who knew her, who'd take a genuine interest in her. Sitting in the corridor, eyes closed, chin in hand, as Rute rehearsed her weekly checklist; whether she was eating well, getting enough sleep and keeping away from boys. Even Rute, poor housebound, terrified Rute, had been more adventurous than she. 'Caterina, I've joined the library – have you read '*How Green Was My Valley*, by Richard Llewellyn?' – the v's and w's transposed. Cat smiled at the recollection. Rute's cheap menus, such as breast of lamb stuffed with porridge oats – 'There's nothing you can tell me about poor cuts!' – or potato cakes made with bacon and dried apricots. As if she hadn't known that Cat lived in a cell-like room with no cooking facilities, or that she was supposed to be eating in Hall. She'd been living a lie; she'd belonged neither with her mother nor at college; she belonged nowhere.

The film club where she'd first met Bill, the anonymity of the enveloping dark, Vincente Minelli's film about Van Gogh, *Lust for Life*, and her infatuation with Kirk Douglas. Jean Renoir's documentary about his father, the unforgettable image on the screen of *The Young Renoir with Gabrielle Renard* and how, suddenly entranced with portraiture, she'd felt her own life literally changing before her eyes. Renoir's eulogy to Renard, delivered by the narrator in a gruff French accent: *She taught me to see the face behind the mask*

64

and the fraud behind the flourishes. Pity that hadn't taken root; pity she hadn't seen Bill's face behind his mask before it was too late, or found the fraud behind his flourishes.

Bill had already graduated and held a junior position in the local bank. Her horizons widened to include his friends, the pub, the cinema, Johnny Dankworth gigs in Cambridge and Ronnie Scott, only to narrow again next morning as she rushed through the empty streets to catch lectures, to write up last minute essays and to lie about their ineptitude.

Her panic, when she realised she was pregnant, her Principal's rapid dismissal of her, how the words above the arch of the old building, *Educational Establishment for the Training of Mistresses* were no longer amusing, for her three years at college had come to nothing. She'd boxed up her books and hauled them to the nearest charity shop, piled her clothes into suitcases, and, in the pouring rain, went to find Bill. She'd sat shivering over his cheerless electric fire, watching his face for his reaction, and totally unprepared for what he did say.

'Cat, you don't want to get rid of it, do you?'

'No. No, Bill I don't.' She'd seen some of these women and there was something about their faces afterwards, some sore, colourless, impenetrable look, which told her that abortion was not a straightforward option.

She remembered how he'd taken both her hands in his, and proposed to her. Those hands, so small compared to hers, but so effective when it came to hitting. She remembered how she'd tried to pull away, to be sensible. 'Bill, I just don't want to put any pressure on you, that's all. I really, really don't!' and his look of obstinacy, how he'd gripped her wrists so tightly that she'd had bruises for days. He'd never been rough like that before and his brusqueness made her shrivel inside. But then, of course, she'd given him a shock; it was understandable.

He seemed to know what she was feeling and his manner changed; he became kind and encouraging.

'You're miles away, Cat. Whatever you thinking about, stop. Look, I know it's a risk, but we've a baby on the way...' He gave a light laugh and pulled her closer. 'So just say "yes". Why not?'

Driving blindly up the motorway, trying to be fair, it seemed necessary to remember that, at the time, she'd felt nothing but relief and gratitude. She'd taken the train home, and desperate to confide in her mother, she had steeled herself to speak; she could have laid her head in her lap for very weariness, but Rute rushed at her with her own troubles as though her life depended on it, almost as if Cat had never been away, and the moment when she could have confided was gone.

Rute was planning an extended visit to America to see her sister Hannah for the first time since the war, and was terrified of the long flight across the sea. Too cowed by her pre-natal burden to let her imagination stretch, Cat said little to allay her mother's fears, and two weeks later, Rute flew out. On the eve of her departure Cat told her about her engagement, but all Rute seemed to care about was whether Bill had good prospects; there was no mention of meeting him, and as for love, it seemed irrelevant. Cat didn't mention her pregnancy.

No one, later, would ask Rute, 'How was the journey? You were all right, were you, on your own?' or, 'How was Hannah? You find out what happened to her after Zwickau?' How could they? No one except Cat knew the details of Rute's life, and she was too preoccupied to ask.

Cat had three weeks alone in the house and apart from a couple of visits to Bill, she spent most of the time drawing. She took a three mile bus journey to

West Wycombe, surreptitiously sketching her fellow passengers, then climbed the chalk hill to the Hellfire Caves and sketched the tourists. Afterwards she took the bus back into town to buy some paints and to re-stock her mother's larder. This time she didn't draw, but gazed, unseeing, out of the window, her hands over her swollen stomach, over the growing life within.

She remembered their Registry Office wedding, how she'd wondered why her replies seemed so mechanical, but by then she'd felt mechanical for a long time. The weekly checkups at the hospital had been worse than essay tutorials, the waiting room crammed with pregnant women with wedding rings, whose only conversation concerned the merits of breast feeding or the new-fangled disposable nappies. She felt totally estranged from them, sick in body and mind, but she reminded herself that Rute had been in a similar situation and during their one transatlantic call she finally confessed that she was pregnant. Later she asked herself, had her mother really said what she thought she'd said?

'You might have told me earlier. I could have embroidered some baby clothes for you. Matching baby clothes, just think!'

A week later, on her mother's return, bronzed by the Florida sun, a very pregnant Catherine Feugler in a white charity shop maternity dress, and a disturbingly florid William Adamson were married.

2

There was something else Cat might have said earlier. Sometime during their brief engagement, she might have told her future husband that her mother was Jewish, not that she'd thought it any more relevant than that she had once been a pianist. It only came to light in the Registry Office, at Rute's audible hiss of satisfaction. 'He will make you happy. You can forget poverty, Green Street, put it behind you. He is *rich!* The look he gave Cat, a steely-eyed, reddened-ear look, was so profoundly disillusioned that she had recoiled.

Bill was appointed deputy manager of Lloyds Bank in Beaconsfield, on the strength of which he had taken out a mortgage. It was a small isolated house at the top of a valley, but it was on a bus route and near enough to High Wycombe for Rute to visit, which she did regularly until warned off by his hostility. By then their pattern of life was set and for Cat it was full of fear. His mood changes were terrifying, one minute he was gentle and affable; the next, edgy, petulant, winding himself up to a vicious temper. The slightest domestic problem could provoke his wrath; late meals, the smell of nappies, crying babies, and six months into their marriage, in the middle of an argument, he slapped her hard across the face.

They stared at each other in consternation. He immediately apologised and took her in his arms. 'Honestly, it'll never happen again; I just flipped; please believe me, Cat.'

But she didn't believe him. She felt a huge weight of dread at her heart. She didn't know what to do, and when it happened again, she knew the rot had set in.

Even as toddlers the twins dreaded his key in the door and she was already saying to them what she would continue to say into their adolescence – 'Oh, don't mind Daddy; he's just a bit tired, that's all; why not just go outside and play?' or 'Let's see what's on television, shall we?' Later it became, 'Oh, do *something*, but please, please, just stay out of Daddy's way.'

Bill tried to explain his behaviour. It saddened him, he said; he didn't know what possessed him.

'Of course,' he said, 'all violence is wrong, but especially in the home.'

'Yes,' she said, 'it is.'

He loved their home, he said, and he wanted her to know that on the very rare occasions when he drank too much, it wasn't because of her. He loved her; he loved her very much; he couldn't begin to tell her how much he loved her. It was just work, he said; it stressed him out. He joked about it. 'Plenty more to walk into my shoes, you know; got to keep my face on the radar'.

For weeks afterwards, things were better between them, and he even suggested they had another child. Cat was silent; she didn't trust him, but he took her silence as a personal insult, and if, after that, he hit her or slapped her or pushed her, or deliberately tripped her up, he would find other excuses for his conduct. He said she didn't understand what a miserable business it was to come home to 'a mucky house, bickering kids and no proper food on the table.' In spite of his drinking he liked his food, and the lack or it, or its poor quality, became a huge issue between them. 'I can't eat out all the time, you know – you want to bankrupt me, or something?' Aware of how sparse were her culinary arts, Cat searched the library for cookery books, but bewildered by the plethora of titles, she turned to her mother. 'Oh, I should have taught you how to cook,' said Rute, shamefaced, and gave Cat her copy of Mrs Beeton, but when Cat took home to read in the kitchen she realised that the pages were almost pristine – obviously Rute had rarely opened it.

The Preface read, *There is no more fruitful source of family discontent than a housewife's badly-cooked dinners and untidy ways.* Right, she thought, so it's all my fault, is it? *A mistress must be thoroughly acquainted with the theory and practice of cookery, as well as be perfectly conversant with all the other arts of making and keeping a comfortable home.*

It was not to be. 'What a piece of *shit*,' he said of the steak she then prepared for him – 'Why can't you remember I like it rare?' or 'You know I hate cod; it's for kids', or, of her lamb casserole – *'Stew?* Bloody lorry driver's *stew*? Oh, for Chris'sake, get me a beer.'

He told her she was manipulative, dull, *old*. He said he felt trapped. Cat had always believed she was dull; old she was not, except that her hair was greying, as had her mother's at about the same age – yet wasn't *he* older, too, with his receding hairline and his paunch? But *trapped*?

'It was you who proposed to me, back then,' she said. 'I didn't want to put pressure on you, remember?' But she also remembered how she'd colluded in their marriage and she felt his snarl of contempt was deserved. Later, with his fists, he used the word 'emasculation'. He was heavily-built, and his fists hurt. She knew, then, that she'd been right to be wary. Nothing had changed and there'd be no more children.

The years went by. She could have left him, as Rute frequently implored her to, but she didn't. Time and time again she told herself that, now that she had learned to cook, now that the children were older and more observant, now that he had a more senior position in the bank and was earning more, things would get better. She knew she was deceiving herself.

She couldn't have left him. How would she manage, where would she go? Without qualifications and never having worked, how could she cope on her own with two children? Two children who knew their father's rages but, when he was quiescent and affectionate, loved him dearly. If she fled, he'd only find her; his rage would find them out.

She was thirty-five and she reckoned she'd told more lies than one person should be capable of in a lifetime. Sometimes, she even believed them herself, those petty fabrications, those inane, grey excuses. 'Oh sorry, we can't make that date; Bill's got a meeting.' Or 'Sorry, Bill's out; he's busy; his train is late; the car broke down; we can't come; we can't go; the children need; James has a school function; Deborah, a dental appointment...' Lies which did little more than cloak her fear, the fear that she'd be seen in public with bruises, the fear that one day he'd hurt the twins, the fear of police, of social workers, of the whole paraphernalia of 'care'. To lose the children, to have them taken from her... They were her one joy in all that misery, the one shining light in all that conflict, and she couldn't imagine life without them. She certainly couldn't desert them. At night, when she dreamed the resurgent dreams of childhood, it was they, the twins, who disappeared into the black hole, and it was a place where she couldn't follow.

During the day, alone in the house, she took refuge in her painting; compositions of fruits or vegetables, the view into the garden, or an old coat hanging from a hook — any and everything that suggested structure and tone. Her pencil mapping was a realistic record of what was in front of her but in her colour work she explored the resonances of light and tonality, the three dimensional body-evoking shapelessness of the old coat or the fruitiness of the fruit. Occasionally she would paint her own reflection in a mirror, and find there a similar fecundity that, despite her deep unhappiness, showed in the bloom on her cheeks, on her forehead and in the shine of her hair. She would search with her eyes her own eyes, exploring, probing; trying, with the brush, to soften the penetrating gaze of the self-portrait.

If she mentioned her painting at all, it was with typical self-effacing modesty, with the result that people dismissed it as 'little hobby', a term Bill sneeringly flung at her, and as she thought her work amateurish and mediocre, at one level she believed them. But she was driven to it in a way that belied that superficial assumption. She continually felt that she never quite achieved what she wanted to achieve, that there was always more to learn, especially about colours and how to make them. She learned to stop work before she actually needed to, so that she could clear up before anyone came home and still have time to make the beds, empty the washing machine and rustle up a meal.

Her evenings were spent arguing with Deborah over her untidiness or missed assignments, or with James, about which television programmes he could watch, which books they should or shouldn't read, and pretending to herself that these were no more than the normal, everyday battles of family life, that everything was well, that there was nothing to fear.

Of the twins, Deborah was the more intransigent, but Cat always assumed that her daughter's exaggerated response to every little mishap was normal adolescent behaviour, a stage simply to be borne with and accommodated. But sometimes, exhausted, unable to sleep, she worried that Deborah must sense how hypocritical her parents' marriage was and feel utterly suffocated – but, to suffocate one's own daughter? Cat loved the twins equally, but she yearned towards her daughter in a way that she felt her own mother had never yearned towards her and she looked forward to the day when they might enjoy a more equal companionship. And yet she also kept her at arm's length. The idea of unburdening herself to her, as her mother had done to her, was utterly repellent.

James was milder by nature and more aloof, so

whether the twins discussed their parents with each other, she didn't know; even the thought was humiliating.

When Rute looked at her askance she said, 'Oh, Ma, don't blame Bill; it's not his fault; he's good to us, really; it doesn't happen often; he's just got a bit of a temper, that's all.' She was perfectly aware that by excusing him she was conniving with his behaviour and she hated lying to her mother. If Rute noticed a cut or a bruise or heard him shouting, she said, 'Oh, I hurt myself and he's just upset about it; I banged into, ran into, bumped into – it was my fault, really'. But his demeaning words and his profanity became a growing ulcer in her mind, a sore incapable of healing. She longed for another life, a different sort of life; another love, a different kind of love, an affirming, devoted, more equal love, but she knew it was a chimera.

3

Bill was not averse to blaming Rute for the tribulations of their marriage. To be saddled with an archetypical Jewish matriarch as a mother-in-law was a lethal combination, he said, a double whammy. Privately, Cat sympathised, and but for his spite it could have been a joke they shared behind her mother's back. There was open warfare between them, a vicious cycle of attack and counter attack, which, as Rute turned up every Sunday morning and stayed for lunch, drove the twins from the house and antagonised them forever.

Cat made excuses for her mother, similar to the ones she made for Bill. 'She's all alone; she hasn't got anyone else; she gets depressed; she's had a hard life; naturally, she wants to see her grandchildren.'

In extremity she appealed to her mother. 'Ma, he's only being provocative. Why rise to his bait?'

'I know I do,' Rute muttered. 'Hook, line and stinker.'

Food was Rute's panacea for all ills, and after she had gone Bill would dance mockingly round the kitchen, exaggerating her accent in a high falsetto. '"Gif zem a bit of steamed fish, Caterina, it verks vonders with ze digestion," or "Caterina, vy not make zem soup with dumplings; I expect zey're chust hungry; werry comforting, soup viz dumplings."'

If Rute deeply disapproved of Bill and was distressed for her marriage it was his racist remarks that angered her most and one day she reached the end of her tether.

'You do know,' she said, fighting back with some relish, 'that Deborah and James are Jewish names. You do know that, don't you, Bill? Your own name is Jewish – Adamson. Have you never thought to research your ancestors?'

Bill flushed with rage and his mouth curled with

disgust. He stood up from the table, rearing over her.

'How *dare* you speak to me like that? At *my* table, in *my* house... If you think you're welcome here, you're mistaken.'

He leaned so hard on the table that it tilted and his plate slid off on to the floor and shattered. He bent down to retrieve the pieces, clattering them together, and began to hurl them at Rute, who swung away, her arms raised to protect herself. Cat sat rigid with dismay and the children were open-mouthed. She nodded to them to leave the room and a moment later she heard them giggling on the stairs.

'Just... just get out, will you,' he roared, his spittle flying, 'before I do something I'll regret!'

Rute fled. Cat heard the back door close behind her and then her diminutive shape flashed by the dining room window. Bill got to his feet and slammed out of the front door.

Cat didn't go after her mother. Like an automaton she began to clear the table of its debris. She put the broken china in the bin, and stacked the rest in the dishwasher. She felt stunned at how quickly their quarrel had escalated. She looked out of the window. Rute was walking tensely up and down the garden path, muttering to herself, looping her necklace round in her hands. Then she reappeared at the back door. She leaned against it as if she was very tired.

Quietly pleading, she said, 'Caterina, can't you stop him saying these things? I'm sure he doesn't mean them, but he... he can be very stern sometimes. Sometimes he's so much like my brother, like Reuben was. Can't you do something?'

Cat shrugged and shook her head, her eyes closed and her expression blank. Rute gazed at her sadly, and then turned away. Cat finished loading the dishwasher and put the food away. Then she washed the saucepans, drying them carefully and sliding them into the pan drawer. She mopped down the surfaces and folded up the tablecloth. She took off her apron and hung it on its hook and only then did she go out into the garden to her mother.

She found her sitting on the damp grass under the willow tree, as remote as in the old days of her childhood. Cat sat down beside her; she would have put an arm round her shoulders, but Rute leaned away from her, averting her eyes. Her face was ashen. She looked shocked and dazed. She left soon afterwards, refusing a lift. Cat watched her from the door, wearily dragging her feet. She stood at the bus stop a long time, dry-eyed, and bent.

Cat went after her. 'Ma, come back in the house and I'll ring for a taxi. You can wait ages for a bus here on Sundays.'

Rute shook her head impotently. Opposite, tucked into the hedge, was a telephone kiosk and, turning her back on Cat, she began to cross the road.

'I am perfec'ly capable of ringing for a taxi myself.' Then, fumbling in her purse, she turned. 'Have you coins? I have no coins.'

'I'll get some.' Cat rushed back to the house, but when she returned Rute was nowhere to be seen, and when she telephoned her later there was no answer. A month later Rute was gone. She packed up her little house in Green Street and moved to a small housing estate on the outskirts of Coventry. She never came to their house again.

If Cat had asked, 'Why Coventry?' Rute would have said, 'A lottery!' but in fact the answer was as plain as the nose on her face. Coventry was far enough away to make a clean break but still within reach of Cat, should she be needed. Between them silence descended, a silence broken only by polite phone calls. The intimacy of Cat's childhood and youth had dribbled away, sunk into the damp grass under a willow tree. All that she could hope for was that, in that big, sprawling multicultural city, her mother might find other

Holocaust Survivors, be able to unite her story to theirs, and find friendship. Whatever friendship meant. In all her life Cat could think of no one she called friend.

Except, of course, her mother. After all this time, Rute's magnetism was still strong; there was nowhere else she could go, no one who knew her as her mother knew her, or who would understand. Now, driving helter-skelter towards Coventry, all she could hope for was that somehow Rute had found the grace to forgive her and would give her a bed until she found a place of her own. She could say that to her. She might accept that. The prodigal daughter.

She was off the motorway, on the Coventry bypass, at her mother's door.

4

'Oh my poor Caterina, what has he done to you this time?'

Except for her hair, which was almost completely white and still caught up untidily at the nape of her neck, Rute had hardly changed. Now over sixty, she was slightly bowed but still slim, and although her hands were parchment-dry and slightly liver-spotted, her knuckles swollen from years of laundering, her eyes were bright with intelligence and she still moved and thought like quicksilver. She bent for Cat's case, took her by the arm and rushed her into the house.

Exhausted, but intensely relieved, Cat prevaricated. 'A door, Ma. Just a door.'

Rute looked sceptical. 'Always you say these things. Always bomping into things...'

'But I'm leaving him, Ma.' Cat faced her mother, her hands limp by her sides. 'I've left him.'

'Truly?' said Rute gently. 'For good?'

'...Or ill.'

'But your *children*, Caterina? How can you leave your *children*?' Her first thought, always, though she had not seen them for years.

'Ma, they're *grown up*. Deborah went ages ago, you know that. And James won't come back after college. Kids don't, these days.' She felt suddenly overwhelmed by the strain of the last twenty four hours. 'Look, can I just go to bed for a while? I didn't get much sleep last night.'

Her mother watched her from the bottom of the stairs, her fingers already groping for her necklace, and as Cat turned back the covers of the bed in the single bedroom and drew the curtains, she remembered how Rute's father had fought tooth and nail to protect his family and she wondered how wise she had been to come. As a child she had wondered at the manner of that fight. The phrase 'tooth and nail' had remained with her, along with a nightmarish image of an old man in a swirling shabby caftan bouncing off an unseen enemy, his beard unkempt, his fingernails dirty with grime, his teeth bared like a wild animal, his figure disproportionately large against the backcloth of his cowering family. An image she knew to be inaccurate, reconstructed by her own powerful imagination – he had not been there when they were taken away – but teeth, nails, sound and fury had entered her dreams, together with the other nightmares. Yet, in spite of the continuing anguish of those nightmares, and in spite of the passage of thirty or more years, and in spite of the fact that she was now a grown woman with children of her own, children not much younger than her mother had been when she recounted her stories, it was her mother she had sought, in a way that she had not done even as an adolescent girl. She should have managed on her own, but that evening, when the pain in her eye became almost intolerable, and Rute, her lips taut, threatened to call her doctor, she gave way to a panic that was almost childish in its intensity.

'No, you mustn't... I don't want...'

'Caterina, he may have damaged your eye! You want to go blind, already? You should have gone straight to Casualty!'

'Then what? The police? I can see OK, really I can. I drove here all right, didn't I? Just get me some salt water, would you?'

The telephone shrilled. 'That'll be him,' her mother hissed, as though Bill could hear.

'Don't tell him...'

'Of course not!'

'Lie. Say anything. Say I've been and gone. Don't say...'

'Don't worry, Caterina,' Rute said significantly, 'I know how to keep the silence.'

Their eyes met, acknowledging their mutual history,

and the ringing stopped, its echo in Cat's ears for hours.

In the womb-like sanctuary of her mother's house, she slept the profound, dreamless sleep of emotional exhaustion. Waking was another matter. She lay rigid for hours, her arm clamped behind her neck, the events of the last two years crowding in on her.

The day Deborah left; James, sitting at the kitchen table, his dilapidated school bag at his feet, one knee jigging nervously, hands dangling, wrists showing – both the twins were tall, with the slender delicacy of youth, and James was fast growing out of his clothes.

'Sit down a minute, Mum...'

Cat perched on the very edge of her chair, shoulders hunched, arms pressed against her chest, her legs knotted, dreading what she would have to hear.

'She's gone to London, Mum.' He was seventeen, his voice at the half-broken stage, one minute gruff, the next high-pitched, and he hated it. 'Says she'll sleep on other people's floors.'

'*Whose* floor?' Cat demanded, imagining drugs-sex-and-drink. She was bitterly hurt that Deborah hadn't confided in her or even said goodbye. 'Where? Did she take any clothes? And why tell *you*, and not *me*?' She saw the pain in his eyes and snatched back the words. 'I mean *as well*; me as well!' By which she meant, 'Me first.' Then, with gritted teeth and flying hands, snapping the words, 'Who does she know who even *lives* in London? And why *now*, suddenly?'

It seemed a rejection of the worst kind, and Cat suddenly realised how her mother had felt the day she had looked to her for protection and been denied. She put her face in her hands and wept.

James was embarrassed for her and loyally evasive. 'Mum, she did promise to keep in touch.'

With *you*? With *me*? *HOW?*' she screamed, but he

merely gave a non-committal shrug, grabbed his bag and ran upstairs.

Bill, when she told him, was incandescent with anger, and not only with Deborah. The white-faced James got his full share of wrath and Cat another bruise, but it was only when he made no attempt to find his daughter, or none to which he would admit, that Cat began to be suspicious.

'It was you, wasn't it?' she shouted. 'What did you say to her?' She went up to him and for the first time in their married life, laid hold of him violently and shook him. '*What have you done to my daughter?*'

'You're being ridiculous,' he said quietly. 'I haven't said or done anything. Look to yourself, Catherine, and for heaven's sake, get a grip.'

James, when she confronted him, closed his eyes against her and turned away. 'Oh, please don't ask me, Mum – she said not to say.'

He had tears in his eyes, and out of compassion for him she left the matter alone, but her anger against her husband mounted. She moved her things to Deborah's room, and that night she wet her daughter's pillow with her tears. The sense of loss, of something irretrievably broken, was indescribable.

Lying in the narrow single bed, basking in the still, quiet warmth of her mother's house, Cat imagined how Deborah might look, two years on. Tall, willowy, confident and smiling? Or cast down by hardship? Now, perhaps, she'd find her again, and not just Deborah, but James as well.

Two days she slept, fed with her mother's newly baked bread and thin soups, nursing her bruises with a piece of stewing steak – all that Rute could afford, and which, afterwards, she served up to Cat as she sat hunched over the kitchen table in her mother's pink candy stripe dressing gown.

Then questions; Rute tenacious, arms afloat, her

green eyes slits in her wrinkled face.

'So, what's been happening? You ready to tell me, now, Caterina?'

'Ma, I said, already,' she muttered, through a mouthful of food. 'It was a door.'

'That's just silly, Caterina. He's *eine Trottel* of a man! I don't know why you protect him, the *schmuck*.' Her accents were guttural with contempt, and Cat found a grin. 'And why now, may I ask, when you left it so long? So many times have I said you could have brought the twins here...'

'What, and disrupted their whole lives? He was all right with them, mostly...'

'Mostly? What's mostly? And Jakov gone a year? So why not a year ago you leave him?' She shook her head, exasperated. 'How many times have I told you, Caterina? Sometimes you just have to run!'

It was the word 'run' that did it. The tears which Cat had repressed for so long burst out and she put her hands to her face, covering her eyes like a child. Rute looked aghast, completely unaware how the word had resonated, how it not only underlined what Cat had just done, but had also resurrected one of the worst moments of her childhood.

Into the light-shot darkness of her fingers comes the memory of that deserted playground, the boy's contempt as he pelts her with stones, a blond, square-headed boy dressed, inexplicably, in *lederhosen*. A boy who has long taunted her with her race, who now seizes the day. Boy? No, he's a lout, ugly and oafish, and she cowers from him, balled against the grimy wall, 'Jew! Jew!' ringing in her head. Why wasn't *he* bullied, with his crew cut and his silly *lederhosen*? What had given her away? Was it Rute? Her accent, the residual odour of her charity shop clothes?

Rute comes at last, a tiny, dark haired woman dwarfed by the school railings, which she clutches with both fists; her shriek, 'Run, Caterina, run!' ringing across the playground. Later, wiping Cat's tears with a soiled tissue, she demands an explanation. 'Why he fight you, anyway?' and adds vehemently, '*Dämlich* people! You mustn't provoke them, Caterina! What you say to make him...?'

'I called him a *Trottel*, but only half-way through. He started it.'

Rute gapes in delight. '*Ach, zo!* But you haven't told him you are Jewish, have you?' Pure grit abrades her accent. 'Hide it, Caterina! Don't tell anyone, no one at all! In future use the bus and I'll meet you in the town. That *dummer Hurensohn* tries it again, you *run*!'

5

Cat woke as a couple of local newspapers were dropped on the bed; the Coventry Times and the Ad Mag – a fruitless endeavour on her mother's part since Cat had no intention of taking 'a pleasant' terraced house in Bedworth, or a refurbished flat in Earlsdon, or whatever else was on offer in 'a desirable location near a thriving multicultural city'.

'But, it's what you want, isn't it, a place of your own?'

Yes, thought Cat, but decidedly elsewhere; not near her mother and not merely up the motorway from Bill.

Over the next few days Rute tried another tack, pressing Cat to stay on with her, at least for a while. You're in shock, she said; you need rest and care, and a break from decision-making. This was said almost wryly, in full awareness of their chequered past, but Cat would never put herself under her mother's thumb again; they could not go back. Yet she realised what a pang her mother must have felt when, under a cushion on her chair, Cat discovered a copy of *The Lady* and found in those auspicious pages what she was looking for. It was an advertisement for an old sail loft on the Thames; she liked the sound of that, and it was cheap. Carefully she cut it out with her mother's sewing scissors – 'Not *paper*, Caterina, please! How many times...?' and put it in her purse. She phoned the agent and arranged to view the place the following day. He was a bookseller in nearby Swanscombe, an elderly man with a pronounced Welsh accent.

'When you come into Swanscombe, turn left by the station. That's the High Street, see – I'm on the right, towards the top. You can't miss it, and I'll have the keys ready.'

She set off early. Rute, on the doorstep, looked old, gaunt, ashy-grey, as desolate as the mist that hung over the streets, reminiscent of the day Cat started secondary school, when her mother shoved her out of the door almost roughly, her face puckering, and in the afternoon, when they met in the town, said she'd just pottered around all day. Laughing, self-accusing. 'I've been very busy doing nothing.'

On the motorway the mist thickened to a pale, swirling fog, as dark as evening, and the traffic was nose to tail. It was like driving into a black hole and she nearly turned back, so evocative was it of her nightmares. Those nightmares had journeyed with her throughout her life, like a piece of furniture moved from house to house with an unwanted present mouldering in one of the drawers. They had coloured her waking hours and filled her nights with dread, but now, strangely, they kept her going. At least they told her who she was, that she had substance, individuality, a past and potentially a future. Like her mother, she knew she had the capacity to stand back, to hope, and if not to forget, to go on.

And, finally, to escape the marital home. She'd learned silence; she'd learned acquiescence; she'd learned not to answer back, but with flight always in mind she'd looked forward. She abandoned landscapes and Still Life and concentrated on portrait painting. She took a number of commissions, small canvases which she completed quickly, with growing confidence. She watched her post office account grow steadily, month by month, until even she was awed by how much she'd earned. To add to it she offered art tuition at the local college. Bill never knew that after he left for work, she would put on her make up and rush down the hill to her class. Every little bit of money she earned she hoarded like a miser. Eventually she blew it all in on a small second hand car, a silver Renault 5 with a dented wing – as hers was, she thought; as hers was. She housed it on their forecourt, used it rarely, and kept the tank full. Bill looked on with disdain, but also with reluctant admiration. 'Ah, the little hobby maketh the shekels, does it? Wow.' She had no concrete plan but what she called her escape fund empowered her and bred within her the first seeds of hope. Stage one, to find the means, had been accomplished; stage two was to store up courage, a commodity she felt that she'd always lacked.

It was not until six months later, after James had left home, that the final showdown with Bill came. In the interim, things had unaccountably improved; he drank less, and was less violent, as if his behaviour to Deborah had sobered him. He even booked a night for them both in a nearby country hotel; there was a man, he said, he had to meet on business; it would help to have a wife around. Any invitation from him was rare, and while she treasured his intermittent absences, she had seen this luxury hotel from the outside and the thought of staying there for a night was irresistible.

They went down to dinner together. In the bar, he downed several glasses of beer; over dinner he shone; he was affable, agreeable; he consumed a bottle or more of wine; after dinner he became truculent and his business contact began to look embarrassed. The evening dragged on, as with bright smiles and banal chatter, Cat sought to make amends. Suddenly Bill stood up, took her by the wrist and dragged her to the lift; once in the room his accusations filled the air. That bloody man downstairs, she was *flirting* with the bloody man; making eyes at the bastard; she was a bitch on heat, and now he'd give her what for. He hit her in the face, and she reeled backwards over the bed.

Her first thought was her painting. 'My eye! Oh, my eye! My God, you've damaged my eye!'

He threw himself on top of her, his face suffused with blood. He tore at her clothes and fumbled with his own. Why, he's going to rape me, she thought, and fought him all the way. But he was drunk, ineffectual;

he collapsed at her side, panting, his sweat staining her face. She lay as he had left her, on her back, and listened to him snore. She felt nothing but disgust. Her eye felt twice its size, and she dragged herself out from under him and went to the bathroom. There she soaked a flannel in cold water and, leaving the light on, settled down on the sofa, pressing the flannel to her temple.

What had happened had the force of destiny. It liberated her, and that night there were no gabardined men in her dreams, no tramp of angry feet or black, smothering hole, but merely a hint of violin, played behind closed shutters. It was a light, happy sound, almost ethereal, infinitely preferable to Bill's stertorous breathing and she wanted to hear more. She woke early, content and full of hope.

As soon as she heard movement in the corridor, she got up, quietly packed her suitcase, left it by the door, and shook him awake.

'Bill, get dressed. We're going home. I'm leaving you.'

'Whaaa...?'

'Give me the car keys.'

She soaked the flannel again, wrapped it in a plastic shower cap, took her suitcase to the car and waited in the driving seat, holding the damp package to her eye.

'But this is *my* car!'

'You're not fit to drive.'

As they drove back through the quiet streets Bill cast sideways looks at her, anxious, sheepish, penitent, but Cat didn't speak until they were home.

'I'm leaving you, Bill. I said I would, and I am. And don't for one minute think of finding me. I'll never forgive you for what you've done to us, me and the children.'

She got out of the car, opened the front door and went quickly upstairs. She went to the medicine cabinet, found some aspirin, and swallowed three tablets whole. She walked into the bright clear light of Deborah's room and took her childhood teddy. From James's room she took a small Hornby train. She packed a couple of suitcases, put in the toys and took them downstairs. All this time she'd kept her car keys in her hand. Bill was standing on the gravel, wearing his habitual, derisive sneer, but when he saw her rucksack with her painting kit, his expression changed to alarm.

She climbed into her car, fastened her seat belt, turned on the engine, and put her foot on the clutch.

'Where d'you think you're going?' he shouted, banging his knuckles against the window.

'Somewhere south,' she lied. 'Anywhere. To the seaside, perhaps. To peace and quiet.'

'Oh yeah!' He stood back, laughing. 'Just who d'you think you are? You stupid bitch, don't you realise, all I have to do is get in my car and follow you? '

Questions akin to her those of her teacher, and she made the same response. She put her foot on the accelerator and drove away. Quite easy, in the end, except for her black eye.

6

Her journey south from Coventry had been time-consuming but uneventful. After St Albans she turned east on the M25. Aware of overhead speed warnings gleaming through the fog, she kept to her lane, dutifully followed the car in front. Ahead was the Dartford Tunnel, and once through it the fog was replaced by a sky of sweet, incandescent blue. As she looked the white orb of the sun finally broke through, clothing the grey sprawl of factories and tower blocks with an opaque, luminous vapour and turning the wide expanse of glittering water into vivid orange. It filled her with delight – a splash of real colour on an otherwise toneless palette. With each mile she became more elated, the stress of the journey forgotten. The idea that her new life might mean a completely new world, a world of colours and reflections, was almost overwhelming.

She saw signs for Gravesend, Gillingham and Herne Bay – places she'd heard of but never seen. Swanscombe was further on, its sprawling town centre set back from the seafront, the High Street a plethora of small shops and a distant view of the flint and brick parish church.

The bookshop was an unprepossessing Edwardian building with tinted windows squeezed between a Sixties Co-op and a hairdresser's salon. When she switched off the engine the sense of the absolute quiet of the seaside town was almost unnerving. Where was everyone? Well, commuting, she supposed and smiled to herself; she'd told Bill she was going south, to the seaside, to peace and quiet, and here she was. She checked her face in the rear view mirror. The bruise had yellowed and she reached for her sunglasses – absurd in such weather, but first impressions mattered.

She got out of the car and stretched, glancing up at

the almost illegible sign above the bookshop: *Antiquarian Books – R Dilwyn Williams*. Inside it was a seedy, ill-lit sort of place, like a charity shop at the wrong end of town, its sloping shelves crammed with cheap paperbacks and, on the threadbare carpet, crates of dog-eared manuals tied with orange twine. So much for antiquarian books, she thought, and wondered fleetingly how the business kept afloat. Behind the counter was an elderly man with greying hair and bushy black eyebrows that met over the bridge of his nose. He was pale and unsmiling, and his forehead seemed sculpted by perpetual anxiety. He regarded her with polite disinterest, and then with concern.

'My, that's a fine bruise you've got! Hurt yourself, have you?' The slow Welsh accent of their telephone call.

Ignoring his question she said, 'I've come about the flat. Catherine Feugler? We spoke on the phone yesterday....'

'Ah, yes, Miss Feugler. But *The Sail Loft* isn't really a flat, see.' He gave her a warm smile. 'Sorry to give you the wrong impression, is it? It's actually a considerable building. Used to serve the old barges – you know, for drying the sails? After that it was the manager's house. There's an old paper factory next door with a connecting bridge...'

She cut him short. 'Really? I can't wait to see it.' Leaning against the till was a bulky envelope, her name writ large in black felt tip. 'Are those the keys? OK if I drop them back when I've finished? Won't be long.'

'I've made you a little map...'

She took it from his hand, smiled her thanks and left. She was grateful to be out in the open air.

Back in the car she looked at the map, working out which way she had to go. Apparently her way led inland at first before swinging round once more towards the river. She put it on the dashboard next to the magazine cutting, and slowly coasted down the hill towards the estuary. It was effervescent with light and intensely alluring, and she turned from it with regret. She came to a small housing estate and then a country lane. She passed a row of disused factories with rusty corrugated iron roofs; she glimpsed dilapidated chain-link fencing strung with papery convolvulus, splintered pallets piled with whitened bricks, the forlorn detritus of a bygone age. Here the lane narrowed and became increasingly pot holed, the encroaching banks lined with nettles and brambles and the tired yellow heads of ragwort, but she could smell the sea and she knew that, somewhere over that hedge and across the fields, was the estuary. The hedge stopped; she was now driving between sodden, unfenced pasture, empty of cattle and darkened by winter rains. Occasional stunted hawthorns, angled against the wind, raised their gnarled branches against the ashen sky.

She knew she was intuiting the place with the dark poverty of her marital experiences, and imagining a history of which she knew little, but it was such a desolate approach that she was strangely glad of it. if she took this place she could be alone, if she wanted to. It was ugly, grey and moribund, but only those who had business with her, or those she invited, would venture along this lane; with anyone else she could, if necessary, take evasive action. As to how, with only one way out and the river at her back, she would have to discover.

A little further on, silhouetted against the water, was a small cluster of buildings connected by a covered timber bridge, and immediately the little press cutting in front of her sprang to life. Here was her destination, her long-awaited sanctuary – possibly. If the bridge was sound it could be her exit strategy; she would have the run of the place, literally.

By now the exquisite gold of the estuary was subsumed in grey, and heavy clouds were forming. Cat parked on the slipway, facing the water, and sat for a few minutes watching the tide move sluggishly past, amber brown and viscous under the gaunt, frowning shapes of the warehouses across the river. Then she peeled back the flap of the envelope. Two keys dropped into her lap, emblematic of the freedom that she craved, and which she might now achieve. It struck her then, how similar this was to her mother's experience, both of them escaping − whatever it was that Rute had escaped − both of them seeking refuge and the space and freedom to build a new life.

As she got out of the car she spotted a seabird of some kind flying towards her across the estuary, hugging the choppy water. As it approached it rose overhead to reveal its long, silver neck and black underbelly and, spellbound, she turned to watch it go. Behind her, set well back on the slipway, was a high, two-storey building, a Cape Cod look-alike of clapboard and brick with a steep mansard roof. What struck her most was its huge window, which encompassed the entire frontage of the upper storey, and she found herself imagining how it must have seemed long ago; a vigilant, slightly authoritarian eye surveying the great panorama of the estuary − the wharves, the sprit-sailed barges and the red, square sailed trows. She could almost hear the noise, the sheer bustle and commotion of a river at work. Now the window was badly cataracted by salt and grime, the planks caked with lichen, like the silvery green of hoarfrost. This, then, was *The Sail Loft*.

Across the slipway was the disused factory and she crossed the greasy cobbles to explore. The front jutted out into the water, but at the rear, through a dense thicket of nettles and brambles, she could just discern the remains of a chimney, its brickwork encrusted with soot. She made her way back to the slipway and, cupping her hands, she peered through the metalled windows. In the oblique light cast by the river she could just make out the dark, oily bulk of vast pressing machines, and the peculiar, outlandish shapes of huge vats. It seemed a still, lifeless place, locked in time, a time when people were smaller and hungrier, and within it was such an extraordinary sound of muffled whimpering that she recoiled. It came to her, then, that it was only the creaking of an old building, settling in the running tide.

She turned away and climbed up the rickety flight of steps that led to the main door of *The Sail Loft*. From here she could see thick fog sweeping in over the estuary and the water level was visibly rising, banking up against a concrete pier and dangerously close to flooding.

Well, I'm not compelled to live here, she thought. I can find somewhere else, given time. But I haven't time. Bill will soon find his way to Coventry.

She had romanticised enough.

7

It was the window she wanted to see. Everything else, the accommodation, the kitchen, the bathroom, would have to take second place. More than anything else she wanted to see it open, to let the light stream in, the intense white light that is reflected from water and in which she could paint. The room itself was huge, its walls covered in flaking paint, and apart from a few solid wooden cupboards it was empty of furniture. The window stretched from floor to ceiling, and she went straight up to it and tried to open it, but it was festooned with cobwebs and the lock was stiff. At last it gave and she pulled at the handles, wrenching the doors sideways. For a moment they juddered awkwardly in their metal gullies and then they were free. The light flooded in, dazzling her. Outside was a narrow balcony, its rails fractured in places, and she stepped on to it gingerly.

To her left was the paper factory; to her right a heavy industrial barge was chugging upstream, its heavy prow raised slightly against the flow, the pulse of its engine borne towards her on the breeze. As she watched, it disappeared behind the factory and immediately its noise ceased as though someone had switched off the ignition. At the same time, as if out of the wall itself, a flight of swans appeared, their wings beating gently and their elongated necks stretching towards the sea. The effect was enchanting, intensely moving, and in a moment she was sobbing, huge gulping sobs which shook her whole body. That's what it means to be free, she thought, chasing her sleeve across her eyes, and – this is the place; this is where I'll live. Wiping her tears, she turned back into the room and closed the windows.

Can't do this, she thought. Can't cry. Can't give in. Have to get on with it. Get a *life*.

Upstairs was a small box bedroom with a tiny, metal-framed window and next door a shower room decorated with small white tiles, cracked and fissured with age. The walls were begrimed with finger marks, and Cat smiled, thinking how Rute would have said, 'What, a battle in here already?' She'd have had a field day in this place. The taps were stiff but after a clanking sound in the pipes, a jet of brown water bubbled out and she stepped back hastily, afraid for her shoes.

She spent an hour looking round then locked up and went back to her car. As she drove away she was euphoric. It was a good place; it would suit her, and she looked forward to telling her mother about it. With luck, she'd be home before nightfall. Only then did she remember; she was never going home again.

'First impressions, Ma, OK? One, cobwebs, and lots of 'em.' She grinned. 'Two, a huge room covered in… probably silt. Three, a very poky kitchen. An OK bedroom with a plank bed; next door a sort of working shower. But, Ma, you should see the windows in the main room! They're the height of the ceiling and you can fold the whole lot back like a concertina. The light's superb, just what I'm looking for.'

'A safe haven,' said Rute enviously, distorting the word with her strong accent.

'Yes,' Cat replied eagerly, 'all that, and more. And, Ma, a boat came past and then a flight of swans.' She hesitated, afraid Rute would think her sentimental. 'It was magical, almost like a painting by Magritte.'

'Magritte?'

'You know, that Belgian who does dream paintings. Has a different fix on reality. He once painted a man's pipe and wrote under it, *Ceci n'est pas une pipe*. He meant that the painting wasn't a pipe; it was an image of a pipe. So you have this boat, and it's a solid wooden structure, but then these wonderful swans fly out, mysterious, like ghosts, but, oh, *much* more real than the boat.'

'Wasn't the boat real?'

'Of course, but the *swans*, Ma. They're what made me...'

'Maybe they did,' said Rute quietly. She was sitting very still, her wrinkled hands loose in her lap. 'But 'gritte', it sounds like grit, *ja*? Courage. Facing up to things. Feet on the ground, Caterina. *That*'s the reality.'

Cat sat back, slightly deflated. 'Well, it also sounds like 'greet'; saying hallo... And that's what I'm doing, aren't I?' She lifted her arms. 'Hallo, the future! Hallo, new life! Hallo, a studio of my own; hallo to the *swans*, Ma! Because that's what decided me, you see. Everything else, the light, the size of the place and everything... the window... All that was brilliant. But the swans... They seemed so *free*, Ma....'

'Well, an omen, perhaps. *Ein gutes* omen*, Gott willens.* 'She paused. 'Cup of tea?'

'I'll make it. You're still drinking lemon tea, I notice.'

'Why change, already? Lemon tea is good for you. When will you go?'

'Oh Ma, I haven't thought. As soon as I can, really. In a week or so, probably.'

'Well, good for you.'

Her mother seemed resigned to her leaving, almost stoical, and Cat felt a surge of tenderness for her, that after all those years they had finally come through.

'And I'll get the telephone re-connected,' she promised, as she brought in the tray. 'Except, never, never tell him where I am. I couldn't stand it if he found me. But you must come and see it when I'm settled.'

Rute ignored this. 'But your children, Caterina. You're just abandoning them?'

Cat studied her mother's worn, lined face, her eyes, wincing with grief, and her heart softened.

'Ma, I'm not abandoning them,' she said gently. 'I've

96

told you, they've long ago cut the umbilical cord. As for the rest, it's empty, mere dross. It's already... un-longed for.'

'Un-longed for?' A compound phrase outside her mother's vocabulary. Or perhaps not. 'You don't long for your children?' Her voice was almost inaudible. 'How can you not long for your children?'

Cat was hurt. 'Ma, I wasn't meaning them! Of course I long for my children! If I could undo what's happened to them, I would. They'll blame me, of course,' she added bitterly. 'They won't understand. I've made certain of that. But I can't undo it, can I? That's asking the impossible.'

'No, you can't turn back the clock...'

Cat put her mug back on the tray and leaned back wearily. 'Even that's not true, is it? You just move the hands. But you can't undo damage. You ought to know that, the sort of memories you have. It's an elusive thing, memory, isn't it? Easily romanticised. 'Rose-tinted', they call it. Strange, isn't it, how people use colours: blue moods, brown study, green-eyed jealousy... And yellow... most people think yellow is the colour of light, Van Gogh included, yet look what it did to him! The light has a lot to answer for, don't you think? No, some things are much better hidden...'

Rute looked bewildered, as though Cat was unhinged. In fact she was now extremely sleepy, the ideas running together in her head. It had been a long day.

'But, Caterina, the *kinder*...' Rute insisted, as if from a great distance. 'They'll have to know...' She looked wretched.

'Oh, I'll tell them something. Meet them somewhere. Talk on the phone.' She laid her hand over her mother's. 'I won't lose touch with them, Ma.' Not more than I have already, she thought bitterly. 'I'll need to find a job, though. Have to pay for it somehow.'

97

Rute got to her feet. 'Ah, I've had an idea about that. Wait here a minute...'

She left the room and Cat heard her quick step on the stairs. She came back with a large brown envelope clutched to her chest, and without a word, she handed it to Cat. On its left hand corner was an indescribably unpronounceable address:

Bundesentschädigungsgesetz,
Fehrbelliner Platz 1,
Berlin.

'What's this, Ma? It's not your savings, is it? I can't take your savings, Ma!'

'Take it,' insisted Rute. 'It's only money. Buy yourself some freedom, Caterina.' Her accent was suddenly harsh. 'And it's *nat* my savings; it's my latest reparation money from the Cherman Government. I've never touched any of it. I wouldn't touch it with a barge-pole. Blood, sweat and tears money. The blood we share, Caterina, and you know all about sweat and tears, in your own way. So take it!'

Cat didn't argue, but took the envelope in her hand.

'Now give it back, Caterina – I have to cash it. You can have it as a lump sum. Hah!' she exclaimed, tossing her hand at Cat's eye, 'a lump sum!'

8

Cat stayed with her mother a week and then moved into *The Sail Loft*. The intervening days were a time of joy, except when Bill rang, wanting to know where she was, but Rute was good at dissembling, a talent that always eluded her whenever they said goodbye. Five days later a letter arrived, forwarded to her from her mother; the words, in Bill's handwriting, 'Gone away', like a hunter's horn in diminuendo or a coldly indifferent epitaph. She had to grit her teeth to open it.

If Bill had known what it was he might never have sent it on. It was a commission from Wycombe Strike Command to paint the portrait of a retired general, and it promised a good fee. Cat wondered how they'd heard of her, but she also knew how potent word of mouth could be. This would be a new life, the life of a professional portrait painter, and she was exhilarated. She held the letter in her hand for a long time, wondering if she could ever brave a return to High Wycombe, and eventually she wrote back, explaining that she had recently moved house and requesting a brief postponement.

First she would make contact with James, and through him, with Deborah. She longed for them both. At last she might discover what had made Deborah leave home when she did, and why she had stayed *incommunicado* for so long. They'd be easy together; they'd have drinks on the balcony; she'd cook for them, as in the old days, and they could walk by the river. They might make fun of the place in their different ways, but everything would be enjoyed, all things reconciled. Or would they? It seemed that she was still possessed by fears. Above all she feared their censure, even if completely unintended, and she procrastinated – first, she thought, I will spring clean my nest. Meanwhile, Deborah's teddy and James's Hornby train waited for them on her bedroom windowsill.

She had prepared for the cold with a couple of halogen heaters and a pile of heavy sweaters from Rute's favourite charity shop. The hardware store in Swanscombe provided the wherewithal to decorate, and she shopped for food at the Co-op. Driving back and forth over rain-soaked roads, the car buffeted by bitter easterly winds, she was again thankful that to traverse those sodden marshes would be an ordeal for any but the most persistent visitor. It wasn't a lonely business, setting up home again – far from it, though it did give her a queer feeling, one day, when she absent-mindedly knocked against the telephone and discovered a dialling tone. Except for Rute, she had no one to ring, so she brought her up to date.

Afterwards, sluicing whitewash over vast walls with an enormous spade-shaped brush, an activity designed for introspection, she found herself pondering her mother's question, why she had waited so long before leaving Bill. Easy to ask, but other than safe-guarding the twins, impossible to answer. As if safe-guarding them wasn't reason enough. Now she wondered at her own feebleness. She could have just walked out the door with them, found somewhere to live and a job; there were supportive agencies for people like her, had she not been too frightened to approach them. But the twins would never have understood, anymore than they'd understand now. They'd have been petrified. Better to stay, sweat it out; at least she'd given them stability. Or so she hoped.

Standing immobile at the huge window in the studio, watching a muscular wind harrying the surface of the water, she spoke the words out loud.

'I've done it. I've really left him. And no one, *no one,* will ever bully me again.'

She recalled the day of her solemn vow, how she bargained with God that if he'd sort out her marriage she'd lie passive on the bed she'd made for herself;

she'd forgive whatever needed forgiving and let her anger and frustration sleep. It didn't work, but then, she wasn't in God's club. She was certainly unschooled in prayer, but Rute used to say that the *Kol Nidre*, the prayer used on *Yom Kippur*, was very good for getting out of such bargains if God didn't come up trumps. All such vows or promises – careless, unrealistic promises, she'd said, made in the heat of the moment – excused for the current year. But God didn't come up trumps, and she was left to battle on her own.

Cat was fully aware of the tricks that memory can play on a vulnerable mind, and therefore how false that memory might be. When she looked back into her childhood it was always Rute's silence she recalled, a silence that was only broken when she began her stories. The loving intimacy they had shared in the small house in High Wycombe, her mother's dark humour, her warmth, her vivacity, her courage, her quirky, intelligent mind, had all paled into insignificance, buried by the need to always protect or propitiate her. This, together with the years of marital conflict, and the appalling self-deceit which had accompanied it, had warped her perception of the world. She had created around herself a wall of pretence, a shield, a fence against all incomers. Constructed in childhood, shored up during her marriage, frequently patched and mended, it had become impenetrable. It was part of her, now, and how could it be otherwise? Perhaps, at last, she could learn how to dismantle it.

She was guaranteed the Strike Command portrait but, in the interim, she still needed paid work. She pored over the advertisements in the local newspapers, the notices in Swanscombe library and in shop windows. Greenhithe Post Office wanted a sorting clerk; the Sea Front Nursery School a teaching assistant; Swanscombe Royal Hotel, waitresses, and there were endless advertisements for shelf-stackers and till managers. She took none of them. They would steal time from her painting; they would steal her precious light. Yet, far from being demoralised, fragile and brittle as she was, she was full of hope, sometimes even carefree.

One day she met R. Dilwyn Williams in the street. He was still pale, still unsmiling, and the lines on his forehead seemed even deeper. Belatedly, they introduced themselves.

'Everyone calls me Ricci,' he said. 'And by the way, *The Sail Loft* – it's a bit run down isn't it? You want it decorated? Sorry, I've not been in since the old guy moved out.'

'A coat of paint is fixing that. I'm used to a brush – I'm an artist.' The word tripped off her tongue. 'Incidentally, I'm calling it *The Studio* now.'

His face brightened. It seemed lit from within, and she felt a spark of interest. His was a face she could paint.

'I could exhibit your work, if you like,' he said. 'My window's empty normally. I specialise in antiquarian books and the sun might damage them, see?'

His strong Welsh lilt made a song of the words, but what sun, she thought, as they walked up the hill together, and incidentally, what antiquarian books? It had apparently slipped his mind that she had seen for herself how ailing his business was and she wondered why he was deluding himself. She could recognise self-delusion; she was an adept.

'Want to sign the forms, since you're here?'

Preserving her anonymity, she signed her maiden name.

'I wonder, can I sub-let?' she asked him tentatively, an idea forming in her head. 'It's a big space.'

He looked at her speculatively. 'I'll ask, but I don't see why not. The old boy needs all the funds he can get.'

She smiled at him. 'Me, too.'

'Tried the college? Their life-drawing tutor's just gone off sick. Heard it in the shop, see. Two evenings a week.'

She started work a few days later. Her students were keen but amateurish, except for one. Gustave Mons was a tall, rangy man in his mid-twenties who, by the end of term, would have transformed the rather graceless poses set by the middle-aged female model into sensual, vividly-coloured nudes reminiscent of Matisse. With his square head and an unruly shock of red hair, he cut a distinctive figure in the class, but presuming a German descent she initially gave him a wide berth. Then someone let drop that his parents were Jewish refugees from Bergen and, shocked at her prejudice, she made an opportunity to speak to him. It turned out he was a potter by trade, and conveniently for her, was looking for somewhere to live with a bit of workshop space.

'My parents are off home for a while. They've a place in Haacht, in the Brabant. I've an uncle still living there; or rather he went back after the war.'

'You live with your parents, normally?'

'I do. They're great people; gave me a good start in life. If I strike out on my own I can pay them back a bit.'

Cat was touched. 'You said they were going 'home'. You're Belgian, too?'

'Sort of. There're quite a few Belgians round here, refugees from the war. Haven't you noticed them? They wear a lot of wool and both the women and the men wear flat caps, the older ones, that is. I don't think of myself as anything, particularly. Except Jewish, of course.'

She was surprised. 'You identify yourself as Jewish?'

The full blue of his eyes was turned on her. Anything less like the Jewish stereotype could rarely have been found. 'Of course. Don't you? You're Jewish, aren't you? You must be, somewhere in your roots, with a name like Feugler.'

'And why life drawing, if you're a potter?'

'Dunno really. Shape, form, general skills, observation...'

Every detail of his face was illuminated by the white light from the windows. Cat thought, he looks honest and straightforward enough, and surely far too young to be any sort of threat to me. Into the silence she said, 'I've a studio on the river and I need a tenant. Care to see it?'

The following morning he biked over and she showed him round, and then they sat down in the window with their coffee.

'So, what do you think of the place? We'd each want some privacy,' she added firmly, 'but given you keep the boundaries...?'

His eyes had been darting restlessly round the room, appraising it. 'Mmm... clay work here – I'd clear up after myself, sweep it clean – but where'd I put the kiln? It needs a level floor, preferably somewhere else. Toxic fumes, an' the like. I suppose I could build something outside... Apart from that, it's great.'

'There's a storeroom downstairs with a concrete floor. Would that do?'

'Probably, with ventilation. Can I see it?'

'It's a bit of a mess. Smells awful. I'm afraid I took one look and shut the door on it.'

He grinned at her. 'Sounds like you found a dead body.'

Cat laughed and got up. 'No, just some mouldy rolls of paper and some old paint cans. Come on, I'll show you.'

She took the iron key and led the way downstairs but the storeroom looked even more squalid than when she'd first seen it.

'No, I don't think this'll do, after all. It'll be a

Herculean task to clear it out and it's far too damp; you'll get pneumonia.'

'Yiddishe-Momme!' he scoffed, giving her a knowing look. 'Don't worry; the kiln'll dry it out. Just look at this stuff, though!' He hauled one of the bales of paper upright against a wall and watched the wood lice run. 'Ugh, what a waste!'

She chuckled. 'I know. We'll have to get rid of it. '

'So, what's the rent?'

She had to be hard-nosed, she said, and he nodded warily. Finally she proposed a rent-free month, provided he cleared the storeroom out first.

She locked the door behind them and put the key in his hand, a symbolic gesture betokening a slight surrender of her freedom, but it felt easy and natural. He retrieved his bike and then he stood on his pedals for a minute.

'You don't mind if I bring my girlfriend round sometimes, do you? Julia, she's called. She's a hairdresser, lives in Swanscombe. Parents a bit iffy – Orthodox, you know how it is. We won't get in your way. I agree about the boundaries.'

9

Gus moved in a few days later. Together, they carried his boxes from the hired van up to the main room, not her preferred arrangement, but for the time being, unavoidable.

Let loose on the storeroom he set to with a will, clearing out the rubbish and scrubbing and whitewashing the walls, as she had done upstairs. Mostly she left him to it, but one day he came rushing in and said that he'd found a door. He was as excited as a child and begged her to go and see for herself.

'It's pouring with rain,' she objected, 'and it's probably just a cupboard.'

'The key's still in it and it's too heavy for that. Come on, we don't know till we see it, do we?'

It wasn't a cupboard but an entrance into a high concrete stairwell which led up to the warehouse behind and then, as they later discovered, to a blocked up doorway in the studio. Her exit strategy had been there all along – through, down and out. The warehouse was totally empty, clean, and as dry as tinder, and its wooden floorboards and square metalled windows under the steep incline of the roof gave it character, reminding her of the Victorian schoolroom of her childhood.

'Wow, Cat, this got potential!' In his enthusiasm Gus grabbed her arm and she stiffened; other than Rute, it was the first time anyone had touched her since Bill. But Gus was oblivious. 'Don't you see what this means? I could partition off another room, stick a door in. We could even take another tenant!'

She regarded him suspiciously. 'Who're you thinking of? Julia?'

His mood changed abruptly. His face reddened and he glowered at her, his chin jutting out. 'No, of *course* not Julia!'

Cat cringed, raising her arm as if to ward off a blow, and Gus's eyes widened in amazement.

'Hey, cool it, Cat, *cool* it. It's just that Julia and me... Aw, hell,' he said shamefacedly, 'I didn't mean to upset you.' He took her arm placatingly, but she'd had enough. She shook him off, turned her back and walked away.

'I am going from here,' she mumbled. 'I'm going...'

With a heavy heart, she made her way back to the kitchen and sat down on the chair, her head in her hands. She was trembling.

She asked herself if she had over-reacted. Surely Gus wouldn't hurt a fly – or would he? He couldn't know how she would interpret even a hint of temper as an attack on her inmost nature. Even so, that was no excuse, even if he was having a rough time with Julia. But perhaps temper was habitual with him.

She heard him close the storeroom door, and fearful of close proximity to him in the tiny kitchen, she got up and crossed the studio to the window. There, in that illusion of space, gazing over the wide estuary, she waited for him. The rain had stopped and a feeble sun was breaking through the driven clouds, clothing the water with a golden lustre, so poignant a reminder of her first visit that she could have wept.

A whole lifetime had passed since she had lived with Rute, but now, childishly, she found herself longing for her. Rute would have told her to leave him to it, to find somewhere else, to run. She would have liked *The Studio*, the warehouse, the river – the whole set-up. She would have understood Cat's love for it, but she would still have told her to run.

Cat hadn't told her mother what she felt about the place, how it seemed to have been waiting for her to come along, not just offering a sorely needed foothold and the freedom to paint, but offering, for the first time in her life, the chance to grow, unhindered and untrammelled. Now all that seemed threatened.

107

Well, she thought, I've found a place to live and I'm not about to abandon it. Gus can leave. I'll simply tell him, give it him straight. Yes, that's what I'll do... Or maybe I should pretend nothing's happened, then write a note for him and be out when he got it... That might be best...

He was at the door, sheepish, uncomfortable, gauging her mood, but by then she was back in the kitchen, busying herself with the kettle. Her words came in a rush.

'Wasn't that a great find?' She gave him a radiant smile. 'And you're quite right about another tenant. I'll ask Ricci if we can. He might know someone.' She made the tea and rinsed out two mugs. 'Or we could put an ad on the college board. We could use the warehouse as a gallery – I don't mean commercially, but to house our stuff, impress the clients, if we get any. We could light it with spotlights, give it ambience.' She took a tea towel and wiped down the surface. 'I could have the walls opposite the windows, and you, the rest of it. That storeroom's got a solid ceiling, did you notice? Fireproof, in case of accidents...' Immediately she regretted the word. 'Not...not that you'll have accidents, of course. I didn't mean that... I'm not worried about that...'

'I'm sorry I shouted at you.'

She dropped her head, her hands stilled. 'Yes. Well.'

'I won't do it again. Ever.'

She turned to him, her eyes pricking. 'So you say now...'

'I mean it. I never really shout, to be honest. But Julia...'

'But this isn't just to do with Julia, is it?' she said wearily. 'Whatever's wrong between you, well, I'm sorry, but it's not my business. And actually it's irrelevant,' she added, gathering her courage. 'You'll always find a reason, if you want one. That's part of what I meant by boundaries. Look, hadn't we better call it quits, while we can?'

He didn't approach her, didn't try and touch her, and she was grateful for that.

'There's no need,' he said quietly. 'I won't, I promise. Ever.'

Cat sighed. 'OK, then. Let's leave it for now.'

'Let's have that cuppa,' he said gently, 'and we'll talk about this crackpot gallery idea of yours. We aint got parking, for a start...'

If Gus was bewildered by Cat's reaction, or if he simply thought it masked a deeper malaise that he felt unqualified to name, he didn't show it. For a few days he trod softly around her, busying himself in the storeroom, but the episode was allowed to fade gently away. Naturally they differed occasionally, but in all the time she knew him he not only never raised his voice to her again, but became quite solicitous, and developed an affectionate nickname for her: 'Miss Cat.' Gradually she warmed to him again and they established a mutually satisfying pattern of living, where, in the main, they led a separate, slightly bantering, courteous existence, devoid of actual friendship. But Cat wasn't looking for friendship; simple harmony was enough for her. After all, there was something of a generation gap.

As there was with Julia, who she encountered one day strolling half naked out of the shower, a towel round her head, and who gave a little giggle of embarrassment and fled. It made Cat feel old to have two such young people in the house, and also sad to have missed those years with Deborah and James. Julia came and went like a wraith, although anyone less wraith-like could rarely have been encountered. She was a well-built young woman with dyed black hair, and Cat wondered if they would ever share anything resembling a common language.

Occasionally they shared a take-away in the

evening, delivered by Saul, an Afro-Caribbean with three-foot-long dreadlocks, who so often stayed late that he felt constrained to acquire a CD player for them on which to play his jazz. It was the endless screeching of the gulls, he said; it got to him. A bit of music was what they needed, to drown them out. Cat liked the gulls. She also liked the jazz. On fine evenings Julia and Gus would put on a CD and, with the windows thrown back, gyrate to the music, while Cat would take her drink out to the balcony and watch the leisurely passage of the elongated black barges with their lone pilots, or just gaze, mesmerized, at the river as it swirled down to the sea. But she was still determined to ask Ricci to find another tenant, if he could. Someone to stand between them, if necessary.

Gus slept in a walk-in cupboard off the warehouse, which seemed to agree with him, for although he was late to bed each night, he was always clear-eyed the following morning. Cat slept in her little loft room, less agreeably. She was plagued by nightmares, not just the old ones, fed by her mother's stories, or more recent ones in which Bill figured with raised fists and snarling sarcasm, but also about Deborah and James as defenceless children who, in the dreams, she failed to protect. On waking, she found this bizarre, for although they'd hated Bill's shouting and frequently shrunk from him, they loved him and she hadn't ever seen him hit them. Was this indicative of paranoia, perhaps an echo of Rute's experiences, or – struggling for truth – was it a perverse desire that they should somehow have acknowledged her sufferings? In her heart she knew it would have been impossible for them to have come through totally unscathed.

Yet, although each morning she woke up tired and jaded, by mid-morning her new-found optimism had reasserted itself. After all, Deborah and James were no longer children; they had both made new lives for themselves away from home, as she was doing. They were safe, and one day they would be reconciled and the truth would emerge. What that truth was, she refused at that moment to contemplate.

10

Although the pay at the college was good it was completely insufficient for her needs, so she sacrificed a morning of light and added another class. Her students were curious about her work and she took in some old pieces to show them. They were intrigued about the colours she used, and she invented a useful metaphor to explain what she called, with brief, self conscious pomposity, her *modus operandi.* Colours were like people, she said; they behaved one way on their own and quite another in company; this one was stable, plastic; that, opaque or dictatorial. But isolate a bully, she said, with a sideways glance at her marriage, or mix him up with stronger characters, or challenge him with transparency, and his capacity to dominate becomes diluted. Their reactions were interesting; some regarded her with a blank, rather quizzical stare while others were more perceptive and saw it as deep an insight into their private lives as she had done with hers.

She became a demanding tutor, impatient with token painters, and would constantly challenge them with questions.

'Who, other than artists, really examines colours?' she asked. Or she'd say, "Light' and 'dark' are weasel words, so try to identify their colour. Is light merely different tones of white, or is it any colour, so long as it's in proximity with a darker tone? And shadows, are they just a darker tone of the same pigment, 'sown on' like Tinkerbelle's, or are there lighter colours within, local colours?' Another time she said, 'Don't think of greys as just black and white. Remember, the American euphemism, 'neutralise', which means to kill. Greys aren't neutral; they're the palest tone of other colours...'

'But what are you doing right now?' they asked, and

she had to justify her idleness with the lame excuse that she had only just moved in and was still sorting herself out. 'What I really want to do is...' and it was then that the idea was born. She would do faces, a great frieze of them; portraits of contemporary life, if she could find enough people to sit for her.

When the weather was fine she took her students to paint landscapes *plein air*; inside they painted Still Lifes and self-portraits. One of her best moments came when her students started, not just to look, but to see. 'Oh, yes,' one said, 'now you mention it, I can see a bit of pink.' Or blue or green. 'Isn't that amazing? I never saw that before!' 'I nearly went off the road,' one said. 'I saw this man walking down the street, his face glowing in the sunlight, and I thought, now what colour is that; how would I paint that? Nearly crashed the blinkin' car!'

They said the class had changed their lives, and the need to be articulate was changing hers, opening windows in her mind, and she found herself learning alongside them. She grew in confidence; on college days she took pains with her hair, wore fresher clothes, put on a bit of make-up, and set off already exuberant. Soon her studio space was littered with sketches and small canvases, not faces yet, but tentative explorations of local scenes. She painted shop fronts in different light; she painted fields and pasture in different weather; she painted street scenes. The river she did not paint; it was too whimsical, too tyrannical in its moods, too demanding of her fragile emotional state. She began to use larger brushes and purer pigments; she keyed up her work so that it gradually became more vivid, yet, at the same time, more subtle. She marvelled that in the space of only a few weeks her whole visual perception of the world had changed; maybe her eyes had developed ducts or pores; they seemed like sponges; could soak up images.

Meanwhile the tide rose and fell; seagulls mobbed

low flying cormorants, and the impending Spring brought guillemots, sandpipers and skuas, drifting upriver from the marshes to sweep over the river and pace the shale beneath her window.

It took her two weeks to gather the courage to phone her children, both of whom were living in the outskirts of London, although not together. Deborah was a junior account executive in a PR company, and James was employed in a firm of engineers, and when they didn't return her calls she excused them to herself, assuming that they were too immersed in their own lives to be able to find the time. She grieved over it, but it was also a respite. She told herself that perhaps it was just too soon, but in fact she was still running scared.

In the end it was Deborah, not James, who finally returned her call, and Cat was delighted; it was the first time she had heard her daughter's voice in over two years. But there was no telephone hug, such as 'How good to hear you, Mum, after all this time!' no apology for her abrupt departure or her extended silence but an immediate and very painful reference to Bill.

'Dad told us you'd left him – he'd never have left *you*, you know.'

Cat didn't reply; she was reluctant to justify herself, or to accuse Bill to his own daughter. It only underlined for her how effective she'd been at camouflage, but when Deborah asked her where she was living, she still hesitated, too heart sore at that moment to listen to her daughter's natural, but disparaging, judgement.

Eventually, she said, 'Deborah, does it matter? I'm simply where I ended up. We can still meet.'

'But *where*, Mum? Are you all right?'

'Yes, Deb, I'm all right. It's good of you to ask,' she added politely, suddenly conscious of how little she knew of this daughter of hers, who she'd not seen for so long.

'I asked Granny, ages ago. She wouldn't tell me *any*thing...!'

'Granny?'

'She said you'd tell me when you were ready. I *ask* you! That is so, like, *not* the way to get me on her side! Another thing – you know she's getting headaches?' Her voice sounded bitter, angry. '*You* caused that, you know!'

'Yes. Probably.'

'Then tell me where you *are*! I don't see why you won't even... tell me where you *are*!' There were tears in her voice. 'Oh, Mum, why won't you trust me?'

Cat went cold, rigid with shock. The memories surged back; oh, from far, far back; from the time of her childhood, from the time of her own questions and Rute's endless prevarications. Why, then, replicate them? She named the place with difficulty, the words dragged out of her, constrained by love and guilt.

'Swanscombe, Deborah, on the Thames.'

'Like, in a *boat*?'

Cat laughed shakily. 'No, Debs. That might have been a good idea, but no. Find Greenhithe on a map. Swanscombe's nearby. This place is a bit further on, right on the river. Look, why not come and see for yourself?' She had finished with evasions.

'James, too?' Protective of her twin.

'Of course James, too.'

There was a silence. 'I don't know, Mum. I don't think we can, yet. Is that OK with you?'

'That's perfectly OK, Debs. In your own time, darling.' Once again she hesitated. 'But please, Deborah...please, please don't tell Dad where I am. I couldn't... And please believe me, darling –' Her voice broke. 'I've never, never, stopped loving you.'

'Yeah, well.' A pause. 'I knew it was him. I just knew.' Cat heard a sob, and the phone went dead.

Time would heal, she thought, as eventually she

wiped away her own tears; you can't un-relate blood relatives, especially your own children. One day, she hoped Deborah and James would understand, and perhaps forgive.

11

Two months after Cat moved into *The Studio* Ricci appeared at the door. She was taken aback, thinking she should have heard his car, but it transpired that he had walked down the lane from the bus stop. She assumed he had come with news of a prospective tenant, but he looked so utterly worn out that she almost ran from him. She felt in no condition to listen to anyone else's troubles, having quite enough of her own.

She was still wary about putting herself in a position where she might be faced with awkward questions, and Ricci seemed equally private, but he'd always been straight with her and she trusted him. Like her mother, his expression was completely masked until he smiled, when his face appeared to split open, revealing an inner luminosity. His complexion was markedly pallid, or maybe his dark Welsh eyes, under the bar of his eyebrows, dramatised his skin tones, draining them of colour. Now the sculpture of his face seemed even more chiselled than usual, as if he was labouring under some strong emotion, and sheer courtesy meant that at least she should offer him a cup of coffee. He chose tea, and then said what he had come to say. At first he was unable to meet her eyes, but then he seemed to gather himself.

'All the time I was walking down the lane,' he confessed, 'I was wondering how to put this. It's my bookshop, you see; well, my whole business. It's taken me some time to admit it, far too long, but the fact of the matter is, I've failed. It's my pride, I suppose; wouldn't let me face up to it.'

He looked up and met her gaze. 'But I've reached the stage when I have to, now. I'm sorry to land this on you, is it, when it's nothing to do with you, really."

'Oh, Ricci, are you sure?'

Tentatively, she reached out a hand to him, then withdrew it. It wasn't her pity he had come for.

'I'm sure,' he said heavily. 'I've made hardly any profit over the last three years; I've got into arrears over the lease and now the car's gone. I had to sell it to meet my debts. Oh, I can stay there; I'll let out the rooms over the shop. If that doesn't work out, well, I'll have to think again.'

'But where would you live?' she asked naively.

He looked down, embarrassed, then met her eyes shyly. 'Well, I thought, here, actually. If you don't mind, that is. You're looking for a tenant, aren't you? I could afford that; I wouldn't clutter the place or get in the way of your work at all.' His accent became more pronounced. 'I'll still have the shop so I'd only sleep here, see; have a sandwich by myself, not to be a trouble...'

'But there's no second bedroom. Gus just uses a walk-in cupboard.'

'No, I know that. I see you've decorated, by the way – it looks good – but I thought, maybe Gus could partition something off for me.'

He looked white, humiliated, but she saw that he was putting a brave face on it, and matched his mood gravely.

'Mmm, he always said he'd do that one day,' she said. 'But I warn you, his girlfriend Julia sleeps here sometimes. Well, most of the time, actually.'

Ricci frowned. 'Does she?'

'You know her?'

'If it's the same one. There's a Julia who works at the hairdressers', next door to mine.' He was quiet for a moment, and then he said, 'Well, it's still a big space. Is it big enough? I'm getting desperate, see.'

The question was not whether the space was big enough, but whether *she* was big enough. Privately, she doubted it, but agreed that he could move in as soon as Gus could get a room ready. Then she realised that if Ricci had her room and she slept in the studio she could paint in the night if she wanted to. She already had daylight bulbs for dull days; she could use those.

'OK, then, Ricci, that's settled. And there's no need for Gus to do anything. You can kip down in the loft if you can cope with the cold.'

His smile evoked her mother smile, grave, secretive and enigmatic. 'I've coped before and I can again. And it's best I'm apart from you all. I have to get myself together, you see. If I can.'

With the advent of Ricci the pattern of life became more settled. He had an inner stillness which Cat mistakenly took for tranquillity, as she was to discover. Living alone, as he had done for years, he had learned to cook and for the first time Cat looked forward to meals being more than merely functional. In the evenings she and Ricci ate together, while those he dubbed 'the youngsters' ate on the hoof.

In truth, Gus and Julia were never quite relaxed with Ricci, whose expression, when he looked at Julia, was of someone who knew things about her which she knew he knew and might have preferred him not to know, and Gus followed her lead. But Cat was glad Ricci was there; she was between them all in age and he made her feel younger. She also felt she'd been lazy, even sluttish in her habits, but his natural domesticity reproved her and set her straight. He also brought some sorely needed furniture, including an enormous bulbous sofa, which in no way satisfied fire regulations.

Richard Dilwyn Williams had been a Far Eastern Prisoner of War, a FEPOW. It was the clue to his whole identity; it was the most important thing that had ever happened to him; it was the vital imperative of his whole life and it was the key to all his personal problems. That he had such problems Cat knew by the sounds overhead at night, but it was the sombre, unsmiling Celtic triangularity of his face and his huge, haunted eyes that most reflected it. Maybe it was heartless of her, she thought, even craven, but she was reluctant to get involved. She sensed that behind those large eyes and that deeply wrinkled forehead was a story, but if so, she didn't want to hear it. She'd heard enough stories, enough to last a lifetime.

Then something happened which brought her up short. He had called her to the telephone and afterwards had said, 'That old lady on the phone...'

Cat had laughed. 'Oh, that's my mother, Ricci. She's not old. Well, about your age...'

'That's old. Jewish, is she?'

'Yes, actually. How could you tell?'

'That particular accent. And your surname's German, isn't it? I thought she must be Jewish.'

Later that afternoon all three of them were the main room, Gus working on a slab pot, and Cat was struggling with a painting. The structure was there but the colours seemed dull and lifeless and she dipped her brush in a bright vermillion, thinking to warm them a little. Ricci wandered between them aimlessly, obviously unsettled. He stopped by the easel for a few minutes and then moved on to Gus. Cat was deep in her work and not attending to him, but the word 'nightmares' jumped out at her.

She heard Gus say, 'I'm afraid dreams aren't my province, old chap...' and she heard Ricci's reply. He spoke almost sullenly, the words wrenched out of him, 'You Jews do stick together, don't you? *Iesu Grist*, I'm living in a Jewish enclave.'

Cat was taken aback. Gus hadn't raised his head but she stopped working completely and looked across at him, affronted.

She gave a derisive laugh. '*Enclave*, Ricci?'

He looked abashed, then slightly vindicated. 'Yeah, a ghetto in microcosm.'

'I thought that's what you implied.'

Ghetto. That small staccato word, spoken as her mother had spoken it, with a dying fall into silence. She felt a surge of anger. She wasn't a child of ten anymore and she knew perfectly well what a ghetto was. It was offensive of him and her mouth clamped shut. She threw down her brush, picked up a sweater, and cheeks tight with fury, walked out of the room. She took herself down the rickety stairs and found a place at the back of the factory by the ruined chimney where she could be alone. It seemed a long walk. She felt stunned.

Eventually, endeavouring to find excuses for him, she decided an obviously anti-Semitic comment such as that might have had its root, however oblique, in a number of things; perhaps merely an attention-seeking attack on the *status quo* – after all, all of them were younger than he was and more preoccupied. Or that he wasn't Jewish and they were, or something else entirely. But whatever he meant, why had she taken it so personally? Why hadn't she just given him a light-hearted response, along the lines of 'No, Ricci, the glue between us aint that thick; it's just how it's happened to pan out.'

Or was it? She shifted uncomfortably on the damp bricks. Some conjoined blood, perhaps, some shared root or branch; some mutual Ashkenazi temper, unconsciously mediated between them, which left him always on the outside. So wasn't he merely fighting back? He probably didn't mean anything by it, she thought, so what am I doing, skulking here?

She knew what she had done. She had done what she did best. She had run. But at least she knew, now, *why* she'd run, and why she'd always run. She understood it, with all its darker resonance. It was, literally, to escape. To escape when things got tough. To escape, when she felt, in her innermost being, diminished by a darker, stronger force; out of count, nullified; when her hopes or expectations had undergone a reversal, her very integrity compromised. It was her mother's pattern, to escape. It was what had happened to herself, in her youth; it had happened with Bill, and now it had happened again, simply because of that nasty little word 'ghetto' and the bitterness with which it had been uttered. She hadn't expected, from Ricci, such hostility.

She knew what she had to do. She didn't need to explain her absence. She just had to extract the sting. And if Ricci was attention-seeking, well, she must attend to him, that's all, and in the future, be more sympathetic. And if he really was anti-Semitic she'd just have to educate him otherwise.

She got to her feet, walked across the slipway and climbed back up the steps. On the table were traces of oil paint where she'd thrown down her brush, the bright vermillion lit to radiance by the stark light from the huge window. Ricci was reading the newspaper, his feet up on the sofa, and he didn't look up. He probably never knew that she'd been gone.

12

Later that week, perhaps regretting his momentary surliness and thinking to do her a service, Ricci introduced Cat and Gus to Rudi Marks, a gallery owner in the town – another Jew, as it happened, so obviously Ricci wasn't anti-Semitic.

The Art-Marks Gallery was situated in a red brick stable block behind the High Street. It was an attractive venue and after Rudi had examined their portfolios without demur, he offered them a summer show. They came home jubilant, but their second visit, some weeks later and after they had both put together a huge body of work, was less agreeable.

'Now, the catalogue,' said Rudi briskly. 'I've got your CV's and titles so it's ready to go to print, but…'

'Don't we want an image or two?' interrupted Gus. 'Something eye-catching? Or, since our CV's aren't that riveting, something that sets us apart in some way? Like, I dunno…'

'That's my job,' said Rudi. 'And I've an idea about that.'

Gus grinned and made a mock salute.

'What I want is precisely that, something that sets you apart. So give me a brief statement, say a hundred words. Your roots, you know – what makes you what you are. We're all Jewish, so why not cash in on that? That'd be eye-catching. And it's the right time for it; you have Black shows and Gypsy shows; why not Jewish shows? Let's be innovative! Let's be cutting edge!'

Cat gaped at him. She thought it an appalling suggestion and she glanced at Gus to see his reaction, but he seemed unfazed.

'What, cutting edge in *Swanscombe*?' she said under her breath. 'Well, Hirszenberg's dead, and I suppose if you can't get a Rothko… How did you know

I was Jewish?'

Rudi gave her a dark look. 'Ricci mentioned it. And don't be facetious. You want to pull out, we'll give Gus a one-man show.'

She was about to say, 'I might,' but Gus gave her a nudge, and she shrugged.

'OK, I'll think about it,' she said, hating herself for compromising.

'Do that,' said Rudi lightly. 'And while you're thinking about it, don't forget the Press. They'll be at the Preview, so give 'em the personal touch.'

Cat felt her stomach lurch. She hadn't considered the consequences of publicity – what if someone showed the article to Bill? As far as she knew, he hadn't pushed Rute for her whereabouts, but she couldn't be certain of his other channels. Some months had passed – maybe he had given up. He surely wouldn't be content with just not knowing.

Rudi looked at her intently. 'Still worried, Cat? Now don't go all *verschämt* on me – I'm taking a firm line on this. Marketing is key.'

Cat made noncommittal noises and escaped. She was furious. She felt that her whole equilibrium had been chucked up in the air and come down in pieces.

Gus caught up with her as she reached the end of the mews, but she was oblivious to him. School was over, the street busy with traffic, the pavements crowded with harassed women, pushchairs and fretful children; nearby a bus pulled out; a car hooted and there was a screech of brakes at the crossing, yet all these sounds seemed muted, as if heard through water. Gus, tall and lanky beside her, was speaking, his hands gesticulating as if she was deaf and had never learned lip-reading. She had time to consider the absurdity of this before she sensed the echo of what he was saying, and then the sounds rushed in like the tide, and with them, the panic. Rudi had her neatly in the palm of his hand; she could never explain to him her need for anonymity. Nor could she explain to Gus, who, totally insensible to her mood, and with keen self-interest, was talking excitedly about the sort of publicity a good review would bring.

'I'm not doing it,' she said under her breath.

'What, the catalogue piece? No choice, if you want to exhibit.'

'All that 'roots' rubbish,' she scoffed, evading the Bill issue. 'It's just so... irrelevant to who we are. It... it sticks in my craw.'

'It probably won't even leave Swanscombe,' said Gus quietly. 'If that's what you're bothered about.'

She studied him closely. He looked away shiftily, then, as if realising at last how brittle she felt, he said gently, 'I'm not stupid, Cat. Look how you reacted that time, when I... And there's a mark on your finger where your ring was.'

She felt dazed.

'Cat, you don't have to tell me anything. But you want to sell your stuff, don't you? I know as hell I do! So just say where you trained, an' leave it at that.'

She rallied. 'Well, that's on my CV, isn't it? And you know I only had teacher training...'

Instant recall: Rute, teaching her what she called 'basics' when she was eleven. The names of colours and then a coded word, 3D. As usual, her mother was ironing, hunched over the board, her shoulders tight with strain, her face contorted by heat and weariness. When asked to elucidate she replied almost petulantly, 'Oh, Caterina, just draw what you see, OK? Whatever seems to come out is short, and whatever goes across is long.' This would not have helped much, but Cat, struck by her mother's posture, had already stopped listening and was sketching her portrait. Degas had done it earlier but she didn't know that at the time, and soon she was drawing and painting other faces. She sold her first one to a neighbour in return for a year's pocket money, thirty shillings, in those days a small fortune. Rute was delighted; her weekly house-keeping was five shillings and it let her off the hook for a while.

Uneasy with her silence, Gus gave her a sideways look. 'Come on, Cat, think of the shekels...' and for a few yards they were able to walk side by side before being separated by a crowded bus shelter. It occurred to her that she could just walk away, but she had never been adept at evasive action, except retrospectively, when she could be quite inventive about what she should have said or done.

'Oh Gus, I don't know what to think. I'm not going to argue about it anymore.'

They walked back to the car in silence. Cat unlocked it, tossed her bag on to the back seat and, after some difficulty with the ignition, they set off.

'This car'll let you down one day,' he muttered. 'Bit of a junk heap, admit.'

It was just one more intrusion into her privacy. 'You don't have to ride in it.'

'It's like a getaway car.'

'It *is* a getaway car.'

13

It wasn't an argument, really. It didn't have that quality of wounding which can shatter a relationship, but nevertheless it would take a long time to be resolved before she could finally have a bit of peace.

That evening she telephoned her mother to ask her advice. She omitted her anxiety about Bill; she simply said that as Rudi Marks seemed intent on marketing them as Jewish artists she was tempted to withdraw. Her mother's reaction was completely unexpected. It nagged at her, what her mother said, so sadly said; it stayed with her; and afterwards it was always at the front of her mind.

'Ach, I have not brought you up to be a good Jew... no, I have taught you to hide it.'

The whispered words, the tired, slow enunciation; Rute always slightly husky, vestige of long years of habitual concealment. Cat could picture her blue-veined hand at her throat, as wrinkled as autumn apples, her long sinuous fingers fidgeting with the delicate gold and silver bars of her necklace, her large green eyes in the heart-shaped cameo of her face staring widely down the phone, taut with memory, sensing the shadows of the past.

The fact that they were Jewish was something Cat rarely thought about. They had never gone to synagogue and she never heard Rute pray. The only day in the Jewish calendar to which she was faithful was Yom Kippur, when she would wear a frown and a headscarf and serve up a fatty breast of lamb stuffed with greasy herbs. The rest of the time she'd kept her Judaism safely under wraps.

But she had always kept a *mezuzah* fastened to the lintel with a bent nail, on which, with the barest and most fleeting touch, she would exercise her exits and her entrances – which she excused by saying it was a memory thing, like Roman Catholics did with holy water; she said that if you touched the doorframe before leaving a room you never forgot what you were going to do when you left it.

Cat knew her mother was astute, if only after the fact. Her philosophy of life demanded that, if she couldn't understand or grasp something, or when she understood only too well and felt beleaguered, it was far better to paper over the cracks than to discover something unpalatable. She might even reconstruct it for her own comfort, meeting it head-on with her own brand of sardonic and fatalistic humour. Her guile was totally instinctive, a survivor's instinct, so it was with some surprise that Cat listened to her now, and wondered whether her mother had reached a stage in her life when she was having some regrets.

'Always we had to hide it, Caterina, always... I thought it best... You never know what or who...' A space, a soft acquiescent sigh. 'Maybe for you it doesn't matter so much... Not these days. But in Germany...' She gave a little *moue* of distress.

Cat said gently, 'Ma, all that's in the past.'

'Then what's the problem?' Rute sounded almost impatient. 'If it means so little to you, why ask?'

Put on the spot, Cat retreated. 'Look, I'm sorry I mentioned it. It doesn't matter, anyway.'

'It always mattered to me.' Rute spoke sharply, and Cat knew that there would be no gainsaying her, no room for discussion and no hope of compromise. 'It had to matter. But going out to say you're Jewish? That amazes me – so risky! But if it does not matter to you,' she added firmly, 'well, it should! What you are, from where you come...'

Cat smiled to herself. How contrary was that? Typical!

'It's no big deal, Ma. Let's forget it, hey?'

'Forget? *Ja*, you just try and forget!' She sighed again. 'Well, I blame myself... But this review... Oh,

Caterina, just take care... Ask yourself who will see it. Ask, will it help you or hinder you, for them to know you are Jewish? That's what you have to ask. And if it's 'no big deal',' she added shrewdly, 'then what's bothering you? Is it Bill?'

'It's just that, if he sees it...'

'Cate*rina*, he will only see it if someone shoves it under his nose! He *ist Spiessbürger,* a Philistine! No, have courage; let them say what they like!' Her voice was warmer now, less anxious. 'And, Caterina, I am so very proud of you that you have this exhibition. I just wish I could see your work... but I am not so very well at the moment.'

'Ma?'

'Ach, don't worry yourself, darling. It's something or nothing. I am old now; a headache here and there, what is that? Not every day, just sometimes. And I am a little... how do you say, the vertigo? *Ja,* some days I am just a little dizzy.'

Cat recalled her mother's grey, ashy look, and thought, how selfish I've been! I just thought she was just anxious for me, grieving for the children...

'You want me to come up? I will if...'

'*Ja,* well, sometime would be nice. Come when you can. When you are not so busy with your own concerns.'

That night Caterina Feugler examined her face in the mirror, not with her usual cursory check for smudges of paint, but to seek traces of her Jewish birth. She'd no idea if her father was Jewish, but was there *nothing* of him in her? Wasn't she like him at all? She remembered her mother once saying, how could you be? Now she asked herself, why not?

Like her mother, her complexion was olive, her nose slightly more aquiline, and she had the same auburn hair, greying now, and green eyes. She'd inherited her mother's high cheekbones, but they were also found in other races. She grinned to herself. Such a pity not to satisfy those myths so beloved of the Gentile mind, that a typical Jew was round-shouldered, hook-nosed, scheming and submissive! Then she sobered; of such was prejudice built and formed, hostility manufactured. And yet there were other reasons that evoked hostility. The Jewish belief that they were a chosen nation, that their mind-set encompassed not only theology but land, particularly Israel, and specifically Jerusalem. It ghettoised them, and perhaps that was the root of the conflict.

Or that their survival depended on making money. People conveniently forgot the mediaeval prohibition on usury and their subsequent reliance on the Jews for financial security, but they hated them for it, and their hate had little to do with their religion or its teachings; the whole basis of European law and ethics was Judaic. In all other ways the reality of the Jewish people was similar to any other ethnic group; they were as unprepossessing or appealing, as hard working or lazy, and as disparate as any race struggling to make sense of the world.

Looking closer she realised that she was now older than Rute when Rute first began to tell her stories, and she saw not just their physical resemblance but something more, something other. Her face was not completely unmarked. This vertical crease between her eyes that spoke of repeated strain and tension, these shallow lines from her nose to the corners of her mouth, a mouth that was slightly pursed, as if silenced. They gave her a lost look, the look of someone who had known profound unhappiness, the look of a woman betrayed. As Rute had been, and as she had been, not only by Bill but by her mother as well.

She turned away from the mirror. Whatever harm Rute had done to her, she'd long forgiven. She'd finished with questions; she would never, now, elicit answers. All that was gone, except at night.

14

Cat had been at *The Studio* five months and it was now May, with all its natural plenitude and hours of prolonged sunshine. Each day she promised herself to fix a date to see her mother and each day she put it off. Instead, she took her sketchbook to the streets and sat on benches or low walls, people-watching. She drew quick charcoal sketches on a pad of heavy cartridge paper. She went to the railway arches and to the shopping centre, or wherever she could find people sleeping rough. They lived in murk and she drove out to find them in murk, the early mist that invariably clung to the marshes until burned away by the mid-day sun, and she returned in the evening haze down a lane of white blossom, radiant on the hawthorn. She was encouraged by her work; she felt she was developing, that what was in her to express was being expressed, without constraint, and at the end of each session she felt invigorated, at peace with herself and ready for more. She would do the General, when? Later, when she could no longer work outside. She'd visit Rute, when? Later, when the rain came.

Her subjects were a cosmopolitan bunch of druggies, alcoholics and refugees. Each weather-beaten face, each distinctive pair of hunched shoulders, each gnarled hand of yellowed fingers, tucked into mittens or wrapped in rags or clothed in fingerless gloves, and clasped round mugs of steaming tea, quietly found their way into her sketchbook. Eavesdropping on their desultory conversation was enlightening, and she was amazed that their abject poverty could be even partially redeemed by such dour exchanges. Each expressive mouth recited stories of separation from homeland and family, of running battles with Customs and Immigration, of dark journeys in the backs of lorries. Each voice concocted fairy tales about the new opportunities awaiting them; every feature spoke of anxiety, of the long delay for refugee status, of the equally long climb up the social scale, of hopes for stability; hopes fed by delusion and foiled by bureaucracy, exploitation, poverty and inadequate education. And every pair of eyes rehearsed the inevitable, downward slide into cardboard homes, a catalogue of errors where each sad page spoke of myths and half-remembered truths, papered to the damp brick walls where they huddled. She was riveted, an increasingly angry and protective witness, yet helpless to do more than paint her tender testimony.

Back at *The Studio*, she painted their faces on to unprimed panels of beautifully-grained oak scrounged from a builder's merchant. They all belonged there, to a greater or lesser extent, and their collaboration with the paint and with the grain of the wood seemed almost tangible, emerging from the flat surface to congratulate and to accuse. They'd sell one day, she was sure, if not immediately.

In defiance of her Orthodox parents, Julia took up permanent residence at *The Studio*. That was their business, but it didn't help that Ricci already disliked her. She was the butt of his only Jewish joke, which he repeated for effect, glancing at Cat as if it was a passport into her life, a declaration of solidarity with which to salve his elderly, or Gentile, conscience.

'There's a heavy Jew this morning,' he'd say, in his wonderful Welsh lilt, 'but it looks set to improve later on.'

If he'd only said it once it would not have caused such friction between them but, as Julia was distinctly overweight, it was painfully apposite and he enjoyed saying it. On the first occasion she contented herself with a venomous glance, but when it happened again, she fought back.

'Old men are so *boring*, aren't you, Ricci?'

Sometimes when Cat returned she'd find Julia in tears. 'Why's he getting at me, Cat? I aint done nothin' to him!'

'Can't you just ignore him, Julia? He's had a rough time...'

'Oh, the poor git, I feel sorry for him, I don't think. 'Course, it's OK for you, isn't it? You're not the one he's getting at.'

Cat felt helpless. It saddened her that Ricci, a good, kind man who she would have expected to be sensitive to people's feelings, could be so cruel. One day, to add insult to injury, he came home shorn of all that remained of his hair.

'Well, that's that, I'm in profit at last. Poor Julia, but life's too short, my love...'

Certainly, thought Cat, life was too short for him to bus all the way to Gravesend to find a barber when he could have gone to the salon next door to his shop. She was sure he'd done it out of spite and she turned on him sharply.

'Ricci, I'm sorry, but Julia's always beautifully groomed. If you can't be civil to her just leave her alone! This is my home, and the last thing I need is acrimony of any sort. So stop it, will you?'

Julia looked at her blankly, shocked by her outburst; Ricci looked sheepish, but Cat, as she left the room, was amazed at herself. To think she'd had it in her to be so forthright!

That night she woke to hear him raging and the thump of the mattress. She found herself thinking, poor old chap; he doesn't deserve such horrors. She didn't ask herself whether he was longing to talk about what troubled him but was loath to burden her.

In the morning she was gentle with him, which surprised them both. Defensive though she was, Ricci had found a way in and, obscurely, she was grateful. Since his 'Jewish enclave' remark, when she'd walked out on him, Ricci hadn't mentioned his nightmares again or the anguish he went through at night, and she felt that if she'd pressed him, he might have confided more. Instead she'd warded him off, not because of his quarrel with Julia, but because of her reluctance to get involved. But maybe her experience on the streets, scrutinising and drawing people of all kinds and dispositions, had made her more receptive to someone else's agony, and she was glad to be given another chance.

The following night Ricci came to her partition door. Cat was fast asleep and in her dreams everything was lit to harsh lamplight, although against the metal windows the dark night pulsed, as if wanting to infiltrate. The curtains were open wide – but in the studio there were no curtains as she needed all the light that the never-never God must willy-nilly give. Those were but the slight cotton things she'd hung in James's bedroom to shut out the glare of the streetlamp, and in front of her was little James, Rute's Jakov, rubbing his eyes, swaying on the threshold of her bedroom in High Wycombe.

'I had such a bad dream, Mummy, such a dreadful bad dream.'

'Come into bed with me.' The words like cotton wool in her mouth.

'Oh, I couldn't possibly do that!' Ricci reared back as though stung, and James slipped away, swooping to maturity.

'Ricci? That you? What's the matter?' Cat sat up stiffly, her mind whirling.

'Give us a hand, would you, Cat? I'm having a dreadful night, with dreadful, dreadful dreams.'

Dreams within dreams. Themes within themes.

Cat roused herself. 'Hang on, let me get up. I'll make us a cuppa.'

It was cold, so she dragged her duvet off the bed, and they sat under it on the sofa, hugging their mugs for warmth. Beyond the windows the water glistened, silver lights under a blue night sky. Then Ricci began to speak.

As a young lad, he told her, he'd stand on a local railway bridge, train-spotting, noting the number plates in a little black book. Three weeks into his posting in Burma, never having fired a gun in anger, he was captured by the Japanese and the book was found. Assuming the numbers were frequencies they searched him for a radio, and when they failed to find it, tortured him. Finally, they strung him out between two benches and a whole platoon marched over him.

'That's what they did to FEPOWS,' he said bluntly. 'Sorry to shock you, is it?'

For the first time Cat touched him of her own volition, briefly placing her hand over his, where it lay heavy and motionless on top of the duvet. When Ricci took up his story again, he spoke hesitantly, almost anecdotally, the threads of his story woven together like coarse fabric, full of knots and twists and turns, and it set the hair on the back of Cat's neck on end and filled her with a deathly chill. He told it trembling, with dry eyes, the melodious lilt of his voice belying the horror of his words, while outside the sky lightened to a green glow and the town woke its muffled din.

'*The Kwai*, you've heard of that; that's where we were. The film was nothing like. Everyone else is working in the gorge, but I can't, the state I'm in. So every day I cart the bodies back for burning, usually at sunset, with the river glowing red. Beautiful, really, except, well, 'rivers of blood', you know. And the Japs are beating me with their canes, real bamboo canes, Cat; they cause terrible ulcers when they break the skin. And in the dream I'm being beaten down this path to the river... And then it's like a film, Cat, sort of re-wind, and I'm sort of reversing up the path. Then I go on again, and I get to the river, and all these bodies are there, with the river blood-red, then back goes the film, and down the path I go again, and so it goes on, Cat, five or six times a night...'

'How often, Ricci?'

'Just said. Five or six times a night.'

'No, I meant how often have you dreamt this?'

'Oh, every night. Every night since the war.'

If Cat thought the Jews had a monopoly on suffering she was mistaken. No one had promised it wouldn't happen again, here, there or elsewhere; Rwanda, Yugoslavia, the Sudan. The Burma War was concurrent with the Holocaust, she remembered, and therefore with what had happened to her mother's family. It all seemed so long ago, and she found herself marvelling how, so many years on, even suffering such as Ricci's had not been overlaid, not only because of the Liberation, but because he was so passionately absorbed in his books. Inanely, she put it to him: hadn't being free, and the sheer weight of time and his dedication to his work, helped him to put the trauma behind him?

'Ah, Cat, you don't understand,' he groaned, rubbing his face. 'Trauma doesn't work like that. You're never free; you can never put it behind you. Oh, you try and block it out. You even start to wonder whether it's all an illusion or whether the dreams just exaggerate it. But it's beyond exaggeration, Cat.' He dropped his hands. His face was flushed, and there were beads of sweat on his forehead. 'And it's no illusion; the daytime's the illusion, you see.'

Aware that her response had been facile, even crass, Cat began to apologise, but he stopped her.

'I'm just glad that nothing's happened in your life to teach you these awful things.'

He edged himself off the sofa, and Cat got up too. There were noises above, as of elephants waking; groans and thumping about, and they could hear Julia in the shower, squealing her morning pop songs.

At the door, Ricci hesitated, gesturing towards the

ceiling with his thumb. 'I was foul to her, wasn't I? I did apologise, you know. It's no excuse, but these dreams, they leave me in such a bad mood...'

Small Welsh voice, diffident, child-like, and Cat was touched. 'You're OK, Ricci.'

Ricci smiled down at her. 'No, I'm not. But you are. You've been so comforting, Cat.'

'Me?'

'Yes. You listened, you see.'

Perhaps she had, but at a cost. On succeeding days she found herself thinking more and more about her mother, her extraordinary history, complete with evasions, and how it had impinged on her life. Her own nightmares had diminished, rubbish swept aside, but after listening to Ricci, they hit her storm-force.

15

Conscious that she had procrastinated far too long, Cat rang Strike Command and warmed up the portrait commission. She also phoned her mother to tell her about her influx of tenants.

'Caterina, are you sure what you're doing is wise, to surround yourself with men?'

Cat hadn't given it much thought, but considering her blip with Gus, and yes, her other blip with Ricci, perhaps it was a hopeful sign, demonstrating that she was no longer so vulnerable as to tar every man with the Bill brush.

'And you'll come and see me soon?'

Shamed into action, Cat promised to go up the following day. She left Gus doing a large slab piece to the Ornette Colman CD which pizza-Saul had lent them and which she had played to death. Even Ricci, normally a devotee of Bach, was slowly being converted and could often be heard tapping its pulse on her ceiling. She took Saul's Coltrane for the car and, as a present for Rute, a second hand record player from the charity shop in Swanscombe. She had tested it on Glenn Miller, which she threw in for good measure, it being music of her mother's era. It was only when she was halfway to Coventry that she realised that Rute, with her high-brow training, might find the lyrics utterly trivial and foreign, but it was too late, then, to get anything else.

The further she got from home, and particularly when she passed the junction to High Wycombe, the guiltier she felt that she hadn't visited her mother earlier. She should have paid more attention to Deborah's accusation that she had caused her mother's headaches, and Rute, herself, had hinted at poor health. She'd been good to her when she left Bill, much more perceptive of her needs than when she'd left for college all those years ago, a move she had taken as personal criticism. Given how bleak she must have felt, it had required a lot of courage for her to have managed on her own.

She found her mother fast asleep on the sofa wrapped in a blanket. She had dark rings under her eyes, and she slept with her hands balled under her chin, her lips compressed against any hint of her condition. Cat went through to the kitchen to see if lunch needed attention, but the oven was cold and, except for a solitary packet of butter, the fridge was bare. Cat sat by her mother for a long time and then she laid her hand gently on her forehead. Her temperature seemed normal, but when she stroked her forehead more firmly, trying to rouse her, Rute merely frowned and clutched feebly at the blanket. It seemed that she was refusing to wake and Cat became seriously worried. She telephoned the surgery, and eventually the doctor came, examined her mother and then rang for an ambulance. Cat followed it through the city, parked, and then sat in the waiting room for two hours while they got her on to a ward. They would do immediate blood tests, they said.

'What for?'

'Oh, the usual. She may just be anaemic.'

'Can I see her?'

'I'm sorry, but not just now. Can you come back tomorrow?'

Cat drove back to the house and tidied up, though the place was 'spic unt span', and the next morning she returned to the hospital. She bought a filled roll which she consumed in the lift, brushing the crumbs away guiltily on to the floor — and a yellow pot-Mum for Rute.

In the corridor outside her mother's ward, a nurse stopped her and laid her hand on her arm.

'I'm sorry, dear, you should see the Sister, I think.'

'Why? I only want to visit my mother, give her these

flowers.'

'Well, the Sister does need to see you before you go in.'

'Oh, I see.' Cat looked around, unseeing. 'It's... cancer, then?'

The nurse looked at her with compassion. 'You should really talk to the Sister.'

Cat waited by herself in a side-room until the Sister came bustling in, slowing abruptly and immediately solicitous, her plump dry hand on Cat's arm.

'I'm sorry, dear. Nurse tells me you know.' She indicated the upright chairs. 'Shall we sit down for a minute?'

'I don't need to sit down.' Cat's voice was brittle. 'What is it? What's the matter with her?'

'You need to prepare yourself... It's not good news, I'm afraid. You see, the initial tests have revealed a shadow on the brain...'

'On the *brain*? My *God*!' Cat slid her hand to the wall to support herself, but unconsciously recalling Rute's dislike of finger marks, she fisted it in her pocket. 'Is it operable?'

'Well, we'll do more tests,' said the Sister, 'but, from what we've seen, probably not. It's a massive shadow, and you need to think of her age...'

'She's not that old!'

'And there may be secondaries.' She looked at Cat, appraising her. 'Now, I have to say something to Mrs Feugler. Would you like to come with me?'

'Does she need to know?'

'Eventually she'll *have* to know.'

'So what will you tell her?'

'What do you want me to tell her?

'...Tell her the truth.'

Cat followed the nurse down the corridor, her mind reeling.

Under a thin hospital blanket Rute lay inert, her eyes open. The Sister bent over her, talking softly.

Rute listened calmly, and then turned her face to the window. Her eyes collapsed, washing the green into pools. She inhaled deeply and, under her hospital gown, Cat saw the gleam of her necklace against her throat. Rute turned back, saw Cat's distress and took her hand.

'Don't cry for me, my darling.' Her English was unhurried and barely accented. She took a breath. 'It's the last great journey, *liebchen.* But oh, Caterina, I did not think it would end like this!' A tremor went through her, then she was serene again, her eyes bright with unshed tears, a twist of amusement and self-deprecation on her lips. Cat could hardly meet her eyes, join green to green. 'Just, don't let me be cremated, OK? That man, who shall remain nameless – may his name be blotted from the Book of Life!'

'Which man, Ma?'

Enunciating clearly, 'Hitler. If I am cremated he will have won.'

Once more Cat returned to the house, put out the 'rubbidge', wrote a note to stop the 'milch', locked the 'vindows', 'svitched' the boiler down to low, and bolted the back door. She pushed the record player under her mother's bed for... later. She knew little about terminal illness and imagined that after the first crisis was over, Rute would be sent home. She'd need to get help in; she'd ask the hospital about that. Until then she intended to spend every free moment at her mother's bedside but on her return to the hospital the Sister met her in the corridor.

'Don't come too often, dear,' she said. 'Not more than once a week. We want her to settle in, don't we?'

'Settle in? But she'll be going home soon, surely!'

'Well, it *is* terminal, you know.'

'Yes, but she's not actually *dying,* is she?' Cat was aware that her voice was high pitched and she tried to moderate it. 'How... how long has she got?'

'I'm afraid there's no way of telling.' The Sister looked at Cat closely. 'Look, would you prefer not to know or do you want to hear it straight? You strike me as...'

'I think I'd like to know... whatever there is to know,' said Cat faintly.

The Sister was brisk, and perhaps it was best that way, thought Cat; best to be aware.

'Well, there's a pattern to these things, you see. With some cancers there's a period of remission but not so often with the brain, so it can be very quick. But if she responds to treatment she could live for weeks, though I warn you, even then we may have to keep her in.' She studied Cat's face. 'Or you could try a Hospice, if you prefer. We have to consider incontinence as well, and there's a possibility, you see, it might affect her eyes.'

'Her eyes? You mean she might go blind?'

Rute, *blind*?

'It's possible. I'm sorry; you said you wanted it straight.'

'Did I?' Cat whispered.

'Well, you have to be prepared...'

The motorway seemed endless. At home everyone was out, but Gus's new slab-pot was on the steps drying in the sun, elegant, as narrow as life and indented with swirls. Someone will put flowers in it, she thought, or some twigs, a Chinese arrangement of Yin and Yang.

Later, in bed, she opened *The Night Trilogy*, the Elie Wiesel book her mother had given her years ago, but she got no further than the foreword by Mauriac. The words leaped out at her – *trainloads of Jewish children at Austerlitz Station on their way to the gas chambers*, and Wiesel's rejoinder, *I was one of them* – nightmares come to life, and she laid the book down. Instead, she picked up her little copy of *Four Quartets*, found *East Coker*, and by the time she was ready for sleep had read it through. Over the long, fluted years of her meandering this little leather-bound dog-eared book had always solaced her, had always been relevant to whatever she was doing or thinking.

Home is where one starts from...

Later, unable to sleep, she fetched a canvas. Outside the darkness slanted against the window and, except for the low gurgling of the tide, all was quiet. With a few sweeping charcoal strokes, tender and faint, she mapped out the arms and the hands and then fleshed in the planes with body colour. She painted her in her chair, her embroidery on her lap, her fingers still, her cameo face serene, a small, uncomplaining smile on her lips, her eyes bright and affectionate. Rute. Ruth Feugler. Her mother.

16

The weather had been warm, if humid, and two days later when she returned to Coventry her mother's house felt fusty, already un-lived-in. Cat threw open the windows, breathing in the fragrant air. In the living room everything was as she had left it, the notepad on which she had written the note to the milkman still lying on the arm of her mother's chair. Outside the garden was already showing signs of neglect; the grass was long, brown-patched, soaked with... Jew. She smiled ruefully, recalling Ricci's pun. Many of the annuals had died for want of water and weeds were rampant. In the kitchen she searched for something to nibble, but except for a box of Matzos and a bottle of salad oil, the cupboards and bread bin were empty. In the fridge the pack of butter was rancid, and she threw it away. She was puzzled. What had her mother been eating?

Upstairs, she unpacked her bag in the single room then used the bathroom, drying her hands on a small hand towel by the basin. Rute's bath towels, with their little flower motif, were neatly folded on the rail, and the laundry basket was empty.

In her mother's bedroom was a bow-fronted chest and she opened the top drawer. Inside were small piles of underwear, carefully folded with home-made sachets of rosemary lying on top of them – 'Good against moth, Caterina.' As she pressed them they crackled slightly, their pungent scent rising – *Rosemary, for remembrance.* In the wardrobe, Rute's outmoded dresses and skirts hung in cellophane covers, the cleaners' tickets still fastened to them with safety pins. Completely baffled now, Cat went onto the landing and opened the airing cupboard door. Inside, the sheets and pillowcases were arranged in precise rectangles, each with its embroidered flower motif.

Had her mother *known*? Had she exhausted herself, just to leave it tidy for her daughter?

Rute seemed to have stabilised; her eyes were brighter and someone had washed her hair. After two more days footling around between the hospital and Rute's house they became restless with each other, and she was grateful when Rute said, 'Ach, you have your own life to lead.' Among other things she still had her contribution to Rudi's catalogue to attend to; it was now long overdue, yet another victim to her procrastination.

'No, no, not at all,' she said. 'I'm glad to be here. But tell you what, how if I'll shoot off now and get some jobs done at home, then I can be back in a few days – that OK?'

On the way home she stopped off at the bookshop in Swanscombe and asked Ricci if she could borrow his typewriter, and he took her to his back room. On his desk was a little pile of books, some with leather covers, others with broken spines. The top one, *The Mystical Poetry of Thomas Trahearne*, had a battered yellow cover covered in polythene, obviously his attempt to preserve it.

'What's this? I've never even heard of Thomas Trahearne.'

'Oh, he's an English poet of the seventeenth century.' He took the book in his hand and opened it at its bookmark. 'Listen to this. What do you think of this? Um, yes, here we go.'

He began to read.

All appeared new and strange at first, inexpressibly rare and delightful and beautiful... My very ignorance was advantageous. I seemed as one brought into the estate of innocence. All things were spotless and pure and glorious: yea, and infinitely mine, joyful and precious. I knew not that there were any sins, or complaints or laws. I dreamed not of poverties, contentions or vices. All tears and quarrels were hidden from mine eyes...

Oh, poor Ricci, she thought, how apposite; the regret and longing for lost innocence, or perhaps the wishful thinking of someone just released from his Prisoner of War camp.

'Speaks to you, does he?' he said.

'He obviously speaks to you! I expect you read a lot, closeted here.'

'I did, but not so much these days. This is pretty heavy-going and some say a bit outdated, so it suits me down to the ground.' He grinned at her, closed the book and replaced it on top of the pile. 'Well, I'll leave you to it.'

She sat there for a few minutes, trying to focus her mind on her exhibition catalogue and then she began to type.

Catherine Feugler has been painting portraits for many years

Pause, wipe her furrowed brow – new page; they'll think she's a has-been.

Catherine Feugler is a professional portrait painter, and as such is a keen observer of the human condition. Her explorations in portraiture attempt to reconcile the disparity which, in facial characteristics, exists

Um...

between form and the necessarily partial revelation of personality...

Yuk. Pretentious waffle. Yet compared to some of the esoteric drivel she sometimes read in galleries it was actually quite lucid, if you worked at it.

Catherine Feugler welcomes commissions.

She examined what she had written. Did people know why faces were flawed, how the happenings of life shaped them like clay? This should be Gus's piece, perhaps, but no, painting was equally malleable. And

Rudi wouldn't care so long as he got something. Take a firm line, Rudi, and see where that gets you, but give me space.

At home again, she worked on her portrait of Rute. Rute, weak in her hospital bed; Rute, perched on the easel, watching it progress; Rute, here, there, elsewhere, in her beginning.

Saul arrived with a take-away and they munched together. He had long begged a portrait from her, so she dragged out a fresh canvas and to his delight, set to. Saul was Caribbean, a third generation immigrant, tall, broad-shouldered, with three-foot long dreadlocks which Julia once plaited for him late into the night, the others somnolent on sofas and cushions.

'Got plenty of black?' joked Saul.

'I don't actually need it,' she replied absently. 'There's no black in nature except in charcoal, and even that has a blue-ish sheen. No, I'm using mixes – what we call tertiary colours. *Pace* your ancestry, Saul,' she smiled.

'*Patches?* Oh well, you know best.'

Later she asked, preoccupied, 'You know Saul's a Jewish name?'

'Man, you can't be serious!'

'Old Testament.' And the New, the persecutor-misogynist-preacher man.

'I never heard that before! My folks would have no truck with *Jews!*

Cat didn't flinch. Quietly, she laid down her brush and went to bed.

From there it went downhill for a while. It was the beginning of the end for Rute, the end of the beginning for Cat, *mittel*-times for Ricci. Cat could read him like a book. He might return alert and stimulated after a day in his shop, but those times were infrequent. He seemed without purpose, his eyes dark and his forehead ridged with pain, and he would wander aimlessly round the room, 'just making a nuisance of myself'. But it was he who took the telephone call from the hospital and hovered attentively at her side when she phoned back. Her mother had developed a clot on her lung and needed an operation. The Sister mentioned quality of life and offered Cat an interview with the surgeon.

'He's one of the best in the country. He's concerned that you know he's doing all he can.'

'Kind,' Cat said slowly, 'but no... no... it's OK. If my mother's agreed. Thank you for telling me. When will it be?'

'Well, soon. We think early Friday morning. It'll be keyhole surgery so she shouldn't be too sore. '

Cat thought quickly. Today was Tuesday. At last she had made a firm date with Strike Command and was due to start her portrait of the American general on Wednesday. It was an overnight stay, and she could easily go on to Coventry the following morning.

'...Right, I'll be there in four days.'

'You mean Thursday? But the operation isn't until Friday.'

'I meant Friday.' So, today was Monday; she had gained a day.

17

It was the silence she heard first. She woke with the sense of the river uncannily holding its breath, the waves rebounding off the factory walls with a dull pulsing echo, like a heartbeat. She crossed to the window and peered out under the mist. It was high tide, and beached in the murky shallows was a black inflatable dinghy, its outboard motor belching fumes, and two men clad in luminous yellow waterproofs were dragging something across the turgid water with long metal hooks. It slithered along the side of the boat and someone swore. It was a body, its flesh bloated and white, with waving tendrils of skin like fins on tropical fish.

'Don't look, Cat. Come away.' Gus, shivering by her side. 'Come on, I'll make us all a cuppa. We're lucky Julia's out for the count – she'd throw a fit!'

He took two mugs outside for the men. Ricci appeared, his eyes swollen with sleep, or the lack of it; he took one look out of the window and collapsed in a heap on the sofa. Cat bent over him, crooning, stroking his sparse hair.

'It's OK, Ricci, it's OK.'

'Oh, my God! My gracious God!'

'It's OK.'

Later, the boat and its contents gone, Gus spoke into the silence, striving to be rational. 'I'm surprised it hasn't happened before. Wonder who it was? Probably a drunk or something.'

'Or a suicide,' said Ricci.'

So do all memories drown and sink.

Since she was awake, Cat packed up her studio into her little car and set off for High Wycombe. She drove slowly, partly because she was still unnerved by the morning's events, but also because she was apprehensive about returning to the town where, as far as she knew, Bill still lived. The journey was uneventful, but as she drove down the hill from the motorway, she was surprised to find that her recollections were less focussed on her marriage than on her childhood. The steepness of the hill reminded her, not of struggling home with heavily laden shopping bags, wondering what sort of mood Bill would be in, but of a tilting bus ride with Rute to the narrow stream on the common where they had paddled, and the clump of high rocks on which they clambered. And her memory of the railway station was not how it was when she met Bill off the train after he lost his licence, refurbished, with new lamps, but as it had been when she'd left for college, with old-fashioned bottle green paintwork and blackened iron lamps. She could even recall the ravaged expression on Rute's face as the train came in, how she pushed her away – 'Go, Caterina, chust go!' and how her lonely figure in her shabby coat receded down the platform, her head bowed in denial, as if her daughter was vanishing into oblivion. And on her return she was always at the station to greet her and to help carry her bags up the hill, as Cat had carried her mother's shopping as an adolescent.

All those were true memories, if blurred, but it came to her then, that she must have distorted her memories of childhood; Rute had not been as disengaged from her as she had always thought. She did play with her; she did take her out; she did watch for her coming; she did care. She found herself blushing with humiliation; to have maligned her like that was pure arrogance. To think, only recently, she had *forgiven* the harm her mother had done to her, with her silences and her evasions and her endless, nightmarish stories. No, it was *she* who needed forgiving. Fleetingly she wondered what else in her life she had falsified – but perhaps memory was always at fault and never tallied with reality. Bill's violence had been real; her love for her children was real, but her mother's ghetto and her escape – had they been real? She could hardly ask her, now she was so ill. No, Rute was leaving her, irrevocably, and the time for questions was almost over. Cat knew the death of a parent was a natural process but nevertheless her thoughts were desolate, and to dismiss them from her mind in order to be alert, professionally competent and friendly with a complete stranger, seemed at that moment the hardest thing in the world to achieve.

Following the signs to the Base she turned off the main road into a wide avenue lined with tall beech trees, their scent intensely aromatic. The house was set back among trees, with a wide sloping gravel drive and welcoming tubs of red camellias under the portico. The General was at the door, and he greeted her with his full name in the American way.

'Hi, now you're Miss Feugler.' He shook her hand with vigour. 'Edward Henry Barber at your service ...'

He was tall and broad-shouldered, his eyes deep-set and very blue, and Cat felt a rush of confidence – I can paint this man. They had English tea with English scones and melting butter, and then he went up to change into his uniform. Cat laid out her cloth and paints, checked the direction of the light, set up her easel and waited.

The General returned wearing full dress uniform, and she felt an immediate frisson of unease. She tried to focus on his face but her eyes kept returning to the harsh blue of his uniform, to the way the cut of it narrowed his waist and squared his shoulders, to the devoted shine on the buttons. What have you been up to, she thought, wearing this stuff? She found herself wondering how Rute would have coped, and how long it would have taken her to run.

He was striking rather than handsome, if slightly frayed at the edges. His face was angular, his hair and

151

eyebrows silver grey, but his features were unusually asymmetrical, one side alert and focussed; the other almost introverted, more appropriate to some Parisian bistro poet than to a seasoned soldier. Such characteristics were hardly imperfections, and normally they would have filled her with glee but instead of taking time to stop and think, to get beneath the surface to what might emerge as personality, her distaste for his uniform took precedence. This was far too simplistic, as she was to discover.

Sensing something, he waved at his chest and asked, 'You OK with this outfit? It's protocol for military portraits...'

'Yes, of course,' she lied. 'It's what I expected you'd wear. Shall we start?'

Squeezing tubes furiously she tried to pull herself together. If she let herself, she might enjoy painting the Still Life of his accoutrements, the great swathe of braid on one shoulder, the peaked cap perched on his lap, the medals and ribbons and the buttons, the polished upright chair. His 'outfit' might redeem itself if she could distance herself from it a little. Seated, his height was less obvious, but he still had that slightly scrawny, refined look of a lean, middle-aged man in good shape. He sat very erect with his knees apart, and as the pose seemed natural to him, she decided to keep it. Usually she encouraged people to introduce into the composition some discreet symbol of their life, not to impinge, but a private communication: this was what I achieved and how I want to be remembered. General Barber chose a small brass figurine of an oriental dancer; a pun, he told her, on top brass. Later he told her of its connection to Korea and 'Nam.

'You want me to sit still?'

She smiled. 'Quite still, but I need you to relax. Not if it gets uncomfortable. Reasonably. If you can just remember the pose and what you can see behind my head, that would be great.'

152

It was her usual blurb, and sometimes she put chalk marks on the chair as a reminder, and a little square of masking tape on the wall, but not here, not on a four-star General's antique wheel-back chair or his William Morris wallpaper.

'Reasonably I can do.'

Cat knew that if people were told they could relax, they immediately felt less threatened. And it was a threat of sorts, to come under the scrutiny of the brush. They would suddenly feel vulnerable, when they had spent their lives masking whatever vulnerability they were born with, or which they had acquired in the sheer heck of living. As Cat also knew, just by looking in the mirror.

'It'll save you looking glum,' she offered, 'which tends to happen if you sit very still. You'd get lost in your own thoughts...'

'And how d'you know they'd be glum? Yeah, you're right – too much of that and I'll end up looking like Methuselah!'

She gave a light laugh. She liked his humour but she needed to concentrate. Palette knife poised, she stood back, assessing his skin tones, and then bent to mix some colours. It was very quiet, and when he spoke again she was startled.

'Newspaper?'

'Sorry, what did you say?'

'I'm asking, can I read the newspaper?'

This was unforeseen and she hesitated. 'I'd rather not, if you don't mind. Your face will be too, um, down.'

'Down? You mean depressed? Because it's all bad news, anyway?'

She felt slightly exasperated. 'General, I need to see your eyes, you see.'

He squinted sideways. 'Mmm, I get a real good view of my drinks bar.'

'Tedious for you,' she smiled. 'You could listen to

some music, if you like.'

'Music? I don't know any music.' His eyebrows lifted. 'Well, dance music? Jazz? No, we'll be fine as we are. OK, Girl, let's go!'

Blank canvases are naked until clothed in paint. Her first marks seem particularly intrusive, like a weal or a bruise on bare skin, but her expectation is that under the slow caress of the brush the face will eventually recover, to emerge whole and healthy again or at least no worse than it was before. Inherent is struggle, the risk of losing spontaneity or that the final image might lack truth, if facial likeness is truth at all. And, as with any truth, does interpretation help or hinder?

Slightly self-conscious, her spread feet replicating the position of the easel, she mapped out the plan with fast sweeps of thin paint. The weal became a line from which she would develop other lines; the bruise redeemed with slight, but significant, adjustments of tone, so that the first marks, the first impressions on the canvas were more evoked than applied.

First impressions didn't matter as much as people said they did; they'd mislead her; they'd close her eyes and she'd stop learning. It was the *story* that counted, how the body articulated the happenings of the years, R.S Thomas's *bent bones fractured by life*. Yet with this portrait it was a long time before her first impressions gave way to that necessary, deeper understanding, much longer than was usual with a new subject. It was the uniform; it got in the way.

Whole arm movements, accelerating now, and suddenly the risk lessened and she grew in confidence, engaging with his face, the shape of his shoulders and the distinctive angle of his head, *still, but still moving*. Eliot, this time. She felt alert and in tune with what she was doing, and the poetry flicking through her mind helped; it was in her, part of her life, inseparable from her hand and eye. She was also ready to hear his voice again, for how he talked would influence how she described him, although she mightn't be really listening. As usual, she found herself hoping that this time she might express more profoundly the close relationship between her subject and his world, and how his features had been fitted together to reveal his uniqueness.

She was aware that he was looking at her with mild curiosity, but then he was unaware of her fretting and hoping and the struggle with risk. Perhaps he was still at the wary stage, wondering what impression he was making or whether she thought this was an ego trip for him. Which, she thought, it might very well be. Next, he'd say how absolutely fascinating it was to watch an artist at work – and it seemed that it was, for he said it, to which she mumbled something polite, and hoped she wasn't seen scrubbing things out.

It wasn't long before he began to fidget. He crossed and uncrossed his legs, each time tilting his head towards the window, as if hankering to be outside. He seemed unable to sit still for more than a few minutes, and he had absent-mindedly tossed his cap over the figurine. They had done less than an hour, but Cat threw down her brush. That got his attention.

'You done for today? I'm game to go on, if you like. It's been, what?' He glanced at his watch. 'Golly, under an hour – seems more.'

She gave him an admonishing glance. 'General, I know it's tough, but this needs to be reciprocal. You need to focus as hard as I do...'

'Hell, I *am* focussing!'

'Good. Can you remember the pose?'

He looked surprised. 'Sure I can! I'm still here, aren't I?'

Cat smiled at him. 'Where's your hat, General?'

18

General Barber had a light touch in conversation and the laughter lines around his eyes and mouth belied the austerity of his rank and gave him a certain benevolence. Cat was drawn to him. Considering his rank he seemed unpretentious, which spelt a lot. He seemed to have been a serious soldier – whatever that meant in his context – but he revealed a deep compassion for the underdog. She may not have seen his depths but she saw that, and she decided to emphasise it if she could; separate, as it were, from whatever his history had been. His white hair was cut close to his head but not too close, and within it she found the cool flesh tones by the temples and the blue lights above his ears that corresponded with his eyes. She repeated the same hues in the thin skin of his hands, and ensured that the violet-red shadows cast by the curtain were reflected on the back of his neck and in the upward plane of his wrists as they disappeared into the cuffs of his jacket.

He was behaving himself now and it became a pleasure to paint him, but again, she was conscious that their scrutiny was mutual, his expression intent and curious.

At length he said, 'You work very fast. You make me quite breathless, watching you.'

'I always work fast in the beginning. I try and get lots of ideas out all at the same time.'

'That don't muddle you, some?'

She let that pass. 'It might muddle you, but it don't muddle me.'

A bit later, he said, in his gravelly drawl, 'You're very serious, Catherine.'

She smiled. 'It's a serious business, General.'

'Call me Ed,' he growled. 'You look very... fierce.'

'Well, I'm concentrating.'

'I beg your pardon, Catherine!'

'Think nothing of it, Ed!'

She painted until the light went, and then stood back. She had caught something of him, his strength and his humour, especially in the eyes. It was only much later that she began to ask herself why, in her blindness, she had failed to perceive his vulnerability, particularly since she had long prided herself on her ability to look beneath the surface, to discover the soul behind the eyes, as she put it. The uniform still made it impossible to see him more than skin-deep or to ask the necessary questions that could have revealed his depths, the shadowed side of him that she would totally fail to comprehend.

Later, she would blame herself for this. Much might have been averted.

'I always reckoned on retiring to the States, but my wife's buried over here and somehow I can't see myself going back to a place where I've not lived since my youth. I'll park my clogs here when the time comes, and they c'n put up a slab for me somewhere.'

'Mmm, complicated. Where was it you lived?'

It was their second session. Ed was silent much of the time, but occasionally he'd make a remark like this, as if he was thinking out loud. Cat became accustomed to it, as a deep background tune to her painting. He didn't seem to expect a reply and his eyes lit up.

'Cincinnati, Southern Ohio. You know the place?'

'Never been.'

'Oh. Well, I've a daughter there, Marie-Beth, married to a farmer. She comes home regular, though. I send her the fare.' He spoke with a wistful tenderness which was more eloquent than any words.

'How did she meet him?' she asked, frowning over her work.

'You wanna know?' he echoed, betraying his Mid-West roots. 'You really wanna know?'

Cat looked up, startled. Was she intruding?

'It's a joke. She met him through me. He was one boot soldier I booted out. He couldn't march, he couldn't aim straight, and to cap it all, he turned out pacifist!'

Cat smiled, her brush suspended. 'I always thought Daw's Hill was an Air Base.'

'Lady, the Military's everywhere. We keep the Base on its feet.'

'So, what happened to your myopic peacenik?'

'My myopic peacenik?' His face split into laughter, open and guileless. 'That's good. That's very good. My myopic peacenik!'

'Well,' he drawled, 'he stayed on with us for a while. I couldn't send him home, now could I? Marie-Beth would've crucified me. I got him a live-in job on a farm, over at Lacey Green. Now, here's a funny thing,' he added. 'We used to have dinner parties, my wife and I, mix up soldiers and airmen, you know, and we had to say to Marie-Beth... "Look here, Beth-honey, would you and Frank" – that was his name, Frank, he was a Stevenson, still is – "would you and Frank go upstairs for a while, amuse yourselves, while we have company?" Now, can you fancy that? Me, her *Pa*, for God's sakes, telling my own daughter to go upstairs with her boyfriend?'

He slapped his thigh, knocking over the figurine, which crashed to the floor.

He gave her his daughter's room, and after a late supper of fried ham and fruit salad they parted. The house had few rooms but they were spacious. Downstairs there was a 'lobby', a sizeable kitchen, and a huge dining room with a long, beech table stretching from end to end, surrounded by a dozen matching chairs. Upstairs, the drawing room where Cat was painting him was furnished with a huge three-piece suite, his drinks bar, some bookcases, and a glass-fronted cabinet cluttered with army memorabilia. Beyond that were his bedroom, another room that she didn't see until later, and his daughter's, with a cupboard-size *ensuite* bathroom.

His daughter's room was small but comfortable. It had a white wardrobe, a diminutive white desk, a single bed with a white headboard, and a portable white television. It had pink curtains, a matching pink counterpane and a frilly pink rag-rug on the carpet, a school project, perhaps. The walls were festooned with coloured prints, faded and curling at the edges; Everglades and Florida Keys; adolescent pin-ups of the Beatles, a sultry Robert Redford, Harrison Ford with his crooked grin, plus a huge torso of Mick Jagger, his pouting lips and hairless chest dominating the wall, hip-line belt just visible. On a shelf above the bookcase was a plethora of worn teddy bears and above, school photographs of girls in hockey gear in age-ascending order, doubtless from Beth-honey's years at Wycombe Abbey School. There wasn't a speck of dust anywhere. It was like a shrine, and Cat wondered how old his daughter was, and in spite of what he'd said about sending her the fare, when she'd last been home.

She bathed and went to bed, opening her Elie Wiesel, which she had brought simply to feel closer to her mother, but soon laid it aside. She preferred something less taxing, such as the sound of the breeze in the trees. She slept well for the first few hours. Then she woke, terrified, to the sound of planes.

As a child, she had been accustomed to see light aircraft overhead, flying in to the airfield at Booker, but this was a deep, almost menacing, sound and it was still in her head. Was this the source of the dream she had experienced as a child, and which had frightened her so much that she had shouted out? She always woke in her mother's arms, marvelling that Rute had come so swiftly, and concluding that she was already awake. The dream had long since faded from her memory, consigned to oblivion by the necessary disassociation of the intervening years, but resurgent now, merely because she was once again in High Wycombe and Rute at the forefront of her mind.

She had never discovered why the sound of the planes should have disturbed her so much, or why they did now. She felt cross with herself; she was a grown woman; she'd had plenty of time to grow out of it, but this time she was not in her own small bed and Rute was far away in hers and she was terrified.

In the morning, over a waffle breakfast, she asked casually, 'General, did you hear planes last night?'

'Call me Ed. You hear planes last night?'

Cat grinned self-consciously. 'That's what I'm asking you.'

'What, big 'uns or little 'uns?'

'Biggish.'

'Nah...'

Cat's heart sank. The sounds had been as real as if she was a child again, hearing their slow progress across the sky above the ceiling of her room.

'You get used to them,' he said through a mouthful of waffle. 'I never hear them now.'

'Oh.' She was relieved. 'But they still fly?'

'Yeah, they still fly. They're Chinooks; they make a hefty noise. We police the world, the US of A, you know that?' he said with some irony. 'We police the world.'

Cat promised herself that on her next visit she would take time out, take a nostalgic tour, go and sit by her mother's old house and try to discover what made her so afraid all those years ago, whenever there were planes in the night, very high up in the sky.

19

As so often happened, the third sitting did not go well, and Cat found that she was compelled to put aside the military aspect and dig deeper. Almost instinctively she felt that beneath that too-amiable exterior must reside a more complex character, but if so, it was hidden. Perhaps he masked it; perhaps his profession had colluded with him in subverting those aspects of the child in him, or the uncomfortable youth. Surely there had been a struggle somewhere in his life that had enabled him to reach such tranquillity, for tranquil he seemed, in a way she envied and thought unattainable.

He told Cat of an episode with an officer who'd gambled away the bar profits, and how he'd confessed to Ed in tears. After the disciplinary committee had relieved him of his rank, Ed had stayed alongside him and privately helped him back on his feet. Cat's prejudices – that people in the armed forces were brash, their humour coarse and lavatorial, that there was no room for sensitivity or vulnerability or compassion, that those more feminine attributes would undermine the job of work they had to do – were turned on their head. Painting him became more difficult, not less, and she nearly reached the point of regretting her instinct to look beneath the surface. She could have left it as merely the portrayal of a man in uniform, but that would have been half-baked and mediocre. She floundered on, hoping that eventually something would emerge to lift her blindness and she would suddenly discern what had hitherto been veiled to her.

The following day she drove up to Coventry, approaching, with some trepidation, the concrete block where her mother lay. Or, given the plethora of buildings, whether she would find her at all. Despite the faded maps or the waist-high coloured lines that should have led her, like the simplest maze in a child's puzzle book, to the place where she was meant to be, she always ended up elsewhere. She would hug the empty corridor walls, fighting the double doors that swung open in her face, pushing when she was supposed to pull and *vice versa*. Or she'd take the wrong lift, get out at the wrong side, or find herself in the basement surrounded by baskets of soiled linen and machines belching steam, the pale air full of nameless shadows. The inevitable, suspicious glances or the resigned questions, 'Can I help you?' 'Lost, are you?' and the ensuing convoluted directions which she immediately forgot, merely left her feeling foolish, inadequate and old. Others seemed to find their way all right. It was only she who was incompetent, who retreated with a hasty apology, 'Sorry! Sorry!' – echoes of ball games on hot beaches and midsummer courts after Wimbledon. Even when she'd made the journey several times she could still make a silly mistake. That much she knew about structure, already.

Rute was sleeping, and for a while Cat stood gazing down at her. A cage was over her chest and from under the sheet a tube stretched up to a saline bottle; over the bed a wire to a heart monitor bleeped quietly, its red zigzag pulse both reassuring and alarming. This was keyhole surgery? She gently touched her mother's shoulder and Rute's tired eyes slanted towards her, hazel-green.

'*Liebling...*'

'Hello, Ma.'

'You brought the *kinder* to me?'

Her first thought on waking; her first concern, always.

'No, Ma, just me, I'm afraid.'

Pause. 'You had something to eat?' Her voice was very weak, slurred and rough from the anaesthetic

'I'm fine, Ma. Are you OK? You're not in any pain, are you?'

Silence, while her eyes closed. 'They had to cut me in the end. I have *nineteen* stitches!' Her eyes opened briefly and Cat caught the hint of green. 'You want to say something to me? You want to tell me something?'

'No, Ma. You sleep.'

'You go on home then, leave me be. I'm fine. Just... zo sleepy. There's a bit of cooked chicken in the fridge... no, I ate it. Get yourself...'

'It's OK, Ma. I'll come again later.'

'Have some pickle with it.'

Cat left the hospital and walked up to the Canal Basin, where she bought a sandwich. She sat on the bank in the sun, watching the water and grieving – for Rute, for her children, for all the lost years. On her return Rute was awake and the cage had been removed. She was sitting up against a heap of pillows, trying to reach her bedside table.

'You want something, Ma?'

'My tees.'

Cat didn't even know she had false teeth. There were certainly no obvious gaps. On the bedside table was a cup of black tea, the teabag still in it, and beside it a tooth glass. The teeth turned out to be a small plastic plate with a single tooth on it. Cat passed it to her and she slipped it into her mouth. 'When you bury me,' said Rute, reaching out for her tiny 4711 bottle and rubbing some over her wrists, 'put in a bottle of this, as well. And bury me with my teeth. I do not want to go *nackt und stinkend* into the next world. I might see someone I know. But,' she giggled, 'that is not very likely, is it, when you come to think. They have all gone up in smoke.'

She reached for the cup.

'You got them to make you lemon tea?' Cat asked, smiling.

'Ach, they don't know how to make it! They look at

163

me as though I am from outer space! It's a very respectable drink, lemon tea.'

'It must be cold now.'

Rute sipped it and pulled a face. 'It is. I waited too long for that damn sachet to infuse! It's not real lemon, I can tell you that!' Her lips curled with contempt. 'Camomile-something, and no spoon to smash it with. I ask you!'

Cat took the cup from her. 'Shall I make you some, if I can find a lemon?'

'Ach, would you do that for me, *liebling?*'

In the ward kitchen was a fridge with an assortment of coloured plastic tubs, each lid labelled with a scrap of paper: 'Edna Sanders, one scoop – breakfast'. Edna's box was blue; 'Joan Meredith, prunes', was dirty white with chewed edges; a yellow box read 'Teabags – Mabel Bachelor', one of which Cat furtively stole. No lemons, but – eureka – a plastic yellow bottle of lemon juice, 'Charlene Wright'. Cat thought, thanks Charlene, whoever you are, I'll have a bit of that if you don't mind; you won't miss it.

Walking back with the tea Cat studied the names over the beds. Charlene was opposite Rute and Cat smiled at her, guilty and grateful, and the woman stared back with a fleeting tentative smile.

'You want anything else, Ma? Fruit? Biscuits? I know, how about a truffle?'

'Ach, those truffles! We spent a fortune on those truffles, you and me.'

'Not a fortune, Ma.'

Rute's eyes sparked. 'A *fortune*, I tell you! Well, *ja*, I could eat a truffle. But, can you get one?'

Cat stood up. 'I'll go and check first. I'll have to hunt, so I'll be a little while.'

'Take all the time in the world, my darling. I'm not going anywhere, as far as I know. Ach, my mouse is already watering!'

Cat took her little car and sped into the town, but

by the time she had parked and found the bakery they were pulling down the blinds.

'We're shut, luv, I'm afraid.' A strong Midlands accent.

'Oh...I didn't want much. I'm visiting my mother in the hospital... She used to bring me here when I was a child.'

Emotional blackmail, Deborah would have said, but Cat was desperate – but what a place to be desperate, in a baker's shop! Some desperation.

'Before my time, I expect. OK, then, but you don't mind if I bolt the door behind you? What was it you're wanting?'

'A few truffles?'

'None left, ducks, but I can soon make you some.' And for the fist time in her life Cat saw how they were made; a concoction of scrunched-up marzipan, some crumbs of chocolate cake, bits of cherry from a stale sponge cake, some nuts from a battered Florentine, all of which were rubbed in chocolate powder. Cat took note, for studio treats.

'No brandy, I'm afraid,' the woman smiled.

Brandy? Rute used to feed her *brandy*, on Shabbat?

'How much do I owe you?'

'Nowt, m'dear. It's for your mother int' hospital, you said.'

'Yes, but I must owe you something.'

'Dearie, we used odds and ends, which we're not really allowed to do. Anyway, till's locked for the day.'

Tears sprang to Cat's eyes. 'You're very kind!'

'Don't think owt about it. I just hope you find your mother better. Look, I'll make you up a little cake box. They might squash in't bag.'

She took a flat sheet of white cardboard, folded it along the perforations, lined it with a paper doyley and put the truffles in.

'There we are. Done and dusted. Well, goodbye, luv. God bless!'

She waved Cat out, and bolted the door behind her.

Local colour, she thought; light in darkness. Not everyone lives in the shadows.

It gave her great pleasure, after Rute had had her truffle, to put the remainder into the fridge for later, and to label the box: 'Ruth Feugler, morning and evening for three days.'

20

Cat reached the General's house in the early evening and found the lamps lit and an open bottle of red wine warming on the hearth. Ed was wearing a chequered shirt and slacks, and he slumped deep in the armchair with his long legs crossed at the ankles, lazily relaxed. Cat sat opposite, less relaxed, and wishing she had been able to paint him like that, in casual clothes and in that warm light. Later he put on some Ellington, very softly, and she saw he had the same Coleman CD which she had left behind with Gus. As she sipped her drink she watched the play of light on his face and occasionally glanced over to the easel, which she had draped with a cloth.

'You want to start work again?'

'No, not tonight. The light...'

'But you would, wouldn't you, if it weren't for the light? You only work in daylight?'

'I can work in any light, providing it's consistent. No, I'm happy just sitting here.'

'Then put your feet up, lady, and let's talk.' He paused, and then he said, 'Catherine's a pretty name...' He pronounced it 'purty'. 'But you don't use it, do you? You call yourself, what?'

'Just Cat. I sign myself Cat-Fugle. A bit quirky, I know, but it's what people call me when they can't say Feugler, which is most of the time. And I've never really liked 'Catherine'.'

'*I* like it.'

She was amused. 'You mangle it. 'Care' and 'thrin'. It's not me.'

'Cat's OK, too, but why shorten it?'

'Well, you shorten yours, Ed.'

He acknowledged this with a grin. 'You know what a 'fugle' is?

Cat was intrigued. 'No, tell me.'

'It's either a wingman,' he said, 'the guy who leads in the planes, or a soldier posted on the flanks to send out signals. *Flügelmann*, in German. Fugle's probably a derivation.'

She regretted asking. 'Anyway, a flugel's a trumpet, I think,' she said uneasily, 'a sort of horn.'

He chuckled. 'Yes, same function, originally. It's German: *flügelhorn.* '

Cat exhaled. To hide her tension and to change the subject, she said, 'Tell me a bit about you.' She was going to change her signature, too.

He gave her a potted history of his childhood in Cincinnati, but skirted round his various postings as though they were inconsequential, and Cat didn't ask for details. She was more interested in hearing about his family, her own being lost to her, and she wondered how he had got it so right, for he spoke about his parents and his daughter with deep affection. When it was her turn, she told him how Rute was in hospital and a little about her art and her teaching. She told him she had twins but she didn't mention Bill and he didn't ask, but then he hadn't mentioned his wife either; maybe he was still grieving and assumed she was, too. He sat very still, his blue eyes grave and intent, as if he was hearing more than she actually said and reading between the lines. He did ask about her 'Pa' and what his profession had been, but seemed unfazed by her illegitimacy. 'A silent presence?' he asked, to which she replied, 'Not even that. More a silent absence.'

'Well, you've legitimised yourself,' he said, which she thought a lovely thing to say, however dubious, and her heart warmed to him. The room was very quiet when she finished, and there was no sound outside from traffic or planes. She went to bed exhausted, slightly tipsy, but content, and that night she didn't dream.

The next morning the General had a meeting at the

168

Base and Cat decided to use the time re-visiting her mother's old house in Green Street in the west of the town. She was prepared for changes, and true enough, on the hills rearing up on the opposite side of the valley, which she remembered being clothed in beech trees, little box houses had sprung up, following the contours of the hills, and there were no trees to be seen. Oh, she thought, they have cut down those stately trees, what a shame! But a child hardly notices such things, so why the fuss? A green protest with no root in anything.

Green Street had gone down in the world, or maybe it had always been down. Parked cars lined the narrow street, its curbs littered with drinks cans and cigarette packets, and on a wasteland between the houses was the assorted debris of urban life; a sodden, dilapidated armchair, a television with a smashed screen and a couple of battered shopping trolleys from Somerfield's. It came to her, then, that she'd been a young woman when she'd left home, just eighteen, and in her early twenties when she had visited Rute, so surely she would have seen those changes as they happened. Perhaps she was only dwelling on her childhood memories now because she was seeking the root of her nightmares, and simply hadn't seen the changes as they happened, but surely, the houses seemed smaller than she remembered, and more grim. Their window frames were decayed to the bare wood, the glass obscured by grime and the curtains drawn untidily, as though, inside, someone slept.

On corner of Green Street and Jubilee Road there was a small, windowless mosque, its glossy white walls and narrow tower picked out in green and she saw that, on its tiled porch, was a neat row of shoes. To find in that place an echo of the innocents, the thousands who died in the camps, wrenched her heart and she sat gazing at them for some time before turning away. And there, right in front of her on the corner, was her mother's house, with the same ramshackle chain-link fence separating it from the area of grass and weeds. At the side of the house was a single upper window. Her bedroom window.

But now what? All this was futile; to understand her nightmares she needed to be *inside* the house, in that bedroom, and that was impossible. But she might discover something if she just went to the door and knocked, although she did wonder what reaction she'd get if she simply said she was looking for her mother.

The door was opened by a frowsy young woman with a half-smoked cigarette in her mouth, a soiled tea towel tucked round her waist, and from the back of the house came the plaintive wail of a child. She squinted at Cat through the smoke impatiently – and a bit suspiciously, Cat thought.

'Yeah? *Darren, shaddap, will ya!*'

'I'm sorry to disturb you, but... Well, I used to live here and...'

'So...? Unaware of Rute's prohibition, she leaned one hand against the already greasy stain on the woodchip wallpaper, blocking the view, as though Cat was demanding right of return.

'My mother and I... My mother's name was Feugler. I wonder if you remember hearing of it...'

'Foogler? *Darren!* Raucous, over her shoulder.

'Feugler.'

'Sounds German to me,' she said, reaching forward to flick ash across the step. 'Or Jewish. Not many of them round 'ere. Blacks, yeah, and Pakis, plenty of them... no Jews, though, far as I know. 'If there's any, they'll live in the richer end of town, know what I mean?' She shrugged in distaste, and made as if to shut the door, then relented, curiosity getting the better of her. 'You actually lived 'ere, then? This house?'

'Yes, as a child.'

'Well, sorry, but I can't let you in. I don't believe in

strangers. Got a child here...'

Cat reassured her. 'No, that's all right. I suppose it's changed a lot, anyway. But can you tell me about... say, what's at the back of the house, or anything?'

'OK, let's see. There was a big apple tree, if that 'elps. My bloke cut it down. Said the roots were damaging the foundations. I dunno, but we never got much fruit off of it. Two years ago, that was.'

Ah, the apple tree! There can't have been many apple trees in Green Street, theirs planted solely because *apfel strudel* was cheap to make, and with home-grown apples and dried fruit it might last a week. When Rute acquired theirs it was a spindly thing, not much taller than Cat, but she had obviously planted it too close to the house. Cat could recall few apples on it, and even fewer *apfel strudels*. Three years later, and before the branch could possibly bear Cat's weight, Rute constructed a swing. 'Again, Ma, again! Do it again!' 'Ach, childt, I'm exhausted viz pushing you. Let's go in the house, make some potato cakes together...' Grated apple and potato, running with honey...

It was coming back to her now, how the branch broke and how Rute walked her up to the hospital. Just below her kneecap was a tiny, silvery-white crescent-shaped scar, overlooked through years of washing and drying and plastering on sun creams. But oh, the poor apple tree!

The woman saw Cat's dismay and said defiantly, 'Well, it was our tree. Waste of space, ask me. Killed the grass, what bit there was.'

'And was there a hedge with a wooden gate in it, into a lane?'

'Well, the service road. If there was a gate, it's gone. There's no 'edge. There's a new fence, though,' she said brightly. 'Somerfield's built it just before we come.' She seemed interested now, and anxious to please.

'Thank you.'

She looked surprised. 'That it, then? Tell you what, you c'n see inside if you like. I only said that to... It's not very straight, you see.'

'No, I've kept you long enough. Your child...'

'Oh, don't fret y'self about him – *he's* all right. OK then, see ya.'

She closed the door and Cat went back to the car. She had no definite plan, just to sit in the car for a while and look up at her bedroom and try to recollect how being in it felt. She adjusted the back of the seat so that she would relax, folded her arms, and prepared to empty her mind. Again her eyes were drawn to the solitary window, a small sash window, half-open at the bottom, and she thought briefly of Darren, and hoped the woman would close it before he fell out. Grubby curtains fluttered across the windowsill, but Rute's would have been *Clean and Fresh-smelling with Daz Washing Powder...*

Through the dusty glass the faint image of a child's face peers out, her figure dwarfed by the height of the window. Her hair is dark, her face oval, her eyes large. Then she's gone. Of course, she's watching from the other side of the street, watching from her little car. Now she runs down the alleyway towards the tiny front yard, but swings round suddenly at her mother's voice: 'Don't run out into ze *street*, Caterina!' A woman comes out of the alleyway and takes her hand. She is carrying a large bundle of washing, wrapped in a sheet; the corners tied together – 'Let's make rabbit ears, Caterina'. The woman's hands are red with perpetual laundering – 'Turn the mangle with me, Caterina,' – giggling and panting with effort, the grey water pouring back into the wash tub, the hot steam rising, sending condensation down the windows. Later, endless ironing, the woman bent over, pushing and thumping the old steam iron, the daughter chewing her pencil at the kitchen table, the Degas pastel painting. 'Oh, just draw what you see, *liebchen*.'

This was an ordinary house, a house like all the others in this street, except to her, and ghosts hung around it – her mother's stories, papered to the walls and now shredded into woodchip – the gate to the lane to the school; the back garden with its patchy, ill-kempt grass; the apple tree with its broken swing hanging immobile from the broken branch, the slightly tilted wooden seat green with lichen, the ropes frayed, like memory.

Cat is inside the room. She is lying in bed, watching the curtains drift in the breeze, and from the pattern of the fabric she contrives animals; a dog's head, a squawking bird, a fish, a dragon. The room is cool but she is warmly tucked up under... not a duvet; they came later, but a German feather eiderdown, brought back, no doubt, from Israel. Beyond the window, the sky is not yet dark, but Rute comes in and closes the curtains.

'Time for sleep, *liebling. Leyleh toph.'*

'Layle minucha, Ema.'

Modern Hebrew. Ritual and remnant of her time in the kibbutz.

The quiet time of the night. Deep sleep, very deep, very profound, very still.

She wakes, terrified, to the sound of planes, very high up in the sky; the sound falls away into a bottomless pit; there is a cacophony of violins; they shriek discordantly out of the shadows; clouds crush the walls of her room; they are caving in, not violently or noisily, but like solid blocks of cotton wool, inexorably caving in; they fall slowly, gently; they touch her face; they *cover* her face; she thinks she's woken but she's *inside* the dream and she can't get out. But Rute is here, trembling, crying, and she is in her arms. Her necklace trails across her face; she can smell her *eau de Cologne* and mixed with it, her fear. She holds

Cat tightly, too tightly, so tightly that she cannot breathe.

'It's all right, *meine liebling*, my darlink, my precious Caterina. I'm here. You're safe now. Quite safe.'

The landing light spilling across Cat pillow, but her mother loved her, and it's enough.

So. What did it mean?

Allied bombs? But when? Rute was in Palestine by then. Perhaps the story of the bombs. Not her mother's story, but someone else's, the larger story. Was it that which overwhelmed her, the thought of the bombs raining down over her people while she was safe in her bed in the kibbutz? The chatter of the crickets, the hot humid restless sleepless night; she, distraught and guilty, for she was alive in the Promised Land while, in a country of broken promises, they descended into hell?

And not just the planes, but the other, unforgotten images, distorted or not, and the terrified waking, was it her fear or her mother's fear? She had been a child of what, five or six? Woken in the night, suddenly, out of a deep sleep, by the unexpected grip of her unspeakably grief-stricken mother? Was it possible, was it remotely possible, that the dreams hadn't woken her at all, that what had woken her was her mother's necklace, sliding over her face, gentle as cotton wool, being scooped up into tense arms, clutched fiercely, held passionately, while Rute had passed on her own horror and dread?

Cat sat in the car, frozen, sweating, immobile, her heart thumping, and she knew it was so. She knew it was the truth. A weight lifted from her, like a voice: you don't have to bear this anymore. Hand it back. You're not the victim here. It's not your story.

Not my story? I can't own it, terrifying though it was? She was angry, resistant. When, O absent Lord, does her story stop being *my* story, or mine, hers;

Rute's nightmares, *my* nightmare; Rute's memory, *my* memory; Rute's root, *my* root? Maybe I *need* this burden, have you thought of that? Did I say I wanted to lay it down?

No! I simply needed to *understand*.

21

To her amazement she discovered that the oppressiveness of the uniform had diminished, and she was able to start work without distress. She filled it in quickly with broad brushstrokes and then took the colour upwards to where it resonated on the downward planes of the face, the chin, under the nose, the lower eyelid, the temples. Then she took it sideways, down the length of each finger. With a tiny brush she found the complementary colours, the warm, luminous oranges, the sweet greens and the delicate violets. She looked at Ed and Ed watched her looking at him, while outside birdsong competed with the distant hum of traffic and an occasional overhead rumble.

When at last she stood back, she felt completely content. She was getting there, achieving something, though as yet she knew not what. She turned away and began to clean her brushes.

Taking this as a sign that the sitting was over, Ed got up and stretched.

'You are a hard taskmaster, Catherine.'

Cat glanced at him, surprised. He was frowning, and his face looked pinched.

'I don't mean to be!' she said. 'I did say you could move around... I'm sorry; I sort of get absorbed...'

'Don't mind me; you're hard on yourself, as well.'

He went to change, then came back into the room, fixing his tie.

'We're going out tonight.'

'We are?'

'I thought, why not a take-out, but, hell, I've changed my mind. There's a little place I know down the valley. That OK with you?'

'Ed, I'd like that, but I've nothing to wear.'

'You'll do fine as you are,' he growled. 'But help

176

yourself to anything of Marie-Beth's. My wife's things, I got rid of them a while ago. You'll find something of Marie-Beth's in the closet. Take your time.'

Cat took a long bath, scrubbed her oil-stained fingers, washed her hair, and chose a white school shirt and navy cardigan to go over the cleaner of her two pairs of slacks.

'I look respectable?'

'You look....'

'Mutton dressed as...?'

'No! You look swell.'

He brought his car round, a large BMW, an automatic. The seats were pale leather, the dashboard polished walnut. It floated up the hills out of High Wycombe, across the motorway and down the other side towards Marlow.

'We're going to the Hambledon valley. There's a place there by the stream which'll do us fine.'

They entered a small village, pulled up in the pub car park, and found a table in the window. A log fire, low oak beams, crystal sparkling on the polished tables, hovering waiters. Another world.

They ate, they talked, they laughed, the air cleared by truth and tears. She was comfortable with him and content to be there. Afterwards they strolled by the stream, their steps soundless on the dirt-track, and watched the darkening water running by. He took her arm just above the elbow, and strangely, she didn't mind. His hand was warm, the pressure gently fraternal.

'Cat got your tongue?'

'Very funny. No, I'm just enjoying the water.'

'With 'Cat-like tread'.

'Oh, ha ha.'

A bit later he said, 'You'll come and see me again?'

'I'll have to come again. I'll work on the background and stuff at home, but then I'll need another sitting, if that's OK. I shall need to link everything together.

Anyway, I'll have your jacket.' She was taking it home to work on in the braid in the interim.

'Don't leave it too long. That jacket's a bad fit. You don't want it not to meet around my waist.'

'Oh, it won't be as long as that. Anyway, you're in good shape, Ed.'

'You think so?'

'Now you're fishing for compliments.'

'Well, hey, why not? Location's right. And there has to be some compensation for the trouble you're causing me.'

She was silent. He was opening up a completely new world of teasing and friendship. She thought it took a long time to make a friend. Perhaps she was mistaken.

'I'll come up next week.' she said, after a bit.

'I'll look forward to that.'

'We missed you, Cat.'

This from Ricci, while Gus hovered with a take-out. A take-out? A take-away.

'Your hair's grown.'

'Julia, it's only been two days.'

'Well, it looks longer. You want a trim?'

She looked at Cat dubiously, making snip-snip signs in the air, but knowing the answer.

'No thanks, it'll do for a while. I might hack at it later.' Provocative.

Ricci put an arm round Cat's shoulder, unsmiling. 'Your mother, Cat – she OK?'

'She's OK, Ricci. Thanks for asking.'

She looked at him with new eyes – a Survivor.

'You had a good time with the General?'

'I had a swell time.'

Ed, on the easel and Rute, propped against the wall, faced each other across the studio, Rute slightly tremulous; he rather Teutonic, now Cat thought about it, with his square forehead and his intensely blue eyes, but she put aside that distasteful thought. Something struck her, then, about both sets of eyes; a veiling, an inwardness, which she couldn't explain, yet which, because she had painted them, she must have seen.

She picked up the portrait of Rute, took it over to Ed, and formally introduced them.

Rute, don't look now, but I think this man is giving value to my life. Did you have someone like that, Ma, someone who made all that fighting, that constant battle for survival, worthwhile?

That night she dreamt the planes dream again. Inside it, she was indignant, and the dream halted, its finger to its mouth, startled by her outrage – now that I understand, how dare you come back and bother me? She forgot how she had railed against the idea of letting it go. She decided, therefore, to stay with it, and the show glided on. Now she understood it she wanted to scrutinise it, seek clues within it, to find within it more than just an intimation of her mother's fear. I don't need to be here, she told herself; I can just turn around and walk away, be my age, snap out of the childhood memories or pretend they're just distorted. No, she couldn't do that but she could let go the grasp of the sounds and the images. She stayed with it until the end, and there was no terrified awakening, no bottomless pit of darkness, just a gentle fading into deep sleep, and then the muted drone of a barge passing over Fiddler's Reach. It was nearly morning, and the cold green light of the water was creating a series of dancing, luminous flames on the ceiling, which floated like Tinkerbelle, now here, now there, now elsewhere.

Above her bedroom there were other sounds, less whimsical, less serene. Ricci, in his troubled sleep. Cat lay very still, straining her ears, but she heard nothing more. Then it started again. The clock said nearly five.

He sounded so frightened that she couldn't just lie in her bed listening, not after what she had learned. She pushed her feet into her canvas slippers, threw on a wrap and made her way up the stairs. She touched the closed door with the flat of her hand, lightly brushing its surface, and then tapped gently.

'Ricci!' A stage whisper. 'You OK?'

Julia opened the door of the box room, scowling, dishevelled. 'Cat? Whatcha doin?'

'Julia! Why're you sleeping in there? No, don't answer that.'

'Gus is firing his bloody kiln,' she grumbled. 'Takes him a day and a whole night, you know that? Tickling it, he calls it, every five minutes. Could do with that meself, sometimes!' She gestured to Ricci's door. 'What's up with 'im, then, the old man? There's no bloody peace anywhere in this place, an' I gotta job of work to do tomorrow!'

'It's OK. He gets bad dreams, that's all.'

''That's all'? You must be joking! He was like it last night, too. How boring is that? He's like a kid – why can't he control himself?'

'Julia...'

'Now I shan't go back to sleep again. I shall have to move out if this carries on...'

Something in Cat snapped. 'Well, move out, then, if that's what you want! No one's keeping you! You're not actually paying rent, are you?'

Julia turned away huffily: 'Oh, be like that! It's OK for you – you don't have to sleep next door to him!' The door closed behind her.

Ricci had gone quiet, but now there was a new movement as he climbed out of bed and then the sound of bare feet padding towards the door.

'Cat? What's going on?'

In his faded pyjamas he looked frail and vulnerable, his eyes bleak and haunted. There was a sheen of sweat on his upper lip and the lines on his forehead seemed more pronounced. Hadn't he known he was calling out?

'You were dreaming, Ricci. I'm sorry...' She turned to go.

'Wait a mo.' He ran his hand over his face, and hitched up his pyjamas. 'You don't fancy a cuppa and a sofa, do you?'

'Come on down. I'll put the kettle on.'

Soon they were once more ensconced on the sofa and he was rehearsing the same dream as before; the beating, the path, the sunset, the blood-red river, the bodies, the rewinding and fast-forwarding, the endless repetition; nothing new. Her heart went out to him, but it proved to be a longer, and more intricate, conversation than she had anticipated.

She began by asking him if he was ever 'inside' the dream, whether he could find any point of recognition within it, like a sort of 'out of body' experience. She knew where she was going with this, but she wanted him to try and distance himself a little.

Ricci frowned. 'I do recognise it, but Cat, I was there four years and I did come to know it very well.'

Four years; the same length of time as Rute, in the ghetto.

'But no conscious acknowledgement?' she asked. 'Like: "Oh hell, I'm dreaming that dream again"? It's just that... well, I dream, too, sometimes – oh, nothing like yours, Ricci; just a left over from childhood thing, but sometimes I am aware that I'm dreaming. In my head I know that the reality's different, of course...'

'I told you, Cat. For me, the reality *is* the dream. It's life that's the illusion.'

Cat was silent. This was far too deep for her.

'Yes,' she said hesitantly, 'but you're a survivor... You've...'

'What, made a new life? Hardly! The old one overlaps too much. Anyway, go on with what were you saying.'

Deep within Cat a new truth formed, muted, faint, a small light only, how the old life could overlap... She tried to gather her thoughts.

'Well, it's about levels, surely, or layers. Take the unconscious level, that's very deep, isn't it? Then, near the surface, there are hopes and expectations, things you might have thought about or talked about. But somewhere in-between is memory... And if your hopes and expectations have been thwarted, somehow, like, I don't know, shifting tectonic plates or something, well, whatever's thwarted them has taken over, so they can't be on the surface anymore.'

She was struggling for clarity. 'So where do they go? You don't forget them, do you? They're as much part of you as, say, your arms and legs – part of the body of who you are. So maybe they're in your memory... And whatever's thwarted them is there as well. Overlapping.' She twisted round to him. 'Ricci, that's terrible! Completely opposite influences, battling away in your unconscious! My God!'

'Yes.'

They looked at each other. Her expression was horrified, but he was impassive.

She bit her lip. 'You know all this already, don't you? I'm just...'

'Some of it. I've read a bit about it, see, over the years. I told you, you can bury yourself in books.' He laughed wryly. 'I get very few customers, Cat, and those I do – well, it's a hideaway for them, too, some of them.'

He rubbed his eyes, which were tired and bloodshot.

'But, Ricci,' she said, hesitantly, 'what if, during the day, there's a trigger of some sort? Is that why it gets repeated at night – like pain routes? Amputees say that when they're under stress, they get pain in the same limb, real physical pain. They do say that happens.'

'Well, I do get physical pain, but that's just what's

left over from... what they did to me, and that's not so bad. What's bad is the mental pain.'

'Yes, I realise that. But I'm talking about *routes*, Ricci – the way the body always responds in the same way to the same trigger. So if the pain you have a mental pain, it's your mind which expresses it, which is maybe why you get nightmares.'

Ricci paled, and his eyes became very dark. 'So you're trying to tell me it's all in the mind, that I'm mad or unhinged? I'm not, you know.'

Cat was frightened for him suddenly, and searched for some way to mitigate what she had said.

"No, but maybe a bit disturbed, perhaps. Bound to be, aren't you? Anyway, we're all disturbed. You, me, everybody. It's what life does to us. It's how you deal with it that...'

'I think we've proved I don't deal with it,' Ricci said shortly. 'And actually, I'm finding this a bit tough.'

'I know you are,' she whispered. 'We should stop, shouldn't we?' She made to get up. 'I'll get us some breakfast, shall I?'

He surprised her then. He seemed to gather courage. He sighed and said, 'No, it's OK. Go on with what you were saying.'

Cat looked at him doubtfully. 'OK, if you're sure.' She sat back and thought for a minute. 'I was talking about pain routes, wasn't I, and the trigger. So maybe the trigger is guilt or fear, or maybe other issues entirely – unresolved issues, Ricci, dating back from God knows when, which you've never come to terms with. Not just what happened in the camp, but perhaps something from your childhood. Or that, when you should have been at home in Wales, the powers that be couldn't keep you safe...'

Ricci gave a wry laugh. 'I was beaten regularly as a child. I never expected to be safe. Don't look like that; it wasn't for anything dire; nothing at all, really. That generation, I suppose, and growing up Chapel.

Cat put aside the awful image he had conjured. 'Well, and here you were again, being punished for something you hadn't done. That little black book and the numbers. The radio...'

His whole body jerked. 'Look, I told you there *wasn't* a radio!'

'It's all right, Ricci,' she said gently, stroking his arm. 'I know there wasn't a radio.'

'No, there wasn't.'

'No, I know.'

He was breathing heavily and his eyes were very dark. 'Well, look at that,' he sighed, wiping his forehead with his sleeve. 'The lies we tell. Cat, there *was* a radio, but I only found out later. I didn't know it at the time. That's the first time in my life I've admitted that. Just goes to show...'

Cat could feel his heart thumping in his chest. It worried her. It was suddenly clear to her that she must tell him something about herself, something about her mother. Not too much, not enough to burden him, but enough for him to realise that he wasn't alone. She slid off the sofa and sat facing him on the rug.

'I know a bit... I mean, I understand what you must be feeling...'

He touched her hand briefly. His was clammy, like damp parchment. 'I expect you do,' he said politely.

'No, let me finish.' Cat had to nerve herself to speak. 'Remember saying you were glad nothing had happened to me? Well, things *have* happened to me. I'm what's called 'a battered wife'...' Ricci's head snapped up, his eyes huge. 'That's why I moved here, to escape. So I mean it when I say I understand what you must be feeling...'

'That black eye of yours...'

'Yes. And that's not all.' She took a deep breath. 'My mother was – well, is – a Holocaust Survivor. She grew up in East Germany, Ricci, and then... she came to England as a refugee. She told me things... about it all.

So that's where *my* dreams come from. What I've been feeling, why I wasn't very... kind... to you at first, stemmed from that...'

'You've always been kind.'

'Well, I didn't feel it. And I'm not telling you all this to... to somehow justify my behaviour, but to let you know that I do understand what you're going through. In so far,' she added, 'as a second generation can.' She looked at him closely. 'My only concern now, Ricci, is whether we should be talking like this at all, whether it's bad for you...'

'No, it's not bad for me,' he sighed. 'It's OK. I'm fine.' He met her eyes. 'Thank you for telling me, Cat. Do you want to say more?'

'No, not now, if you don't mind. Not about that.'

He was quiet and after a moment, Cat said, 'OK, if you're sure you're all right... Where were we? Yes, I was about to ask you why you survived while your friends didn't...'

'Now I do wonder that!' he exclaimed. 'So many of them, Cat. You end up thinking, what's so special about me? That's something I shall *never* understand!'

'No. But *grief*, Ricci. Part of the dream may be grief, for all those bodies, the horror of it all... So, maybe, in a way, you're holding on to it, the horror... You keep rehearsing it, as though it's unbelievable...'

'It *was* unbelievable. What human nature could do, the depths of depravity, the... I haven't told you the half of what went on.'

'Yes, well, that's part of it, too, isn't it? Maybe you thought, I can't believe I'm here. It's an absolute nightmare...'

He gave wry laugh. 'And I'll wake up and find myself back in Wales? Yes, there was a bit of that. But chiefly, you know, that was association. It got very cold in the camp at night, unbearably, like when I was growing up. We used to get slag from the pits, but...' His eyes met hers, warm and affectionate. 'I told you I could cope with the cold, didn't I, Cat.'

'Ah yes, you did. When you first came.'

'It's a small thing, but you feel it more when your belly's empty. And you don't forget it, Cat. You forget nothing. If you did, the Japs would have won. It would be an insult to the dead, to forget.'

'You're saying you can't forget, or you won't? You refuse to forget because it would be insulting the dead? Is that what you're saying?'

He shifted uneasily. 'Partly, if I'm honest. Not consciously refusing. I don't *want* this dream, Cat.'

'No. And I suppose that's where the battling comes in. But what happens during the day, to trigger it? The physical pain?'

He was silent. 'No, I don't think so. It's not anything special, you know.' Oh, how Welsh he sounded! 'Just life in general...'

'But, Ricci, why hang on to it so much, then? It sounds as if it's sort of ruling you. OK, you were a victim, but you don't have to go on being a victim, do you? Can't you let it go?'

'What was that you said?'

'What?'

'About... being a victim.'

'Well, if you can be aware that you're dreaming, you can say, "that was then, this is now, and I'm not a POW anymore. I'm free. I'm an old man..."' I mean, "I'm not a soldier anymore..."'

'I know what you meant, Cat.'

Cat found a grin. 'Sorry. I just thought that, if you can say, "Oh, this is that dream again," and at the same time say, "I don't need to be here anymore," maybe you can stop it, turn round, give the Jap a punch on the nose, and go home... No, I don't mean that, but you can walk away, can't you, if you're aware that you're dreaming? Maybe the dream's a sort of skin,' she said slowly, 'like a membrane over your memory, between what you know of life, now, and what you remember of it then. And if you can surface a bit, that makes a sort of thin place, doesn't it? They say you only dream when you're sleeping lightly. So maybe, if you could wake yourself up...'

'You think you can control it like that?'

'Yeah, well, I dunno.' Julia had suggested just that. 'You could give it a try. It worked for me.'

'It did?'

'Yeah.' Cat struggled to her feet and stretched. 'My dreams don't bother me anymore.'

'You know,' he said, looking up at her, 'I don't know a single FEPOW who doesn't have nightmares. It... it smashes everything; your peace of mind, how you cope with your work, even your sex life. I've known so many FEPOW's whose marriages have broken up. They don't talk about it much, just as they didn't talk to their wives when they got home. They can't, see. Some of them were newly-married; you know how it is, they say, "Marry me now, 'cos I am going to war" – I know it's a cliché, but that's what lots of them did – then they come back all churned up, completely different men, and the wives, well, they don't know how to deal with them. They think, well, he's home now; let's get on with it; make up the time we've lost; get a place to live; have a kid or two... Then everything goes pear-shaped, and the wives, they say, "Talk to me about it, get it off your chest," but they can't, Cat, they can't talk about it. It's all too... It's a real – what do they call it? Conspiracy. A conspiracy of silence...' His voice trailed away.

'This happened to you?'

'Oh yes,' he said quietly. 'I've never spoken about this before. I couldn't, see. I didn't make any fuss, I just let her go. What did I have to offer her? I never had anything to offer, not before, and not since. Oh, you may think it self-pity, but it's not; it's the truth, the simple bare fact of the matter. And all that about my marriage, well, it's in the past now. I sorted that out ages ago. But even so, it takes the heart out of you, you see, literally, and there's very little left. Oh, Cat, it's a life sentence. That's what *she* said. She said, "It's like a life sentence, being married to you. You're like an empty shell".'

He struggled out of the chair and went to the window and looked out, an old man caught up in his memories.

Cat's voice was small. 'You can hear the sound of the sea in an empty shell.'

Ricci swung round. 'What a beautiful thing to say!' His face was dark against the white light of the morning. 'Oh well, I know its all clichés. That's half the trouble, but the fact is that the clichés are true. You *are* empty. You *are* a shell. And the heart *has* gone out of you. I'm afraid there's no sound of the sea, Cat, or anything else. I've known men who've come home and they've *never* spoken about what went on, and what they suffered. Never. It doesn't go away, you see. Far from it, it comes back, again and again and again and again and again.' He slapped his thigh gently, punctuating the words. 'It haunts you. The FEPOWS, we try and forget, but we can't. It's too deep. It's part of who we are. And there aren't many of us left. Our ranks are thinning, as they say whenever we meet, but it's true, people are dying off. We meet at the Citadel every year and every year we march. Oh, we can *march*, but we can't *talk*! Those of us who're left, well, everyone has these nightmares, and life... Well, life's such a struggle, I can't tell you. You eat and you sleep and you make conversation and you do your work, but inside – you're just a mess. Disturbed, as you so rightly said.'

'Well, maybe you shouldn't meet, then. I didn't know you kept in touch with each other.'

'It's keeping faith, you see. They're family. The Citadel – that public place is the only place to really hide.'

'Well,' Cat said slowly, 'maybe that's why it carries on hurting you. Maybe you should tell them you're not going anymore...' She spread her hands. 'Oh Ricci, I'm not very good at what you call family. I don't think I even know what it means. But I do think you can take control. I really do, especially in the dreams.' She subsided.

Ricci's shoulders lifted, an infinitesimal shrug. 'Well, you may be right. Look now, I'll give it a go. I'll try anything, but it'll be a bloody miracle if it works. It would be good, though, wouldn't it, Cat, not to have nightmares anymore, or to have nice dreams, instead? Or even no dreams at all. I could live with that. That would be easy. Then I could tell the others.'

'Yeah, but there's one thing more. Our nightmares, Ricci. It came to me recently, that they might be a gift.'

'A gift? Now you've really lost me!'

'Maybe I've lost myself,' she said with a laugh, 'but mightn't they be there to help us understand? Then, maybe, you won't need to carry on hiding.'

Rute is everywhere; in the flurry of ripples on the water, is her lined face; in the sun's reflections, deep within the green depths under the bridges, are her lit eyes, and on the pebbles, exposed by the low tide, her blemished hands. The gentle curve made by the shadow of a sloping breakwater on the shingle expresses completely her narrow, slightly osteoporotic shoulders, a line so controlled and precise it might have been drawn by Matisse. Her portrait looks out across the room but since her operation she has grown beyond it, diminished within it, and it's already out of date.

22

While Ed's portrait dries off a bit, Cat continues to build up her body of work for Rudi Marks, more *Faces*; the secret lives under the arches and in the cardboard boxes by the railway station walls. She is unable to tell what draws her to these people, rather than Gus's wartime refugees or the factory workers or housewives she sees on the street, or the boatmen. Every day her sketchbook fills with the tired, expressionless faces of the shadow lands, their weathered cheeks ingrained with muck and weariness, their clothes redolent of rot and mildew. She is familiar to them now, and when she arrives their hollow red-rimmed eyes gaze at her in welcome. She is surrounded with welcome, with their inoffensive, self-deprecating humour, as pithy as a Harold Pinter play.

'Pleased to see you, Miss! Take a pew. Wan' a drink? Bob, make the lady a cuppa coffee, will ya?'

'Wotcha paintin' today, then, Cat? Who you gonna draw today, eh?'

'Dust down that seat, Tom; she don't wanna sit on your muck! Put her some newspaper down, for Christ's sake – no, not that one; that's for loo roll. *God*, he's a stupid booger... savin' your presence, Cat. '

They sit close to her, slightly inebriated, so that she is within the intimate odour of their embrace. And it *is* embrace; there's no violence offered, as with her un-lamented husband. In rambling, muttered, incoherent tones, slurred with drink, they confide their histories, and she is hard put not to pack up her easel and run. Instead, she stays stuck still, drawing, listening, trying not to hear.

A newcomer arrives, gypsy-dark, maybe a Bosnian refugee, her scarf as bright as bunting, and she settles down in front of her with a cheerful, unfathomable, smile. If Cat hopes to see her mother in her, she is disappointed; this is not Rute, merely rootless-ness. Her eyes behind her lank hair are vacant and confused, the universal eyes of the itinerant, the dispossessed.

She recalls an Iris Murdoch story of a young woman commissioned to paint the retired headmaster of a private school. Initially titillated by the whole idea, he soon begins to ask himself why he's agreed to be painted by this inexperienced chit of a thing, and he attempts to mislead her. Instead of wearing his usual shabby corduroys he digs out a suit and a bow tie, but his post-retirement paunch is uncomfortable in them. It's an entertaining moment, when she mildly suggests he puts on something more casual, and he realises she has found him out.

Later, enchanted with the painting, he arranges a formal unveiling. The art master, a difficult, caustic man with a stutter, comes to view it and the girl waits nervously for his comments. At last he stammers, 'Ah yes, my dear, it's a f-fine picture, but the m-mass of the cranium, my dear, the m-mass of the cranium! Do you not know that, behind, there is a b-brain?'

Since reading that, when Cat starts work she thinks, the mass of the cranium, get the planes in, Cat; make it bone, and make the flesh that hangs on it communicate something of this breathing, living, sentient being in front of you. The lines of her mapping are tentative, faint; they let in the light; they declare, this is not the be-all and the end-all of this person; wait for it, let the colours come. Her task becomes a matter of listening to what the eyes are saying or the slant of the head, of finding the cool indentations in the temple lobes, the warm, expressive contours of the lips and the soft strands of hair at the back of the neck, which, with her thumb, she smears into the background.

And she thinks about edges, that there are none. The edge of the canvas merely states what's *here* and *there*; a different way of looking, that's all, like

Magritte; a way of time and place and surface. Even in life drawing, she thinks, as soon as the person breathes or moves the lines are irrelevant. There's no edge, no periphery, no absolute boundary which can't be permeated by space and light. The edge is an absolute, like a sharp, unforgiving wire, and it must give way to life, to space, to freedom and fresh air to breathe, and of course to planes. Yes, she thinks, it's not lines but planes that enable us to relate, to slide with delight into what surrounds us.

This is not flirting with illusion, but gravely submitting to the discipline of her craft. So she stands back, takes time, spends time, uses the time thinking. Trying to scrutinize, to understand, to draw what she sees. Until, with delight and amazement, she senses that there is nothing false where truth will not eventually emerge; no veil, which may not finally be lifted and no deception so deep that it's completely closed to revelation. Revelation, the ultimate convergence point between the known and the unknown, between past and present, between illusion and truth. And since, in these *Faces*, she cannot find her mother, she is not averse to searching them for something of herself, a certain resemblance or an expression in the eyes, occasionally caught, like the likeness of a previous generation spotted in a rear view mirror...

And what of those who will look on them in the exhibition? If they take time to linger, not only will they find themselves exposed to a slice of life they've previously avoided, but find stories that are an echo of their own, a new awareness that compels them to move from what is comfortable, but unchallenged, to an unknown place where they never thought to be. To their own uncertain memories, their forgotten dreams, their hidden places where they shove everything they want to forget. An interaction will have taken place at a deep level, and maybe that's all she can hope for, and that someone will buy them, for her bread and butter.

From flat, textured wood she evokes the tender mystery of three-dimensional face and form, and she does it out of the miracle of seeing and believing, with a stick with a few strands of hair in it and a bit of pigment. As each panel is finished, she hangs it with its comrades to dry on the bare white walls of the warehouse. At times she visits them, and when she switches on the light they leap from their sarcophagus, their eyes following hers, waiting for the light of day, hungry for recognition. Or liberation.

23

A week later Cat packed the canvas into the car for her final session with Ed. How fervently she wished that she could have painted him with a similar fierce passion that had possessed her with her *Faces,* but she felt a commissioned portrait prohibited the imposition of her face on the face of her subject.

'You want I get a bed ready?'

It was good to hear his voice. She imagined him standing in the 'lobby', dressed in slacks, slightly stooping for the phone, or sitting, knees apart, on the stairs.

'Only one night, Ed. I must see my mother and then get back.'

'You're busy? I mean, you've got other work at the moment?'

'Bits and pieces. I've a show coming up.'

'You have? Wow, I'd really like to see that! Is it open to the public?'

'Oh, yes. You can come to the Preview if you like.'

'Heck, if you inviting me, Catherine, invite me, then! None of this, "if you like", business, as though you don't care one way or the other!'

Cat did care. 'OK, Ed, I'd be delighted if you'd come to the Preview. If you can spare the time...'

'Well, I don't know,' he drawled. 'I'll just consult my schedule... Mmm, let me see. Yeah, if it don't take too long I guess I could fit you in.'

It made Cat happy and excited, that someone was so interested in her. It made her rich.

'Ed, that's very gracious of you, but I haven't told you when it is...'

She spent a good day with him, slept in fresh sheets in his daughter's room, and set off for the hospital the following morning. Rute was not on her ward, and her absence hit her like a smack – another person in Rute's bed – and she turned on her heel and fled down the corridor to the Sister's desk. There was a short queue, and she waited impatiently.

Perhaps I should have phoned, she thought guiltily. They've been trying to contact me, and I've been out or on the road.

The Sister was looking at her enquiringly. Stumbling over her words, Cat said, 'Mrs Feugler, she's not in her bed. Has something happened? I'm her daughter...'

'Why, of course, my dear! Catherine, isn't it? Well, she's had a little turn for the worse so we've moved her to a single room, that's all. Why, did you think...? Oh, I'm so sorry, but she's as well as can be expected...'

Under the circumstances. The words remained unsaid, and Cat followed her down the corridor, her stomach churning.

A white room, very light. White walls, white ceiling, white office blinds on the white-framed windows, white linen. Through the open window a fresh breeze blew in, redolent of limes. Tea, *mit limon.*

Wires from Rute's wrist and chest, the monitor ticking; tubes disappearing under the bed; her tired, bony, liver-spotted hands flaccid above the sheet, her face pale and faintly yellow. There were dark lines under her eyes, her cheeks looked sunken beneath the bones and her hair was greasy, lifeless, the Gently-Covers-Grey faded, washed out.

'You can wake her if you like. She's only sleeping.'

'Thanks, I'll wait a bit, I think.'

'As you like, love.'

Cat pulled up a chair and sat down. She would not touch her mother yet.

Rute, my mother. *Ema.* Ma. Do you know what feelings sweep over me as I sit and look at you?

Silence is a dark, window-less room, full of nameless wraiths. Open the door but a crack, and the light streams in and takes possession. The shadows seem less menacing, their threat, as they make obeisance to the light, less obfuscating. So can I reach my mother with my whisperings?

Did you know, Ma, that when you shared your story with me, you made it mine? Did you know about my nightmares? You couldn't know; I kept them from you, and only the other night, with Ricci, let in a chink of light. You see, Ma, I belong to a generation not afraid to speak of dreams. People, these days, will not despise or condemn you for your dreams, for fear they might reveal overmuch reality. Or madness. They will not reject you for a dreamer nor repudiate the night-time visions. They know they speak of truth. Dreams, if they're let, can exorcise the demons of the day.

Your years of silence, Rute; the ghetto, of which you'd never speak. Was this terror, or simply a gritty determination to put it behind you, to make a new life for yourself in a new place? Or because you refused to transmit to me your racial fear of all things German? Ach, *Mutti*, you could not hope to succeed in that! But why forestall my questions all these years? Why the unanswered riddles of your life? Where *were* you, Ma, during those four years when your parents disappeared into darkness?

Your silence, Ma. Was it simply because you refused to be party to revenge, to retribution, to the hunt for the guilty? Or did you think you were unclean in some way, or tainted? But what courage, Ma, to start again, and what unshakable hope, to have a child!

And yet. What is the opposite of Diaspora, Ma? Gathering? Or concentration?

Elie Wiesel told it, the way it was, for some. (At last she was getting to grips with him. Not enjoying it, but it was compulsive reading. It made her think.)

Wiesel describes a man and a woman who meet in the camps. She has lost her children, he his. After the war they marry and have a child of their own. But the child knows that when they look at him they do not see him. They only see the children who have gone before. He is not invisible, but un-see-able.

It was not like that for me. You were very strong, almost too strong, I think. You didn't conform to the stereotypical craven Jew, which everyone recognized and expected. You hid your Jewish-ness in public, you battled with appalling memories, with grief, poverty, hardship, loneliness, fear, but you kept faith with your child.

A story is told of a small boy, neglected by his parents. One evening he enters the drawing room where his mother sits absorbed in the television. Without turning round, she asks, 'Is that you, darling?' The boy replies, 'No, it's only me.'

It was not like that for me. It took you a long time, didn't it, a very long time, before you could say you loved me. Yet love was all you gave – everything you gave me was for love. I'm proud of you for that, Ma, for your strength, your unconquerable hope, your indomitable courage. You humble me. And I'm grateful for all that we had, the intimacy, the sharing of troubles, even the telling of your stories, however partially or untimely told. You were always there for me, Ma.

Be merciful, God, if you exist. Let her go without pain. Let her not suffer, now, as she suffered before. *Let her go gentle into that goodnight*, in dreamless sleep.

At last, Cat put her hand on her mother's arm.

Rute woke smiling.

'Oh, Caterina,' she said clearly, 'I knew it was you. I could see you in my dreams.'

24

It had been a long summer, a time of intense stillness, bright light, and beneficent warmth. Cat asked the Sister if she could take Rute out for a drive but, with some reluctance, she demurred.

'But there's a little park behind the hospital. You can go there if you like, but use a wheelchair. It's really for staff, but I'm sure nobody'll mind. Just sit with her a bit in the shade.'

'What d'you think, Ma? You'd like to do that?' Now would be a good time, if there was any time at all, to ask about her childhood.

'I am going aus? How perfec'!' Already pushing back the sheets.

'Hang on, love,' said the Sister, 'while I get rid of these wires and things. But don't be too long.' She glanced at Cat. 'She tires easily and, in any case, it'll be her supper time soon.'

Third person singular, my Ma.

The Sister had hardly turned her back when Rute said in disgust, 'Supper? What supper? You should see the food here, Caterina! *Mein Gott,* you should see it! You should taste it, already! Junk! Haven't they heard of pickled herring? Always the cottage pie, and pastry, bread and potatoes together. *Unt* fish, with bones in, I ask you! I am forever spitting. I wouldn't give it to my worst enemy. Well,' she added, dourly, 'I might give it to that man, that louse....'

The Sister reappeared with a wheelchair and they were on their way. Cat negotiated the lift with care, waited for inward-opening doors, struggled over the uneven pavement and, with a real sense of achievement, crossed to the garden, a verdant green bordered by hedges.

'Where would you like to be, Ma? Here, on the grass?'

Rute sighed, already exhausted. 'Over there, darling, *unter den* trees, where I can watch the leaves for a while.'

Silver birches, clustered together in a copse, with pendulous yellow leaves that danced in the slight breeze. Cat sat on the grass by her mother's side and studied her. Her skin seemed thin, transparent, the dark rings under her eyes more pronounced. Over the last few weeks she had lost weight, the bones of her face seemed more prominent and her hair was wispy, betraying the pink of her skull. In her hands Cat could see each creamy metacarpal, each blue vein. She was as fragile as a flower.

With a sinking feeling in her heart, Cat knew that there was no way she could disturb her mother with questions; all that now remained was to attend to her. But how long, Ma? How long have you got?

'How are your eyes, Ma?'

Rute leant her head back and breathed deeply, her face luminous in the light. 'My eyes? Why my eyes, already? They are as usual. Why you ask about my eyes?'

'No reason.'

Presently Rute said slowly, 'You know, my darling, they say I can't go home again...'

'Yes, they told me, Ma. I'm sorry.'

'...But, you know, darling, I never much liked that view from the front room. Just cars...'

She was thinking of the little house in Green Street. The Coventry house was equally small, one of a cluster on an estate. Rute would spend hours at her window, watching the children in the playground opposite; they reminded of butterflies, she said. That was all past and done with now. The playground was deserted, the butterflies gone, for Rute had forgotten.

After a few minutes, watching her, Cat said, 'Is the food really bad, Ma?'

'Oh, *nicht* zo bad... *nicht zo* bad, really. I am just a

complaining old woman...'

'Not old. Don't say that, Ma.'

'But complaining, *ja*?' Rute's eyes snapped open, roguish, full of mischief. '...*Unt* last night we had semolina! With *jam*!'

'Oh, that's good.'

'But you know what else we had? Pork! Oh, *mein Gott*, I do like a bit of crackling! My father would turn in his grave – if he had one.'

'Excuse me!'

They had been laughing together, but now they glanced up to see a florid, full-bellied man approaching them across the grass, wearing the cheap grey uniform of a security guard. He was shaking his head officiously and Cat's heart sank. He positioned himself in front of them, menacing, blocking out the sun.

'May I ask what you're doing here? This is a private garden, for the use of hospital staff only. Visitors are forbidden...'

Verboten.

'We were told...'

'I'm sorry, it doesn't matter what you were told. I must ask you to leave...'

He waited, jowl jutting, hands on hips.

An angry retort on Cat's lips, but Rute squeezed her hand. 'Don't, *herchen*,' she whispered, 'don't provoke him.' She looked up at him where he towered over her. 'We will go now,' she said with dignity. 'We didn't mean any harm. But thank you for putting us straight. We wouldn't want to offend.'

Furious, Cat got to her feet, pins and needles in her legs. She crossed her arms over her chest, holding herself in.

'If you wish to make a complaint about us,' she said softly, 'please do so. All we're doing is just sitting here quietly, enjoying a bit of sun, and we aren't going to leave. We will leave in a few minutes, when she...

when we need to go in. Until then, you will kindly leave us in peace.'

She had said 'leave' three times, indicative of incipient stress, and his eyes gleamed. He opened his mouth to speak but Rute spoke first, a whisper, her white fingers fluttering in distress, catching the light.

'Liebling...'

'*No*, Ma!' Cat looked at him grimly. 'My mother is on Ward... which ward are you on, Ma?'

Which block?

'East 3,' said Rute faintly, pulling her hospital gown closer round her neck.

East 3 was the cancer ward, though they didn't call it that. Cat knew it and so did he. He had the grace to look away.

'East 3,' she repeated firmly. 'So speak to the Sister if you have a problem. She told us we could come here.'

'Hmmm!' He turned to go. After a few steps, he spoke over his shoulder. 'Just a few minutes, then. OK? I'll be watching.'

Rute spat the word under her breath. '*Nazi!* They are all the same! No room to breathe Gott's free air!'

But her eyes were inward, and her thoughts, elsewhere.

'Take me back, Caterina, would you? Take me back, now.'

He couldn't tell they were Jewish, of course. He couldn't know how his officious manner resonated with her mother, or his uniform, or how being identified by a place and number might echo in her mind like footsteps in a darkened corridor. Nor did Cat suppose that others wouldn't have responded as her mother had, not wanting to make a fuss. But his mind was already closed against them, shuttered with branches even before he stood under the trees; to him they were merely intruders, anonymous. Yet, with their history, or rather Rute's history and Cat's intimate knowledge of it, they were bound to over-react, to see the pattern of the yellow star and the rhythm of cowering placation: you're surely not making me leave; I hoped to die here; I know you find us hard to stomach, but a bit of space, only, is what we ask, space to live the life we love, to study in the yeshiva, to listen to our rabbis and learn from our mystics, to teach our children and to eat our food. To carry on doing what we have done for years, in our tradition.

Echoes of Elie Wiesel. Cat had come to know his voice.

Then, my God, *thanking* him for putting us straight! The straight uncompromising message: *No Jews Here*, on every door on every house on every road! Wait, here's another road, we'll lead you down it, we'll even take you there! This one goes everywhere and nowhere, to all places and none; it is endless; it is one-way; home is always elsewhere.

The story of persecution, everywhere.

And Rute? She would have gone like a lamb. Silently. Unresisting.

Suddenly Cat's mind lurched. Was there, in her defence of her mother, a veiled criticism? Who was *she* to plead her cause? *She* wasn't on the trains, the transportations, the long marches, or in the ghetto. *She* didn't lie for hours half-starved among the dying, crazed with dust and darkness. Bodies bear marks of such things, souls get numbed even by the story of them; each day becomes a task of beating back the memories, a struggle neither to forget nor to remember. Who was she to tell Rute, with her deep inner wounds, how she should react? Only a *child* of a Survivor, whose experience she'd not tasted except in story-telling.

And yet. How many, at the last moment, showed any resistance, however futile, or any sort of rage? *Do not go gentle into that goodnight; rage, rage against the dying of the light* – to put their oppressors to shame. For that was all it had taken for this particular bully to crumple. Cat almost felt sorry for him. Coals on his head. He could not have known, in his unctuousness, what he had brought on them.

Ah, surely her mother had spoken truth to her in her stories...

On the way back to the ward Rute was silent, and Cat wondered what she was thinking. Or remembering. Rute gave no clue until she suddenly mentioned her brother's name, her brother who she had not seen for years.

'Caterina...' Her voice, from the front of the wheelchair, was weary, lethargic. 'I would like to see Reuben, if he will *komm*.'

'Uncle Reuben?'

'Who else Reuben? I would like to see him again before I die.'

'Ma, I'll ring him up. Would you like me to do that?'

'*Ja*, give him a ring. You know where to look for the number?' Her accent was becoming more pronounced, as if she was losing her hold on the English. 'My address book, by the phone.' Her little bony thumb emerged from one side of the wheelchair. 'But, on the one hand, will he come, after all these years?' Her other thumb emerged. 'On the other hand, he will never come by his own. He is afraid of travel-ling. He is afraid of many things, Reuben.' She shrugged expressively. 'On the third hand, if he comes he will bring his wife, Amit. I like her; she is an old friend. Once we were very close, Amit unt I... So speak to Amit. She is a good woman. She haff sense.'

Now they were in the lift. 'And, Caterina...'

'Yes, Ma?'

'Have your *kinder komm* to me. I would like to see them again. If they want to, that is. I don't expect they'll want to.'

'Ma, you'll get tired, all these visitors.'

'Zo? I'm tired now. What's a little more tiredness, already? I know what it is to be tired, *unt* I would like some visitors.' Her voice cleared. 'I am dying, Caterina. But nat yet. I will wait a little longer, see the family. Will you do that for me, *liebling*?'

'Of course. I'll get on with it straightaway.'

In the corridor to her room, Rute said, 'Caterina, chust one thing more I ask.'

'Ma?'

'Haf the funeral in a church. My friends, some of them will be affronted, but no matter. For a long time now, I haf been a believer. But say *Kaddish* for me when I die. There is no other way to go into the next world.'

Back in bed, snuggling down under the white sheets like a child, she said, slowly, slowly, and with the sweetest of tired smiles, 'You know, Caterina, the earth is millions of years old... and, *Gott willens*, will last millions of years longer... Well, my sweetheart, I have to tell you, I am chust zo glad that I am here now, to spend these precious hours with my darling daughter who I love so much, so very, very much.'

25

Cat drove south, bleak, anguished, already grieving, chock full with her mother's love. On the back seat, the cloth had fallen away from the portrait and, in the rear view mirror, she could see Ed's eyes, scrutinising her. She would have to hand it over soon, and then there would be no more Ed. Sometimes it was hard to let go of a painting, and this time it would be very hard. He was the only one who'd fully understand what she was feeling, and she couldn't wait to get to him. She was tight, tense, a hard knot in her belly. The traffic was heavy, but she kept in the fast lane, and when at last she reached the junction she swung across like a lunatic and had to brake hard at the top of the slip road. In the lay-by was a police car and she slowed again. She drove slowly down the hill, slowly turned right into his tree-lined avenue, slowly pulled up the drive and parked the car. The hand brake squealed loudly as she yanked it up.

She ran up the steps to his front door and rang the bell. The windows were open and she could hear music, not Mozart or Beethoven, the music of the camps, played while people queued up for death, but jazz, the Colman she had left behind.

He was at the door, leaning towards her, welcoming, concerned, tall, rangy, nose-beaked, wide-shouldered. She threw herself into his arms. She couldn't speak.

'Why, Catherine! Is it your mother?'

Chust don't ask, OK?

Later, when she was once more curled up in the easy chair opposite him, Ed spoke to her of death. He sat very still, his hands loose on the arms of his chair, his blue eyes unblinking. As he marshalled his thoughts there was a slight frown on his forehead, and when he spoke it was slowly, his mid-West accent hardly noticeable

'I never told you my wife's name, did I? Well, it was Anne. When she died I thought I wouldn't be able to manage. I used to tell her she'd get well, that everything would be as it was before, but she knew better. They used to say what a fighter she was, though I don't know, even now, what that means. Is it fighting, to deny the inevitable? Is it lack of fighting, to accept it? Or is it grace? She got very tired before she died, and I think that was my fault...'

'It's not a matter of fault.'

'Catherine, there was a multitude of things. I got married late; maybe I didn't have the skills. But I loved her very much, and she held on for weeks. She got very thin... hardly slept nights. *God*, she was weary, and so was I. We'd sit, holding hands, or me reading across from her. Bits of them endless, like Jane Austen, and some of them perfectly dreadful, like Hardy.' He smiled. 'I'd have preferred Le Carré or something. But you see, she was waiting for me to let go, and I knew it. So, one day, y'know what I did? I got down on my knees and I prayed.'

He waved his hand in the direction of the landing, a gesture startlingly resonant of El Greco, the hands similarly pale, the fingers long and sinuous.

'I was across there, in the bedroom. Anne was down there in the dining room where I'd made up a bed. She could see the garden better, and she liked the garden. Anyway, there I was. I got down on my knees and I said to God, "God," I said, "why don't you just take her? I'm ready." I said, "I've held on too long and for that I ask your forgiveness." And then I thanked him for her life, and our life, and for giving us Marie-Beth and then I got up. Shortly after...' He hesitated and looked away. 'Well, never mind that. But that night Anne got the best sleep she'd had in months. She was at peace, you see. She knew I wasn't... keeping her. It

206

set her free, Catherine.'

Cat was silent. Part of her was focussed, listening, but she was also becoming increasingly irritated that he always mispronounced her name, that he had fashioned something out of it that even she didn't recognise, and which she had told him she disliked. But mostly she heard what he said clearly enough.

'Now,' he drawled, shifting his position, 'I'm not telling you all this to get your sympathy. I don't need it. Nor am I saying it's all in the past, because it aint. You can't spend years together and not miss 'em when they're gone. What I'm saying is that, death, dying, aint all bad. When someone's very ill, like your Ma is, and like my Anne was – well, they get sort of fixated that things can't go on as they did before; they can't go back, and it's no good, in the end, resistin'. From what you've told me, your mother lived a good life in the end. She had you for the better part of her life and she had her health till now. But don't be surprised if she waits for the family and then just goes to sleep. Now, that's not a bad sort of death as these things go.'

Cat was silent for a long time. Eventually she said quietly, 'Ed, you had Marie-Beth and Frank. I can't imagine not having her around. I feel so... alone.'

He leaned forward and put one finger on the edge of her knee, a careful, slightly admonishing gesture that went straight to her heart.

'You're a grown woman, Catherine, with kids – and that'll all come all right. You're not alone. If you think that you're quite wrong, lady. You've got me.'

'Then will you call me by my name, please!' Cat spoke almost fiercely. 'I'm Cat, OK? Not Catherine. Just...Cat.'

Cat used Ed's telephone to ring Israel. Amit picked up the phone, her voice as clear as if she was in the next room.

So sorry to hear about Rute. Yes, they'd come, of course they would. When? Now? In a week? How long had she got? No, Reuben's not here, he's in the garden; things are not so good on the kibbutz these days; he gets a bit of peace in the garden. The place is full of old people and the work's not getting done. We've had to close the orange groves and the olive factory. The kids are leaving for the city; they don't want to work on the kibbutz any longer. They are not idealistic like we were...'

Cat interrupted. 'So, I'll let you know about Rute?'

A huge sigh down the phone. '*Ken, b'vakashah* – if you will.'

Then, her heart in her mouth, Cat rang Deborah, but Deborah was her father's daughter, difficult, argumentative, and intransigent.

'Mum, there's no way I can get time off. I'm flat out. You don't know what it's like. PR demands very long hours, OK? I've got this job in the Press tent – my promotion hangs on it. We're doing an event in Birmingham, at the NEC...'

Cat hated acronyms. 'Well, it's not that far to come, then, is it? She's your granny, and she's dying. She's particularly asked to see you both.'

'That's right, do the emotional blackmail bit! That's so, like, *you*, isn't it? Well, I'm sorry, but it's not as if she ever took any interest in *me*. She wouldn't even tell me where you were! So why should... OK, OK, I'll come, but I don't know when. Probably one evening. That OK?'

There, in Ed's gracious house in High Wycombe, Cat sat on the stairs and sobbed. How could things have got so bad between them? What had she done wrong? She hadn't neglected Deborah. She was hardly painting when Deborah lived at home. Well, not much. Her life was completely focussed on the family, trying to compensate for the lack of a father's presence. Like her mother, perhaps. Meals, bedtime stories, helping with homework, the school run, fetching, carrying, clearing up after them, ironing innumerable school shirts,

208

making packed lunches... All the usual things. There wasn't much to do wrong. Yet, despite all her efforts at camouflage, Deborah still seemed to regard her with dislike and suspicion. Maybe she'd had caught her out in too many lies.

But Rute? Why pick on Rute? "You have everything you need, Deborah? You want I give you some money?" "You hungry, Deb? You want I cook meatballs for you and Yakov?"

In the days when they had plenty and Rute, nothing. But she'd always sensed the deep malaise in the family, and for her the panacea for all ills was either food, as Bill had so roughly pointed out, or distraction. "You want to go shopping with me, Deb? You want some new clothes?"

"No thanks, Gran. Don't *pester* me, Gran! Oh, Gran, leave it out, will you? Just leave me alone! I'm going to my room, and my room's *private*!"

When Deborah left home Rute was shattered. For her a community had broken, the community of the family, which because of her upbringing was sacrosanct, and afterwards, on the telephone, it was Deborah she always asked about first.

Cat pulled herself together and rang James.

'Hell, Mum, 'course I'll come. Is it urgent? I mean, nothing's going to happen in a hurry, is it? Shame, really, she was a great lady in her own way. You were close, weren't you? Pity she was such a loose cannon. No, what am I saying? Sorry, Mum, I didn't mean that, but she *was* a bit odd, wasn't she? Anyway, I haven't seen her for years.'

Past tense. For him Rute was already in her grave, and he, insensible to her suffering, had moved on. But he was a gentle soul. When he sees her, Cat thought, when he hears her voice, he'll be glad he came. So she told herself.

26

Cat worked on the portrait all the next morning, a bonus session, and Ed sat quietly while she tweaked it. The hours sloped by and the sun went round. She was procrastinating and she knew it. It was finished really.

'Do you know when something is finished, Catherine? Now that's not meant to be a significant question,' he added, 'though it might be. I meant your painting ...Cat.'

Cat saw how he had corrected himself and she was grateful.

'Well, sort of. But you think you've finished, and then you find all sorts of things...' She laughed. 'No, I'm just fiddling, Ed.'

'Well, don't fiddle. It's great as it is. Just sign it.'

Cat did as he said. Having no alternative she signed it *Cat-Fugle*, but there was a heap lot more she could have written.

Ed got up and came and stood in front of it, loosening his jacket.

'How is it, compared to what you usually do? Up to standard?'

'I'm not sure.' But Cat was sure. She would have liked to start afresh. 'I'm still too close to it...'

'Yeah, I can understand that. I think it's great, though. It's just a pity I won't own it myself. It'll hang in the Officer's Mess. There's a whole rogues' gallery there, but this'll be the best of 'em. Yeah, this'll be the best.'

'Will there be a formal unveiling?'

'God, no, they'll just shove it on the wall. It'll need framing though.'

'I could see to that if you like,' said Cat diffidently. 'My picture framer gives me a discount.'

'Good idea.'

So, she thought, I shall have him a little longer.

Surely this can't just disappear into the ether, this closeness, which has become more to me than... Well, let's just say it's been different from how I envisaged.

Ed left to change his clothes and when he came back he was already speaking and Cat turned from where she had been looking out of the window.

'...we have the rest of the day. Let's go out somewhere – make use of it.'

They drove down into Marlow and parked behind the High Street. Ed had brought a rug, a bottle of wine, some cheese and French bread, black olives and a couple of apples, and they found a place on the towpath. He had forgotten to bring glasses so they drank from the bottle, a little bit of intimacy that forced itself deep into her mind. The river wound its way, ducks quacked; geese flew; swans approached in stately fashion for their non-existent crumbs; boats, skiffs and canoes went by at speed... Such energy in the water and such laziness on the bank. Throughout the whole summer it had hardly rained.

Afterwards, Ed lay back on the rug, his hands behind his head, his eyes closed. Furtively, Cat took out her sketchpad and started drawing him. She would have something of him, she thought defiantly, for the empty days ahead.

'These last days have meant a lot to me,' he said slowly. 'I expect all your customers say the same, but I'd hate to lose touch, Catherine.'

She heard him with delight, not just because of the words, but also at the way their thoughts ran on twin tracks.

'But we hardly know each other, Ed.'

'Oh, I think I do, a bit,' he said languidly. 'Enough to be goin' on with, at any rate. We could do some jazz concerts – you like jazz, don't you? After a bit of that we'd know each other quite well.'

Cat gave a light laugh. 'What about my work, Ed? And you can't even decide what to call me!'

'I'm getting there, but it hell is difficult! I like your name... Catherine. Yeah, I like it.'

'But nobody else calls me that... Anyway, it's not just my work...'

He lifted his head, his eyes gimlet-sharp. 'So what else?'

She hesitated. 'I need to get something sorted... It's about my mother, Ed.'

'Well, talk on!'

'You remember I told you she's German-Jewish?'

He nodded, waiting, and she leaned towards him and then hesitated again. When she spoke, her words came in a rush. She told him how silent her mother was during her childhood, and how that silence had only ended with the telling of her stories. She told him how graphic the stories were, and that she still had nightmares about them. She described the nightmares as they had happened, in sequence. She told him about the shut tram doors, about the street full of gabardined men, about the echoes of violins, about the black hole. She left nothing out. She told him about the planes, and how she'd sat outside her mother's house in a last ditch attempt to try and understand why they had frightened her so much. She told him about her mother's necklace, sloping against her face like gossamer web, about her mother's fear. She made no mention of her marriage, but she told him that the whole experience, the silence, the stories and the nightmares, had shaped her, and shaped her choices in life. Again and again she found herself returning to how secretive Rute had been, about the gaps in her story which she'd never been able to resolve, about the black hole. All the time she was speaking her head was down, so as not to see his reaction. Fleetingly she found herself marvelling that she could trust someone enough to bare her soul like this, and she wondered if *he* trusted her. She wondered if this was how her mother had felt, all those years ago; afraid of not being believed; afraid of losing respect afterwards; afraid of being thought... what had Ricci said? Unhinged. Or of exaggerating. It struck her, then, like a lightening strike, the reason why her mother had told her those stories when she was ten. At that age she was a captive audience, too young and too trusting to ask awkward questions.

She raised her head. Ed was sitting rigid, half-upright on the picnic blanket. His body looked planted on the ground. He didn't look as though he wanted to run. He looked aghast. He looked concerned. She could read sympathy in his eyes; they were moist, the life in them blunted. It was for her sake they were blunted, and taking courage, she went on. It was the gaps, she said, that worried her most; the unexplained four years of her mother's youth. But time was slipping away from her; her mother was dying; too ill, at the moment to question, but if only, if *only* she could have found some answers, she could have let it all go, long ago. She could have had closure.

She had been speaking for a long time, while Ed listened soberly, but now, at her use of this Americanism, he smiled briefly.

Cat did not return his smile. She had to know what it had cost her, she said; she had to know the truth. At this he looked sceptical, but Cat insisted.

'I *need* to know, Ed. Sometimes I feel I don't know who she is. Therefore who I am. And if I don't know who I am, how can y... how can anyone else?'

'I reckon I know who you are,' said Ed easily. 'But what you've described can't be the sum total of your memories – people are both loved and hated into being, I think.'

'*Hated?* My mother didn't *hate* me, Ed; she *loved* me.' She could have added, though I've only just discovered it.

'Yes, I know it's a strong word – but people can love you and still neglect you. Look,' he explained, 'for

213

'neglect' read anything that crushes you; for 'love' read anything that builds you up. Of course your mother loved you – otherwise you wouldn't have achieved anything in life. She also, obviously, neglected you. Well, that's about par for parenting, I reckon. As for truth, well, it's a strange animal. It can be very elusive, you know. Have you ever heard of false memory syndrome?'

'No, what is it?'

'It's where things are factually incorrect but strongly believed – or the other way round, denying what's true.'

'But she's *Jewish*, Ed. A Jew would never deny what's true – what, all those camps, all that loss?'

'I said, it can also mean behaving as though what's false is true.'

'Why would anyone do that?' she said impatiently. 'Anyway, I'm talking about who *I* am, not some theoretical...!' She stopped, took a breath. 'Ed, I'm as Jewish as she is...'

'So? You talk about it as if it's a handicap, or something.'

Cat's eyes blazed. 'Ed, of course it's a bloody handicap! It's been a handicap all the way through! The whole Jewish *history* is about handicap! Without that handicap there'd have been no segregations, no beatings in the street, no camps – at least for them!'

She used not to be particularly conscious of being Jewish. All that had changed, perhaps when Rute got ill. Or maybe when she was painting Saul or her *Faces* or listening to Ricci. Or at the old house, God help her, working through her dreams. She didn't know when it changed, but it had.

'The history matters, Ed,' she said quietly, 'and I don't want to... to relegate it to the level of anecdote, or to think of my mother as just one remnant of an amorphous mass. And dismiss it.'

'She's your Mom. You'd never think of her as just

214

one remnant of an amorphous mass.'

Cat hesitated. 'No, but if I'm honest, maybe that's just what she is. Lots of people are, Ed. Like those *Faces* I've been painting – what are those guys, but remnants? And Ricci, he's a remnant, isn't he? It's even how I feel about myself, sometimes.'

'Not remnants, Catherine; survivors.'

'Yes, I suppose.' Cat looked down river, unseeing. Tears pricked her eyes, and she tasted salt. Then she said, the words rusty on her tongue, 'I love my mother, Ed...'

'I know you do.'

'...and I'm losing her. Maybe all those stories were a way of... bequeathing something to me, teaching me something, maybe even warning me of something, though why, I don't know... But I do have to take notice. There may come a day when it doesn't matter, but right now... Now she's actually dying, I realise I've been struggling for years...'

'Catherine, I know you've been struggling for years,' said Ed soberly.

'How can you know? I never said anything!'

'It's in your face. Look, you stand there, painting me – and you know perfectly well where *I'm* looking. I've seen you've been tussling with something, and it sure as hell wasn't the portrait. But this identity crisis of yours, if that's what it is, well, there comes a time in everyone's life when they have to say enough's enough, and start to look forward. I did it myself when Anne died. You learn new ways, where to put your energies, what to commit to, who to love, what to hope for. And you don't start by dragging up the past. In any case, if it's what I think it is, it won't be very pleasant.'

'No,' she said, thinking of Elie Wiesel. 'No, it won't be pleasant.'

'And who was it said, "The past is another country"?'

'But it's not *in* the past,' she muttered rebelliously.

215

'How can it be, if it's still affecting the present?'

'Well, of course. But it was your mother who was in the cattle trucks, or the ghetto, or wherever, not you. It was your mother who lost her family in the camps, your mother who had to survive, not you. *Her* roots, *her* memories and *her* life. What I'm saying is, you haven't put down roots, not yet. Oh, you were born here and you live here...' He shook his head, a wry, slightly exasperated smile at the corner of his mouth. 'But your country – it's more than just a piece of real estate. And, incidentally, the place where you live isn't even that, is it? More a sort of squat, from what you tell me.'

'It's not a squat! It's a very special place to me!' Cat's mouth quivered. 'It practically saved my life, when...'

He reached out quickly and touched her arm. 'OK, sorry, I didn't mean to denigrate it.'

'And Ricci's there... I love Ricci. And my teaching, my painting...'

He smiled. 'I know you love Ricci, Catherine. And your work's great. It's probably outstanding, though I'm no expert. But painting doesn't help that much, does it? Obviously.'

They were quiet for a long time. She glanced across at the river, running past. It should have looked dark and forbidding, as bleak as she felt; not glowing in the sunlight, as though oblivious to what was taking place on its banks.

Ed took her hand in his. 'Look, I don't mean to dismiss your home, and I certainly don't want to dismiss your painting. No, it's too important for that. But on it's own it doesn't root you enough.' He paused. 'You know, the danger is that if a person without roots becomes attracted to others without roots they can get drawn in; a sort of downward spiral. Like the guys you're obsessed with in those *Faces*, for example...'

'I'm not obsessed!'

'Well, take Ricci then. Until he met you, where was he going, but down? It all seems to have the same theme, doesn't it? It's always someone else's story you're trying to find, when what you need is to make your own, and build on it. Which is the very opposite of what you intend to do with your mother's memories.' He rubbed his forehead. 'Personally, I think you need to break away.'

'She *made* it mine,' Cat muttered. 'Telling me all that *made* it mine.'

He hesitated. 'Yes, but you're looking over your shoulder all the time. Your Ma, your kids – I don't know why you left your husband and I'm not aiming to ask – but Ricci and those two kids at your studio, even your down-and-outs... I bet you've had none of the attention you've handed out, over the years. Do any of them see you as you really are, rather than what you can do for them?'

Cat glared at him. 'How do I *know*?' she shouted. Then, bitterly, almost inaudibly, 'People see what they want to see.' She felt numb, pared away. She had revealed too much. This was friendship? She was afraid of what he was saying. She felt it could damage her and she'd gain nothing but turmoil. At that moment she felt more vulnerable than she'd ever felt in her life.

'This is terrible,' she said. 'You make it seem as though I've never grown up...'

'Not at all.' He brushed his fingers over her hand. 'I'm not blaming you for feeling the way you do. Don't think that.' He grinned. 'Perhaps you're just too good a listener. But maybe the time's come to put it behind you...'

She flicked off his hand, suddenly angry. 'What? You're serious? Put it behind me? How can you say that, after all I've said?'

He sat back, his expression suddenly tense. 'Are we quarrelling?'

Cat was mute.

'Trust me, hey? Just trust me. It's just that you've got to realise where your mother ends and you begin.' He picked up the bottle of wine and gestured towards her with it, but she shook her head. 'Also, Catherine,' he said, pouring his drink, 'just think, if you never discover more than you already know, could you cope with that level of mystery? With not necessarily finding the answers? Or that the answers you do find may not be that palatable?' He took a sip, and wiped his mouth with the back of his hand. 'Look here, Catherine, this is obviously a big deal and I'll help you all I can – though I don't quite see how you'll accomplish it. And I promise to try and understand, but in return,' he said seriously, 'you promise me you'll watch out for yourself. It won't do you, or anyone else, any good, if you make yourself ill over this.'

They were quiet then, staring at each other.

He put his hand over her clenched first and shook it gently. 'You know,' he said gently, 'when and if we meet, there are also things...' He hesitated. 'Well, I'll just say, I'll give you my full attention. But someday... well, I might need yours.'

Cat frowned. 'What do you mean?'

'Never mind. But will I have it?'

'Of course. If that's what you want.'

Cat felt stronger, then. He was wide of the mark sometimes, but she didn't want to lose him, and she wasn't losing him. They stood up and Ed folded the blanket. 'So, how're you going to set about things?'

'Oh, I know what I'm going to do.' She helped him gather the picnic things. 'I can't ask *her*, can I, but her brother is coming, and when he does I intend to ask *him*.'

27

The day the exhibition opened they woke to heavy cloud banking up over the estuary, and a surly river which, in the hot, muggy air, seemed to shudder against its banks. Cat looked at the sky anxiously, and hoped it wouldn't rain for the Preview. It might stop people coming.

The warehouse was empty, the walls bare. Rudi had packed up all the *Faces* plus the portrait of her mother, marked NFS. As each one went into bubble wrap Cat made her farewells, having no idea who'd come home after the show. Her Eastern European woman winced as her face was covered and, as they were shoved once more into darkness. two of the down-and-outs grinned malevolently. *Got tired of us, Cat, have you? We've not seen you recently. Making money on us now, are you? What price your pity, eh?'*

Rudi appeared in the doorway, wiping his hands.

'All done, and I've brought you a copy of the catalogue. I should have shown you the draft, but hey, what does it matter? It'll be a good show, one of the best.' He leaned over her wolfishly. 'You got anyone coming tonight, or do I have you to myself?'

Cat backed away from him. 'Just us lot, Rudi, and a friend. Not a painter or anything,' she said airily, as he leered at her.

'Oh. Oh, right. OK, then, see you tonight. Don't be late.'

Cat made herself a cup of coffee and settled down in the window to look at the catalogue. Rudi had done them proud. She turned to the back, to the potted histories.

Catherine Feugler is a Jewish artist...

It was the only part he had edited but she expected it in a way, and found that she didn't mind. Being

Jewish was like a tide that had washed to the front of her mind. It would recede again one day, but, as she had told Ed, that day was not yet.

A step on the stairs. Ricci had smelt the coffee, and Cat watched him pour himself a cup. He looked better, less fraught, his forehead less lined.

'You sleeping any better, Ricci?'

He sat down with her by the open window. Below, the river lapped greenly, the warm composty smell of its silt-encrusted shores rising in their nostrils.

'I am, as a matter of fact. I did what you said, and it was amazing; I could see myself standing on the path, looking at myself from outside.' He gave a light laugh. 'I felt very sorry for myself, I can tell you. It was uncanny, like a hallucination...'

'But you still dream?'

'Yeah, but now I do get an occasional night off. That's progress, isn't it?.'

She laid her hand on his arm. 'It's terrific!'

'When they come, though,' he said lightly, 'it's almost worse. Bonfire, bodies and blood.' He laughed ironically. 'Not to fuss about it, though. I'm not making this up, you know,' he added, seeing her shrinking expression. 'Attention-seeking...'

'Ricci, I never imagined for one moment that you were!'

'At least it's not every night. Last night there was a point when I sort of said what you told me to say, 'I don't need to be a victim anymore.' Out loud, I said it, in the dream...'

'And what happened?'

'The Jap guards, they just laughed.'

'But the pattern's changing?'

'Oh yes, the pattern's changing. They never laughed before.'

Since Ed was coming to the Preview Cat took care what she wore, and from her meagre wardrobe selected a long black skirt and a silver top, silver earrings and a broad silver necklace from the charity shop, and black sandals. She looked OK, she thought, if a bit hoary.

'You coming, Miss Cat?' Gus, at the door, was dressed in crumpled jeans and a black tee shirt printed FBI.

'I'll wait, I think. Ed Barber is coming.'

'My, a four star General! Honoured, I'm sure! Chose the right shirt, didn't I? OK, I'll see you there, then. God, it's hot.'

Cat stood by the open window, tasting the salt on her lips. Above the heavy clouds the sky was a vivid dark blue, and both were reflected in the water, a pure ultramarine shouldering up against raw umber. Quickly, she found the right pastels and opened her sketchbook.

Julia was at the door. 'Ready? Cat, you're not *working*, are you? Um, Cat, your hair – it's really shaggy; d'you really want it like that, or shall I do a quick...?' Snip-snip in the air.

'Have we time? I'm expecting...'

Julia looked flabbergasted, Cat capitulating, and then she rallied. 'Course. Won't take a minute. I'll just get my things. But don't dare change your mind while I'm away! And clean up your nails!' Her excitement at the prospect of at last getting her hands on Cat's hair was almost comical.

She draped a towel round Cat's shoulders, while Cat kept an eye on the slipway. Sure enough, half way through, Ed's smart car coasted down the slipway, and she could see him peering up at the warehouse and frowning.

'Hurry, Julia, he's here.'

'You got a man at last?' Julia stared out of the window. 'Wow, will you look at that car! Sit still, would you, I haven't half finished.' She began to giggle.

Footsteps on the outside steps and Ed appeared in the doorway, wearing a lightweight suit, a white shirt and a narrow, rather old-fashioned tie. He ducked his head to avoid the lintel, an actor on a strange set.

'Right place?' he said, grinning. 'The right night? Or you want me to go away again?'

'No, come in, Ed. Sorry, won't be a minute. Julia's just...Look, come and sit down, you're making me nervous.'

'Cor blimey, he's a looker,' Julia whispered. 'Bit old, though, innee? Cool tie, though! Where'd you pick 'im up, then?'

'On my travels. And he's not old.'

A flurry of scissors, the towel whipped away, a quick breath in the region of her ear, and she was gone at last. Cat picked up the necklace, and made to put it round her neck.

'Here, let me do that. Why, you're trembling, Catherine! Don't worry – it'll be great. You look... great. Stunning.' He looked around. 'So this is where it all happens?'

'Yes, Ricci's upstairs, Julia and Gus are below, and I'm in here.'

'Great. Fantastic views, too.'

'Not just a squat, then?' said Cat, *sotto voce.*

'And where's that, across the river?

Cat was relieved he hadn't heard. 'I'm not sure exactly. It's not an area I've explored.'

'Difficult to access, I should think. Well, show me round later. I can't wait to see this work of yours. Aint it hot?'

They took Cat's car for easier parking and set off up the slipway.

'The rain's coming,' he said, as they drove up the lane. 'The sky was a really muddy blue on the way here, and there was this fantastic double rainbow; you shoulda seen it. I never realised before that the second one would be back to front.'

28

The cobbled alleyway leading to the gallery was lit by ancient gas lamps, acquired by the elder Marks and converted to electricity, and the newly-painted carriage doors had been flung wide. In the already crowded room Cat recognised several faces, an art critic here, a journalist there, a few of her students and the mayoral party. A cameraman, dressed in a navy tracksuit, was nudging people into groups; tummies in, busts out, false smiles applied, his sidekick with her notebook, taking names.

Rudi, the ubiquitous three-piece suit and spotted bow tie incorporate, bustled towards her looking anxious, his shrewd eyes assessing Ed.

'Ah, better late than never, hey, Cat? This your friend? Hi, I'm Rudi Marks. I'm running this show so if you want to buy come straight to me. Cat, see how I've hung your work? Tell me what you think. Hot, tonight, aint it? Let's get you both a drink...'

Cat took hers and went to see how Rudi had hung her *Faces*. Instead of invisible wire he'd used large-gauge galvanised chains suspended from a metal rail, and in spite of herself she thought, Rudi's good; he sees things; how chained the homeless are to their way of life. Gus's exhibits, slab pots of all shapes and sizes, were arranged on narrow, moss-coloured pedestals, scattered with flotsam from the river, seashells, roots and driftwood. They looked wonderful, and Cat wished she was rich enough to buy one.

People were buying and Rudi was kept busy. By the middle of the evening several red dots had appeared on her work, including her Eastern European woman. Ed was in a corner of the room, deep in conversation with Ricci, and later they were out in the comparative cool of the street. She was glad for Ricci, but wondered how much Ed could take. They were not, obviously, just talking about the weather.

At dark, there was a lull while the heat rose and fell like a blanket, then a bright flash of lightening split the sky, followed by a rumble of thunder. Then the rain came, sudden and torrential, the first rain for weeks. Those outside rushed in, shaking themselves and chattering excitedly, but Cat thought, I knew this was coming. I could smell it on the air.

After a while she was impatient to leave. She had her mother's intolerance of crowds, and in spite of the rain the room was still airless; she needed to be alone again. She glanced around for Ed, but he was talking to Rudi. OK, she thought, full circle, come on Ed, get me out of this, but they seemed deep in conversation and she turned away. A moment later Ed spoke at her shoulder.

'Ready to go? I want to see my portrait again. Let's do our leave-taking and push off.'

Cat made her excuses to Rudi and looked round for her picture framer, but he was already approaching.

'Hey, that's a great portrait you've got there, General. Wow, she really caught you! Aren't you the clever one, Cat? You want to take it tonight? It's in the workshop...'

'You want to ...Cat? We may as well. Then I can take it home with me.'

Not yet, Ed. I'm not ready. I want to have it a bit longer. I just want you to look at it, and then come back to *The Studio* with me, even if you can't say my name without a pause in front of it, as if you've forgotten who I am.

'That'll be fine,' she said.

Her picture framer passed her the key. 'Now look after this, Cat – I know what you're like! I'll pick it up tomorrow, on my way in. Just lock up behind you, will you, darling? By the way,' he added, 'your paintings are great.'

They drove silently through the streets, the

windscreen wipers futile against the rain. They could hear the roar of the sea as it smashed against the walls, the spray rising like phantoms in front of them. The promenade was swamped, the gutters sluicing with muddy water. It had even flooded into the workshop, but the portrait was safe against the far wall, the gold frame gleaming at her through the bubble wrap. It will match his braid, she thought dully.

Ed picked it up. 'Oh, it's light. I thought it would be heavier.'

'It's only the weight of the frame. The canvas is nothing.' She felt miserable.

'You OK?'

'I'm fine. Let's get it into the car.'

She locked the door. The car was nearby, and hitching up her skirt, she hurried to lift up the boot.

The painting wouldn't fit. What had been an easy fit without the frame was now impossible. Cat felt as though a load had been taken from her shoulders. Laughter rose in her throat and she began to giggle. Ed shook his head at her, chuckling. The rain poured down on them as they stood in the puddles, laughing.

'It's not meant to be, is it?' he said at last, wiping his face with a spotless handkerchief. 'Oh well,' he said regretfully, 'you'll just have to bring it up next time you come.'

Next time.

At *The Studio* she changed into jeans while he dried himself off with a towel, and she called through the door. 'I saw you talking to Ricci...'

'Yeah, poor guy. He told me about his dreams. You've been swell to him, Catherine.'

'I've not done much. And I bet he didn't say 'swell'. You hungry, Ed?'

'Famished. Those canapé's just whet my appetite. You got a take-out nearby?'

'Nothing's nearby, Ed. You saw that as you drove in. Yesterday's pizza?'

About midnight the phone rang. They were sitting on the sofa, listening to jazz and nattering, their empty mugs on the table in front of them. She had no presentiment, no weight of foreknowledge, no sense of dread.

'Maybe Gus needs a lift.'

It was the hospital. Her mother had had a stroke.

Cat packed an overnight bag, scribbled a note to Ricci, and they left. At the last minute Ed offered to take her all the way to Coventry. He was ahead of her on the stairs and he turned, his face sombre.

'Come on, you need the company, and you're tired anyway.'

It was tempting. She would have liked Rute to meet him, but in the end she said, no, I don't know what I'll find, and he accepted that. He drove up the slipway in front of her, and in spite of the spray, they kept in convoy all the way along the M25 to the M40. By then the rain had stopped and the sky was clear. She watched his tail-lights, the shape of his head intermittently lit by passing cars. Just before High Wycombe, he signalled and pulled on to the hard shoulder. She punched her hazard lights and drew in behind him and stopped. Ed got out of the car and came towards her, and she got out too, easing the ache in her shoulders, and went to meet him.

'Ed, we can't stop here. It's against the law.'

'Just for a minute, to say goodbye.' He took her hands. In the orange light of the streetlights his face was luminous, the pupils of his eyes very dark. 'I shall be thinking of you, Catherine. All the time. Is there anything I can do, to make things easier for you?'

She hesitated. 'You could ring Israel for me if you would. Her brother ought to know, and it costs a fortune from the hospital. I'll pay you for the call – oh, my bag's in the car.'

'Leave it. Just tell me what time to ring.' He took

out his diary and held it to the light. 'The time difference is OK, but I don't want to wake them too early.'

She smiled. 'But the number's in my bag as well.'

On her way to the car she thought, dear Ed, he's so considerate, first to me, then Ricci, and now my family. Surely, if a friendship was capable of ending it had never existed in the first place. She reached for her address book and gave him the number.

'Ring about nine, if you can. They'll be up by then.'

He took her in his arms, a brief, fraternal hug. 'You'll be OK? This isn't going to be easy, Catherine.'

'I'll be all right. It helps having you around. Even,' she added, wryly, 'if I get stuck with 'Care-thrin'!'

'Yeah, I'm around, lady, whoever you are.'

They set off again. He turned up the slip road and Cat saw his car in her rear view mirror as it went over the bridge. Less time than it would take him to drive it she imagined him negotiating the roundabout, turning into his road, driving slowly up to his garage. She imagined the security lights going on, the electronic garage doors opening, the car going in. She imagined his face in the light, his key in the door, the door closing, and soon after, the security lights going off, the blind façade of the house closed for the night. An echo of jazz.

A hundred yards later the orange glow of the streetlights stopped and she came into darkness. With empty roads it would take her just under two hours. She put her foot down.

29

Rute's face was twisted, her jaw slack, her mouth open. She was very yellow and she looked skeletal. There was a trickle of moisture under her eyes, as if, in her sleep, she wept. Her hands, those beloved, blemished hands, were limp on her chest, like a pious Renaissance painting. She was wired up all over the place. The monitor ticked, zigzagging redly. Lights flashed on and off. Little bubbles came from between her lips and Cat took a tissue from the box on her bedside table, bent and wiped them away.

Outside, the dawn was breaking, radiant with light, an incandescent green. The lift clanged, and there were voices. Someone walked past the open door with a trolley laden with white, primly-folded sheets, its wheels squeaking intermittently. Other doors opened and shut. Nearby someone said, 'God, another shift!' and there was the sound of laughter, quickly hushed.

Silence is a wall all by itself. It doesn't need bricks or stones or barbed wire.

It was the silence of her roots she minded.

At about nine-thirty she got up, stretched, and went to the phone. Ed had rung Israel and they were coming. His voice, down the phone, was grave, focused. She rang Deborah and James, left messages on their answer machines; rang their mobiles and left another. When she got back, Rute was as before. She waited for her to wake. Her mother, she was always late.

A diminutive nurse arrived on sibilant steps, Chinese or Singhalese, and Cat found herself marvelling how she could do her work, fetching, carrying, steering heavy trolleys, lifting patients. She bent over Rute, propped her wrist against her tiny waist and took her pulse – how many wrists had she supported thus? She wrote on the chart, and smiled at Cat.

'There's a canteen downstairs, Miss.' She had a reedy, heavily accented voice. 'Maybe get a cup of coffee, something to eat?'

'I might, a bit later. Thank you.'

Cat must have dozed. Her watch said nearly eleven. Rute was as before, the slant-eyed nurse standing over her.

'Will she wake, do you think?' asked Cat, rousing herself.

'Oh, Miss, she not in a coma; she wake ver' soon; ver', ver' soon.'

'Is there... I mean, will she... Is there a danger of another stroke?'

Perhaps the Sister would have said, oh, no, dear, whatever made you think that? Oh, no, she'll be as right as rain in a few days. But this one had a different philosophy.

'Miss, if stroke come again, think God's mercy. *Zūntáng* – Mother very tired, poor lady...'

'You're saying that she might not actually wake up again?'

'Oh, no, I not say that. *Zūntáng* wake soon. If she not wake soon, I say His mercy. You think of Mother. You think His mercy, Miss.'

More accented utterances were to follow, which, if Cat could have thought about it, she would have thought surreal.

'Ca-wina, you 'ways bin goo' dorwa t'me.'

A good daughter? Rute's eyes were open, mere slits of hazel-green.

Praise God. Praise be to you, Master of the Universe, for you have given me back my mother. Cat leant over the bed, took her hand. Did she know her touch as well?

'Feel... funny.'

'Yes, Ma. You've had a little stroke.'

'Oh, ha' wi?'

Pause, while she took it in?

'You lowely dorwa, di' I tell 'oo?'

'Yes, Ma, you told me. And you're a great mother. You really are. You've always been there for me.'

'I twyd... In spi' o' ewy-fing.'

In spite of everything.

'Don't talk if it bothers you.'

'No, iss alwi'. Not mush ti'e leph.' Her eyes looked sore, red-rimmed, the strain, perhaps, of keeping them open. Or the tears she shed while she slept?

Just a little time, that's all I ask. But she said, not much time. How does she know? Is *this* God's mercy?

Let her go, Catherine. Ed's voice.

'You sleep,' said Cat, struggling with her throat. 'Go back to sleep again, Ma.'

'Ca' I?' Testing.

'Yes, have a little rest. When you wake up Reuben will be here. And Amit.'

'Oh, goo'! Zo gla'.' Rute closed her eyes.

Elie Wiesel tells a story of a native of Lodz, who, faced with destruction, got down on his knees and prayed. In God he put all his slender hope, for only He could rescue his family. Yet, in the end, only this man was saved from the camps. Since then, when he prays, he thanks God *in spite of everything*. Life had treated him harshly, but God still gave him mercy. He still gave him joy.

For her mother this joy was simply a joy in living, which, once discovered, she never lost. Previously she'd been continually looking over her shoulder, which was how Ed had described herself, now she thought about it. But as long as Rute could keep the two of them together – secluded, maybe, but inviolate, herself the chatelaine – she was content.

As for Bill, she did not know how to deal with his rejection of her.

'Why does he not call me 'Mutti'?' Or, 'You not have any friends? Why does he never let me meet them?' Or, 'Why, Caterina, does your husband *schmirk* at me behind my back? With the *kinder*, for Gott's sake!' And, 'Caterina, your husband is very like my brother Reuben sometimes. He can be very schtern.'

Yet, through all these years of struggle, her mother had never despaired. Cat had seen her weep sometimes; heard her weep more often, but in spite of everything Rute had always been a person of immense spirit, passionate, quirky and caustic; a dragon spitting fire, warding off the demons in her life.

Past tense? No, just memories.

The hospital offered her a bed. She declined, but her heart sank; things were moving inexorably towards their end, and she hoped Reuben and Amit would arrive in time. But the thought of taking Rute's brother to Rute's house to sleep in Rute's bed was intolerable, not when he had refused to speak to her all those years, and she decided to find a small hotel near the hospital, where she could stay with them. In the corridor was a telephone kiosk, and she stood under its orb, scanning the telephone directory and making the booking in a voice that seemed strange to her, not her own. From her children there was nothing but a stony silence – yet how could it be otherwise, she told herself, when she'd no mobile phone? Perhaps they'd just turn up.

When she returned to the ward she was not allowed in. She glimpsed Rute, almost naked and surrounded by nurses, and one came out and said they were treating her for bedsores. Cat waited in the corridor until they had finished.

Rute lay on the bed as if she had never been disturbed; still, tiny, reduced. Was she waiting for Reuben, unconsciously conserving her energies? Cat sat by her side and watched her for a while, but then she became restless. She needed something to do, something to read, perhaps. And how would she feel, knowing someone was scrutinising her while she slept? She felt in her bag for her little poetry book, but slipped it back again. *Four Quartets* haunted her. Why did she ever learn it?

Four quartets. Bill, the kids, and herself. Yes.

Rute, Reuben, Amit and herself. Two.

Gus, Ricci, Julia and herself. Three. She was in all those worlds.

Was there a fourth? What should the fourth be, and was she in that, too? Was Ed in it? Her thoughts were rambling. But she had found her way around the hospital. She had learned her mother's cell-like room. She had learned again her mother's face, though she would never paint her thus – she was no Lucien Freud.

In the drawer of the bedside table lay a Gideon Bible; the Psalms, Proverbs and the New Testament. But how many Jews feared to open it, in case they found a gospel of rejection? It depended where they looked, of course. In the first few pages there was a sort of menu; for depression, read this; for despair, psalm that. The psalms were OK, Cat supposed, for desperate people dipping in. People who didn't know their way. After all, they weren't requiring an exegesis.

She felt in her bag again; at least she knew her way around Eliot.

...wait without hope, for hope would be hope for the wrong thing; wait without love, for love would be love of the wrong thing; there is yet faith, but the faith and the hope and the love are all in the waiting... pointing to the agony of death and birth.

30

Reuben and Amit sat in the back of the car while she chauffeured them to the hospital; occasionally she snatched glances at them in her mirror. She asked about their flight, the security checks and the weather in Israel, but they were tired after their journey and uncommunicative. Amit was tall and willowy with tanned, leathery skin, her white hair pulled back in a large bun on the nape of her neck. Stray hairs were escaping; caused, Cat supposed, by the friction of the headrest in the aeroplane. She was wearing a cream cotton two-piece suit and heavy costume jewellery, which seemed incongruous but which Cat suspected she habitually wore. Reuben was also white-haired; he was stockily built, and wore a shabby suit with a white, open-necked shirt which revealed his gnarled throat and the dry, silvery hairs of his barrel chest. His uncompromising, weather-beaten face bore no resemblance to Rute, his twin – except that his eyes, like hers, were green. He walked with a pronounced limp. While Amit expressed eagerness to see Rute, he was silent; the same tight-lipped, introverted silence that Rute used to have. They went straight to the hospital, for Rute was sinking.

James and Deborah were standing beside the bed. It was the first time she had seen them together for two years, and they looked beautiful. Cat drank in their likeness to each other, their smooth skin, their slimness, their height, their glossy hair, their *youth*fulness, and suddenly filled with compunction and a rush of affection, she lifted her arms to hug them.

'Oh, you're here, my darlings. Deborah, after all this time!'

But Deborah was looking at her as if she was a stranger, flinching away from her, her eyes dark with dismay, and James's face had paled. Glancing at him,

Deborah stepped out of her embrace.

'Mum, we've been here simply *ages*.' She glanced at her watch. 'I *told* you, I really don't have the time for all this...'

Her lack of feeling was incredible, her rudeness outrageous, but Cat hastened to placate her.

'Sorry, their train was late.' Instantly, she heard the echo of all the excuses she had made for Bill, and, for a moment, she was dizzy. Putting a hand to her forehead she heard herself mumbling, 'I'm glad you've come, though. Thank you.' And wondered, fleetingly, why she always took the role of appeasement.

'She isn't even *awake*, is she?' persisted her daughter. 'So it's all a bit pointless, really. I mean, like, *sorry,* but I don't see why we're here. It's too late, isn't it? Oh, Mum,' she said, exasperated, 'why do you always do this?'

'Do what? What have I done now?'

'Why do you always leave things so *late?*'

'Did I leave it late?' asked Cat distantly, recovering her courage. 'You could have seen your Granny any time, you know.'

'And Mum did leave messages, admit,' said James quietly.

'*Yes,*' hissed Deborah, 'when it was already bloody-well too *late*! All this is her fault, anyway. It was *her*, leaving home, caused this it! *Really*, Mum! Sometimes I think... Oh, God, I dunno. Sometimes I just... don't know who you *are* anymore!' She clamped a hand over her mouth, and exhaled noisily, shaking her head in frustration.

'Well,' said Cat, smiling through her misery, 'then it's just as well *I* do, isn't it?'

Amit glanced at her. 'It's OK, Deborah,' she said, laying a conciliatory hand on Deborah's arm. 'Doesn't it make it all worth while, just to be together again?'

Deborah shook her off.

Bill taught her how to function like this, Cat thought

bleakly; to think that everything must be my fault. But now it has to stop.

'Deborah, control yourself!' she said sharply. 'Remember where you are!' She looked pleadingly at James. 'Talk to her, Jake.'

He stiffened. 'Oh, don't call me that, Ma!'

Cat felt a great wave of weariness sweep over her, and James, seeing her expression, gave her an apologetic smile. 'She doesn't really mean it, Mum. She's just upset. And call me whatever you want.'

Cat looked at him. 'OK, but we're all upset, and I don't want your Granny to hear. So let's leave it now, shall we? Look, your uncle and aunt have come all the way from Israel, and we haven't even welcomed them properly.'

Belatedly, they shook hands and snatched air kisses, but Reuben's eyes were distant, moist, fixed on Rute, as they had been, Cat realised, throughout the conversation. He seemed to have the capacity to detach himself from what was uncomfortable, or to pretend it wasn't happening. I could have done with a bit of that, she thought; it might have been very convenient sometimes.

Amit tried to make conversation with Deborah and James, but it was obvious that both of them were itching to leave.

'Better go, Mum,' James said eventually. 'Got a train to catch.'

'You didn't drive up?'

'Mum, the traffic's horrendous and I've got exams. I told you. On the train I can work on my laptop. Debs'll give me a lift to the station.'

Cat glanced at Deborah.

'I'm in Birmingham, Mum,' she said, looking elsewhere. 'I told you that as well. I may as well go straight on. No point in coming back here, is there? She's not going to wake, is she?'

Cat turned away for a moment, pushing back the

hurt. 'OK, darlings,' she said brightly, 'you'd better get off then.'

'Yeah,' said James, 'but you'll let us know when she... you know, when the...'

'Yes, James, I'll let you know.'

Cat was crying inside, for all of it, for her memories, for those children of hers who were so estranged from her, for Rute, for all the hurts, for all that had been lost.

The door closed behind them and she left it like that for a moment, and then opened it again, as the Sister had told her to do, although right now she would have preferred the privacy of a closed door. Reuben was by his sister's bed, his eyes bleak, holding her hand. He seemed set to stay like that for some time and suddenly Cat could bear it no longer. She had to get out and breathe Gott's free air.

'I'll leave you alone for a bit, OK?' she said. 'I'll be just outside. Fetch me, would you, if she wakes, or anything.'

She knew Rute wouldn't wake again. She had seen the last of her green eyes.

'Don't let Deborah upset you,' whispered Amit, as she left the room. 'She's grown into a bit of a baggage, that's all.'

'She's *not* a baggage!' returned Cat loyally. 'She's the most wonderful daughter who ever lived and she's had a hard time. '

31

Later they went to the hotel and Reuben and Amit settled in. The hospital promised to call if there was any change.

'How long can you stay?' asked Cat, as they sat down to the meal.

Reuben didn't reply. He was still wearing the same clothes in which he had travelled, the collar of his open-necked shirt frayed and worn. He looked grim and rather forbidding, his face etched in lines of tragedy as if he had forgotten how to smile. There was little courtesy in him; even at the station he said no word of greeting, either to wish Cat *shalom*, or to commiserate with her for her mother's illness. He was, as Rute had said, a real *kibbutznik*.

It was Amit who answered.

'We can stay a day, *liebchen*. We'll come back again, when... you know...'

What, only an evening and a day to sit with Rute, and for Cat to discover what they knew of her mother's story? In that case, she thought, we'd better get on with it.

Conscious of the lateness of the hour and their fatigue, she started hesitantly.

'Uncle Reuben, I'd like to ask you something, if I may.'

He gave a little shake of his head, immediately on his guard. 'Well, go on. Ask.'

'Can you...Can you tell me a bit about my mother? I know most of what happened to her, but there're some things... There are parts I don't know, and I'd be really grateful if... You see, I'd like to sort of get it clear in my mind.'

There were others in the room, couples dining, and Cat spoke quietly. A solitary man sat at the table in the window, and for a moment she was distracted, speculating who he might be. Then the food came, omelette and salad for her, fish for Amit, and for Reuben, soup and French bread.

Again, it was Amit who answered, not Reuben, who stared at his bowl in silence, as if trying to identify what was in it – not Reuben, the brother.

'What do you want to know, exactly?' She also was guarded.

'Just... small things. As I say, I know most of it. I've grown up with the stories. But there are one or two gaps...'

'Well,' said Amit, 'tell us what you know. But, Caterina, remember that tonight we are sad, and a little tired.'

Cat felt rebuked, but also dismayed. 'Leave it,' she said quietly, shaking her head. 'It doesn't matter.'

Amit pursed her lips. 'No, it matters. You should understand your mother's life. How else do you know from where you come?'

Cat was astounded by her intuition.

'So, Caterina. Tell us what you already know. Just the bare bones.'

She began in the middle, which seemed as safe a place as any.

'Well, I know that she went to Israel,' she said slowly. 'I mean Palestine, as it was then. And a bit about my father. She once mentioned something about a coal barge, but it was no more than a mention, and that somehow she escaped....'

Reuben's eyes snapped up, icily green; he was about to interrupt, but Amit placed her hand on his sleeve, a gentle, quiet, protective gesture and he subsided. He looked down at his plate for a few seconds and then he put a piece of bead into his mouth. He chewed slowly, as though his teeth were bad.

'...and about the transportations, and the yellow star. And about... about how Hannah was... I'm sorry, I know this is painful... how Auntie Hannah was got out of Zwickau...'

Again Reuben's eyes were on her, wide, staring, and again Amit forestalled him.

'...but what I don't know about is the... the ghetto. Ma never talked about those four years. She talked about almost everything else, but she would never talk about that. And I must admit... I've always wondered why.'

Amit gave a long sigh and glanced anxiously at Reuben.

'...I know about the house, too, in Zwickau, and the piano lessons with Artur Schnabel, and about your father, Uncle Reuben, that he was a Rabbi...'

Amit coughed, interrupting. 'Caterina, let me, first of all, tell you a little bit about how things are at the moment.' She smiled kindly. 'If you come to Israel you should understand our history. Even if you live in the Diaspora, you should understand.'

She took a drink of water, pushed away her uneaten food, and folded her arms on the table.

'Our kibbutz – Yagur – is near Haifa. It was one of the first kibbutz to be built after the War, and Reuben and I, we were some of the first pioneers. Ach, those days! We were so full of idealism! But, you know, Caterina, we have seen the peace recede again and again. We have watched our children go off to the army, and our grandchildren too. The anxiety... I cannot speak of it.'

She gave Reuben a fleeting glance, her eyes worried.

'Now,' she said heavily, 'because of the political situation, life in Israel is not quite fulfilling our dreams anymore. So much suffering... Do you know how many suicide bombs there've been in the last few years? Tel Aviv is only nine miles from the border, Caterina – nine miles! Well in reach of their rocket attacks. But, *Gott danken*, we are not yet bitter. We do not want, utterly, to give up our hopes, or even now, our dreams. But you see, there are similarities...'

'Similarities?'

Was this Rute's story or her own?

'Caterina, the Jews suffered in the *Shoah* – my Gott, how they suffered! But the Palestinians, under this government, they suffer too. Now, there is no comparison. The *Shoah* was on a completely different scale and it was unique. But, suffering is... suffering. And not every Jew in Israel has what we call a Holocaust memory. Some are from Ukraine or Africa and this government listens to them. It has to, to stay in power, so they make these restrictive laws. The Palestinians, they cannot go where they want, or work where they want, or go to school where they want...'

She was becoming agitated. 'The same as it was for us in Germany – the pattern is being repeated. Ethnically, too, we are similar. So, you see, we dislike some things very much. Like the building of settlements close to the Green Line and in the Territories; illegal, you know, under international law. Land appropriation – there are shepherds there who've worked the land for generations. It belongs to them, and to the olive farmers. Now there is little shepherding; the sheep have gone and so have the olive groves. And they're extending the wall all the time – as though we've not had enough of walls!' she added impatiently. 'In any case most of these settlers, *pah!*' she said contemptuously, 'they're not Israelis; they're not from out of our communities; they're Americans! *They* won't compromise with the Palestinians over land; oh no, *they* say God promised it to them, from the Nile to the Euphrates.'

Rute's story, Amit? Please? While there's yet time.

'Now, many of us think this is... how do you say? Fantasy. We don't believe it, but the others are too powerful for us, and they get all this funding from America. We *hate* the way things are for the

Palestinians. We *hate* the bulldozing of olive groves, the repression, the violence, the shelling. But, Caterina, we also hate and fear the suicide bomber very much. We must defend our land...'

Her voice changed to a whisper, as though she didn't want Reuben to hear, and she spoke behind her hand. 'A friend of ours, you know, he was Palestinian, a Christian-Arab-Israeli; he ran a café in Haifa; he was a victim of a suicide attack. One of their own, you might say!'

She was in full flood. Why was she not answering Cat's questions? What *was* all this?

The waiter came and cleared away, loading their half-empty plates on his arm, squashing the food. He flashed the menu again, and when they shook their heads, gathered up the crumpled napkins and left. Immediately Amit lit a cigarette and inhaled deeply, blowing smoke across the table. Cat glanced anxiously at the *No Smoking* sign, but the room was emptying, and no one seemed concerned.

'We cannot get on with our lives,' she said. 'And while we're constantly thinking about our security and pouring money into defence, we cannot solve our own internal problems like water and immigration. Serious problems, which we're not addressing. Genesaret is down eighty percent, and people say, we're going to have to solve the water problem one day, why not start now? It's the same with the peace, Caterina. It has to be sorted out one day, so again people say: why not start now? Somehow we have to learn to co-exist.'

She took a sip of water. Again she put her hand protectively on Reuben's arm, stroking the wrinkled flesh of his wrist tenderly, and Cat wondered where she was going with all this and when she was going to get round to Rute.

'People like your uncle, you know, they used to have a voice, but now they're afraid to speak out.' She leaned forward. 'You mustn't judge us, Caterina. We're just so *tired* of perpetual war. We're utterly weary of it. We just want a quick end, and some peace lived for a change. But there are atrocities on both sides and we find that very difficult.'

Her voice was becoming hoarse. 'So, what now? Because of the demographics the politicians want to herd the Palestinians into a small space. If they were able to live where they want, vote how they want, they would over-run us in ten years. They're motivated, and it's the land which motivates them. And if that happened Israel as a nation would cease to exist. It would be Muslim – Shariah, even, with their own religious laws, the strictest possible laws, especially for women; much stricter than Mear Sharim – you know Mear Sharim?'

Cat shook her head. Amit threw herself back in her chair.

'We'll be here all *night*! Listen, Caterina, it's just part of Jerusalem, OK, where the Haredi congregate.' She waved a dismissive hand. 'No, I don't expect you to know about the Haredi. They're Ultra-Orthodox Jews who think they know best how Judaism is meant to be lived. They repudiate everything that is not in Cabbala or the Talmud, which means, you see, that they repudiate Zionism. OK? You got that?'

Cat used to loathe history at school and she was bemused. Amit seemed to sense this, and became more emphatic. 'Now, Shariah Law is ten times – no, a *hundert* times – stricter than Mear Sharim. It is about exclusion and it is about crushing. But you see, Caterina, for Reuben and me, and some others, we remember how *we* were crushed. When they talk of segregating Palestinians, we remember how *we* were segregated. When we see Palestinians being denied their rights, we remember how *we* were denied *our* rights.' She gestured with her cigarette. 'It's just too close to what it was like under the Nazis.' She caught herself. 'Ach, how can I say that? But it's true; my memory is *nicht* zo bad that I can't remember. But others, they do not *want* to remember. They don't even want to *think* about it. And the ones concerned only with religious laws think of nothing *else* but religious laws! Where's the ashtray?'

Cat started, heard the echo of what she'd said, emptied out the sauce packets from their shallow dish and passed it across. Amit stubbed out her cigarette roughly and folded her arms again, her eyes dark.

'My God, after the Holocaust you would not expect Jews would *treat* people in the way that we treat the Palestinians! The Torah talks about being a blessing on the land, not a curse. It talks about how you should *treat* strangers in a strange land.'

She felt in her bag for another cigarette and lit it, exhaling sideways over her shoulder, speaking through the smoke.

'But, Caterina, so many close their eyes against history. For them, it's the Palestinians who have usurped the land, not we, the relative newcomers, who've simply returned to a land which was ours from the beginning of time.'

Not from the beginning of time, Cat thought, with black humour; what about the people they conquered, the Amalakites and the Zebuzzites and the Cellulites, and all the other Ites?

Amit poured herself a fresh glass of water and drank from it, wiped her lips, and tapped the ash of the cigarette into the sauce dish.

'Reuben wasn't always afraid like this,' she said, holding the cigarette up in front of her mouth. 'He was a member of Haganah in the War of Independence – '47-8, I am talking about. Your mother was, too.'

At this mention of her mother Cat came awake fast. 'Yes, she told me she was in the ATS...'

'Which was where she got the guns she smuggled,' Amit replied dryly.

Her fearful, diminutive mother, smuggled guns?

'She could have been shot. But they both felt they had to resist British rule. Your uncle, he was in Acre jail for two years, imprisoned by the British. Did you know that?' She leaned towards him slightly, her eyes bright with remembrance. '*Nicht zo* bad, eh, *liebchen*? Remember those marital visits?' She chuckled, and Cat suddenly saw how she might have been, as a young woman.'

Amit was talking again. 'These divisions, they are not by our will, but they happened. We could have worked together, we and the Palestinians. Some still do, though the press don't report that; they only write bad news. All of us were fighting hard then, for peace and co-existence. But others can be very aggressive and none of us wish to be pushed into the sea. Long ago the Arab League took a vow to obliterate us, to annihilate Israel as a nation, and that has not changed... *Annihilation*, already! Ach, we have seen that before! We know what *that* means!'

32

Amit was finished. There was no more, and merely a trace of Rute. She had gone quiet, into herself. Her eyes were screwed up, distant; her lips pursed; her two spread, slightly arthritic fingers holding the cigarette poised rigidly in front of her mouth, the ash tilting, threatening to drop. An image caught in time. Reuben was also looking away, his eyes glazed; his face, under his tan, was ashen with fatigue. It was late, the hotel silent. Everyone else had gone to bed. Cat's own eyes felt splintered with tiredness, with the strain of the day, and with frustration.

'Well, thank you for that,' she said. 'It's brought me up to date.' She pushed back her chair and got up. 'Do you want coffee, Aunt? If not, I think we should go to bed. You've had a long day.'

Amit sighed, and pushed herself up from the table slowly. 'Ach, I am not so young as I was.' She turned to Reuben. 'I'll go up, I think, use the bathroom. You follow in a minute?'

He nodded, his eyes lowered, his arms on the table, his broad wrinkled brown workman's hands toying with the cloth, smoothing it back and forth. He seemed to be waiting, almost with the back of his head, for the sound of the door closing and her feet on the stairs. At last he raised his eyes. Pale slate.

'Sit down, Caterina.' His voice was thin, high-pitched, but authoritative, the syllables harsh, staccato.

Cat obeyed. Was *he* going to tell her something?

He spoke in a whisper, but precisely, his eyes gleaming. 'Caterina, what you have said, what you said at ze beginning. From where did you get all zis, eh? From your mozzer? You get it from your mozzer? Ach, she always made up *stories*...'

Cat suddenly realised he was very angry.

'What you said, it is... it is a *s-slander,*' he said

quietly. 'Hannah... got out of Zwickau?' He was almost snarling. 'She was *not* got out of Zwickau! She was already in America. She went there for her studies and she lived with a werry religious family. Oh, I know your Western innuendo,' he said with heavy sarcasm; 'I know what you mean. But she was *virtuous*. Unlike your mother – we hadn't been in the kibbutz a *month* before she told me she was pregnant... But would she tell me who the father was? *No!* So I sent her away.'

Cat was stunned.

'You *slander* Hannah's name when you say this. I don't know from where you *got* the idea. Unt ghetto? *We never went to any ghetto!'* He spat the words. 'Unt what is zis about *coal?*' He laughed humourlessly. '*Mein Gott, coal,* already! Unt our *Fater,* a *Rabbi?'*

He jabbed the table sharply with his forefinger. 'He was not a Rabbi, Caterina,' he hissed. 'He was a docktor, OK? From where you *get* all this nonsense?'

His accent was very pronounced, guttural, like hers used to be, like Rute's, and Cat wondered why Amit's wasn't.

'Your mozzer,' he said scathingly, 'she was – how do you call it? – a ro-mantick. Always she had to make up ze stories. Always ze stories. She wouldn't stay with me, you know, on the kibbutz,' he added derisively, apparently unaware that he was contradicting himself. 'Ach, *no,* she had to go and live in the city, in Tel Aviv. Much gut it did her! There was zis *fellow* she have affair viz. He was your own *fater* but you do not ask about *him,* do you?'

Cat's head jerked, a mute negative, but he was still talking, his high voice rasping the room, thick with contempt, the spittle flying from his mouth.

'From Greece, he comes. *Greece,* I ask you! Nat even Ashkenazi. She make me ashamed more than once. Now she make me ashamed again! What she said to you, zese things –' He banged the table with his hand, and Cat jumped. '– *they didn't happen*!'

Cat was quiet, not daring to meet his eyes. When he moved, finally she looked up. He was still glaring at her. The green of his irises was silvered at the edges, and she realised he had cataracts, and his lips were dry, slightly chapped. His shoulders were bowed and his face was intensely pale, as though he was ill. She noticed broken veins in his cheeks and innumerable small moles on his neck.

Slowly Reuben pushed himself up from the table, turned his back on her and went heavily from the room. Cat took a paper napkin and wiped the back of her hand where his spittle had landed and, like an automaton, started to clear the plates. But there was no need; they were in the hotel and her mother, she was in the hospital.

Upstairs she showered mechanically, brushed her teeth, got into bed and put the light off. The pillow was cold, the sheets brittle with old detergent. Outside she heard the distant hum of the bypass. A car came down the street and stopped, its brakes squealing. In the hotel a door slammed, then another, then the sound of talking. Somewhere, incongruously, an alarm clock shrilled, and a little later, she heard footsteps and the sound of a suitcase wheeled noisily along the corridor. She heard the lift clang, then silence. The silence fell like snow, silvery under lamplight.

Cat lay motionless, her eyes open; her hands clutching the sheet to her chin. A child runs down an alleyway, swings under apple blossom. A small woman edges through the crowd, smiling. There is an echo of planes.

Ed, I wish you were with me. I would like to talk to you now.

Ed, I'm glad you're not here. What can I possibly tell you?

She lay still.

PART 3

canvas, wood and other ground

Had they deceived us
Or deceived themselves, the quiet-voiced elders,
Bequeathing us merely a receipt for deceit?

TS Eliot Four Quartets -- East Coker

1

Ruth lay between crisp, white sheets, a hospital blanket over her thin legs, her face pillow-white. She looked immensely vulnerable, like a small, malnourished, wizened child, and it created in Cat an immediate and unforeseen rush of emotion. She yearned to cover her mother's body with her own, take her in her arms, to spoon-feed back into her flaccid frame her ebbing life. *So are all roles reversed.*

In spite of Reuben.

Spite, in his blue eyes – almost in his very skin – exuded from him on their next encounter like a pall. Cat had hardly slept and, to avoid meeting the Israelis across the table, had taken an early breakfast, but on her way back to her room she encountered them on the stairs. They were leaving that night, said Amit, or rather early morning; they were packed and ready to go. Cat had to make herself meet her eyes, but she arranged to catch up with them in the foyer after they'd had their breakfast.

She had woken in anguish, hardly knowing what to think or to feel. Profound grief for a dying mother wrestled with self pity – *how could she have done this to me?* Dancing in her brain were mystic, almost Cabbalistic, images from old nightmares and dream paintings, like the inverted reality of Chagall or Munch. She was inside *The Scream.* She was here, there, elsewhere, fluctuating between the Pre-Reuben time and the post-Reuben time; *that* was before; *this* is now. A battle between heart and head, where she – whoever she was, and she would have to re-think that now – was stuck where she'd been punched, in the solar plexus. Her habitual filial, protective love for Ruth, the tenderness of their entwined memories, was relegated to the Pre-Reuben era; this new, bleak animosity, this new resentment and outrage, were post-Reuben, and the grief was for herself, for the daughter she had been and that Ruth was not the mother she had pretended to be, or might have been.

A fan was blowing by her mother's head, and they had put a special mattress under her. The wires and tubes were gone, though the monitor ticked on, like an oversize alarm clock in an empty room. Her hair was matted, whole tendrils of it lifted slightly in the breeze from the fan, and something in Cat told her she should wash it for her, but another part drew back. Pre-Reuben and post-Reuben.

Reuben sat on the other side of the bed, continually running his hand over his wet face and sniffing. What was he thinking? Was this some ritual of his own which took precedence over his revulsion, so that he was able to dismiss the conversation of the previous night, or forget his contempt? Or maybe he was genuinely grieving. Maybe he was going to the root of things, to their childhood. Cat couldn't tell, nor did she care. It was not her story.

Amit stood by the window, looking out, fiddling with her cigarette case. The nurse came, bent over Ruth and checked her pulse against the tiny inverted watch on her lapel. In her slim delicate fingers Rute's wrist looked gnarled, blue-veined, her knuckles protuberant. She smiled her brief smile and was gone; other stories waiting.

The day advanced; everything was intensely bright, sharply focussed. On the trees outside, where they had sat in the forbidden garden, the leaves were yellowish-green, drenched with sun – which, she'd heard, shines on the just and on the unjust alike, or was that the rain? – and the birds were singing, free to roam where they willed. It was the height of summer and everything was lush, but the clouds were indigo, threatening more rain.

It was evening. She wondered where the day had

gone. Reuben and Amit went to the canteen. A rush of footsteps at visiting time, children's voices like butterflies; the rise and fall of television sounds.

She felt a touch on her shoulder. It was Amit, but for a moment Cat didn't recognise her.

'You should get something to eat. It may be a while yet.'

Cat looked at Ruth; she was as before, her breathing shallow but even, and Cat nodded and stood up wearily. She went down to the canteen; drank, thankfully, a mug of hot tea; bought a filled roll which stuck to the roof of her mouth; went to the washroom and bathed her eyes; thought for a minute, then rang Ed.

His voice was gravelly, deeply warm. 'How are things? You have the Israeli couple with you?'

'Yes, since yesterday. They are leaving early tomorrow morning.'

'So soon? Can't they stay with you a little longer, be with you when...?'

'There isn't... much longer, Ed.'

He was quiet. 'You want me to come up?'

'No-o. No thanks, it's OK. I'll be all right. Ruth is...'

'I never heard you call her that. Are you really all right, Catherine? What's happening there?'

Neither had he called her Cat, but how could that matter, now?

'She's going.' Cat's throat caught and she cleared it silently, struggling to swallow. 'They've given her something...'

'Oh. Yes.' He'd been there. 'That'll help her, you know.'

'I know. I just wish...Ed, I wish I could see her eyes again, just once. I think I could tell, then... I think I'd know...'

'What?'

'No, it doesn't matter.'

An image, suddenly, of her ear pressed to his mouth

and his to hers, in intimate proximity, the silence stretching on for ever with nothing more to say.

'Well, I'd better get back.'

'Wait a minute. Did you talk with your family? I mean with the Israelis? Your uncle? You find out what you wanted?'

'Ed, I must go. I'll ring you later.'

Walking back to the ward she found time to acknowledge that she'd have to compromise with him about her name. She was even beginning to quite like the way he said it. The tenderness of it. She had been starved of tenderness for so long that to be on the receiving end of some of it now was worth all the compromise in the world.

Reuben and Amit went back to the hotel, exhausted, wrung out with their travel and their vigil. Cat arranged for a taxi to take them to the airport though her scant reserves hardly stretched to it. She found herself borrowing against red dots on sales, but all that seemed another world. They made their farewells in the corridor.

'I'm so sorry about all this.' Amit, warm and compassionate. Had Reuben told her what had been said? 'She was a good friend, your mother. We had some good times, in spite of everything. And you'll come to Israel? You'll come, when all this is over?'

No, thought Cat, I won't be going to Israel. She said something – what, she hardly knew.

'Well,' said Amit, watching her, 'I'll come back for the funeral. Not Reuben. He can't manage it again. But he'll sit *Shiva* for her.'

'Shiva?'

'The seven days of mourning...'

'Seven days?'

'Oh Caterina,' said Amit tiredly. 'There's no need to repeat everything I say. For *Shiva* people come. They sit around and talk about the one who has died and they weep.'

Right, turn on the tap, Cat thought, but I wonder what they'll say about Ruth or who was left who remembered her.

'But I'll come,' said Amit. 'Represent the Israeli branch of the family.'

Root, twig and branch.

They hugged, but Amit's expression was preoccupied, anxious. Reuben gave a single, dismissive wave, his eyes averted as though already disconnected, and they left the room. Cat stood by the door and watched them go down the corridor; he favouring his good leg and shuffling a little, like the old man he was; she, just as old, supporting him by the elbow. She was slightly taller than he was, but they were both old people at the end of their lives. They had not kissed Ruth goodbye, but perhaps that was not their way.

Alone again, Cat sat by the bed, and held Ruth's hand, pre-Reuben style. There was a time of nurses and injections, a time of water, a time of ice, pushed gently between cracked lips. The windows were closed against insects, but the blinds were open. The sky was dark, and a gentle rain was falling, pattering softly against the windowpanes, and in the corridor there were wet footmarks. Later, a man came, a black man in a blue overall with a bucket and a mop, and washed down the tiles. His eyes rolled at her from the doorway – see the work I have to do? She smiled at him briefly.

Briefly, she thought of Reuben and Amit. By now they would be in the taxi, on the way to the airport. Who reclined against the other's shoulder, took their rest? Who spoke first of their brief visit to Ruth? Which of them blamed the other for their fruitless journey? Who, in their life together, excused the other's frailty?

A sound from the bed, a movement. Cat rushed to her

feet and put her hands on Ruth's shoulders – so hot! In panic, she reached for the bell; heard its echo in the corridor. This time it was the slant eyed nurse again, a new shift for her, perhaps; she went straight to the bed, bent, and took her mother's pulse.

'She said something?'

'No... a sound... and she moved.'

'Maybe she uncomfortable. I go find someone help me turn her. Wait here.'

Where else would I be? thought Cat. 'Must you disturb her?'

The nurse looked at her in pity. 'Miss, she have bed sores.'

She left the room and returned with a houseman and Cat hovered anxiously. As they turned Ruth on to her side the houseman noticed her necklace – 'Ah, they should really have taken that off, but never mind, now.' Ruth's head rolled; she smiled sweetly and her eyes opened. Those dear green eyes in which there had so long been candour – could they deceive her now? But they were sightless, Ruth already in another world.

'Call us, Miss, if she change.'

Cat sat down again. Ruth was motionless, her breathing a brief, intermittent rising of her chest. On her face was an expression of peace, of serenity, as if she knew where she was going – as though she was floating deep beneath a sea where no current could disturb her, where the memories of wrongs done to her or which she had done were irrelevant. Once again, and with no conscious summons, Eliot spoke for her.

I said to my soul, be still, and let the dark come upon you, which shall be the darkness of God.

This was what her mother had called her 'last great journey, and was she reconciled?

The hours passed, they passed. Cat went to the window and looked out at the shimmering pinpricks of rain, and further away to a long line of red lights from traffic held up on the bypass. Other stories, other lives. An orange aura hung over the city, like a visitation, and high up in the glass she could see a clear reflection of her mother in her white bed – echoes of Chagall again. Her own reflection was more nebulous, distorted by the meniscus of the thick glass. She returned to her chair and took her mother's hand. It was warm but limp. She waited, watching her mother sleep.

A gasp, a sound deep in the throat, and it was over. No time to ring the bell. The monitor shrieked its horizontal line. She died quietly, unobtrusively, politely; now here, now elsewhere.

She lay in the foetal position, like a child, sleeping.

2

Cat found walking away from that room the hardest thing she had ever done. The Sister came in and offered to cover her mother's face, and when Cat demurred, reached up and put on the basin light, then she switched off all the other lights so that the room suddenly appeared more intimate, less austerely white. It was a considerate thing to do; just a pity that she couldn't have done it earlier.

Cat had no idea how long she stayed close to her mother's bed, chafing the still warm hand in hers, the fingers wilted, like a drooping plant. In death, Ruth's eyelids had parted to reveal a hint of green, but her face was already pallid, pinched and empty. Beneath her hospital gown her beloved Tsarist necklace, that long string of bars and tiny silver rosettes that had punctuated Cat's childhood memories, glinted in the feeble light. Carefully she reached out, undid the clasp and slid it slowly out from behind her mother's neck.

She didn't stay long after that; hers was the only breath that disturbed the air. A trolley appeared outside the room, laden with clean sheets; of course, they wanted the bed. Would she be able to bear it while they lifted Ruth on to a stretcher, hiding her bare, emaciated legs, her arms pressed carefully to their stomachs, trying to stop her head rolling for fear of upsetting the daughter, her blind eyes opening?

No.

At the door Cat stopped and looked back. The sight of her mother on the bed, small, sunk into the mattress, silent.

She went down to the night station to tell them she was leaving. The corridor was quiet, curtains drawn around the beds; the night not yet past. The Sister took one look at her, came round from behind the desk and took her by the arm.

'Are you all right, dear?' she said anxiously. 'A cup of tea, perhaps? You look quite white.'

Cat felt white. She felt she had absorbed into her whole body the whiteness of that room. Hair, cheeks, hands, quite white. Drained of life's blood, empty.

'I'm fine, thanks. I'll go now, I think. I just wanted to say thank you for all you've done. You've been very kind...'

'Oh, nice of you to say, but we're just doing our job.' She hesitated. 'You know what happens next? Never mind,' she added hastily, 'someone will be in touch, dear.'

Cat sat in her car for a long time, holding the necklace tightly in her closed fist. When she opened her fingers it slid out of her hand and on to her lap, glinting in the watery glow of early morning. She ran her fingers through the bars, looping it round and round, her eyes dry. Finally she put it round her neck under her shirt, next to her skin. It felt cool, then immediately warm.

Outside it was getting light, the orange streetlamps eclipsed by the early morning blue of the sky, extinguishing one by one ahead of her, like a Pied Piper in reverse. Far above, a plane chalked its passage silently across the clouds and small birds flew up, as if their ears were more attuned to it.

Cat drove slowly back to the house through the empty streets, and let herself in. She felt weary to the bone. With leaden feet, she mounted the stairs to the little room where she'd slept after leaving Bill. She had hardly the energy to turn back the covers, but stripped off her clothes, and in tee shirt and pants, slid between the cool sheets. She was asleep almost before her head hit the pillow.

She woke about four hours later. The sun was

streaming in through the windows on to her pillow, like the glow of the landing light of her early childhood. Remembering that she hadn't rung Ed she phoned him from the living room, kneeling on the carpet, the phone on her lap. He told her how worried he'd been but she could hardly find words to explain. She told him her mother had died in the night and that she was phoning from the house. Ed went very quiet, and then he asked her how she was feeling. She had no answer for him.

'You sound... you sound a bit strange.'

'Oh, sorry, Ed. I've just woken up.'

'You on your own there?'

'They flew out this morning.'

Immediately he offered to come but Cat said no; she had telephone calls to make and a funeral to arrange, but he insisted, so she gave him directions and they rang off.

She went upstairs, straightened her bed and got dressed. Then she went outside into the garden. It was choked with weeds. The sun was hot and very bright, casting strong purple shadows. In the shed she found a small hand fork, a trowel, a bucket and a grey metal wheelbarrow. She knelt down and started weeding. After a bit she noticed a tiny, rather straggly rosemary bush; a recent purchase, she guessed, but now half-strangled by convolvulus. As she cleared them away the scent lifted.

Rosemary for remembrance... pray you, love, remember.

She went back to the shed and found a large fork, dug up the little bush and found a plastic plant pot for it. She carried it round to the pavement and then returned to the garden. She cleared the weeds from the whole of the back border and down one side and filled the barrow with them. The withered petunias and the pansies had sunk on the soil for lack of water and she dug them out, gathered them up in her hands and threw them into the wheelbarrow. The purple of the petals shadowed her fingers, like ink. She fetched the mower, a bright red, long-handled thing with a long red flex, plugged it in through the kitchen window and started mowing. She mowed about half the lawn then raked up the debris into the wheelbarrow. It was now full so she fetched some green plastic sacks and emptied it and lugged them round the side of the house to the dustbin area. She was sweating by then. She did the other half of lawn, then took the mower round to the front and did that, too.

Much later the sky darkened again and it came on to rain, a light, gentle rain that danced in the sunlight. She stood the barrow upright beside the shed and put the tools away, wiping them down with a rag, one of several that she found in a carrier bag hanging up on a bent nail. A tattered vest with little ribbon straps: thermal, size S.

She stood in the doorway gazing at the garden. It looked better. She sat on the step, her knees apart. She felt tired, faint. The rain was cool on her forehead and on her cheeks. She leaned her head against the doorway. Eventually, she slept.

She woke to find Ed standing in front of her. He helped her to her feet. She was stiff, and very cold. It had stopped raining, but the sun had gone. The sky was sullen, grey.

'Oh, Ed...' Her head buzzed with the sound of her voice. 'I forgot you were coming.'

'What's that? You're whispering...'

Strange, she thought, and cleared her throat. 'Sorry. What time is it?'

'After four. I rang the bell but there was no answer, so I came round. Catherine, you look awful. You're very white.'

'It was the room.' She was chilled through.

He put his arms round her and rubbed her back hard to warm her. 'Catherine, have you really been out here all day? Why've you been gardening, after what...

261

There's a plant of some sort sitting by your car.'

'Not all day,' she said, her face muffled in his shoulder. 'I did a bit then sort of took time off. Sorry, Ed, I lost track. I don't know why I did it. It needed doing, that's all, so I did it. And it's a rosemary bush – I'm taking it back with me. Sorry, I'd have put it straight in the car but my keys were in the house.'

'Don't keep apologising. Come in the house.' He took her hand. 'Have you had anything to eat?'

Cat thought about that. 'I had a roll with something.'

'When, this morning?'

'Um, it must have been yesterday.'

'What, nothing since then? For goodness sake, let's get you something to eat! You must be starving.'

In the kitchen she started shivering. She went to the sink and scrubbed her hands. The dirt was under her nails. She dried her hands on a folded tea towel and rubbed it over her face. Ed filled the kettle and it began to make a swishing noise.

'Where's the tea?' He was opening cupboards.

'Here.' She took the old pock-marked tin from the shelf over the kettle. 'I'm sorry, Ed, I'm dozy.'

'You're tired and hungry, that's all. Go and sit down, and I'll bring it in. There's no bread, is there?'

'Nothing. Oh, a box of Matzos.'

Ed was only a little while making the tea, but she had gone to sleep again by the time he came in. He brought buttered Matzos with Marmite but she found it too salty to eat. The tea was scalding. She could feel it in her throat and in her stomach. She looked down. Her knees were dirty with soil and bits of grass.

'Sorry, I ought to go up and get changed,' she muttered. 'I'm too grubby to be in here. She'd hate it.'

He took her arm and helped her up. He banged his arm against the banister as they squeezed together up the stairs. She went to the bathroom, filled the basin, and picked up Ruth's face flannel. It was like cardboard. She soaked it in hot water and wiped her legs and knees, rinsed it under running water and wiped down her chest and under her arms. A 'possible' wash, her mother had called it – down as far as possible. She ran the water cold again and wiped her face, holding the flannel to her eyes for what seemed ages. Echoes of Bill, and that other bruising.

In the bedroom Ed passed her the tea and she drank it thankfully, sitting on the side of the bed, and then he stood her up and helped her undress. He noticed the necklace, fingered it lightly, and asked her if she wanted to keep it on. She nodded, bunching it in her fist. She felt the touch of his hands on her skin as he pulled her tee shirt over her head, a brief, fleeting touch, almost impersonal, but intimate enough to confuse her; she did not want, at that moment, to acknowledge his masculinity. She thought, maybe he's undressed someone like this before, in some bedroom or other. Of course, his wife, when she was ill. She had no room in her mind to dwell on it, but got into bed and turned her face to the wall. She was conscious that Ed stood looking down at her for a long time before he finally left. She heard the door close behind him.

She lay perfectly still with her eyes wide open, unconsciously studying the wallpaper, a repeated pattern of pastel green and blue stripes interspersed with tiny silver flowers. She had never noticed before how the silver of the flowers greyed as they climbed the wall or how, where the wall met the ceiling, they were almost brown, as if damp. The effect of light on metal, she thought; sometime I must have a go at something metal. She closed her eyes and shut her mind against thought. She let everything go; she just wanted to rest. She felt her eyelids quiver, and then she sank blissfully into sleep.

When she awoke it was nearly dark. The house seemed so still she thought he'd gone and she came right awake and sat up. On the bedside table was a note. 'Gone shopping'.

That's OK then, she thought, he's coming back. She got up and went across to the bathroom and had a shower, washing her hair and scrubbing her nails again. Her hands looked old, shrivelled, the skin rippling, the veins blue, and she took some of her mother's hand-cream and rubbed it into her hands. Afterwards she wrapped herself in a towel and went hunting for clothes. She found some of her old jeans in a bottom drawer and a light sweater. Remnants of her youth.

She put out cutlery, turning the stainless steel back and forth in the light and ruminating. She found a couple of paper napkins, two glasses and two mats. Then she went outside, unlocked the car and put the rosemary bush into the boot. The street was quiet, but she could hear the drone of rush hour traffic from the main road. She went back in and sat down on the sofa. She waited in the still, quiet room, surrounded by her mother's things.

Ed brought bread, steak, salad and a bottle of wine, and cooked supper.

3

'I picked up the portrait, do you mind?'

'What? Oh, no, I'm glad. Does it look OK?'

He was wearing, she noticed suddenly, a pair of very dark blue slacks and a pale blue shirt. He looked tanned. His eyes were very blue in the lamplight.

'It looks great.' He chuckled. 'But we had problems getting into the workshop. You'd taken the key with you.'

'Oh... It's in my bag. No, it's in the car. Gosh. But you got in all right?'

'Eventually. Your picture framing friend had another key. I told him we'd had a journey ahead of us, but he said you don't need an excuse; you might have done it anyway.'

'I suppose I might.'

Ruth was always late, and so disorganised.

'Talking of journeys, you ought to get that car of yours serviced. It'll let you down one day. When did you last have it done?'

'I've never had it done.'

'Perhaps you need another one.'

So Gus had said, eons ago, and she made the same reply. 'Sometime.'

They were quiet.

'Anyway, I'm hanging on to the portrait for a while. People are away at the moment, but they'll have a party in the autumn.'

'I thought there wouldn't be a party.'

'Well, rumour says different.'

'And you had space for it?'

'I took something down, put this one up. No problem.'

'Good. I'm glad.' She chewed a piece of meat.

'Gus asked after you. And Ricci. I went to the studio, looked them up.'

'You did? They did? That was nice.'

He'd bought a tart for pudding so Cat tried some, but it dry and synthetic.

'I heard from Marie-Beth,' he said. 'She's coming over in the Fall. She's having a baby at last. She's had some trouble, but she's OK, now.'

'So, you'll be a grandfather, then.'

'That's right. I shall enjoy it. Do you think I can do that; do it properly?'

'I'm sure you can. You'll be a great grandfather.'

He laughed. 'Not yet, Catherine.'

Cat looked at him, mystified.

'Not a great-grandfather, not yet awhile.'

'Oh...' she said. 'No, I suppose not.'

He sat still, watching her, his face serious. She could feel the muscles in her cheeks.

'You're hiding, Catherine, you know that?'

Startled, she said, 'I'm not! What, from you?'

'Well, if not from me, from, I don't know. Everything else, perhaps. Your mother's death, maybe...'

He leaned back in his chair, nursing his drink, one leg crossed over the other. It was dark outside, and Cat got up to draw the curtains. She could hear children playing in the recreation area, and in the opposite house a woman was looking out of her window. The light was behind her and Cat thought, she'll be able to see right in...

From behind her she heard his voice, asking something. She heard the echo, 'Have you cried?' When she said no, he said, 'Don't you want to?' It seemed a strange question – who wants to cry? – so she made no reply, but stood looking across the road. The woman was still there. Their eyes met. In her eyes Cat could see herself standing there – is that the daughter?

'Catherine? You want to tell me about it? You want to tell me what happened in the hospital? With your uncle and aunt? You want to talk?'

Cat closed the curtains. She felt lethargic, disconnected. She sat down on the sofa, clutching a cushion to her chest. Ed pulled up her mother's chair. It was a high backed Queen Anne chair with stumpy mahogany legs, the green dralon with which her mother had covered it worn to a blue-ish sheen. It was a bit small for Ed.

'Come back to me, Catherine.' He reached out and put a finger on her knee; a pause, a breath, a reminder: I am here. She looked at him miserably, picking at loose threads on the cushion.

'Here, let me sit beside you.' He settled himself on the sofa next to her. 'Come into my arms, Catherine.'

She lay back on his shoulder thankfully, his arms round her over the cushion. It felt good, as if she belonged there.

'You ought to talk about it, if you can,' he said quietly. 'Seems to me it's all bottled up.'

'It is,' she said thickly. 'It is bottled up.'

'Then let it out. Speak to me.'

'How...' The words stuck in her throat. 'How do you speak of the unspeakable?'

She told him how her mother had died, quietly, courteously, how the room was suddenly empty. She felt him nod. She told him how warm-hearted Amit was, and, by contrast, how forbidding and cold Reuben was, and how he'd wept by Ruth's bedside, wiping his face. Then she told him what he had said at the dinner table after Amit had gone.

'*She* said her father was a Rabbi, but Reuben said he was a doctor. OK, you might forget things; you might get them wrong, but you don't get something like that wrong, do you?'

'You're talking about your mother?'

Cat looked at him in surprise. 'Of course. And the ghetto – she'd never speak about it, and I never knew why. But I know why now,' she said bitterly. 'Because there wasn't a ghetto, not for her. He was quite adamant about it.' She swallowed. 'Ed, I'm not saying that I *want* there to have been a ghetto, or anything... Or that her experience, whatever it was, wasn't somehow valid without it... It sounds...'

'Don't worry how it sounds. No, you're reaching for what's true, what's authentic. Go on.'

Cat half-turned to face him. 'I always suspected there was something fishy about all this,' she said painfully. 'To anyone else it would have been glaringly obvious. I don't want to say anything against her, but in my heart I think I knew all along... Yet it's taken *this*... having to listen to Reuben. That was... I can't tell you what it was like. It was excruciating.'

'What else did your Mom tell you that you're not sure about?'

'Well, she told me they'd gone to Israel, I mean Palestine, by coal barge. I asked her once – from which docks, I said, and why not a proper ship? I distinctly remember asking her that, because that was the first time I ever looked at a map of Germany.'

'Germany is land-locked on its southern side,' he remarked. 'So what did she say?'

'She got distressed, as though I was catching her out, or something, and she wouldn't answer. Perhaps I should have made her. Stupidly, I didn't.'

'Catherine, you can't make people answer questions if they don't want to. And you weren't stupid. You were young, you respected her, and it was a question of trust.'

'Yes,' she said, 'exactly.'

They were silent, then she said, 'But don't you see, if there was no ghetto, there was no transportation either. I mean, for her. He was angry, Ed, very, very angry. He said it was just a load of nonsense.'

'He said 'nonsense'?'

'Yes, that was the word he used.'

'Have you ever asked your Aunt Hannah about all

this?'

'No, we've never been in touch. She'd be too frail now, anyway, so how can I? I don't know if she even knows about my mother's illness – unless Reuben or Amit have told her.' She twisted round to face him again. 'But what I can't get my head around is why she should lie? Reuben called them stories, but he meant lies. How could someone have a genuinely traumatic, life-changing experience – because, quite obviously, *something* happened to her! – and then, when they're talking about it, exaggerate it so much that it becomes almost meaningless?' She punched herself in the chest, hard. 'And to *me*, her own daughter! A deliberate distortion!'

'Catherine...'

'Wasn't it bad enough without making things up as well? I was terribly young when she first told me all this. Much too young to hear the sort of stuff she told me. Why would she do that? Why tell me things which were frightening and horrible and... and hideous, but hadn't really happened? All those *nightmares...*'

'Why're you calling her 'she' all the time?' he interjected. 'Her name's Ruth, isn't it?'

'Yes,' said Cat stiffly, 'that was her given name. But I'll tell this my own way, if that's OK.'

'Whatever. I just thought...'

'Oh, never mind.' Cat felt exhausted. 'Anyway, I grew up thinking it was such a burden to her that she had to share it, and there wasn't anyone else, so she shared it with me. But, you know, Ed, it was a burden to me, too.' Her words almost ran away with her. 'And what about my own problems? Look,' she said, 'I'll tell you something. You know how I learned about periods?'

'Periods?'

'Oh, the menstrual cycle, Ed. I was eleven, pre-pubescent and my mother sent me upstairs to fetch what she called 'a little package' and to put it on the fire. When I saw it, a soggy little red bundle sitting on the stairs, I was terrified. I said nothing, just picked it up and did as I was told. Now, I thought, I'll be really alone. Anyway, one night she heard me crying and came into me. I told her in the end. I said, "Are you dying, Ma?" She asked me, she *asked* me, Ed, what on earth had put that fear into my head. I said, "The package; it was full of blood." She spoke more sensitively, then, about how a girl becomes a woman. She spoke about the wonder of it, and its grace. But I was too angry to listen. For me there was no wonder, and whatever grace there might have been was sullied by my rage, that my mother always made a mystery of things she couldn't bear to talk about. She was in no way ashamed of herself or her methods. And that was typical of her.'

'What a terrible story...'

She felt exhausted. What she had told him was true but she felt deeply ashamed to be criticising her mother when she'd just died.

'Ed, I'm sorry to go on about it, but if you're a young girl on your own, with no siblings, no friends, who else do you share things with except your mother? All through my growing-up years... But my problems seemed trivial in comparison with what she'd suffered. I already felt guilty because I even existed. Without me round her neck she'd have managed better...'

'No, no, you mustn't say that. You can't go down that road...'

'Oh, *can't* I?' she retorted. 'What about before I was ten? You think she wasn't struggling then? With a young child, no job, no means of support?'

'How *did* she support herself?'

'She took in washing. Scrimped and saved, and what for? To look after *me*! She must have worried herself sick! But now I wonder if she suffered at all, at least, not in the way she said, the ghetto, the camp, or whatever it was... What on earth am I to believe?'

270

She stared at him and then away. 'I don't know what's left. And look what it's done to me!'

She felt him smile. 'What do you mean, what it's done to you?'

Cat lifted her hands helplessly. She'd never told him about Bill, and wasn't going to start.

'My life, Ed. My stupid, broken, *futile* life.'

He was quiet. 'Catherine, I think you must trust your intuition over this. Also, remember what I said about false memory syndrome? Memory is always flawed in some way. But we accept many things as true which we can't personally remember, although I must admit there's usually evidence to help us along; other people's accounts, photos, things like that. Something verifiable. But I understand where you're at. To be told so compellingly that something we've been told by someone we trust, never actually happened is an almost impossible thing to accept. It goes against all you hold most dear. So, as I say, I think you have to trust your intuition. And that may mean just trusting your mother.'

'But that's the whole trouble!' she exclaimed. 'How *can* I trust her? I do it, too, what Reuben said. I've *always* pretended...'

'Pretended things were worse?'

'No, better, actually. Or just... different.'

'We all do that. We wouldn't get through otherwise.'

'As for my intuition, I don't know that I have any. Reuben was so... so utterly categorical.'

'You believed he was speaking the truth?'

Cat sighed. 'Oh, Ed, why would he lie?'

Ed shifted his legs, and she curled up against him once more. She felt sleepy and angry at the same time, and her eyes were pricking again.

'As for the doctor thing,' he said. 'If your uncle's a secular Jew, he might be embarrassed at having a Rabbi for a father and might have thought a doctor sounded less religious.'

'Oh, if *he's* telling lies, it complicates things even more!'

'Yes, it does, and we'll probably never know. It seems to me, Catherine,' he added slowly, his deep voice in her ear, 'that there's more than one question here. I don't want to upset you more than you are already – quite rightly, I may add – but the first question is, why it should matter to you so much.' Cat jumped slightly and he pressed her arm. 'No, I'm not saying it *shouldn't* matter, because it obviously does, but what effect does knowing her story was false – and I'm not convinced it was – have on your life *now*? You need to ask that. Maybe, just maybe, Catherine, it shouldn't matter quite so much, not after all these years...'

She had put the same idea to Ricci, and it was as crass then as it was now. She sat up completely, and turned to face him.

'But I've only just found out! It's fresh in my mind! And I can't exactly ask her, can I?'

'OK, well that's only the first question...'

'No, Ed you don't understand! The number of years is completely irrelevant. You ought to know that – you've listened to Ricci as well! Don't you see, if you're repeatedly told something... if it's underlined again and again and again... and if it gives you nightmares... and if it effects how you grow, how you relate, what choices you make, and if, all the time this is going on, nothing ever, ever gets better...' She choked.

'Catherine, Catherine!' he said gently. 'Just relax. We're going to sort this out together, OK?' He stoked her arm soothingly, and then he did something which no one else had ever done; he laid his warm palm on her forehead. She hadn't enjoyed being told to relax, but she closed her eyes, and breathed deeply. She could have stayed like that for a long time. And she did relax. She could even have fallen asleep.

'Catherine,' he said slowly, 'why exactly do you

believe Reuben over your mother?'

Reluctantly, Cat roused herself. 'Because, Ed, except for me, he was the person nearest to her; he was her twin. And what's more, he's the first adult I've met who actually knew her during those years.'

'That doesn't make him right.'

'But if he isn't, why pretend the ghetto, the trains, the camps, didn't happen? When, by doing so, he denies not only the horror of it all, but its terrible consequences as well. It would have had a shattering effect on his life. I asked Amit direct questions, Ed, and she just went on and on about the situation in Israel, as if *that* had anything to do with it!'

'Something, perhaps. Well, let's sleep on that one. But we've still two more questions to ask.'

My God, she thought; the military mind! But then, she thought rebelliously, he can afford to be detached. But God help me if I ever get into an argument with him!

'The third question,' he continued, 'is what you asked before, why your mother should lie to you – or rather, let's say reconstructed things. Well, people do that all the time, either because they've lost hold of reality, or because they fear not being believed – or sometimes just to get attention. I don't suppose any of those can be true of your mother, not to the extent of making things up and not when she was talking to her own child. And she sure had your attention. So where does that get us?'

Cat was silent, leaving it to him.

'Maybe there was something else, apart from words, I mean. Did anything particularly frighten her when you were growing up? I'm just looking at the options. Something that might have disturbed her deeply, but which she didn't actually talk about with you?'

Then Cat remembered what she should have remembered all along.

'There was something. That particular dream I told

you about. Not her dream; mine. The one about the planes, and how I used to wake up absolutely terrified. And she was always there, and she was crying too. And lately I've come to the conclusion that it wasn't *my* fear of planes which had woken me, but her fear, which she had somehow transmitted to me. Not fear of planes, necessarily... and perhaps not even fear,' she added. 'Grief, perhaps, for those people she knew left behind in Germany. She didn't make that up, did she? So why make up other things?'

She stood up and went to the window again, and pulled aside the curtain. Cars lined the road, glinting under the streetlamps, and the houses opposite were dark. It was very late. She stood there for a moment, trying to settle her mind, her arms folded tightly over her chest.

'All this,' she said quietly, 'it's a revelation in a way. I suppose I ought to be grateful. It shows me what I'm really like. Even to speculate like this, to *ask* such questions about her, my own blood – it makes me... ashamed. All my life,' she said, talking to the empty street, 'I've compromised. Placated. Made concessions. I'm not strong-minded enough, I suppose...'

'Come on, that's a bit hard on yourself...'

She turned to him. '... but I have learned the difference between truth and... lies!'

Ed shook his head, a gesture of protest. 'No, Catherine, it's not that black and white. In any experience people are bound to exaggerate some things and play down others, gloss over some things and bring others into tighter focus. You've got to take into account the grey areas – you know that in your painting.'

Cat could have screamed at him. 'My *painting*? Ed, for goodness sake, I'm talking about matters of life and death! Bone of my bone, don't you see? I need to know the truth, the objective truth of what happened!'

'That's what I'm saying,' he said mildly. 'Since when

has truth been objective?'

Ah, that she could understand. In the making, the distorting. She looked at him without speaking. It had calmed her, as he had probably known it would.

'Ed, if you do it as an artist,' she said quietly, 'at least you're *aware* you're doing it. And you do it to reveal *more* of the truth, not less. She must have known what she was doing, because, otherwise, it's... it's sick.'

He pushed himself up out of the chair, and went across to her.

'Well, maybe she *was* sick. Trauma can cause all sorts of sickness; it's common knowledge.' He wrapped his arms around her folded arms. '*And* nightmares, *and* indecisiveness, even impaired memory, as I know from the men I've served with, and you don't have to be sick to have it.' He laid his cheek against hers. 'But she's still your mother, Catherine, and she made her own choices. She told you what she needed to tell you, that's all.'

They stared at each other for a minute, and then she heard the ticking of the clock. It was nearly midnight.

'Ed, the time! You can stay, can't you?'

'I'm afraid I can't, lady. I have a meeting tomorrow at nine. Some VIP's coming over from Paris. Everyone's away, so they've hauled me out of mothballs. But you'll drop off at High Wycombe tomorrow night?'

'Yes, I'd love to.'

It will be something to hold on to, she thought, while I do what has to be done.

'And don't worry about me. The roads'll be empty. Now come and sit down again for a minute. Go on, relax. There, that's better. Glad to see you obey me. Augers well. Now I'm afraid there's one final question we need to look at.' He hesitated. 'I am not sure how to put it, but it's this...'

He spoke slowly. 'Maybe, in the last analysis, you're

not being asked to *believe* your mother, or even understand her. Just to... to respond to her.'

She looked at him blankly, and he explained. 'Well, we grow up expecting our parents to be right all the time, don't we? Or in the right. Straightforward. Truthful. Your mother, she was always there for you, you said.'

'Yes,' said Cat slowly. 'After my tenth birthday.'

'Well, perhaps all she needed was your response.'

'My response?'

'Yes. To accept her for who she was. So, who was she, to you?'

Cat shrugged, not sure what he wanted from her. 'She was... she was just Ma. She was... my mother.'

'And she loved you?'

She nodded, and couldn't stop nodding.

'Yes, she loved me.' She covered her face and began to cry, deep, heart-felt choking sobs that shook her whole body. 'She *did* love me...' she wailed. 'She did, didn't she? And I ... and I loved her... And I still... I still *do*!'

'Well, Catherine, that's all there is to it. What else matters?'

4

A barrage of questions, a veritable bombardment. No, she shouldn't exaggerate, merely four; the fourth quartet, the unforeseen, insidious fourth quartet. And she was in that world too.

It was not until the next morning, as she strolled round the little garden with her coffee, that it dawned on her that the questions still hung in the air. She had slept well, exhausted but calmed, but now, in the cold light of day, she wondered if the answers they had found were just too superficial, mere speculation, fabricated for her peace of mind and unreliable. So perhaps she should just do what Ed wanted; let it all go, and think of her future instead. Soon she would start painting again, and the thought gave her new courage. If it was roots she was seeking, she could make them in her work.

For the moment she had to do what needed to be done for Ruth. First, she phoned the funeral director and was connected to a very brisk and competent young man.

'You need to phone her vicar, fix a date and time, and then get back to us, OK? And the name of the deceased? Feugler? Was she Jewish, by any chance? If so, you'll want the Rabbi. There's a synagogue in town. I'll get the number. I've got it right here...'

Timidly she interrupted. A church would be fine, she said, wanting to affirm her mother's late conversion.

'Where did the deceased live? Oh, Phoenix Way? Well, her parish church is quite near, just down the road in the shopping centre.'

By mid-morning the date was fixed for the following Monday. The vicar offered to call round and discuss the service, but Cat told him she lived miles away, and needed to get home. Then she remembered that Ruth had asked for the *Kaddish*. She began to look for a prayer-book, and on the way got distracted by other titles; mostly European or Russian, huddled together on the shelf. Thomas Mann, arm in arm with Goethe and Gunter Grasse; Gustave Flaubert, sidling up to Maupassant; Turgenev with Tolstoy, two volumes of Paustovsky's *Childhood* shouldering a slim volume of Chekhov's play, *The Seagull*. If they could speak, she thought, could they tell me the truth of Ruth?

Alongside them were her mother's translations, loose-leafed pages with yellowing canvas spines, her name flowing out from the title page: *Translated by Ruth Feugler*. Two, at least, reminded her of her childhood, of the little stack of dusty second hand books on the breakfast table in High Wycombe, the ones her mother had toyed with and then put away, unable to cope with the brutality of their prose. Had she translated those as well? Had she, at last, heard her father's voice?

The prayer book was squashed like a conscience between two Bible commentaries, large solid tomes in High German Gothic, its black leather cover faded and curled upwards at the back corners, for it was read from right to left. On the flyleaf was a faded inscription, *Matteus Feugler*; Ruth's father, then; the Rabbi – or the doctor. On the left hand page were the phonetics and the German translation; on the right, the mysterious Hebrew characters. She experimented with the phonetics, her voice loud in the empty room, her mother's accent on her tongue. Ah, yes, but was it accurate? She fetched the telephone directory and found the name of a local Rabbi.

A woman answered.

'Sorry to disturb you, but could I possibly speak to –' Cat hastily checked the telephone directory – 'Rabbi Fisher?'

Fischer? Fugle? Flügelhorn?

'Speaking.' Cat was surprised – a female rabbi? But why not?

'Well, my mother's just died in the hospital, and...'

'You want to book a funeral?' The voice was businesslike, startlingly insensitive.

'Not exactly, but you see, she wanted the *Kaddish* and...'

'You want to book the synagogue?'

'Actually,' Cat said, 'it's taking place at the local church...'

'She *was* Jewish, though, or she converted?' Shock-horror? No, resignation.

Cat prevaricated, refusing to explain. 'It's the family...'

'A mixed marriage?'

'*Yes,*' Cat spoke firmly, tired of being interrogated, 'but my mother particularly asked for the *Kaddish*, and *that's* what I'm actually ringing about. I've got the prayer here,' she added quickly. 'You wouldn't just listen to me over the phone, would you?'

'You read Hebrew?'

'Sorry, I meant the phonetics.'

'OK, then, if you insist,' she said impatiently. 'But, *Kaddish*, over the telephone? That's most unorthodox...'

Dead right it's un-Orthodox.

'I'll start then, shall I?' Cat suggested. 'Um, here we go... *Yitgaddal v'yitkaddash - sh'meh rabba b'alma - di v'ra chir'uteh...'*

The Rabbi interrupted. 'You say you don't speak Hebrew? You read it very well,' she added grudgingly, 'but you aren't saying it as though you understand it. You have the English translation?'

Cat hesitated. 'Actually it's in German.'

'Oh, is it?' Cat could almost hear her mind ticking, making connections, getting interested. 'Well then, find a translation. And you need to know when to emphasise some of the words and the pauses. Like this: *yit gaddal*, pause, *v'yitkaddash,* pause, *sh'meh rabba b'alma*, slight pause, *di v'ra chir'u-teh...* and the pauses are also between the 'v' or the 'b' and the next syllable. But short ones, not breaths; like this – *v-yitkaddash*... Study the translation and you'll do OK.'

'But you haven't heard it through!'

'I've heard enough. The pattern's the same throughout. Just study it. You say you don't speak Hebrew? You've been to Israel, perhaps?'

'No. But will I really be OK?'

'If you pause in the right places. And try and find out what's *intended* by the prayer. Have you a Commentary?'

Cat glanced at the rows of books. 'I can find one, I think. I'll have a read of it.'

The Rabbi sighed heavily. 'No, try to *pray* it! But perhaps you don't pray?'

Cat was silent.

'If you don't pray,' the Rabbi asked, now thoroughly exasperated, 'why do it?'

'I said. It was what my mother wanted.'

Yit'gadal v'yit'kadash sh'mei raba. b'al'ma di v'ra khir'utei... May His great Name grow exalted and sanctified in the world that He created as He willed.

Were the camps what He willed? Would this not stick in her throat as she said it? Would it have stuck in her mother's throat? And had it been faith on her part or merely slavish ritual?

She phoned her children and left messages; then Israel, spoke to Amit. They were awkward with each other; neither could finish their sentences.

'Reuben's not well, or he'd come to the phone.'

'I'm sorry to hear that,' she said politely. 'I do hope it's nothing...'

'Well, Caterina, I think he's just very...'

'He must be tired, especially after... Please do give him my...'

'I will. Caterina, are you phoning about Rute's...?'

Cat gave her the time and the place, promised to arrange a lift from the station and rang off. Next she phoned Ricci to bring him up to date.

Gus answered the phone. 'When're you coming home?' he asked. ''Cos there's something here for you.'

'In the post, you mean?'

'No. Well, I'll tell you. A pot.'

'One of yours? Why, thank you, that's amazing! I'm very touched.' And she was.

He sighed. 'Cat, it's no big deal, OK? You don't buy 'em, do you, so, what the hell, you've been a bit down recently, so I thought I'd make you one. It's nothing fancy. For a plant, or something. It's very high-fired so it won't leak at the bottom.'

'That's really very sweet of you, Gus. I can't wait to see it.'

'O*kay*. No big deal, OK? Anyway, see you soon... By the way, you've got sales. Some of your down-and-outs – they'll have to wash, now.' She heard him guffaw down the phone and smiled to herself. 'And the woman with the patterned scarf, she's gone.'

'You made sales too?

'Yeah, some. It was an OK show.'

5

Later she phoned Ed, thinking he would be home, but there was no answer and she felt suddenly bereft. Everything was still, the street empty of traffic, but around her, abruptly, was a tentative, whispering sound, soft as the murmur of awakened sleepers, as insistent as tinnitus. As if the story was not yet finished, that there was more to tell. Or for her to learn. The furniture stared blindly into space, but the walls seemed to shift around her, and Ruth's books and pictures, each mutely suggestive of her inner life, blinked at each other across the room. Other, more private papers whispered to her from her mother's bedroom and she sprinted upstairs. The room was cluttered with furniture from the old house; the familiar oak bureau and the matching chest of drawers and dressing table, an upright chair and a single bed. Beside it lay an old rag rug, its original blue, like the curtains, washed out like cataracts. On the wall a faded print of Vermeer's *Girl with a Pearl Earring* stared at Cat like an accusation, her eyes round, startled, her mouth open in an inaudible mutter. Mutter, Mutti, Mother... where are your clues?

On the dressing table were her mother's outmoded hair brush and mirror, the backs delicately embroidered in plastic-covered blue silk, and a small vase of blue silk flowers.

The dressing table had a top drawer which she opened cautiously, conscious of intruding where she had little right. Unlike her own top drawer, which was cluttered with old makeup and unused jars of face cream, it was nearly empty. There was a small pile of handkerchiefs, some rolls of meticulously darned nylon stockings and, in the corner, an empty bottle of *eau de cologne*, which Ruth must have kept for the sheer pleasure of its paddled shape. For the first time in her life Cat read the tiny, almost indecipherable, words on the label:

ECHT KOLNISCH WASSER
Eau de Cologne&Parfumerie-Fabrik
"Glockengasse No. 4711"
KOLN a. RH. /COLOGNE.

The words sat harshly on her mental tongue.

The key to the bureau was where it had always been, carefully taped on the back. She drew up the bedroom chair, put the key in the lock and slowly lowered the lid.

The whispering stopped.

It was a tiny piece of furniture, revealing several compartments in which three notebooks stood upright, held together by a slightly perished elastic band. Flat on the shelf were two brown envelopes, one labelled *Catherine* – not Caterina, but her given name. With shaking hands Cat opened it, which was easy enough as her frugal mother had licked only the very edge of the flap. Inside was a postcard of another Vermeer, *The Little Street,* showing the gable end of a redbrick house above a cobbled pavement, with a separate gate into an alleyway, a Dutch version of their house in Green Street. Cat turned it over, and felt a paroxysm of grief at the sight of her mother's careful, slightly Germanic script.

My darling daughter Catherine, my angel.

After I die I want you to have my necklace. It has always been my talisman. It is C19 Tsarist. All my life since I was a girl I longed for you to have it. Apart from you, it is my only treasure. It comes to you through the female line, so wear it for love of me, and then pass it on to Deborah.

I will always love you, darling, come what may.

RUTH MATHILDE FEUGLER

Cat held the note in her hand for a long time, running her fingers over the words, her eyes pricking. Then she felt round her neck for the necklace, the necklace of her childhood which Ruth had worn next to her skin, which she had twisted in her fingers when distressed. The necklace that had pooled into Cat's hand at the hospital, and that she had fisted in her hand when Ed put her to bed. Other than a couple of inexpensive watches bought on the market – and once, regretted, from a catalogue – it was her mother's only piece of jewellery; one of two items, she'd said, that her grandfather had brought from his home when he had fled Russia during the pogroms. The other was a samovar, now 'lost', which Cat had assumed meant pawned, probably in his early years in Germany.

But 'talisman'. She thought that was an item of protection. But protection from what?

She picked up the second envelope: *The Last Will and Testament of Ruth Mathilde Feugler*.

A few sentences revealed that, apart from a few goodwill items, her mother had left her all her goods, such as they were, and the house. Her mother's music was left 'to my dearest friend, Leopold Heim'; her books, save those that Cat could choose, to the library; her clothes to the charity shop, Children in Need, 'for the other volunteers'. She'd known that Ruth frequented charity shops, but it was news to her that she'd worked in one. And who was Leopold Heim?

Cat sat at the bureau, poring over her mother's papers. She discovered more about her, then, than she had ever dreamed. The notebooks were her own school exercise books; one recycled as an address book, labelled in Ruth's neat hand and crammed with the names of her friends. Some she had scored through, perhaps as they had died or moved away, or carefully pasted over with lined paper. Mostly Germanic or Jewish names: Blum, Frankel, Heim, Katzenstein,

Muller, Rosenberg, Stein – the list was endless, though there were some distinctively English names, too, and one lonely Asian, Indira Patel. The book was thick with inserts – backs of envelopes, mostly, filled with her mother's distinctive script; old entries in faded, greenish ink, the later ones in blue biro, turned sepia with age, the more recent ones in thin blue felt-tip, as if rootless Ruth was conducting some private experiment in permanence.

Two more exercise books, frayed at the corners; one, *Catherine Feugler Standard V FRENCH,* re-labelled Music Group, the other *ENG LIT,* now Reading Group, together with her mother's current diary, its weekly entries showing that the groups had met regularly in her house.

What music did they play? The Romanticks, as Reuben might have said? And on what? A fiddle here, a keyboard there, a couple of CD's, a discussion, followed by lemon tea or, her other favourite tea, English Breakfast, and Ruth's own tea bread? Cat could remember that tea bread, concocted from raisins soaked overnight in black tea, then mixed with eggs and flour.

And did they read Ruth's own translations? Or did they, for goodness sake, read them in the original, her Turgenev and Mann, her Goethe and her Maupassant, her Victor Hugo... Cat could imagine the conversations, guttural and acerbic, the shrieking cackles of caustic laughter distributing crumbs, homely, slightly barbed comments; the sharp, wily intelligence of those Ruth called her friends.

That was the point. Not only had Ruth survived, she had overcome, but Cat thought, how immensely sad that she hadn't found friends earlier, not only to serve her own happiness, but to lessen the burden she'd laid on me, her own child. In the end she hadn't needed me at all.

A bitter thought, *post mortem*.

Selecting a few names from the address book, she started telephoning.

Ella Adamson, with the slightest of accents: 'To think Ruti is no more! We're on summer recess, you know – my God, Ruti already sent her apologies for September! Do you think she knew, and was saying goodbye? My God, I'm appalled. I could have visited her in hospital. Why didn't she let us know? Well, excuse me, but you want to talk to Leo Heim. He plays with the Birmingham Symphony Orchestra, you know, the violin. Zo, we'll get together for the funeral? Ach, to think of it! In a church, you say? Well, what does the place matter, anyway? It's all the one God.'

Maria Blum, in a rush of Messianic piety: 'Oh the dear soul may she rest in peace she's with the Lord oh the Lord have mercy she's home at last with the dear angels in heaven oh praise Jesus where we all long to be...'

This had to be interrupted.

'Mrs Blum, thank you, but do excuse me; I've other calls...'

'Oh *bless* you, dear... but you need to talk to Leo Heim.'

Rachel Stein's voice was soft to the point of being inaudible, and strongly Germanic.

'You must talk to Leo Heim,' she whispered. 'He was so good to her, my dear. We had finished for the evening, but he went back in to say something to Rute. Then we heard the sound of her playing.' A run of tears in her voice. 'I sink that was the first time she played the piano since Chermany... well, not a real piano, a keyboard. None of us knew she could, you see. She never said. We just thought her a werry cultured woman who liked to listen. Ask Leo about it, see what he says. Ach, well, zo now she is gone.'

Since everyone wanted her to ring Leo Heim, she did so, and asked him to elucidate.

'Yes, we were very close, Rute and I; she was my friend,' he said soberly. 'I'd bring my keyboard, and she'd play her childhood studies for me. No one else knew at first. Look,' he added, 'I'll tell you the story, how they found out. One day, after we thought the others had left, I gave her this old LP, still in its brown cover. You know what it was?' His voice was alight with triumph. 'Artur Schnabel playing Beethoven's Third Piano Concerto. Her teacher, and the piece she'd have played in Dresden. I'd brought the manuscript with me so she could try it on the keyboard. So there we were, with the tears running down her face. She remembered it, you see, every note. And the sound brought the other people into the room, and they gathered round, like she was having her concert at last. And they said, "Rute, your eyes are wet, are you crying?" And very slowly, she said, "Yes, I am crying. I am crying because Gott is so good!"'

Cat listened avidly; this was the first time she had gleaned details of her mother's private life, or who she was to her friends.

'So, with your permission,' he continued, 'I shall play her the *Kol Nidre* at the funeral, the prayer from *Yom Kippur*. You know the words?' He began to intone. '*We will forgive those who may hurt us, whether deliberately or by accident, and pardon fully those who may not keep their promises, obligations or oaths between this Day of Atonement and the Day of Atonement to come.*'

It was exactly the same prayer which she had used when bargaining with God over her marriage, and hearing it again, Cat felt slightly faint.

'You mightn't think those words appropriate for a funeral,' said Leo, 'but I assure you they are. They used them as they walked into the gas chambers – now, how inspirational is that? To the music of violins,' he added ironically. 'But that's Jews for you – always praising God and making music! But of course you

287

knew that already. So for our dearest Rute I shall play my violin, and I'll play her out with the *Kol Nidre*.'

Cat went into the kitchen for a cup of tea, though she'd have preferred a stiff drink. The discovery of the notebooks had shown her mother in a new light but now Leo Heim had put flesh on the bones; he was her mother's 'dearest friend', whose love, uniquely, had affirmed her and reunited her with her youthful aspirations. The thought that, with his encouragement, Ruth had replicated her parent's soirées in Zwickau touched her deeply – *how loud the music behind closed shutters!*

She washed out her mug and put it away, and then went back upstairs to lock the bureau. She was about the lower the lid when she saw that she'd overlooked a blue airmail envelope, standing upright in one of the compartments. In it were two small black and white photographs, tattered at the corners and slightly crazed. One was of a young woman dressed in shirt and shorts and heavy boots in front of lush vegetation – obviously Ruth, on the kibbutz. The second showed a young girl, a head and shoulders portrait, with the word 'Hannah' scrawled on the back. But why had her mother never shown these to her, either when she was a child, when she had asked about her relations, or since?

She sat there for a long time, looking at the photographs and thinking, and then she locked the bureau and put away the key. She was tired again, but she still had the wardrobe to attend to; clues were coming out, and she had to pursue them to the end.

Inside, on the shoe rack, were her mother's worn but highly-polished shoes, two pairs of court shoes, a pair of black ankle boots and two pairs of ragged canvas sandals in a shabby Somerfield's bag. The shelves were piled with linen, and, aware of her mother at her shoulder, she carefully laid them on the bed.

It was were a description in linen of her mother's journey from poverty to relative affluence; poly-cotton sheets, which didn't need ironing, thick white cotton sheets, heavily starched and seam-turned for economy's sake, and below, a cluster of thin kitchen towels, frayed at the hem, each with its hook of white pyjama cord.

Behind where the linen had been was a heavy cardboard box, and she pulled it out, sat down on the bed, and removed the lid.

Inside were brown, curled manuscripts and she could see at a glance that the music would be exciting. Endless lines like railway tracks covered in tiny dots and flicks, with large sweeps and curves above the notation; great runs of black notes, sheet after sheet of it. Above, directions in German Gothic script in a broad adult hand – Schnabel's? – *andante, forte, piano, pianissimo.* Almost there was a sound again in the room, here and gone in an instant, and she looked up, startled. Music from her mother's youth, echoing down the years.

6

Cat drove south to Ed, thinking hard, wet-eyed, occasionally, at the memory of Ruth's secretiveness, but at other times smiling to herself as she recalled some trivial quirk of her mother's character, some accented utterance or acid comment; her tardiness; her smallness; her rapid, crab-like walk; her flying hands; her charity shop clothes. Unperceived, the nights were already drawing in, the rain misting the road, and the droplets of water on the windscreen, illuminated by the lights of oncoming traffic, formed myriads of dripping, luminescent tears.

Long before she reached the halfway point the sky had darkened, and with it, her mood. The necessity to make practical arrangements for Ruth's funeral, her exploration of her papers and the conversation with Leo Heim, had diverted her for a while, but now the questions surged back, and her heart grew cold against her. In spite of the cords of memory which bound her to Ruth, or that she was astounded by her latent talents and delighted that they had come to fruition, over everything there still hung the bitter incongruity of having been deceived.

She found herself wondering, bleakly, uneasily – not quite self-pityingly, but at the edge of it – whether she would ever reach the point of making an objective judgement, or whether it would be a double bereavement, her mother's secrets buried with her. Living with the mystery, as Ed had warned so prudently. For strip away the pretence at truth and memory became wholly false, wholly in doubt; its power to nurture and to teach invalidated. She was glad for Ruth that her gifts had borne fruit, very glad, but as for herself, her past had been wiped away like a name scribbled over, or a page torn out – not brutally, as Ruth's was, but deliberately, methodically, even cruelly, and over a long period of time.

Except, it all depended on whether Ruth's stories were true or false.

But maybe neither, she thought suddenly; maybe they were metaphors – true, in their own way, but not literally true. So, work it out: for coal and grime read attack on Jewish culture and ideology, the loss of jobs, the bookshop burning; the beating of the old Jew in the street. A thin argument, this, but feasible. For shame and guilt, read her survival when others had not. For escape, read fleeing Germany and the oppressiveness of the new kibbutz. Tenuous connections, but they could be made to stack up, with a bit of imagination and a good deal of charity. But what price charity – or even Eliot's *sharp compassion* – if too sharp, too probing, too unforgiving, or if the enigma of her mother was simply irresolvable?

But if Ruth feared not being believed, why mention these things at all? Why not just let them sink into the great morass of unspoken, unspeakable memories? And if memory and truth were in dispute, what, then, was the value of any of her recollections? To what purpose disturbing the dust on a bowl of rose leaves, if under them the bowl is dross, and when disturbed, the leaves fall away into dust and darkness?

Cat knew the answer to that. It was so that she could at least retrieve something out of the ashes; a necklace, perhaps, and here and there a bit of pure, unadulterated, filial affection.

Ed had said to let her go. And I am letting you go, she thought dourly, but not *gently*, am I, Ruth? No, I'm raging, and not just at your death, but at the un-timeliness of it, that it's happened before I took time to ask the vital questions; questions I hadn't known *were* vital until Reuben so brutally shoved doubts into my mind. And if I'm raging, it's not at the dying of *your* light, but *mine* – and with that same childish resentment I'd always struggled to avoid. What else did

Ed say? That the only response was to love? To say that the whole of the truth is not worth the price of a mother's love? To forgive you your bent truth, to say your mind was fractured by life? I'm too angry for that. All my life I have made your contradictions mine own. You have not left me with a narrative that I can in any way own or pass on, and the loneliness of that is beyond comfort. It cannot be rocked, for it is restless; as itinerant as you were when you fled your memories.

Yet by the time she reached High Wycombe something was nagging her that this darkness of mind was of her own making, and that, somewhere above, Ruth rested, serene and innocent, as if those who have died were transformed into a state where they could understand things that are totally incomprehensible to those who are still alive.

The morning was intensely bright after the rain, the summer sun beating back the autumn chill, though the wandering Jew lay heavily on the garden. It pursued her, Ricci's crack-pot joke, as though whenever the grass was remotely damp she was compelled to react like a Pavlov pup.

They were sitting on Ed's patio, the debris of their breakfast on the table, Ed behind the newspaper. Across the garden, sunlight glistened on cobwebs strung between tufts of grass and pink phlox. The tall, slightly spiralling trunks of beeches appeared almost metallic, their leaves a medley of bright green and rusted brass. In the distance, purple undulating hills and occasional clumps of deciduous trees brushed against a cerulean sky.

'I'll come, if I might, to the funeral, Catherine.'

Deep, rumbling tones, the paper lowered; his hands brown and sinewy, the nails pale and precisely manicured.

She met his eyes. 'Oh, Ed, I'd be enormously grateful if you would. Someone I know...'

'Where's it taking place? The local synagogue?'

'No, in a church. Didn't I tell you, my mother converted?'

He was interested. 'Really? How come?'

'It started at my leaving service at school. She heard the story of the Good Samaritan for the first time, and it had a profound effect on her. There'd been an episode she told me about, when she was ten, when she saw a Jew being beaten up, and she'd always felt guilty that she hadn't stop to help. The story probably helped her come to terms with it. Anyway, she began to attend the local church.' She gave a light laugh. 'I suppose it was good for her; she made some real friends there.'

She was quiet for a moment. 'For me, though,' she added, shifting in her chair, 'it all seems a bit pointless, religion, whatever branch of it you choose. I mean, it didn't save anyone from the gas chambers, did it? But she used to say faith was like the sun rising in the morning – it made her see everything in a new light.'

'It had that effect on her?'

'Yes, plus her friends – even her solicitor was part of her reading group. '

'Those groups – you didn't know about them?'

'Well, maybe she told me and I forgot. You sort of get caught up in your own life,' she said lamely. 'I only discovered recently, when I looked through her papers.' She gave a tense laugh. 'She left all her clothes to a charity shop.'

'Well, that's not unusual, is it? I gave all Anne's clothes to a charity shop.'

'Bet she didn't buy them there, though! My mother always looked like a jumble sale!'

'She was really poor, then?'

'At one stage she was. But she'd have shopped like that anyway. Eco-friendly; one in the eye of consumerism, that sort of thing. Ahead of her time. And, talking of which, you were right about my car. But

I shan't buy another; I've found a garage who'll fix the ignition.' She smiled. 'Easier on the planet.'

'So what are your plans for the next few days?' he asked. 'Will you paint, when you get home?'

Cat hesitated. 'I don't think so, Ed. Not yet. I don't know, actually, if I'll ever paint again. No, I'm serious,' – for he was about to protest – 'The thought of trying to look beneath the surface of a person's face seems almost wrong now. Anyway, I don't think I do it very well. Not as well as I once hoped. I've failed in, oh, so many ways...'

'But, Catherine, it's your gift! You're brilliant at it. You can't not paint!'

'I don't know. I'm not sure I can just... go back to doing what I do, as if nothing has happened. I'm a completely different person, Ed.'

'Catherine, look at me.'

His face was half in shadow, but his hair was silvery in the bright light, almost the same hue as his shirt, and his skin tones through the thin cotton were a delicate hint of brown. Cat automatically found herself trying to determine the colours she would use, were she to paint him outside, in the sun.

'No, you can't not paint,' he repeated shrewdly, 'and you've just proved it, if you needed any proof.'

'What do you mean?'

'You were looking fierce...'

Cat shook her head wryly. 'I was concentrating.'

Ed grinned. 'Well, exactly.'

Cat looked away. 'I can't help seeing shapes and colours, but I don't want to take on any more portraits. It's such a struggle, sometimes. And I no longer feel equipped to make that kind of judgement...'

'Judgement?'

Cat tried to explain. 'I mean the judgement of... of the process. What you learn, and what you do with what you learn. You're given *this* face, at *this* particular point in time, in *this* particular mood, then there's *your* particular mood when you look at it, and the particular light. These are givens; they're not choices. But the choices you do make are more intuitive, hardly conscious, and how can you know,' she said painfully, 'that you make are the right ones, that what you leave out doesn't contain more of the real person than what you put in? It's so presumptuous, somehow. Intrusive, almost arrogant. I'm not sure I could be party to that anymore.'

She paused, uncertain how much sense she was making, but wanting him to understand. Yet how much could the military mind comprehend of artistic *angst*?

'If you do it well,' she said, 'you end up painting someone's soul. You sometimes don't see it till later, so then you've got to mask it somehow – at least, I do – otherwise you put, permanently on canvas, the deepest secrets of someone's heart. When they sit down they don't know what they're letting themselves in for, how things will be revealed. Not just negative things, but mostly. Things to do with where they've come from, the sort of childhood or marriage they've had – oh, all the things that life's hit them with. And there they are, sitting in front of me. Me, with all my own experiences, all that... garbage...'

'You sense all this?'

'Sort of. I don't analyse it, but I do see it. I had a client, once,' she went on, 'whose husband commissioned her portrait. "The most beautiful woman in the world" he told me – so that was a no-win from the start. She was seventy if a day, but he absolutely adored her. So there we were, me trying to paint her, while all she did was go on about her affairs – and there were plenty of them I can tell you. All the details of her sex life – London, Paris, Cannes, over there, over here, under this, on top of that...'

Ed gave a bark of laughter. 'A marathon!'

She smiled. 'A marathon for me, I assure you! And all I could see was this... this calculating, screwed up, *manipulative* face, and Ed, I put it all down in paint, every little last bit of it. *Without knowing what I was doing,'* she added. 'Then next day, I'd think, golly, I can't leave it like that! She looks like a well-heeled tart...'

'She *was* a well-heeled tart, by the sound of it. So what happened?'

'I painted over it three times – three times, Ed! Then I put some music on loud and got it finished. The husband didn't like it, but he had to pay me for it; it was a commission. He hung it, too. Later on, one of her friends saw it and she said to me – she winked at me, Ed, and that wink said it all. "Darling," she said – they all call you darling – "you've painted her *ennui*, you've got her to a tee." That silly little rhyme stayed with me for years. It's surprising I've produced anything, when you come to think of it. And *that's* what I mean by garbage.'

'It's not deliberate, you know,' she added, slightly embarrassed. 'It's not some sort of con. It's just the way I look at things, I suppose. Trying for truth.' She felt exhausted.

Ed was quiet, looking at her for what seemed a long time, then he said, 'You're very honest, Catherine.'

'No, I don't think I'm particularly honest.'

'You are. This obsession with truth...'

'Not that obsessed,' she said dryly. 'I just talked of painting over it, didn't I? Masking it. And even with my mother, look where it's got me.'

'Ah, well, let's wait and see about that, shall we? Things are still very raw. Give it time.' He took her hand. 'You'll come through this, Cat, I'm sure.'

She couldn't answer him.

'So, no portraits for a while,' he said, unfolding his newspaper again. 'But, in the interim why don't you paint some landscapes? This is a glorious country, so varied, and with a fantastic light. You have the hills, the trees, wonderful skies, the garden here, your river...'

Something thrilled within her, deep inside.
Ah yes, maybe now I can paint the river.

7

On the way home her mind turned to Deborah – and James, but perhaps he was, by nature, more amenable. Yet he could be secretive, too; she knew little of his life or his private thoughts. As for her volatile Deborah, increasingly she realised how much more akin to her she was, than to Bill, the reverse of what she'd always thought. As she and Bill used to say, jesting, in the days when they were a family and some quality was being discussed – 'She gets that from you; I've still got all mine'.

Yet that was also a false picture, if recent events were anything to go by. Once shaken, it took time and much wrestling to quell the tumult in her, like the currents in the river, which needed a whole night and a good moon to still the waters. Also, in spite of going on about needing space and God's free air to be breathed, she was still judgmental. True, she still hid her feelings, masked the hurts, disguised the pain and sought refuge in her own place, as Deborah did when she ran crying to her room. Except with that officious man in the hospital garden, for Ruth's sake. But why, after all these years, when she'd escaped, and had even learned to bite back sometimes, was she still so unsure of herself?

It dawned on her then, how little she knew about Ed, other than he lost his wife and that he was a retired general with a daughter called Marie-Beth and a son-in-law called Frank. He was perceptive, generous and kind, and she had experienced his tenderness; it was possible that she was even experiencing his love, although she still hadn't tested her heart on that. But of his history, what did she know? She hadn't even asked him about it. She had taken his hospitality, relied on him for answers, or at least to manage the pace of things, and yet how much of him, his life, his way of dealing with the world, did she really know? Perhaps he was just waiting to be asked. But even if she had, she'd been so preoccupied with her own concerns that she probably wouldn't have listened. And still he was patient, still he waited.

It almost made her want to drive back to High Wycombe.

A car in front of her swerved to avoid a spent tyre, and she realised that she was driving on auto-pilot, and that it was dangerous...

But Deborah, she hadn't finished there. For the moment she had to put Ed aside – reluctantly, oh, how reluctantly, must she put him aside! – pursue her thoughts and find some way out of the *impasse.*

So, then, accept it. She, Deborah and her mother were alike; in their exaggeration of the trivial, their hunger for affirmation, their egoism cloaking low self-esteem, their obsessive hiding and hunt for security, their blind refusal to contemplate what they didn't comprehend, their untidiness, their running away... And wrong assumptions? Probably.

I know where you're coming from, Debs; you come from me.

And another thing. It was something of a shock to realise that every time she left the studio she learned something; she felt renewed and stimulated, but every time she returned she regressed, like a snail into its shell. But why? Had she made of her studio a barrier? And in spite of her passion for her painting, or because of it, had she also made of that a barrier? A grim thought, if that was what it had always been. But a barrier to what? Both her painting and her home were life-enhancing, so how could they be barriers as well? Oh, she was getting nowhere, just tying herself up in knots.

Ahead, the light between the trees pooled on the road, silver, shimmering like a mirage, the stark purple shapes of their trunks pulsing in her eyes, and then she was on the motorway, the traffic nose to tail. The overhead gantry signs were bright with warning: Keep Your Distance.

'Signs like that are supposed to *help*,' she mumbled aloud.

But what did it do to Deborah, when she left?

It was a question she struggled with more and more, and there seemed to be something of a light dawning, slowly and sluggishly upon her mind. Why should Debs have scorned her, and say, as she frequently said, "I don't know who you are anymore." She'd said it recently, in the hospital, and Bill had said it, too. So what had she been doing, to replicate her mother's behaviour in such a way to make Deborah say that?

It was OK, wasn't it, Debs, when I was there, doing the household thing, bearing the brunt of your adolescent spite and your verbal rebellion. That's what mothers are for; to absorb whatever horrors were thrown at them and just keep on loving; against whom it was safe to rail, when to rail at anyone else would result in rejection. Who'd always be there, in spite of everything.

But in the end I wasn't there, was I, Debs? When I thought you'd cut the umbilical cord – when I saw, in my mind's eye, a great escape from all that stifled me, I left. But maybe it's never a neat, precise cut, more a prolonged tearing which goes on well into adulthood. And maybe it's not finally accomplished until we can see in ourselves our parents' faults and... respond. Or perhaps, forgive. Ed taught me this, and I didn't even know what he was trying to tell me.

Yet I'd given Deborah no warning. Bill and I, we'd hidden our pain too well, perhaps even from each other. "I don't know you anymore", might have been, for him, an expression of utter incredulity, that, in spite of all his bullying, I was strong enough to live my inner life and in the end to leave him. The strength that comes from utter desperation. He hadn't known what hit him – a bizarre way of putting it, but apposite. He never saw that inside this reasonably capable, domestically-efficient, dubiously-gifted wife was an imprisoned child in the midst of nightmare, struggling for release, misleading both of us.

What was surprising was that she could hardly recall his face, and she knew that if she'd ever looked at him properly, she would have done. To think, she'd lived with him for nigh on twenty years and never really looked at him! It was unbelievable. It was unforgivable.

And then another lightening strike, about her *Faces*. Was Ed right, that her attempt to express solidarity with the lost was to identify with them and find her identity in them? Had that been her motive, and only that? No, there was no wisdom on earth that could answer that.

She was approaching the slip road. Beyond was the river, a wide sparkling ribbon of light between the buildings, infinitely familiar and yet wholly strange, carrying on its current its own duplicity.

She came into the studio with the little rosemary bush tucked under her arm and her small suitcase in her other hand. On the table by the window was Gus's gift, an immense, three-sided slab-pot, intricately decorated with swirls and glazed a matt brownish-green, a colour which corresponded so exactly with the river that Magritte would have jumped on it. It was perfect for the rosemary bush, and she spread some newspaper out on the table and upended the bush over it. Its scent lifted, pungent and aromatic – *pray you, love, remember.*

But she *was* remembering, wasn't she? The question was how to interpret the memories.

She tipped the soil carefully into the bottom of the pot, fed the roots into it and pressed it down. Against the reflected light from the river it looked intensely Chinese, and she ran her fingers along its indented pattern, through the green, oily filaments of the shrub and into the tiny blue flower. She was still admiring it when Gus and Ricci came in.

'Saw your car,' said Gus. 'Oh, you haven't wasted much time.'

'Gus, it's lovely. Look, from my mother's garden...'

'It's perfect,' said Ricci, coming over to look. He touched her arm. 'Sorry about your mother, Cat.'

'Thanks, Ricci. She...'

Gus ran his fingers gently along the seams of the pot. 'You see how it's made, Cat? Three pieces...'

'Yes, I noticed that.'

'It'll never come apart, even if you drop it. Well, it might smash, but not along the joins. And you see this glaze? It's not a ready-made; it's local clay – I told you I'd find clay, din' I? Took me ages to perfect that glaze.'

'It's beautiful, Gus.'

'Imagine, Cat,' he said excitedly, 'thousands of years ago you get volcanoes and things, shoving all the rocks up in the air then down into the river valleys, then thousands of years of weathering, then along comes the farmer, who ploughs it all up, then *I* come, make a glaze of it, shove it back into fire – the kiln, you know – then if it's dropped and shoved in the ground, it'll stay the same for ever, no more weathering, fixed in time...'

'Amazing.'

'And you see it's wider at the base, so it won't fall over? And did you notice the design on the sides?'

'Yes, very complicated...'

'It's not really complicated, not when you look at it...' He tipped the pot slightly sideways, and some of the loose soil fell out.

'Watch it, youngster,' said Ricci, starting forward. 'You don't want to mess up...'

'No, it's quite stable... See, Cat, the pattern's a bit

subtle, like a Celtic knot. It starts here, goes round – oh, sorry, a bit of soil, doesn't matter – and then it sort of works its way up the pot...'

'Wow, that's really something.'

'Oh, God, Cat, don't go all Yankee on me. That General chap's a bad influence on you... But you see what it's meant to be?'

'Gus, leave off, will you?' said Ricci, patiently. 'She's just lost her mother, for God's sake!'

'No, it's OK,' said Cat calmly. '*Is* it a Celtic knot?'

'No, you dummy,' said Gus, tiredly. 'It's meant to lead into whatever plant you put into it. Can't you see? *You* put the damn rosemary in it! A design of roots. After your mother, Cat, sort of in memory. Cos she was dying, an' all that. I thought you'd like it. Root – that's what you called her, innit?'

That evening Cat spent some time on the balcony gazing out across Fiddler's Reach. She sat there long enough to watch the tide go down, the slight salt-breeze teasing her nostrils. Below, the water licked at the walls for a while, then imperceptibly oozed away to reveal the familiar mud and shingle of the shore and the anonymous detritus of that day's tide. Across the scumbled surface of the river, the factories stood clear-cut below the evening haze, their mirror images glowing in the stream and continually broken by the current into yellow shards of light. Occasionally a window would be caught in the reflected light from the low sun, and would blaze out, flashing like semaphore.

Golden windows, Ruth used to call them; a reference to a bedtime story she used to tell. Yes, there *were* other stories, how could she have forgotten? She could still hear Ruth' voice, falsetto for the little boy, deeper for the old man, and the thick accent of Cat's childhood – the 'v's and 'w's transposed.

'Once upon a time a little boy lived viz his mozzer in

great poverty in a grim terraced house on the side of a deep walley. Every evening, looking across the walley, he saw flashes of goldt, and he said to himself. "Oh, how rich they must be, over zere, to have so much goldt!" And he wished he could have some of it, too. He felt zat if they only had a little of it their whole vorldt would be changed. His mozzer would not need to wear cast-off clothes, and he would no longer haff heavy clogs, but real shoes.

One night, while his mozzer lay sleepingk, he slipped out of ze haus. He marked the place carefully in his mind, but when, at long last, he reached it, dawn had come, and the sun was beginning to show over the hill. Though he searched hard, with increasing despair, there was no sign of any goldt, and in the end he began to cry.

An old man saw him and approached.

'Little boy, vy to you cry?"

'I cry because I come for the goldt and it has all gone! I saw it last night from the oder side of the walley. I saw it shining, but now it has gone, and I have nussink to take home to my mozzer.'

'You love your mozzer very much?' asked the old man, and the little boy nodded.

'Then look,' said the old man. 'Look across ze walley, and tell me what you see.'

The little boy looked, and zere, on his own house, he saw the vindows blazing, lit up with goldt. He looked at the old man with vonder.

'Goldten vindows!' he whispered.

'Do you not see,' said the old man, 'that you have all the goldt you need at home? Zere is your mozzer, and she is calling for you. It is not goldt which changes the world, but luff!"

8

The following morning she made three canvases, stretching the smooth cotton-duck fabric across the frames and tacking it into place. However she tried to paint this river, she knew she would be hard-pressed to paint anything remotely accurate, and would be continually adjusting her palette to accommodate the shift of light or the quality of the atmosphere. To be authentic, she'd have to work on several canvases at once, as Monet did with his *Series* paintings of the cathedral at Rouen, where he'd prepared fifteen canvases and fifteen palettes and, as the light changed, moved between the paintings. Cat remembered reading that it was winter at the time, freezing cold, and he was distinctly troubled by the lack of heating and the smells and noise from the market below his room.

She would do the same with her three; she'd find distinctive colour-mixes and make notes about the colour as it changed before her eyes.

Her mind, however, was wayward, and refused to focus. She was still searching the water for her mother, for the sight of her green eyes in the depths, but it was futile; Ruth had gone, and with her she had taken all association she had ever had, however unwittingly, with the river. It was just a river, flowing endlessly past her window, gallons of it by the minute.

By mid-morning she was ready, the phone off the hook. She did ask herself why she seemed unable to conform to the stereotype of the grieving daughter, who would have spent these few days arranging the minutiae of the funeral or writing letters. She found no answer that satisfied her. It wasn't that the painting had gripped her so much that she could do nothing else; more, it was a limbo, and the question was how to occupy it, how to reconcile herself to that indeterminate pause between asking a question and realising that the only person capable of answering it with any integrity had left the room.

For the moment, the light, the colour and the landscape were answers enough, and in fact she felt excited, energised. For the next few hours all her inner conflict – her reluctant, half-longed-for grief, her guilt about Ed, even her sad preoccupation with Deborah – fled, while she concentrated on bringing to life the view in front of her.

The early clouds had been absorbed into a sapphire sky and the factories and warehouses across the river were also blue, but paler, diluted by the atmosphere. The water sparkled with ochre and shafts of reddish burnt sienna, and beneath her it was a vivid emerald green. The only cool tones were in the swell of the main stream, a dull burnt umber. It was all mapped out in front of her, real and true, and she picked up her palette knife.

For the sky she chose cobalt and cerulean; for the buildings the same mix warmed with violet; for the middle reaches of the river she used cerulean mixed with burnt sienna and a dash of sap green to keep it cool. The emerald she muted with yellow ochre, lightened with cerulean blue. In the end the cerulean permeated the whole painting so that when she stood back and looked at it, it glowed with a delicate blue light. She was completely engrossed, and it wasn't until the light changed that she laid down her brush.

She took the canvas off the easel and propped it out of sight against the wall, then took a fresh one and screwed it firmly to the easel. Heavy clouds had formed, necessitating a new palette. On it she made a mound of warm chrome yellow and its complementary, violet blue. She made a second, identical mound, and to this she added a touch of vermillion to make a tertiary red-brown. To a third she added sap green. Instead of staying with cerulean for the sky, she took a

306

risk and mixed cobalt with the vermillion, making a mellow violet which would almost nullify what had become the warm purple-brown of the distant buildings.

By late afternoon the sky looked ominous. She was standing with her loaded brush in her hand, gazing out, when she realised that the colours had completely vanished from the river, and that a lowering mist had obliterated the opposite bank. She took her third canvas, reached for her palette knife, and slowly, speculating, her head on one side, she gathered up all the residual pigment from both palettes onto a third. Then, with fast, broad stokes, she applied the uniform mess all over the canvas. Into that textured chaos she hacked stabs of pure colour; Windsor blue and a luminous Windsor orange, which, in proximity to her river sludge, created a startling abstract effect. Then she quietly laid her brushes down and stood back.

She stayed motionless for a long time, her eyes fixed on the painting. She knew it was the most authentic rendering of the scene that she had yet achieved or could ever want to achieve; it was neither figurative nor abstract, but something in between; it had mood and atmosphere and it had resonance. It was finished.

She was possessed by a quiet sense of joy, which came only rarely while she was painting. The experience had been incredibly intense, so much a matter of focus and attention that she felt completely drained. She had been painting with passion, almost ardour, for she had been confronting and avoiding this river, by turns, for many, many months. Now she had made a bargain with it, painted her own *Kol Nidre*, and she was with it, in it, at-one-with it; her own atonement – flawed, partial, yet undeniable.

Enough. Weariness washed over her and she knew could do no more. In any case, prosaically, she was now very hungry. She washed out her brushes, left

307

them upended in a jar, and went in search of food. There had been no sign of Ricci or Gus all day, and Julia was at work. However, as she was cutting thick doorsteps of bread, the two men came in carrying pots covered in newspaper.

'Exhibition's down today,' said Gus. 'Thought you'd be there. Rudi asked where you were.'

It had completely slipped her mind. She apologised and went to help them. The next half hour was spent trailing up and down the outside steps with bubble-wrapped paintings and boxes of pots. Once she stopped on the stairs and looked anxiously at the light. She didn't mind if the weather was dreary so long as it didn't actually rain, which would distort things beyond what she felt she could cope with. Yet a grey overcast sky, a grey river and grey buildings would, she felt, test her knowledge of greys more rigorously than anything her students might have expected of her. This fourth canvas, she thought elatedly, would be a completely new approach and, again, a completely different palette.

By then she was famished, and since neither Gus nor Ricci had had any supper, she made a pile of ham sandwiches and they sat down together and ate them and talked about the Preview. After a while she got up again, sandwich in hand, and began to mix some fresh colours.

Greys – what colour were they? First, three piles of flake white; into one, burnt sienna and opaque cerulean blue, making a red-green-grey. Slowly now: into the second, sap green, with a hint of cadmium orange, making a yellow-brown-grey; the third, yes, alizarin with cobalt and a dash of burnt umber, making a blue-violet-grey. The dominant lines, of alizarin mixed with indigo, would provide contrast of tone. She started to paint.

'Don't you want to unpack?' said Ricci, amused. 'See what's sold?'

'I'll do it later,' she said absently, 'when the light's gone.'

'It's gone now.'

'Not quite.'

'You working on landscapes?'

'Yes, thought I would for a while.'

'Not got any commissions?'

Cat glanced at him, her palette knife poised. Why was he talking so much? 'I need a break.'

'Doesn't look to me,' said Gus, 'like you're having a break.'

'A break from portraits, I mean.'

Gus got up and stretched his legs and stood in front of her day's work.

'These finished?'

'No, but the weather changed, so I'll wait till tomorrow, hope for something similar.'

'That blue one with the slashes looks finished to me. I wouldn't touch it if I were you.' He stood back, frowning, hands on his hips, studying the painting. 'Dunno about the other two, but that blue one is great. In fact,' he said slowly, 'mind if I copy it in a glaze?'

Cat was curious. 'How would you do that?'

'Not sure. Oxides, of course. A bit of cobalt and iron oxide in an opaque dolomite base, perhaps. Or maybe a white slip mixed with a bit of cobalt and copper carb, with a transparent glaze shoved over the top. I'll experiment a bit. I like the shapes,' he added. 'They're more cubist than you usually do...'

'*Cubist?*'

'Well, they're very simple planes. And I like the bands of colour across the river. And that orange, Cat, that orange is quite radical. Like my pots, in a way. Turn it the other way up...'

He made to do just that, and Cat stopped him. 'Hang on, it's still wet.'

'Oh... yeah, whatever. Well, here's to another joint exhibition. A *blues* exhibition − Rudi'd love it.' He

309

turned away. 'Well, I'll give it some thinks. But they're great, Miss Cat. I admire you... You're not afraid to do something different, are you? You're not afraid to learn.'

Ah, Gus, but I am. Not about painting, but other things. I'm hiding, Gus. Here in my studio, behind my barrier. I'm even *painting* my barrier. I am afraid to learn. Of older truths and older revelations. And of grief, as old as time.

9

Ed's voice, on the telephone, sounded sad and lonely. Marie-Beth, he said, was in trouble again with her pregnancy and wouldn't be coming over.

'Well, maybe I'll go out in the Fall,' he said heavily.

'It's nearly that, now.'

'I know. Anyway, how're you, Catherine? You coping all right?'

'I'm fine. I'm painting the river, but… I'm hiding a bit, I think.'

'You're entitled. Get some rest as well. And sleep.'

She was sleeping, almost too well, her mind insensate. It wasn't just that she was hiding; she was waiting; waiting for the funeral, and then for the funeral to be over, and then for the time after the funeral to be over, when she could, at last, give Ed her full attention. She no longer expected her questions to be answered.

She'd intended to unpack the *Faces* later that night, but when the time came, the windows closed against the comparative chill of the evening, she couldn't bring herself to touch them. If she unpacked one she'd unpack all, and her mother's face was there, waiting to be uncovered from her shroud of bubble-wrap. She wasn't ready, yet, to put her gaze on Ruth's green eyes, to lay her doubts against her mother's cheek, to see her bewilderment mount until she turned away in sadness. Or shame. Or justifiable anger.

But Ruth was not there to be gazed at. She was lying cold in the hospital morgue; she had withdrawn from Cat as surely as Cat had from her, but while Ruth's withdrawal was inadvertent and very final, hers was deliberate, maybe even callous. The truth was, it still had not come home to her that her mother had died, that she would never see her again, either to embrace her or call her to account. It occurred to her that there might be another accounting going on some place else, but if so, it was no use at all to her.

She and Ricci stayed up very late, talking of books and paintings until it was time to go to bed. Gus and Julia had long since gone, impatient with their arty ramblings.

Eventually Ricci gathered up the mugs. 'Time to turn in. Unless you fancy a walk on the marshes? It's stopped raining.'

'Yes, why not? I'm not sure I'll sleep anyway, and it's a mild night.'

They put on their boots, and headed for the stairs.

In order to get to the lower reaches of the river they first had to go half a mile or so inland. Cat was now easier about physical contact and they linked arms. The windows of the flats in the housing estate were blue with the flickering lights of countless televisions, and late though it was, a group of children were riding their bikes around on the pavement, others footing a ball in the hazy glow cast by the street lamps. A couple of teenage girls lounged against the walls, drinks cans in their hands, and as Ricci and Cat passed, they grinned derisively, a middle-aged woman and an old man out on the street together.

Once back at the river they walked along the shingle beach towards the sand dunes and found a hollow where they could shelter. Tucking their coats under them, they sat for a while in silence, watching the river flowing past, glittering under the night sky.

'There was a river in my village,' said Ricci, out of the darkness. 'Place called Llantilio Pertholey, near Abergavenny in Gwent. It was the *Afon Troddi*, joins the *Wye* at Monmouth.'

'Lovely name, *Troddi*.' Cat gestured towards the water. 'Is it like this one?'

Ricci smiled. 'No, it's just a tributary, very narrow, even when it's flooding. Lots of trees, hanging right over; always dripping. Lovely trout for tea sometimes, even if I got home soaked. You get used to rain, where I come from,' he added, his Welsh accent magnified by recollection. 'But water has the same mood everywhere, don't you think? When I was a boy we had picnics round there, on the *Monnow* flood plains, with the little mountain soaring above us; it's not very high, actually, but a steep climb. It used to fill me with awe. *Ysgyryd Fawr* or *Skirrid,* they call it, with a landslip on it called the *Devil's Bite.* From the top you can see right over the *Sugarloaf* and beyond. It was a mix of rural and heavy industry round there, like all the valleys, the canals full of activity; slow-moving longboats, things like that. They're all gone, now, but I used to collect their registration numbers, and of course the steam trains on the Hereford-Cardiff line...I'd stand on the bridge at Cwmbran...'

'Such names,' she said. 'And such memories...'

'Yes, there's enormous power in memories.'

She could see his face clearly, his eyes luminous in the reflected light from the water.

'Of course, the *Kwai* was different again. Much bigger, for one thing. More turgid, for another. At home the rivers are clear and fresh and somehow transparent...' He gave a grin. 'Except in flood. Actually, I've never been back there. I was afraid to, somehow, and there're enough books in that part of the world, especially in Hay. Anyway, you can't go back, Cat, you've got to move on, and you can get lost in a city and yet it wraps you round like a... like a blanket, sort of. Whereas if I'd gone home... Well, I might have felt very exposed... D'you understand, Cat, what I'm rabbiting on about?'

'I think so. What were you going to say about the river?'

He mused, the river whispering its passage to the sea.

'During the war, it meant a good deal to me, my little *Troddi.* It wasn't just my *imagination* – his Welsh lilt breaking the word into syllables – 'though I'd been away a long time. I got terribly lonely, even though we were living on top of each other, and I'd make myself think about it. It sort of calmed me. That was the main problem, the loneliness. And the noise. The noise in the camp was dreadful, Cat. Constant shouting from the guards, telling us to be quiet – ironic that, when you think of it – or someone being beaten. That's a terrible sound, that is. I shall never forget it. Then the noise from the generator, the constant groaning from the men, the snoring – I can't tell you how the snoring got to me. Drove me mad.'

He scrubbed his scalp with his palms, and shook his head in disbelief. Cat put her hand on his arm. 'Don't talk about it, Ricci. Remember those shifting tectonic plates – you're stable, now.'

He sighed. 'I'm not, actually, although it's a good image, Cat. But I'm not really talking about that, see. I was talking about the river; how it made all the horrors seem just that bit less horrible. It was in my blood, I think. Or wherever it is these things go when you're separated from them. Perhaps they get into your heart; you know, that part of you that tries desperately to hold on to the best of things, when things get tough. That river, it gave me peace, oh, so much more than thinking about *people*! It didn't demand anything, see. It made me forget what I was going through. I became more conscious of... of my soul, if that makes sense. As if my body was asleep, but it wasn't asleep, it was walking down some path towards...'

'I know,' Cat said softly. 'Don't *dwell* on it so, Ricci.'

'I'm not really dwelling on it, Cat; I know I'm being long-winded but I'm sort of leading up to something else... It gave me, you won't believe this, but in the middle of all that suffering it gave me a kind of joy. Like Wordsworth says in *Tintern Abbey* – you know the poem? That was the other one, of course, the *Wye*.'

'The bit about *hours of weariness*?'

'That's the bit. And the end bit, about the mind and *tranquil restoration*.'

'It does,' Cat said quietly. 'It does restore the mind.'

'So I'm grateful to be living on a river. I'm not a deeply religious man, Cat, but, well, Chapel's in my blood. River of life, living water, that stuff; Jesus Christ. That's what the river means for me. Feeding, sustaining, bearing me up. In the middle of all that terrible waste of human life, it underlined for me what Wordsworth called *the still, sad music of humanity*. The sense that in other places people still lived normal lives, went to work, played, made love. It was the life beyond – not heaven or anything like that; I don't mean that; or maybe I do, I don't know – but the whole *possibility* of life. Gave me hope, see. And you've got to have hope, Cat. You, particularly, have got to have hope.'

'*Me?*'

'Oh yes,' he said lightly. 'I wasn't talking about me, you know. I was talking about you.'

Cat was quiet. 'I'm not good at religion, Ricci. I'm afraid God-things have passed me by.'

'Ah well,' he said slowly, 'but then, you see, you belong to a generation that looks for signs. Me, myself, personally, I look for presence, even if I don't always find it.' He shifted his legs. 'Oh well, that's all I wanted to say... Let's go back, shall we?

He got to his feet stiffly, and then reached down to give her a hand up, and as they began to make their way along the shingle beach, he kept her hand in his. Cat had always wondered what it would have felt like, to have a father hold her hand as her mother's father had held hers, beside whatever river was appropriate. This, with Ricci, would be the nearest she'd ever get to it. And it seemed he was thinking something similar.

'I never had kids, you know. And you... well, you're like a daughter to me now. Anyway, that's how I feel. You don't mind me saying this, do you?'

Cat felt the sort of warmth within her that she might have felt as a child, and so she said, 'I don't mind, Ricci.' But because he was not her father, she added, 'Yes, we're good friends, aren't we?' She pressed his hand and loosed it, and put her own in her pocket.

A little later he said, 'By the way, that place we were sitting just now – well, you know *The Studio*'s just off Fiddler's Reach? Where we were sitting is called Northfleet Hope. All the stretches of the river have names, though their meanings are long forgotten, I expect.'

'How do you know them, Ricci?'

'Ah well, I have this little book, you see; an old Port of London guide.' He gave a wistful sigh. 'It doesn't give the derivations, sadly. I'd have liked to have known their derivations. Where things come from are important, aren't they?'

They had reached the alleyway and Ricci switched on his torch. In its light she noticed that he seemed even paler than usual, more stooped, and there was something very fragile in the steps he took. It troubled her. She thought: he's not as young as he was; have we walked too far tonight?

'If I could paint, Cat,' he said, 'I'd paint the river. I was looking at yours over supper, which is why I just told you where we were sitting.'

'...I don't understand.'

He squeezed her shoulder and smiled.

'I'm an old man, Cat, so I can say what I think. It's this: when you paint the river, you mustn't just look *at* it, see. You must look *into* it.'

'...I'm not sure...'

'Well, now look, see, the river, it's complicated.' Again, his Welsh tone elongated the word. 'It's like... well, it's like life. Or your portraits. You look at a face, and you identify the features, but then you look into them, and you see what people are really like. You see their presence.'

His voice became markedly more musical. 'What I'm trying to say is that, if your paintings of the river are going to be great – and they've got to be great, Cat, because I couldn't bear it if you missed the most important thing about it – then you've got to show why it's got such power to draw people to it. It's because of the depths, I think. It's only in the depths, you see, that you find hope, and discover what that hope can mean. I don't know anyone who doesn't relate to some stream or other. It's got to mean something more than just some passage of water. No, it means life, and it means hope and it means presence. It's going somewhere, isn't it? It's not *stagnant*. Anything that stays still, dies. So you have to paint a portrait of it, like anyone's portrait, and not be content with just the surface of things. Otherwise, you see, you don't get to realise it for its own sake. You don't get to know the depths. And if you don't get to know the depths, well, you don't get to know the hope. You do see that, don't you?

'I'm not trying to teach you your job, and I'm not trying to preach to you, either. You've got to take time over it, that's all I'm saying. And I'm not saying it's not risky. There's always risk in life, though; you can't avoid it.'

They walked on a bit in silence and Cat thought over what Ricci had said. After a minute she became conscious that he was looking at her anxiously.

'You're very quiet, Cat. Have I offended you – the things I've said tonight?'

'No, you haven't offended me. I'm thinking of three things. Well, two.' The third being that she disagreed with Ed; Ricci was certainly not 'going downhill'.

She said, 'There was a river where I was brought up, too. Like you, for walks and picnics and things. I didn't look into that one, either. It was just there.'

'Well, you were a kid. You take things for granted then, don't you? And the other thing? You said there were two things.'

'Yes,' she said, 'of someone who said that your treasure lies where you least expect it, on your own doorstep.'

He thought about that, and came up baffled.

She hugged his arm. 'You. You make me see daylight.'

His head reared up with pleasure and he grinned at her.

She said, 'So you think that it's OK to look into things? Even if... even if what you find there isn't very pleasant?'

She thought he'd misunderstood her at first. 'Oh, you find all sorts of things in the river,' he said airily. 'Mud and sludge and unmentionable things. Wonderful things, too, like, oh, I don't know, things that end up in museums and places, which would never have got there if someone hadn't started *dredging*. But that's life, isn't it? A real soup. But you can't mind the sludge if you want to go deep. It's the same with my books. People bring in these old tomes, and they want good money for them, but usually they're not that *special*, and you know you'll end up selling them for even less. Which is why I'm bankrupt, I suppose,' he added wryly. 'You've seen my shop, Cat. I'm not deluding myself it's a bit of a dump; job-lots of not very good quality second hand books; house clearance, things like that. Not always in very good condition, either. But just occasionally a book falls into my hands that's really something. A really rare book.' He laughed at himself. 'I tend to hang on to those, so maybe *that's* why I'm bankrupt. But it's always very exciting, the moment when you're not expecting anything and suddenly discover you're holding something precious. It makes everything else worthwhile, all the drudgery of handling things which, in themselves, aren't worth a penny candle, really.'

They had reached the housing estate. The streets were quiet, their footsteps loud on the pavement. A few windows were still lit, and Cat found herself wondering who kept vigil; who was insomniac; who worked away the night hours; who lay, suffering, on their bed.

Another time, she reflected, such things might not have concerned her, but she had learned pity and she had learned compassion. She had been *given* time.

'And in a way, Cat, I also discovered it with my nightmare. I had to... make friends with it before I could come out the other side.'

Cat peered up at his face. 'And have you? Have you come out on the other side?'

'I'm getting there. It's taken me all my life, but yes, I'm getting there. With your help, Cat.'

Me, too, Ricci. Me too, with your help.

10

When Cat got up the next morning, before it was fully light, and let her eyes go to her new landscapes, she immediately saw what Ricci meant about presence. As with all things, she needed to go deeper, into the darkness within. She also needed a vision, and then to be true to it.

It was immensely liberating that there was no 'other' that she needed to please, no expectation of function, as with portraits. If she ever exhibited them the art-viewing public, small as it was, would have to accept them for what they were, as abstract and very subjective statements. Her hope was that a door might open for them, as it had for her, and they'd be lifted out of the humdrum to the point where some deep, unexpressed chord was touched within them, *face à face*. Time and place suspended, as in Magritte.

In portraits she was more inhibited. There was a complete irony in the fact that, between her gaze and the one she was painting, was illusion. Here, in that reasonably immobile figure in front of her, was life, story, pent-up energy, flesh and blood, but he was constrained for the duration to be there, in that place, in that chair. And her aim was not to create an image to look *at* but more an icon that looked outward, that seemed about to speak, to respond, by means of its distinctive, physical characteristics. Such as the tilt of the head or the slant of the eyes – even the size of the pupils – and the inclination of the mouth or the position of the hands.

As for the soul – but no, she no longer trusted herself on that. Certainly the emotions entered into the agreement as from, behind the easel, she attempted to intimate the intimate. It was a mutual scrutiny of such force that, in the end, it would be a matter of debate as to who would remain the stranger.

Cat turned the canvases to the wall and made two new ones. She knew what she had to do. By the time she was ready, the paints on the table and the first canvas on the easel, the sun had risen and the river was glowing with a diffuse and gentle light. She had never looked at it so early in the morning, but in spite of her disregard here it was, running indolently past her window, just waiting for her to notice it.

As with Ed. And, perhaps, her mother.

It was her river, and Ricci's – and for all she knew Julia's too, though she trod more on the surface of things – and Gus's, for he understood depth and meaning. It was homely and familiar. Underneath, however, it was secretive, infinitely variable, and sometimes threatening. Like life. Like love. Like roots.

By mid-morning the sky was aslant with driving rain, the river frothing with bubbles. Cat tidied everything away; it was time to think of other things.

Her cupboard contained nothing suitable for a funeral; nothing remotely smart, other than her silver dress and she could hardly wear that. She wanted to telephone Ed and consult him. Stupid, as if he'd either know or care; nevertheless, she needed to hear the sound of his voice.

'I'd like to buy you a little black number,' he said immediately. 'You'll let me do that?'

This was not what she'd had in mind. 'Ed, don't buy me anything,' she said helplessly. 'I'll probably find something in Swanscombe, even if it means going to the charity shop. You can get some good bargains there. Harrods, Country Casuals, M&S, all sorts of things.'

'Please me, and don't do it. The funeral, meeting Amit again – it's not going to be easy for you. I want you to feel well-dressed, confident. You must have sold some paintings, Catherine...'

She had, and she hadn't even asked Rudi which

321

ones, or even unpacked. Lovely thought. 'OK, I'll splash out. I'll go into Gravesend.'

'Do that. And I'll pick you up, say eight thirty.'

'For goodness sake, Ed, don't pick me up! I can easily drive up to High Wycombe.'

'Not in that car, Catherine; it's on its last legs...'

'Yes, and I forgot; it'll be in the garage. Drat. But then how'll I get back?'

'We're not coming back,' he said firmly. 'Not immediately. We're going to have a couple of days on the Solway Firth. You ever been there?'

'Ed, I've not been anywhere. Where's the Solway Firth?'

'Scottish borders. You'll like it. Wild and empty and full of birds. I've a cottage up there, this side of the estuary. Two bedrooms,' he added tactfully. 'After that I'll bring you straight home. You wanna come for a coupla days?'

'Yes, I'll come with you, Ed.' Capitulating happily.

'Good! Now, what are you going to do the rest of the day?'

'Um, paint, I think. I can get the outfit tomorrow.'

'The funeral's on Monday, Catherine. If you're going shopping, then you have to do it today.'

'But it's only Friday. I can still...'

'No, Catherine. Today is Saturday.'

The patient voice did not crack, not in the slightest, which boded well, considering. If she had needed convincing, that told her enough. Clothes, equals charity shops. Timing, equals late. Organisation, nil. Imagination? Rampant, already.

As Cat began to walk the muddy mile to the bus stop the sky darkened, and she looked up anxiously, wishing she'd brought an umbrella. Why, she asked herself crossly, did she never *learn*? Why was she so unprepared for what life threw at her? There must be some mechanism of the brain that other people had and which she lacked, some early warning signal which she never attended to. What was it she'd said to Ed about her mother's stories? That she'd always suspected there was something fishy about them? Yes, well, if she'd acted on her suspicions she would not, now, be in this predicament.

She thought that it was probably from the time of grandparents that stories began to filter down, and that before then was a nebulous, shadowy time to which it was impossible to relate. But the more people's lives were filled with other relationships, the more they sensed that at least some of what they'd been told had been reconstructed for the sake of comfort, perhaps long ago and more than once. Any family would say the same: some things just don't add up.

In a way, she thought, it was possible to equate the previous generation's stories with landscape painting; they had the total freedom to choose which truths were absolute and inviolate, carved in stone, and which were not. But that what the current generation *heard* was more like portrait painting, where they needed to decide what was most authentic. And then, in their turn, choose what would nurture, and what diminish. To make a new narrative, based only loosely on old, forgotten choices.

She recalled hearing of a black African, who had never in his life experienced racial prejudice, and who was visiting London just after the war. Browsing in some West End department store he became aware that people were staring at him and avoiding contact. There'd been no overt threat and his family had no personal history of slavery, yet he felt a deep frisson of fear, as though his whole collective and racial consciousness had undergone an electric shock. From that moment onwards, this man feared whites.

And that's the point, she realised suddenly, stepping aside to avoid a puddle on the road, our most important memories are not acquired incrementally at all. They're slapped on to us in an instant, like the earthquakes caused by those shifting tectonic plates, shattering the normal pattern of life, knocking our previous hopes and expectations completely out of kilter and forcing a new pattern to be created. That's what had happened to Ruth, someway or other, and that's what had happened to her, with Bill.

Wordsworth had got that right, too. *It is not now as it hath been of yore – turn wheresoe'er I may, by night or day, the things which I have seen I now can see no more...*

And the disruptions that go deepest, she thought, are the ones that people choose to commemorate. Forever afterwards, each attack on humanity becomes associated with where it took place. That particular hill or mountain pass, that river crossing or bridge is now re-named, re-identified by crosses, cairns or plaques – here, in this place, this happened, their increasingly illegible dates carved in unforgiving stone, so that people won't ever forget. And every year the remnants gather and flout their medals, or, alternatively, make the death march again, grateful, humbled, indebted, guilty. Laying their fragile steps on the self-same steps where their forebears stumbled; or maybe not their forebears, but the disappeared ones. Each year more bowed and bent and bony, each year more closely resembling, in their slender frailty, those who had gone before.

Coach-loads visit these places, and it can't be mere voyeurism that motivates them, she thought, but defiance; the need to reaffirm the survival of the human race, and perhaps to marvel. In Auschwitz they're shown the cells, the workrooms, the dormitory blocks and the gas chambers, and afterwards they're taken up the lush green hill into the lush green woods, and there, under the lush green leaves where the grass refuses to grow, they're told: here are the un-named graves of those whose memory is, and always will be,

324

evergreen.

Whether the stories are subverted or endlessly repeated, whether accurate or distorted, people were condemned to generate them with all their humanity or harm.

So what, then, about deliberate lies? Here she was walking a tightrope; in her personal memory she was umbilically linked to all those who had gone before, to Ruth, especially. It was Ruth who'd drawn the map of her inner reality; Ruth, who'd initially shaped her life; Ruth, her icon, about to speak; Ruth, the window through which she still viewed the world.

But what if the window was clouded? As though she was struggling to look through what she had assumed was misted glass, rubbing it with her fingers, yet, all the time, the dirt was on the other side.

By now it was pouring with rain and by the time she arrived at the bus stop, she was wet through. A queue had already formed, and water ran everywhere, rushing along gutters from flooded drains, from umbrellas on to oblivious shoulders and sluicing across feet; it streamed down the windows of the vandalised bus shelter like a Turner Prize in the making. It was with wry amusement that she noticed that people seemed to prefer to wait in the rain, rather than huddle like wet sheep in the queue. She was the same, even for the sake of becoming just a little less drenched than she already was.

After much searching, soaked to the skin and with aching feet, she ended up with 'a little black number', an olive and black jacket with a high collar and a packet of sheer tights. She also bought a foldaway umbrella to add to the plethora of those she had at home, but by the time she had finished shopping it had stopped raining and the sun had come out. Her umbrella stayed in its sheath, olive-coloured, virgin-pure.

11

Ed crossed the studio to look at the little river landscapes, then turned his back, walked away from them, then swung round again. Cat was amused.

'I do that. Things come together more when you step back, don't they? You see the nuances, and the brush-strokes meld with each other in a way that they don't when you're up close and personal.'

'You work quickly,' he said, from behind his mug.

'Only if I know where I'm going.'

'And you knew where you were going with these?'

'I found out as I went along.'

'I'll take them,' he said.

She misheard. 'You like them?'

'I do. I'll buy them off you, Catherine.'

She hesitated. 'They're not for sale, I'm afraid. I'll use them as starting points for something a bit deeper.'

'I'll loan them to you,' he grinned. 'You shouldn't have shown them to me if they weren't for sale.'

Cat laughed. 'I didn't show you, Ed. You peeked.'

'Well, I'll have them sometime. You should always hang on to your best things, Catherine. Keep them in the family,' he added enigmatically.

She gave him a sharp look, but his face was expressionless.

Once through the worst of the traffic she fished in her bag for her poetry book. Ed glanced sideways, his eyes widening.

'My, that's a really old book, Catherine! You had that in school?'

Cat fingered the little book, stroking its worn leather cover, running her thumb over the cracked spine.

'Yes, and it shows, but it wasn't new, even then. It's

my T S Eliot. I thought the vicar might read this out at some stage.' She turned to *Little Gidding* and started to recite – unsteadily, perhaps because of the road surface.

We shall not cease from exploration...

Ed interrupted. 'Oh yeah, I remember this...'

...And the end of all our exploring
Will be to arrive where we started
And know the place for the first time...

Ed glanced across to her. 'He got it so right, didn't he?' he smiled 'Just hits the nail right on the head.'

'Ed, just let me read it,' she said with difficulty, looking up sightlessly at the windscreen. 'I need to just say it through.'

He was quiet.

Through the unknown, remembered gate
When the last of earth left to discover
Is that which was the beginning;
At the source of the longest river
The voice of the hidden waterfall
And the children in the apple-tree
Not known, because not looked for
But heard, half-heard, in the stillness
Between two waves of the sea...

She paused, too aware of memories to continue.

'Is that where you'll stop?' he asked. 'It resolves itself, doesn't it?'

'Yes. Just bear with me, Ed.'

He didn't interrupt again, and she was able to read it to the end.

Quick now, here, now always –

A condition of complete simplicity
Costing not less than everything.
And all shall be well
And all manner of things shall be well
When the tongues of flame are in-folded
Into the crowned knot of fire
And the fire and the rose are one.

'I think you should read it, not the vicar.' Ed had allowed the silence to fall, and Cat had not interrupted it. 'Your mother would have wanted you to.'

Cat pondered this for a moment, looking straight ahead. She hadn't chosen it for her own sake but as a tribute to her mother – *the half-remembered gate, the apple tree...* But he hadn't known about those. Perhaps she should choose a different extract. Was that what Ed meant?'

'I thought it was more about her,' she said awkwardly. 'She called her dying 'the last great journey'. So you don't think it's appropriate?'

'I didn't say that, Catherine; I think it's entirely appropriate. Anyone can find something relevant in Eliot. They don't have to look very hard. He speaks to the centre of things. But I do think you should be the one to read it.'

Cat took a moment to reply, unsure how much of the poem she still regarded as authentic, and she prevaricated.

'I'm afraid I'll break down or something. In any case, I'm already down to say the *Kaddish*. I don't want it to be a one-man show.'

He smiled at that. 'No, if you want to do it, then do it. It doesn't matter if others aren't familiar with it. Most people are, though, and every American child is brought up on Eliot. And Walt Whitman, of course...'

'Well then, *you* read it!' It seemed an inspiration. 'You know it; you've said so yourself, and you've got a lovely voice, Ed. Then it won't matter so much if...

people don't understand it.'

She'd nearly said, 'if my family said "we don't know who you are anymore".'

'They'll think it's just some crazy Yank, intruding? OK, I can do that.' He took her hand and squeezed it.

It was still early, but Cat dozed for a while, hiding in her thoughts. She was aware of the sound of the engine and of the car slowing and accelerating as Ed negotiated the traffic.

Then he said, 'And have you found the end of all your exploring? You've had quite a few days on your own and you must have done some hard thinking.'

'Yes, I've done some hard thinking,' she replied uncertainly. 'That's to say I've had some hard thoughts. Not many, though. I've been painting, and rather shut out other things. So, no, I haven't reached the end, but, as Ricci would say, I'm getting there. And Ed, he's been wonderful, really supportive...'

'Well, I'm glad he cares about you.'

'He does. He's very perceptive, too. It's just that I don't think I've taken in... that's she's dead. Gone. And without answering my questions. I can't grieve. I can't cry. I just feel so shocked at what Reuben told me. So I suppose I've been thinking less about her and more about myself. Does that sound unbearably selfish?'

'Grief *is* selfish. It's allowed to be.'

'But it's *not* grief,' she said despairingly. 'When I think of her now all I can think of is that she... I was going to say, lied, but I know now that's too harsh. It's all so complicated. Perhaps she told me what she needed to, as you said. And if that meant inventing some things... I shall never know; that's half the problem.'

'And the other half?'

'Well, what it's done to me. I feel like I'm floundering about, trying to make sense of a world I was never meant to understand.'

329

'That,' he said, 'is as adequate a description of family life as I've ever heard. It's like Eliot's 'longest river', not that he was referring to family life. You do get plunged into it, though, don't you? Right at the start, at birth. And when you have kids you do begin to flounder. If you knew then what you find out later, you probably wouldn't have 'em.'

'But you have a good relationship with Marie-Beth.'

'I didn't always. I wasn't a very good daddy, Catherine. I've done my best since I've retired, but it's a little late in the day to start fatherin' her, now, when I couldn't be a half-decent father to her before. And, this may surprise you, but I wasn't a very good husband, either.'

Cat was silent.

'How do I know why Anne got cancer?' His voice was steady, unemotional, his eyes on the road. 'I think, sometimes, something activates it. She was under great strain, was Anne. She wanted another child but, well, it was the height of the Cold War; they were building a bunker near Strike, at Walter's Ash, so I wasn't too sure about that. Then she sort of gave up. She just did her voluntary work and the garden. That garden, it's all her doing. When I realised, I suggested it myself, having another child, but it was too late by then. She thought I was only saying it to please her...'

'And were you?'

'Yes, if I'm honest. Too big a gap and I just felt too old. I told you I wasn't very skilled at marriage, Catherine. She had to do without me for far too long. Even when I was home there was always something else to prepare for, or visits States-side, when she couldn't accompany me. Marie-Beth was at a critical stage in school and she stayed home. Marie-Beth needed one of us to be there for her, and it sure as hell wasn't me!'

Into the silence he said, 'So think about that, when you talk of failure. A failed husband and a failed parent.'

'I didn't realise. I'm sorry.'

'I wanted to talk to you about it before. That's funny, isn't it, because I haven't known you that long. Perhaps it was... what do they call it, propinquity? But, hey, I held myself back.'

'You felt like that?'

'*Hell*, yes! It didn't seem fair while you were painting, and later, well, you were tied up with your Mom.'

'I wish I'd known, Ed. But how do you cope? You have this picture of yourself... How do you adjust when you don't match up.'

'You cope,' he said grimly. 'It hits your self-esteem, but you cope. You learn that your picture of yourself aint what the world sees, or your nearest and dearest see. That brings you up short, but it makes you reflect. Given the chance, you try and make amends. With Anne, it was too late; things got broke and things stayed broke. With Marie-Beth, well, I just hope 'n pray.'

'I got it wrong, too,' she confessed. 'I had this image of always being there for the children, doing the domestic thing, getting them started in life from a reasonably secure foundation... But real life wasn't like that. *I* wasn't like that. I felt trapped all the time. Everything got out of control. And I've realised that I'm not placid, I was a bit of a martyr on the domestic front, and it certainly wasn't a secure foundation. I know better, now. I know that what went wrong... was my fault...'

'We can't beat our heads with it, Catherine...'

'Bill did,' she said, under her breath, but he heard and his head snapped round, his face scandalised. 'He...what? Your husband...?'

Quite suddenly it was the right time to tell him.

'He beat me.' she said simply. 'He's a drunk. He's violent. That's why I left him. And *that's* why the kids are the way they are.'

He still looked shocked. 'You can't blame yourself! Kids grow up how they do.'

This was not what she needed to hear.

'*Yes*, because of what we inflict on them! Anyway, *you're* blaming yourself, aren't you? And Deborah blames me all the time. It seems to be the basis of our relationship. She accuses and I... well, I always feel guilty, so I placate, just as I did with Bill.'

'But she's older now,' he growled. 'Surely she understands? I'd have thought she'd leap to your defence!'

'Ed, don't try to save me from myself,' she said tightly. 'Its part of what I have to do, this facing up to things. As you're doing with Marie-Beth, and as I have to do with my mother. As for Deborah, well, when you meet her you can judge for yourself.'

Soon after that they stopped for fuel and a bite to eat. Afterwards they talked more generally, not exactly avoiding personal subjects, but postponing them. But as Ed described the cottage on the Solway Firth, his hand was over hers, for comfort.

'It's a bothy, really. It's near a place called Drumburgh, past Carlisle and right on the estuary. It must be one of the most isolated spots in the country, and you go across wetlands to reach it. Oh, there're villages, dotted along the estuary but once you're at the cottage, you could be anywhere. No streetlights, so at nightfall it becomes really dark; naturally dark, not oppressive, but so that you can see the stars. Then the place closes down till dawn. You wake to the birds and the sound of the water running in...'

'Sounds idyllic.'

'It is. I hope you like it, Catherine.'

'You stayed there often?'

'After Anne died, I did; to sort myself out. Just wait, two days there and you'll see things in a new light.'

'I wonder.'

12

Phoenix Way was crowded with cars and the front door was wide open. The living room was full to bursting with elderly people; oval-faced women with their hair drawn back in buns or cut in harsh pudding basins, the men in the black gabardines and dark homburg hats of her childhood nightmares. One had a patrician head of thick, steel-grey hair and an equally wiry beard; another carried a violin case, hugging it to his chest.

This must be Leo Heim of the Birmingham Symphony Orchestra and the *Kol Nidre*. He was a Goya portrait of Wellington, tall and narrow-shouldered, his face gaunt and hook-nosed between piercing eyes. His long, burnished bronze hair was tied back in a ponytail.

A diminutive woman worked her way through the *mêlée* and introduced herself in sombre tones, recognisable from the phone call.

'*Shalom,* Caterina, I am Rachel Stein.' She took Cat's arm and gripped it firmly. 'Ah, Caterina,' she whispered, 'zo sad about your mother. Ach, ve had such times! I vas part of her music group... *Komm,* let me make you some introductions.' She turned, but Cat forestalled her, indicating Ed.

'Rachel, this is Ed, a friend of mine.'

She shook his hand perfunctorily, her eyes elsewhere. '*Shalom, shalom,* you are most velcome.' Again she seized Cat by the wrist. 'Caterina, *komm* and meet ze oder members of ze groups.'

Whose house *is* this? Cat thought, and disengaged herself.

'Rachel, forgive me, but I must find my children, if you don't mind. I'll come straight back. I really want to meet you all,' she said, over her shoulder. She looked around the room, searching for Deborah and James.

Ed murmured, 'Catherine, there's a young couple in the garden. Saw them through the window.'

She thanked him, told him a little desperately to make himself at home and went out to the back kitchen. It was a small, rather shabby room, with a pitted Bristol sink and a wooden, water-stained draining board, the shelves above filled with old jam jars and chipped vases. It dawned on her that she'd have to spend some time sorting out the house, and her heart sank. Perhaps the groups might like some memento, some reminder of Ruth, and she resolved to mention it. They could come back to the house after the funeral and have a look round. Not the manuscripts, though, and not her mother's first editions, either, but what else was there?

She stopped as if struck. She hadn't arranged a reception, a wake, or whatever was the local name for it – no caterer coming in with salads and cold meats and pavlovas... In any case, she doubted if there were plates and cutlery enough. *Heck!* And what about flowers for the church? No, that was OK; she recalled the vicar saying that the Sunday arrangements would still be in place. But how selfish she'd been! And where was Amit?

She found her sitting on the grass beside a small pile of cigarette ends, talking to Deborah and James. James looked handsome in a dark suit, crisp white shirt and black tie, and Deborah, Deborah, with her long, auburn hair, straight-cut on her shoulders, looked very slim and young in a dark navy two piece trouser suit. They got to their feet and came forward and hugged her. A little taller than Cat, Deborah had to bend her head to kiss her mother's cheek.

'Mum, you OK?' The merest whisper, but at the sound of it and the feel of her kiss, the touch of her hands, light on her back, Cat felt the tears come. She felt utterly old; bone weary.

'Oh, my darling,' she whispered, 'I'm so sorry...'

Deborah frowned and pulled away. 'Whatever for?'

'For everything... for deserting you... for not being

there...'

'Mum, not now, OK? We can talk later – look, here's Amit; she told us not to call her 'auntie'.'

She spoke in a rush, but she did not let go Cat's hand, and then James put his arm round her shoulders. 'You OK, Ma?'

'I'm fine.' She smiled at him. 'Did you bring Amit?' she asked in a low voice. 'How did you find out the flight times and everything?'

'Got it online, didn't I?' He gave her a teasing smile. 'All that passed you by, Mum?'

At last Cat turned to Amit who had got up from the grass and was dusting herself down, dwarfed by Cat's two young ones.

'*Shalom, liebchen*. Reuben sends his love. He's sitting *Shiva*...'

Vere you get all zis nonsense? Ach, your mozzer, she alvays makes up zese stories...

'Yes, you said he would. It's very good of him...'

Her head rocked, deprecating. 'It's customary.'

Their eyes met, and Cat kissed her weathered cheek. It seemed much more than a week since they had met. She seemed shrunken, greyer, the wrinkles on her face more pronounced.

'It's good to see you again, Amit.'

'Are you all right?' asked Amit. 'You look very tense.'

'Oh, well.' Cat gave a laugh. 'It's... you know, today. That's all it is.'

They went back into the house, and stood together while Rachel Stein gathered up her guests and introduced them – like a mother hen, she thought uncharitably. It wasn't that she disliked Rachel; far from it; she was reminded forcibly of her mother, and that, in itself, was good, as though Ruth had family. But it was the way she appropriated to herself the formalities.

Why am I being so small-minded? she thought. I should be grateful. It's much better than standing

336

round saying our names like in a therapy group.

'Now, Caterina, zis is Ella Adamson; she read vis your mozzer...Unt zis is Joseph Blum unt his vife, Matty; we all did music together... Unt zis...'

A woman stepped forward and took Cat's hand. It appeared Rachel was not having things all her own way.

'*Shalom,* Caterina, I am Hanni Deisenberg. I was with your dear mother in our reading group. This is my husband, Danny.'

Hanni and Danny... Cat grinned, hastily changing it to a smile of welcome.

'How did you all meet?' asked Amit, frowning.

Rachel answered. 'It was me!' she said gleefully. 'I met Caterina's mozzer in ze charity shop and ve vent on from zere. Our group, ve are all Survivors! You know vat I mean, Survivors? Isn't zat somezingk? But Ruth vas our centre, our...how do you say it? Our lunch pin.'

A malapropism which another time might have been amusing, but apart from James, chortling in the corner, no one laughed and the introductions continued.

'I am Yan Buber... *Shalom.*'

As the man shook her hand and bowed, Ed stepped forward eagerly.

'Buber?' he asked. 'Not the Heidelburg Bubers?'

'I am of Stadt Nürnberg,' he said stiffly. The Heidelburg Bubers were Christians of long standing. A very ancient family. You knew them?'

Ed seemed embarrassed. 'No, forget it,' he said. 'I was probably thinking of somewhere else.'

Probably one of his postings, thought Cat, looking at him curiously, but another man was already taking her hand.

'Eric Rosenberg. *Shalom.*'

A full-bosomed woman, similar in height to Rachel, but with heavily wrinkled eyes leaned forward and took Cat's hand.

'*Shalom*, Caterina. We've heard so much about you. My name is Elsa Smith. Now, the last time I saw your dear mother, we hosted a little gathering together. Of course, most of us are Jewish but we also invited Mrs Patel, her shopping partner, you know. Ach, the menu was *beautiful*.' She waited anxiously for Cat to reply.

'Let me guess,' said Cat, smiling down at her. 'Chicken livers and pickled herring?'

'*Plus* cashew nut-roast, *plus gefilte* fish, *plus* vegetable *samosas, plus*...'

Rachel interrupted, putting her arm round Elsa's shoulder. . 'Plus *falafel* with *fava* beans, and then *halva* and apple *strudel* to follow!'

'Now what do you think of that?' they cried in unison.

Cat marvelled at how her mother's social life had broadened. 'Quite a spread – and did you listen to...?

'You're all Survivors?' interrupted Amit. She was still frowning.

The man with the violin glanced at her briefly and then stepped forward to shake Cat's hand. '*Ja*, we are all Survivors. You are from Y'Israel?' he asked Amit, still holding Cat's hand. 'From Yerushalayim?'

'No,' said Amit dismissively, 'from a kibbutz near Haifa. There *are* other places besides Jerusalem...'

'Leo Heim.' He bowed and clicked his heels. 'I am playing the *Kol*...'

'Oh,' interrupted Cat and took his hand. 'Thank you,' she said awkwardly, 'for giving my mother that recording. It would have meant a great deal to her.'

'It was a privilege,' he said formally. 'Your mother was a very great lady.'

'These are my children...' Cat introduced them. 'And this is Ed.'

Rachel Stein clapped her hands and they all snapped to attention.

'Now,' she said, looking at her watch, another archetypal Yiddishe-Momme, organising things, 'it's time to go to ze choich. Efferyone knows ze vay? Ella, you traffel viz me. Danny, can you take Eric and Leo? Ze rest off you haff your own carse? Zen, afterwards, I haff arranged saladts and a strudel to follow. You must all komm back hier for tea.'

They went in convoy. Deborah drove Cat, and James and Amit were with Ed, behind. Cat was expecting a red brick church, and was relieved to discover that behind the shops was an area of green space in which stood a flint medieval church surrounded by ancient yews. It seemed a timeless place, a place of peace. They parked the cars, and began to walk up the gravel path towards the porch.

Deborah had been eyeing Ed, and now she asked, 'Who's the guy, Mum? A friend of Gran's?'

Cat took her arm. 'No, darling, a friend of mine, actually. He drove me up.' Don't deceive her, she thought; give her a chance. 'And he's more than a friend, Deb. He's... he's been a rock.'

'Oh. But isn't he a bit... Sorry, I was going to say, a bit old. Can't find another word for it, sorry!'

'Too old for what, Debs?' Cat asked quietly. 'I'm practically middle aged, myself. I'm nearly forty three.'

'Suppose you must be. Sorry, lost track.'

'That's OK, so do I lose track.'

'But you never knew your father, did you?'

Cat was taken aback. *'What?'*

Deborah had been walking with her head down, and now she looked up mischievously. 'Well, I'm glad for you. You deserve some happiness after all these years.'

Cat took her arm. 'Deborah, he's not a father figure, as you so tactfully imply. It's not that kind of friendship...'

'Isn't it?'

'I've known him less than two months.'

'Pity.' She was still grinning. To see her smile like that, lightly, as in the old days, touched Cat's heart like nothing else. 'I'd like to see you settled, Mum, but do be careful, won't you? Don't do anything in a hurry. Not until you know him well.'

Cat hadn't known that her daughter could be so parental, and she looked at her in surprise. 'Oh, Debs, it's not that kind of relationship. And I *am* settled.'

'Well, if so, then unconventionally. Pete – he's my partner...'

'You have a *partner*?'

Deborah laughed. 'Oh Mum, you're not going to be heavy about this, are you?'

'Goodness, what would your Gran have said? Ah, Deborah...' Cat stopped on the path. 'I'm sorry, I never realised... I didn't understand... I didn't take enough thought, when I left Daddy...'

'It's OK, Mum. Anyway, I left first, remember? I'd already left when you walked out.'

Walked out.

'I don't understand,' Cat said, bewildered. 'You've been so... so angry with me...'

Deborah shook her head, her lips compressed. 'Oh, Mum, Mum, Mum, of course I was angry! You think it was easy for me? But when I saw you in the hospital... When you came in...'

'Yes?'

'You seemed so... Well, you were exhausted, of course, but you seemed so *young*, in a way.' Her hand slid down Cat's arm to her hand. It had been years, *years*, since Cat had felt the touch of her daughter's palm... 'Oh, I know I behaved badly. I didn't realise, not till I was driving home. I'd been angry for such a long time and I suppose I was... hanging on to it. But you looked so... defenceless, I suppose I mean. That's what made me cross. It always did, when I saw you like that.'

She stopped for a moment and reached out for Cat's arm, and gratefully, Cat took hold of her hands and grasped them, leaning forward to catch Deborah's almost inaudible whisper.

'Can you imagine being six years old, huddled under the bedclothes with your brother while your father beats up your mother downstairs?' She snatched one hand away and put it to her lips. 'Hearing... hearing her crying and begging for mercy? Hearing the kicks and the... the thumps and the name-calling and... and all the other words that six-year-olds should never hear...? Years and years of it?'

She was fighting back tears. 'Sorry, I'm sorry! Now is not the moment.'

'Oh, God, Deborah,' Cat breathed, 'is that what it was like for you both?'

'What do you think, Mum?' Deborah exhaled, then compressed her lips and looked away. Her eyes, under their neat make-up, glistened in the reflected light from the sky.

'Or when you get older. You can't run away. How can you? You can't abandon your own mother! But who's there to talk to, to share...? You can't bring friends to your house, your Mum's got bruises; your Dad might come home and start shouting. You can't talk to James...' She grinned through her tears. 'He's an idiot! You can't tell anyone – they...'

The tears began to ooze out of her eyes, and she began to sob. There, on that gravelled path, in full view of the funeral directors waiting at the church door, but impervious to what they might think, Cat took her in her arms.

'They... they might have... taken us away from you...' wailed Deborah softly, and lowered her head on Cat's shoulder.

Into her ear Cat whispered, 'Oh Deborah, what happened to make you leave home when you did? I've been wondering for such a long time... Can't you tell me now? Was it me, darling? I really won't mind if it was me; I will understand. Only, please tell me, darling...'

341

Deborah reared back. 'Mum, *of course* it wasn't you! How could you even *think...*?'

She stopped her lips, and then she said, very quietly. 'Mum, I *had* to leave. He... he came to my room. My room was private, Mum – he knew that. I was sixteen... he *never* came to my room. Anyway, we argued about something... I can't remember what... untidy clothes, I expect.' She gave a wry laugh. 'He hated untidiness, didn't he? Anyway, I answered back or something, and he slapped me across the face. I saw his eyes when he did it. And then he kept on slapping me. Back and forth, back and forth, *wham, wham, wham...* He *enjoyed* it, Mum; he *enjoyed* slapping me. Oh, I knew where *that* led, didn't I?' she said scornfully. 'I knew, then, that I had to get away.'

'Oh, Debs, but couldn't you have talked to me about it first?'

Deborah raised her eyes, almost, but not quite, in exasperation. 'Mum, how *could* I? You always hid things; you didn't know I knew! I didn't know where to go, but... A friend in school had this friend in London and he... she... well, it was a he, actually, but who cared; he was gay anyway.' She gave a slight giggle and then sobered. 'Mum, you do understand, don't you?'

'Yes, I understand,' said Cat, stroking her back. Her throat was tight. 'I've got your Teddy, Debs,' she said thickly. 'And James's Hornby train. I took them, when I... left.'

Deborah found a grin. 'Ah, I thought I threw that Ted away. James won't have missed his Hornby train, though... And Mum, he and I did talk, later. He's not really an idiot and we've always been close.' She swallowed convulsively and felt in her pocket. As usual she had no tissues, and Cat took the only one she had, tore it in half, and gave it to her. They both wiped their eyes.

'Waterproof?' asked Cat, studying Deborah's make-up.

'Waterproof. It's always had to be, hasn't it?"

'Feeling better?'

'Minute.'

Cat waited; out of the corner of her eye she saw one of the men flick his cuff and glance at his watch. She couldn't have cared less, but Deborah had seen it, too.

'Everyone's waiting...' she muttered.

'No, it doesn't matter.'

'Yes, it does! It's your *mother*... That's the whole point! In the hospital, I felt it could have been me, losing you... I remembered what it felt like, you see.'

'All those lost years,' Cat moaned.

'It took me a long while to work through, why you hid things instead of... I thought you could have done something to stop it, but you couldn't, could you? Oh, I've known that for ages... it was his eyes, wasn't it? You were the one reason I didn't leave earlier... but I should still have waited till after James's exams. I shouldn't have left him alone. You ought to understand... You did wait.'

'Yes, I waited,' Cat said quietly. 'But I still failed you. And I've missed you so much, Deborah. Can you ever forgive me?'

'Heck, how do I know?' exclaimed Deborah, her head rearing back. 'It's a big word – I don't even know what it means. But, Mum, will you get married to this guy?'

Cat rolled her eyes in mock frustration.

'But if he asks you?' Deborah insisted. 'He must have *some* reason for... OK, I'll shut up. But if he does, well, you're a bit scatty, Ma. Don't be too scatty over this, will you? Just make sure it's right for you. Don't go and...'

'I won't,' Cat said, capitulating. 'And I'll try not to be too scatty.'

13

Inside the scrupulously-valeted hearse, secreted within the polished pine coffin on a bed of plush velvet, of a quality that she could never have afforded in life, was the small body of her mother. She was laid out according to Jewish custom, her arms straight, her blemished hands trapped against her sides, the twin microcosmic coffin lids of her eyes tightly shut.

Cat could see her body under the lid as if it was glass. She thought, irrelevantly, I'm glad that in our culture we close the coffin lids upon the dead. I could not have borne, just now, to lay my hardened heart upon her thawing face. Let me just get through this, she thought; this process, this machination of religion, then, later, later, when I can look upon her death-shrunk eyes without my eyes dilating... She could not finish the thought; it was too elusive, too fugitive; it would not ground in her being. The ground, where her mother would be, by then.

James, Ed and Amit were waiting for them by the church door, together with four undertakers, burly as rugby players, dressed in shabby dark suits and smoking. In a few minutes, she thought, they'll undertake for us, politely and inscrutably, my mother's rite of passage, her passing over, but right now they're taking time off...

Except for one, she saw, who now detached himself and came to greet them, tossing his half-smoked cigarette into the flower bed. With spread arms in the blued air, he gathered them together like a choreographer, guided them through the porch, his hand on Cat's arm and his sour breath on her cheek, and with appropriately funereal slowness conducted them down the aisle past grey white balding heads and hunched navy-blue brown black gabardined shoulders and black homburg hats towards the sanctuary steps, where stood a pair of low trestles.

Cat could not help herself; the theatrical allusions persisted. As if within chalk marks on a stage their little group took their proscribed places in the front pew; she and Ed with the children knit between them like a real family – but Deborah had not let go her hand; she had not let go her hand. Amit's eyes were fixed on the large wooden cross suspended from the roof above the altar, and her lips were moving – warding it off, Cat supposed. Gradually the theatre filled up, except that the cheaper seats were empty.

The stained glass windows were filled with biblical images in bright, garish colours, the walls decorated with a paper frieze of children's drawings in spidery felt tip, Lowry stick-figures, depicting Moses and the Red Sea. Stereotypically hook-nosed Moses stood twig-like, dwarfed by an immense Hokusai wave – that ethnic cleansing of the Egyptians which had no memorial except this topsy-turvy fall into bright Mediterranean blue. And innumerable wars.

Into her line of vision came the hooked nose of Leo Heim, burdened with an upright chair and his fiddle. He placed the chair by the lectern, sat down and began to tune up. Immediately, the vestry door opened and a woman came out and bent over him, animated. He gave an infinitesimal shrug, his mouth a thin, mutinous line, and then the woman sat down on the organ stool and played a single note – an A, probably, but though Leo already had an A he tuned to it briefly and then rested his bow on his knee. The A droned on, a chair scraped – a perfect A – and from somewhere behind her she heard an appreciative, hastily-suppressed chuckle. Leo looked up and she caught his eye; for a moment he seemed bemused, then he smiled back, a tight, wry smile, instantly looking away. He bent, and laid the fiddle in its open case. It was small, red-lined, like a child's coffin.

A patter of rain against the windowpanes, and at

the same moment, as if on cue, the organ began to play, and the vicar entered, dressed in his clerical garb with a purple stole around his neck. On the hem of his black cassock was a short fringe and she found herself wondering if he knew that its origin was the obligatory fringed garment of the Orthodox rabbi. He bowed to the front of the altar, then turned round, smiling, an elderly man with a kindly face and a slight tummy. Organ fade-out; vicar, you're on.

Tiredly she thought, why am I being so...I don't know what I am being so. Critical? No, not exactly, merely disconnected, part of this mostly ambivalent if not openly hostile audience – as if they'd come to the wrong theatre and were seeing the wrong show, but they're trapped in their seats now, with no escape. She could almost taste their hostility and their ambivalence on her tongue.

The vicar was standing in front of her.

'Catherine,' he said quietly, taking her hand, 'will you say the *Kaddish* as the very last thing before we take your mother out? I'll give you a nod.'

Fine, she said, and introduced him to Ed. They shook hands.

She said, 'Can Ed read something from T.S.Eliot? We've brought it with us. A passage from *Four Quartets*.'

The vicar frowned. 'Catherine, my dear, if you'd discussed things with me...'

She was instantly contrite. 'I'm sorry...' she murmured, 'I'm not used to this...'

'No, of course, but that's why we needed to talk through the service. It's a question of timing, you see, at the cemetery...'

'I've been out a lot,' she said, perjuring herself.

He lifted his hand, glancing at Ed curiously. 'Never mind, I expect there'll be time enough.' His face cleared. 'No, there'll certainly be time. It'll only take a minute and Eliot was a great spiritual writer. Read it after the psalm, Ed, all right? I'll give you your cue.'

So he, too, was a choreographer of sorts, and with a slight swish of his robes he mounted the sanctuary steps.

'We're all here,' he said, a touch parsonically – but why not, if that was his trade – 'to say farewell to Ruth Feugler. Ruth was a great lady and much beloved by all of you. I know that many here today are of Jewish origin and I'd like to respect that, so there'll be no reference to the Christian God of Jesus Christ. All our prayers and hymns will have their root in the Old Testament, the Jewish Bible, a precious heritage in which we all share. For the source of our prayers matters less than to whom they are directed. And, like so many here, Ruth was a believer – in her own way and in her own time.'

It was a mild challenge and he paused and looked around – as if seeking impediments, thought Cat, but everyone was mute, their eyes fixed on him.

'Now, part of the human condition, and essential to it, is the search for meaning, and that can only be found in relationship with God. Ruth spent her life searching for meaning, and whether she found it or not, or how she found it, only God knows. So before we lay her in her final resting place, Ruth's daughter, Catherine, will recite the *Kaddish,* the traditional Jewish prayer of mourning that bears witness to the one, true and living God. And Leo Heim will play the *Kol Nidre*, a musical expression of atonement and forgiveness – in which, again, we all share.'

It was gracefully said, and Cat was surprised, even delighted; it changed the atmosphere and from that motley crowd came a real frisson of relief. With a rush of affection, she thought, they're uneasy in church, that's all, but at least they've come; Amit, Leo, all of them, even Rachel Stein, maybe especially Rachel Stein. They must have loved my mother very much to put aside a lifetime of fear and prejudice to set foot in

347

a Christian church. That must count for something, surely? And who knows what stories they've shared? Who knows anyone's secrets, closeted behind the door of their heart?

In the weft and warp of life, she thought dismally, does one small hole unravel the whole, one fabrication in the fabric deny its fundamental unity? – but how could she take refuge in word-play when her mother had been so stricken, so reckless in her quest for identity that she was prepared to distort what most defined it, and risk implausibility?

The vicar walked back up the church towards the door, and there was a hiatus while people shifted and muttered, then a time of rather out of tune organ playing and then a hush, descending like a wave. They could hear his voice from the door.

I am the resurrection and the life, saith the Lord: he that believeth in me, though he were dead, yet shall he live...

Over her shoulder Cat saw that he was leading the coffin in, lifted high on the shoulders of the four men, and she turned away so fast she hurt her neck. She could sense them approaching, could distinctly smell the stale odour of sweat, cheap after-shave and newly extinguished cigarettes.

We brought nothing into the world and we take nothing out. The Lord gives and the Lord takes away. Blessed be the name of the Lord.

The words, quietly intoned, sent a shiver down her spine and she felt Deborah huddling closer. She put her hand on hers and grasped it tightly.

Lord, make me to know mine end, and the measure of my days, that I may know how frail I am...Deliver me from all mine offences, and make me not a rebuke unto the foolish.

Foolish?

They placed the coffin squarely on to the trestles, which rocked slightly. Then they stepped back and walked out, a stiff-shouldered overweight unholy huddle, and the quiet voice continued.

The eternal God is our refuge, and underneath are the everlasting arms...

Really? Everlasting? So where were those arms when...? And refuge? What, exactly, are we talking about, here?

Ed reached across James and Deborah and laid his hand over Cat's hand, still holding Deborah's. He gripped it firmly, and she felt Deborah quiver.

Cat would never speak of this moment. In her mind's eye were images of a gracious house in a small town in Germany, of cattle trucks, of the battered wooden buildings of a ghetto – though for Ruth there had been no ghetto and no cattle trucks. Not for her, but for how many others?

And suddenly it all rang true. When Ruth would not speak of it she spoke for all their silences, Survivors and the children of Survivors, and there, in that very place and in her absence, her presence made her silence a lament.

Leo got up to play the *Kol Nidre*, and from that battered fiddle came a sound so sublime that many were moved to tears. He played as though it was not from another's pen, remote in time, but his own composition and from his heart; the high notes drawn out, plaintive, yearning, the deep notes sonorous, resonant and strong; the pauses prolonged to melancholy. He played it with his mouth agape, gasping for breath, the tears streaming from his eyes, not just for Ruth, but for all those who had gone before. He finished on a rising scale and a last, sustained silvery note of pure heart-rending agony.

No, she would never speak of this; nor how tightly Deborah held her hand, trembling by her side, or how James sat rigid, chin up, a frown on his forehead and his eyes half-closed, as if suddenly enlightened.

She was aware of Ed squeezing passed them, briefly touching her shoulder, and then he was on the steps. He indicated the little poetry book.

'Catherine wanted me to read from this, in memory of her mother and the great love she had for her....'

He looked down at the book, then raised his head again and cleared his throat. His eyes met Cat's and he smiled gently. Except for the sound of birds singing and cars passing down the road, the whole place was completely silent. He was an imposing figure, straight-backed, slim and tall; his face tanned under his white hair. Deborah was very still, and even James, for all his customary aloofness, shuffled nearer. They sat hand-fast, waiting for Ed to begin, but when he spoke, it was not to read the poem but to say something of his own.

'Ruth came from the other side of the world to your community. And I'm not speaking just about geography, though she was born in Germany and lived part of her life in Israel. No, I'm speaking of the other side of experience. Ruth came out of that experience, which I won't attempt to describe, for I've no right, and there's no need. She came from within it to another place, a place she made her own.'

He smiled warmly. 'As one who knows what it's like to tear up roots and put down new ones, I think I can say that a journey of that kind costs, as Eliot says, *not less than everything*. Yet Eliot doesn't speak of the costliness of the journey so much as the costliness of love, although love is itself a journey. Ruth had a great capacity for love. I'm not a member of the family but I've seen it in the eyes of her daughter and her grandchildren, and I can see it in your eyes, her friends. This kind of love, this quality of love, doesn't stay with the person who gives it, but is passed on, reinforced in those who are born in love. And already generated in your lives, for you wouldn't be her friends had you not discovered her as kin.'

He met Cat's eyes. 'These poems speak about

ultimately finding one's home where one started, in a community of love. They speak of simple straightforwardness and honesty. Ruth was a person of integrity. I never met her, but, again, I've encountered it in her family, and they couldn't possess it but for her.'

Cat was dumbfounded. He began to read, but she was so stunned that, at first, she only heard snatches of what he read, and then the images in the words raised other images, actually in colour, which raced through her brain – *exploration... know the place for the first time...* and she remembered her journey to the old house in High Wycombe and the apple tree and her mother's story of the golden windows...

...the source of the longest river – and in front of her was Ricci, by the river in the dark, urging her, with strange and remarkable prescience, to look into things, something that she had half known – *half-heard, in the stillness between two waves of the sea.*

And all shall be well – Deborah and James – *the crowned knot of fire...* Oh, Ma, the camps, the death cells... *And the fire and the rose are one.*

Suffering love, a design of roots tied into one great knot of at-one-ment, the only Jewish festival her mother would observe. It struck her, then, what strange affinity existed between the rose and fire, between love and death. Both were purgative, both cathartic; both necessitated a relinquishment of self.

Beside her, Deborah was very still, her eyes wide open, fixed on Ed, and her face was glowing.

Ed returned to his seat. Cat wanted to weep. She wanted to throw her arms around him. She wanted to howl to the sky, to testify, because he'd understood instinctively what she'd been struggling with forever. He knew Ruth though he had never met her. He dealt with her with almost filial love and affection, and that made him kin.

His speech had not been that of a disingenuous, sentimental eulogy, when those who bore the scars of long feuding were compelled to listen in silence to a white-washed rendering of a character they knew very differently. He'd made no judgements, for better or worse. He'd talked about experience and he'd talked about love, and maybe that was all anyone could hope for, lying deaf and dead in a box. But had Ruth heard she would have wept; she'd have turned in her coffin to embrace him.

He's wiser than I am, she thought, awed to the depths of her soul; more generous, more forgiving by far. As for me, I've nothing to be generous with. I'm miserly in my giving, bitter and empty, drained of all the energy it takes to love her now. Yes, I mourn her... but for the dying of truth, not for my loss. How can I speak of my loss, when I don't know what I've lost? *Who* I've lost. As for forgiveness, as I hope to be forgiven? What's to forgive, when I'm as much in the dark as she is, lying there. I can't even say *lech b'shalom*, go in peace, when peace, for me, is so elusive.

And so she fretted on, miserable, mean and anguished, forgetting Ed, forgetting the promise of new hope with Deborah, forgetting her painting and her success as a painter and her new passion with landscapes. Forgetting all that meant life, and dwelling only with the dead.

Yit-gaddal v'yitkaddash sh'meh rabba b'alma di v'ra chir'uteh...
Extolled and hallowed be His great name in the world He has created according to His will...

Cat stood immediately under the cross, facing the coffin. Her knees were trembling uncontrollably, her voice loud in her ears, and each time she looked up, always before her was her sleeping mother in that long pine box with its gleaming handles...

y'he sh'lama rabba min sh'mayya, v'chayyim aleynu v'al
kol yisrael v'imru, amen...
Let there be great peace from heaven and life upon us
and upon all Israel, and say amen...

...and beyond, the Jewish contingent swayed and
moaned, their hands reaching for their hair as if to tear
it out by the − roots.

...Oseh shalom bim 'romav, hu aa'aseh shalom
aleynu, v'al kol yisrael v'al kol b'ney adam, v'imru;
Amen...
He who makes peace in the high places, may He
bring peace on us and upon all Israel, and upon all the
children of men, and say, Amen.

The moment when the men lifted the coffin, turning
it awkwardly on their shoulders; the moment when the
vicar motioned her to lead the procession behind it; the
moment when Deborah did not let go her hand, did not
let go her hand, and James took her arm on the other
side; the moment when she turned to Ed − come with
us? and Ed shook his head − no, just family − and Amit
joined them; the moment when she looked into the
faces of her mother's friends and saw them wet and
smiling; the moment when her mother's coffin was slid
into the funeral car and the door was shut on her −
those moments would live with her for ever.

Not the long, lonely drive through the city, where
out of the tinted window all she could see were
shoppers going about their shopping, Asian women,
inscrutable behind their black *hijabs,* brisk city-suited
men, heads bent into mobiles, and mothers with
pushchairs under flowered plastic covers, chatting
beside the road, who glanced up at the sight of the
small cortege and then turned away, as if nothing had

happened of any significance, though all her world was mourning.

Nor the burial, too terrible for words. *Man that is born of a woman hath but a short time to live...* The rain, the slippery mud, the false green of the false grass, the descent into darkness. *In the midst of life we are in death... ashes to ashes and dust to dust* – yet she was grateful to have fulfilled her mother's wish, to be buried in the earth, not consigned to flames which would always and forever evoke Hitler's carnage.

What stayed with her, and would later comfort her beyond measure, was the sense of having come out of a sacred moment, of leaving Ruth in the soil of her final homecoming – and the old man at another grave, leaning on his stick with flowers in his hand, who stood motionless, as much to attention as he could, bare-headed in the rain.

Thou knowest, Lord, the secrets of our hearts...

14

By the time they got back to Phoenix Way the rain had stopped and the late afternoon sun was casting a milky glow around the houses. Through the open front door, Cat could hear talking and subdued laughter, and the occasional sound of an instrument. Meanwhile the grass greened and the weeds flourished.

When Cat entered the living room she saw that the furniture had been pushed back, and they had brought in an incongruous assortment of chairs, some white or green plastic, others of striped blue canvas on rusting metal frames – the kind she associated with parked cars on a grass verge, the wife lethargic over the hot flask, the husband bent over his map. For a moment she was distracted, imagining the hasty but tortuous accumulation of these chairs; the wiping down of them, the folding up of them, the stacking of them into cars and the compliant unfolding of them, here, in her mother's house. They were arranged like a waiting room, except that Ruth's chair, the little green one with the Queen Anne legs, was left to one side, its frayed embroidered cushion squarely on its seat and plumped up, as though underlining the fact that Ruth would never sit in it again.

As they came in there was a mutter of *mazeltophs* and the soft clapping sound of fingers against palms. Over by the kitchen door she saw her twins with Ed and Amit. Amit was wearing a repressive frown, and she was not clapping.

In the middle of the room was a solitary green patio chair and someone took her hand and led her to it and gently pressed her shoulders to make her sit. From behind, a black lacy cloth was draped over her head; the overhead light glinted through its pattern and she could feel it tickling her cheek. Powerless to resist, she sent Deborah a wry, helpless look, and Deborah flattened herself against the wall, grabbing James's hand. As Cat sat down there was an immediate hush, then a brief, keening prayer time in Hebrew led by Yan Buber.

I can't bear much more of this, she thought; I wish they'd just hurry up and go.

Then Rachel took Ella by the arm and they went to make tea, and Amit went out in the back garden for a fag, and the kids disappeared upstairs. Cat was about to get up, but someone shook their head at her, so she stayed where she was. Ed bent over her, said, 'Don't worry; we'll be out of this soon. Just be patient; go with it; they have their rituals, you know, and this is one of them; it's not a bad idea...'

Cat nodded, and held on to him for a moment.

Rachel came in with a tray of steaming mugs, Ella with paper plates of sandwiches, to which the cling film still clung, and more cling film was removed from bowls of salad and the lacy cloths from people's heads, and there was the sweet, spicy smell of strudel heating in the oven. People drew up the chairs into groups to eat their food; she heard whispers of accented English, but also whatever else they habitually used among themselves; foreign-sounding, guttural.

The smell of the food brought the kids down, and they glanced over at their mother, concerned, then heaped their plates and disappeared again. A short while later Cat heard the sound of giggles, and, unexpectedly, alarmingly, the laughter rose in her stomach, as it always used to do when she heard them giggle. She wished she could join them upstairs and roll on the bed with them and throw pillows, but someone pressed down on her shoulders again, no doubt an observant Jew, and she stayed where she was, an untouched plate of food on her lap.

Then Yan and Leo picked up their instruments and tuned up together and the chairs were stacked and cleared. Still she had to sit, but the others stood back, clutching half-empty plates, prepared to listen. They started off with some mournful dirge which did not quite rend the heart, but then the fiddle became wilder, and feet began to tap, and a bearded man in a thin, black gabardine coat started a strange dance, circling Cat with small rhythmic soundless steps, his toes in-turned, head down like a matador, his arms raised to shoulder height, and then other men joined arms with him, completely encircling her where she sat, their heads also curved downwards like matadors, their shoulders hunched and tense, their thin gabardine coats flapping against her legs, the women standing by, clapping a-rhythmically, softly, like *fandango*.

It was so much an echo of her nightmares that she had to fasten her feet to the floor.

And the fiddle shrieked and the clarinet burned and they both reached heights of exploration of which she never knew they were capable.

Thin, high, sustained notes, swirling, metallic, descending slides, and startling, contrasting tempo. A minor key that spoke exultantly of rites and rituals; the celebrations of the old, deserted villages and the empty ghettos; endless, ancient music of the spheres, primitive, urgent, and very Jewish. Klesmer music.

Somewhere in there, she thought, I have my roots. It brought with it no joy.

People appeared at the front door; neighbours, who, she thought with compunction, she should have invited to the funeral, or at least alerted. They came, however, not to complain about the noise, but to commiserate. Among them was Ruth's Asian friend, Mrs Patel, bedecked in a silver sari, a string of pearls round her head and a plunging ruby *bindi* between her large eyes, dark with *kohl*, her whole figure so exotic and mournful that Cat wanted to paint her there and then.

They were softly-spoken people, ordinary people, who came and found her or were pointed in her direction, who took her hand where she sat under her black veil, and their compassion was gargantuan. We knew your mother, they said; we knew Ruth, such a kind lady, we're so sorry, she brought me a casserole when my wife died. so sad, we wished we'd known, we could have sent a card, visited her in the hospital, why didn't she tell us she was ill, don't worry, dear, I'll cut her lawn, you can't have everyone knowing the house is empty, so sorry she's passed away, no, we won't stay, well, just a cup of tea, perhaps.

It made her studio seem a lonely place, bereft of community, sterile and self-indulgent. Yet it waited for her patiently enough, and the light was faithful. She yearned for it, and the river, always there. Her eyes were pricking, her ears deafened by the sound, and she longed to be anonymous, to stand, to move, even to cry, but her cheeks... her cheeks were stretched in a grinning rictus of pretence.

Ed stood in front of her and helped her to her feet.

'Am I allowed, now?' she asked, somewhat sarcastically.

'Think so. You want some air?'

'I want some space. The air will do.'

They went outside and made for the low wall in front of the house. Amit was there, smoking, and there was a little pile of cigarette ends at the foot of the wall.

'Hallo, Amit,' said Cat. 'You're wanting some peace?'

'I've been wanting peace all my life,' said Amit grimly. 'I can wait a little longer, till I get to be with Rute.'

They joined her on the wall. It was getting late; further down the road bedroom lights were on and Cat could see movement behind the steamed up frosted glass of bathroom windows. Inside those houses children would be going upstairs, chased to the bathroom, shouted at to switch off the television, nagged about homework, teeth and abandoned clothes. The everyday battles of family life.

I shan't sleep here, she thought, thankfully; when everyone has gone we'll just drive away. We can't leave before everyone had gone. But the kids should go soon. They both have some distance to travel and work in the morning. I'll speak to them about it, she thought, when I go back in.

They sat in silence for a time, while behind them the music raved on and people laughed and chattered.

'What *was* that, in there?' Amit said contemptuously. It was not a question, and Cat made no reply.

'Had you known Ruth long?' Ed asked Amit, making an effort to distract her.

'Nearly all my life. We were good friends once, but we lost touch when she came to England. You know how it is. But those *people*, in there...'

'Were you in school with her?' Cat interrupted.

Amit gave her an absent look. 'In school? Oh, no, this was later. You're very like her,' she added, 'as she was then. You don't look like her, particularly, but you have the same mannerisms.'

'Really?' Cat was intrigued. 'What sort of mannerisms?'

'Oh, I don't know. The way you have of screwing yourself up into a ball when you're tense. Folding your arms across your chest, twisting your legs.' She gave a brittle laugh. 'Rute used to do just that.'

'Really?' echoed Ed, going fishing. 'How was that?'

She glanced at him.

'Oh, she had this way of shutting herself off. She put a real barrier around herself, did Rute. A real wall. She was unreachable. We were seriously worried about her, Reuben and I. We thought she wouldn't make it. We thought she was so tight, so turned in on herself, she didn't stand a chance. She didn't let up for a minute. She went for whole days without speaking. Of course, in those days we all had to struggle. We were quite literally starving and those who wouldn't share, I mean share what they were feeling, they just turned their faces to the wall and, well, just died. There was nothing you could do about it. Of course, things got better in the kibbutz. She opened up, then. I'm talking about the years in the ghetto.'

A little, staccato word, easily missed in their embarrassment about the rituals, half a breath only – and the world tilted, while behind them Yan's clarinet reached fever pitch.

'The ghetto?' Cat heard her voice in her head as her lips formed the question.

'Why, yes, that's where I first met her.' Amit sniffed impatiently. 'Look at you, Caterina! You act as though you're hearing this for the first time. I only mentioned it for *his* sake!' She gestured at Ed with her thumb.

'Well, tell me more,' he said. 'I'm fascinated.'

'Huh, *she* should have told you! Well, I was already there. They came on a transportation from Dresden, she and Reuben. I'm a year or two older but we stuck together. None of us had parents there. Their father went to Auschwitz, but you must have told him *that*, Caterina! Mine too, and then my mother to Belsen. Their mother died on the transportations, in a cattle truck.' She saw Cat's expression. 'You must have known *that*, Caterina!'

'Yes... No... I haven't... What happened?'

'She smothered to death. She died holding Rute in her arms. Rute was only ten and she was small for her age. She went to sleep and when she woke her mother was dead under her. I'm sorry if you didn't know. I wouldn't have mentioned it. *God*,' she said, spreading her hands, 'how did I get into this?'

The horror blinded Cat for a moment, and she swayed, and Ed's arm went round her. She dared not speak to ask the questions. Ed took over.

'You were all there together?'

'Yes, four years. A place called Terezin, near Praha,

360

on the borders with what's now the Czech Republic. Theresienstadt. There'd always been Jews there. We joined them, that's all, the purpose being that we'd all go down together.'

She turned to Cat suddenly, her face dark. 'Look, Caterina, these things happened! It wasn't uncommon. Forty people crammed into a cattle truck... I expect your mother just wanted to hold on to you. She'd be terrified of getting separated.'

She looked at Cat closely as if trying to recognise Rute in her, and then turned away.

'Anyway,' she continued, 'she was wearing a necklace, Rute's mother, I mean, and Rute found it, and put it round her neck. She hid it next to her skin. It was all she could do. No one accused her of anything. Look,' she said suddenly, 'don't make me go through this, OK? This is not so easy for me... Why don't you just tell your husband later?'

'Ed isn't my husband,' Cat said faintly. 'He's... a dear friend.'

'Oh, I thought...' She turned to Ed, glowering. 'You should have said, when you phoned us, you weren't her husband! To phone like that, and you not family... Well!'

'Amit, that really doesn't matter now,' Cat said wearily. 'Please go on. This isn't something I already know. My mother, she'd never speak of it.'

'But, I thought... I thought you *knew*!' she exclaimed. 'In the hotel, you hinted... But I just didn't want... Not in front of Reuben. Can't you see he's suffered enough?'

'I was trying to find out. Ma, she mentioned things and then... she just... refused to say anymore. She sort of...clammed up.'

'Yes, I expect she did,' Amit said bitterly. 'Typical. But you see... Oh, for goodness sake, Caterina, you're a middle-aged woman – don't you know *anything*? Where have you lived, all these years? It's what people do. When the memory is too awful. When they can't face...'

Cat burst out crying.

The tears spurted from her eyes and she gave a great howl, her mouth wide open, and Ed's arms came round her fast. She turned and hid her face in his shoulder, her eyes thick with tears. The sobs wracked her chest and she felt as though she would choke. She could hardly breathe; she thought, this is going to kill me.

Over Ed's shoulder she saw someone in the house swing round and twitch the curtain aside, and she pulled her face away, and clamped her hands over her mouth. 'Oh... I thought it wasn't *true*...!' The words squeezed from her.

'My God, of course it's true! What, you think I lie to you?'

'No... no... But Reuben...'

'What's this with Reuben, already? Why you suddenly talk of Reuben?'

'No,' said Cat. 'It doesn't matter.' She gasped and took a few deep breaths, trying to pull herself together.

'Go on, Catherine,' murmured Ed in her ear, 'go on; get it out of her!'

'Please, Amit, carry on. I'm sorry...'

'That's o*kay*,' she said slowly, glaring at Cat suspiciously. 'It's a hard thing to hear, I know that. Just don't do that to me again, OK?'

'No. Please go on.'

'O*kay*,' she repeated. She looked shocked. 'I'll fill you in. But just the bare bones, OK? Don't ask me how it *felt*; my God! I don't want another storm like that one.'

She took another cigarette from her bag and lit it, inhaling deeply and blowing out the smoke. 'OK, no problem.'

'Just the bare bones,' Cat agreed.

So now, at last, when she'd entirely given up hope,

the truth was coming. Already she was coming back to her, her mother, Rute; wafting towards her with open arms, as insubstantial as a ghost. Cat felt a tentative surge of joy, like the swell on the river after a boat has passed. She could feel her pulse under Ed's hand, and the sobs settling in her throat. She could hear the music behind them in the room. Up the street a car stopped, and people got out. Doors slammed. They stood on the pavement, looking over, and then disappeared into a house.

Amit was talking again.

'So, the ghetto, Terezin, OK? It was a fortress town. It was actually very gracious, architecturally, I mean. Huge houses of brick and stone; civic buildings; but in the middle was the old ghetto, wooden, ancient, and that's where they housed the children, mostly orphans, like us. The conditions were terrible. We starved, Caterina, all right? You cope with that? We ate out of dustbins. We ate rats and mice and other vermin. We ate potato peelings. We soaked old shoe leather in rainwater – my God, how it rained! – and tried to chew it. A cabbage soup would last for days. We did have bread, a loaf a week, but it had to be carefully rationed, and if you shared your bread, you died. And clothes. We came with whatever we could carry at the last moment. Some people had whole *suitcases* of clothes. And blankets, treasured books, and jewellery – clocks, watches, fancy heirlooms, costume finery, anything. *Junk*. All of it was exchanged for a cabbage, a few root vegetables, an ounce of flour. Reuben had an old samovar – God knows why he brought it. It was his father's, he said, but we had no fuel for it, anyway. We sold it for bread... My God, a loaf of bread could cost you your mother's jewellery. Caterina, don't *look* like that. I'm telling you the truth. And all the time Rute had this necklace. She wore it always, next to her skin. She refused to part with it, even when Reuben got angry with her. He said, "Would you rather die?" She said, "I would rather die." She said, "One day, I might have a daughter of my own. I've got to have something to give her."'

Cat's stomach lurched but Amit made a gesture of contempt.

'*Stupid!* she said angrily. 'Adolescent and stupid – you know what she's like, how romantic she can be, how full of dreams. We had more sense, Reuben and I; we knew we'd left behind whatever dreams we'd had. We told her; we said, "You don't know from one moment to the next whether you'll even survive!" She herself was still a child, for God's sake. But *so* stubborn! That's when she went into herself. Refused to speak for days....'

Cat made a bad mistake, then, a very bad mistake. She felt under her jacket for her mother's necklace. 'Was it this one?'

Amit gasped. '*What?* Let me look at it, Caterina.'

She reached out and took hold of it, fingering the delicate gold and silver bars, taking the weight of it in her hand.

'My *God*, Caterina,' she said savagely, 'this could have saved some lives! And she kept it all these years?'

'Yes. She always wore it. Even in the hospital. I... I took it from her neck when she died...'

Amit grimaced. 'Ah, so history repeats itself – well, it always does. But my God, to put my eyes on this again! Well, you're lucky to have it,' she said heavily, tossing the necklace away in disgust. 'It's Russian, you know. It's worth a great deal of money, Caterina.'

'Yes, I believe it might be.'

Amit shook her head in disbelief. 'I'm glad you didn't show it to Reuben! It would have killed him. I don't know what it would have done to him! To think, all these years! He would have taken it from her by force, but after what had happened to her, he couldn't use force. But he was very, very angry. He was furious. It makes me furious just to look at it, even after all this time!'

Cat hid it from her eyes, not just to save her feelings. Her disgust polluted it somehow. She slipped it down her blouse against her skin, where Rute had worn it, in the ghetto.

'What happened to her?'

Amit breathed out, running a hand over her face. 'God, I can't get over seeing that necklace!'

'I'm sorry, Amit. Leave it, will you?' Cat said faintly. 'Let's leave it for now.' Amit glared at her, as if she'd been rude. 'I meant, what had happened to make Reuben not want to use force? To get it, I mean. To get the necklace.'

'Rute was attacked. We'd been there four years by then and she was sixteen years old. She'd never even been in the company of boys who weren't family and this was a grown man, the bastard. You led a very protected existence, you girls. I mean, Hannah and Rute did. That was the way with those old Orthodox families. *God*, Caterina, you know all this! Why do you make me...? OK, OK, I suppose this was something else Rute wouldn't tell you.'

'I knew something had happened. Not the details.' Her heart was pounding and she pressed her first against it hard.

'My God, she wants details, already...' Amit threw her hand in the air. 'She was attacked, OK? And after that she was never the same. She turned her face to... Oh mein Gott, *enough*, already!'

'I'm sorry, Amit,' Cat said. 'Please go on with your story.'

'Huh, a story she calls it!' Again her hands seized the air, the cigarette clutched between her fingers, and a shower of sparks flew.

Cat waited. 'What happened next?'

Amit lit a new cigarette from the stub of the old one, inhaled deeply, and blew out the smoke. 'We escaped,' she said shortly. 'Got away. Went to Israel.'

'Yes, but how?'

'Oh, I forgot, she wants details!' said Amit, with heavy sarcasm. 'OK, Caterina, see if you can cope with this.' She paused, gathered herself. 'You have to imagine coal trucks, sort of metal bins on wheels, high-sided things which used to transport coal to the ghetto. You have to imagine,' she repeated, sighing with exasperation, 'old buildings very close together, and a low bridge, about twelve feet high, which joined them and went over the road underneath. Where ordinary people lived,' she added grimly, 'who had real food and real clothes and real fires. Camp followers, Nazi women. *Pah!* We used to watch them from the bridge, and their cheeks, their cheeks were rouged and their bellies were fat. And they walked properly. They didn't shamble about like we did. They weren't *weak.*'

She paused, drawing on her cigarette and screwing up her eyes against the smoke. 'These coal trucks, they went on tramlines through a pair of heavy wooden gates. Manned by the Nazis – well, soldiers; I don't know if they were Nazis. You couldn't hope to get out that way. But if you were prepared to take a risk, jump from the bridge, then you stood a chance, just a slight chance...'

'My God, Amit...'

'Yes. Precisely. Well, you get desperate. And you couldn't go alone. You had to go with someone else. You all had to jump together. That's what we did. and we'd nothing to lose by then, anyway. The ghetto was becoming too crowded – there were over a hundred and fifty thousand people there by then, and the Germans were clearing it out, transporting people deep into Germany – I don't need to tell you the places.

'That October there was a special children's transportation. Every day children disappeared, street by street. When they came to our street – it was very early one morning – Reuben came rushing in where we were sleeping, and said, 'Now! We have to go now!

Otherwise we'll never get out.' So we took some bread and a few onions wrapped in a blanket, blacked our faces with coal dust, and we went. When the empty trucks came past we climbed over the bridge on to the parapet – it was lower there – and then we held hands, and then... Then we just jumped.'

She stopped, her mind far, far away, in empty days, empty lands.

'You were all right? You landed safely?'

'Rute was all right, but she was in the middle. I broke my arm landing.' She held it up. 'Look, I can't straighten it properly to this day. And Reuben smashed his ankle. It never healed properly. You noticed he walks with a limp? Well, that dates from then.'

'You got away?'

Amit's mouth gaped and she looked at Cat with irritation. 'For God's sake, Caterina, of course we got away! Would I be sitting here now if we hadn't got away? All the time we were huddled under sacking in that open truck it was snowing. We nearly froze to death. We went to a port on the Black Sea – I don't know where; I never saw the name. The truck was loaded on to a ship – you know, a container vessel, and it took us all the way to Cyprus. Five days in the hold; complete darkness, and by then we had no food. But we didn't know for sure we'd 'got away', as you put it, until we stood on the soil of Palestine.'

15

Cat realised that the music had stopped, and that it was very quiet. Rachel Stein stood over her. 'Ach, here you are! Your jungsters are sleeping upstairs, Caterina. You should get zem to go home.'

Cat got to her feet stiffly. 'Yes, I'll tell them. Rachel, thank you for everything. I'm sorry I haven't...'

'We vondered vere you vere, Caterina,' said Rachel reproachfully. 'On ze one hand, I understand you haf your aunt to see.' She nodded at Amit, who looked away. 'On ze ozzer hand, you should nat have left your guests so long.' She wagged an arthritic finger. 'On ze third hand, you should come inside ze house if you want to talk.'

It was her mother's voice, her mother's idiom. Cat felt a rush of affection for her and Ed's mouth twitched with amusement

'We'll do that,' he said, getting up. 'Amit, you come on in, too; it's getting cold. When folks have gone, you'll finish your story?'

Amit shrugged. 'Always story! Well, I'll finish. There's not much more to tell.'

They went into the house. Everything had been cleared up, the plates, the glasses, the cutlery; the chairs had been stacked and the curtains drawn. People left quickly, and the room was suddenly empty, drained of sound, though the walls would vibrate for years. Cat felt guilty, grateful, and very tired. But also energised, somehow, buoyed up; at last things were coming together.

She woke the children with a mug of tea, got them freshened up and down the stairs, tidied the bed, washed up their dirty plates and mugs, remembering the old times, when they had lived at home.

Amit and Ed were sitting quietly in the living room, and Deborah was squatting on the floor, her arms on her knees, whispering to him softly, her eyes alight. Cat supposed she was at the age when anything could impress her and Ed's performance in the church had evidently done just that. She's like me in this as well, Cat thought — too quickly charmed. James stood by, grinning sleepily. Amit seemed lost in her own thoughts, disconnected, waiting to go.

Cat hugged James closely. 'Bye, darling. Thank you both so much for coming.'

'Yeah, well, no big deal, Ma. Keep in touch, OK?'

'You're taking Amit back?'

'No, she's going by train. I'm taking Deb to Birmingham.'

'Well, let's meet,' Cat said. 'Do lunch. Or you could come to the studio.'

'Does that rule out lunch,' smiled Deborah, getting up, 'if we come to the studio?'

'Darling, just come; spend the day. Bring Pete if you like. You as well, James — I expect you've got a partner, too.' He grinned sheepishly. 'Mmm, why am I surprised? Look, I'll ring you both up.'

'OK,' said James, 'but we'll come on our own, Mum, the first time.'

Cat saw them off, feeling old. She waved from the front of the house, and then stood quietly on the pavement, savouring the darkness. Then she closed the door, switched off the upstairs lights, and went into the living room. Ed was sitting silently, his hands loose on his lap. Amit was looking round as though she was in a different culture entirely; foreign, in more ways than one.

'So, I'll tell this, and then I'll go,' she said. 'I need to catch the last train. You can drop me at the station?'

'What time's your flight?' asked Ed.

'Seven. I can sleep in Departures.'

'You can't sleep in Departures!' Ed protested.

'Oh yes I can!' she said emphatically. 'It won't be the first time. I've slept in worse places.'

'You could sleep here for an hour,' Cat suggested. 'It's not ten yet, and we can order you a taxi for later.'

'Look, leave it, will you? I can decide for myself. Just let me get this, this *story* over with, and then we'll go, if you don't mind. In fact, there's nothing more to tell. We stayed in that ship till it docked in Cyprus. It was before the exclusion zone was put in place – you know,' she added bitterly, 'when the British stopped refugees going into Palestine.' Almost she would have spat.

'How did you survive on the journey?' asked Cat. 'I mean, without food.'

Amit coughed suddenly and put her hand to her throat.

'My mouth is dry,' she said hoarsely. 'Get me a drink, Caterina.'

It was Ed who went, and Cat heard him turn on the tap in the kitchen. She and Amit looked at each other.

'Is he Jewish?' she whispered.

'...No.'

'Well,' she sighed, 'that is *nicht* zo bad. You ought to break free... I won't expect you to come to Israel after all this. Why should you? You know your father wasn't a Jew?'

'Oh, Ma told me he was. She said his name was Aaron Rosensweig.'

'Hah!' she scoffed. 'The Rosensweigs weren't proper Jews! They were so-called Messianic Jews; Jews who had converted. Aaron Rosensweig came from Greece or Malta or someplace. Sephardi, but a convert. I saw him once, in Tel Aviv. He was there with Rute and the baby – that was you, of course.'

'I was born in Israel? But Ma told me...'

'Caterina, of *course* you were born in Israel! Where did you think you were born? Haven't you got your birth certificate?'

Cat shook her head. 'No, I've never seen it. It may be among my mother's papers, but if so, I haven't found it. I always thought I was born in High Wycombe.'

'Well, you weren't. You're Israeli by birth. And your father was very proud of you. Pity they didn't marry, but Rueben... Well, Reuben loathed him. His excuse was that he wasn't Ashkenazi, but that wasn't the real reason. He'd have hated anyone who came between him and Rute'.

There was nothing to say, and by then Ed had returned with the glass of water, so they didn't discuss it further. Cat did wonder, though, whether her father, being a Christian, hadn't influenced Rute in that direction, but now she'd never know. She'd look for her birth certificate, though.

Amit took the glass eagerly and drained it, and then cradled it in her lap as though for comfort. Ed sat down again and Amit looked at him blankly.

'You were talking about the ship,' he reminded her gently. 'About food. About surviving.'

'Ah. Well, we stole, OK? We sent Rute. She was small and she wasn't injured. In any case, after all that fuss about the necklace, she deserved... Well, I won't go over that again. We sent her out at night and she got it from the mess quarters, or wherever. Left-over rice, mostly. Raw potatoes. Tomatoes. That kind of thing. Luxuries to us, what there was of it. We survived, OK? *Enough*, already!'

Cat was going to let her go. They had their coats on, when Ed suddenly led her into the kitchen. They talked quietly, their faces nearly touching; Amit close by, in the downstairs closet.

'Catherine, ask her about Reuben. Why he told you it was a pack of lies. See what she says.'

'Ed, I can't. She's an old lady; she's tired. She just wants to get away. It doesn't matter, now...'

'*Ask* her,' he urged. 'Otherwise, you'll never have closure.'

371

Cat held on to him. 'And then we'll go?'

'Then we'll go. It won't take us long. With empty roads, a couple of hours. You'll go to bed, and wake up beside the estuary.'

Amit came out, wiping her hands.

'My God, Caterina, your mother was a case! She had a plastic Star of David hanging up behind the door. You know that? My God, a plastic Star of David!'

'Amit,' Cat said, 'would you come and sit down for a moment? There's just one thing more I want to ask you. One last thing, then we'll get you to the station.'

Amit shrugged and went back to the living room and sat down, her thin arms folded round her coat.

'Amit...' Cat began, and couldn't form the words.

Ed took over. 'Amit, Reuben said some things to Catherine, in the hotel. I think that's what she wants to ask you about.'

Amit glanced at Cat and frowned. 'What things?'

Cat couldn't meet her eyes. 'He said... he said Ma had... made it up... about the attack on her. He said there was no attack. He said her pregnancy was a slander on Hannah's name...'

'On Hannah's name? Why on Hannah's name?'

'Something to do with... purity...'

'Purity? No, he wouldn't have said that. He'd never have spoken about purity...'

'No, I forget; he said virtuous. And he said... I am sorry, Amit, but he was very angry with me. He said my mother always made things up, and that it was all nonsense. He said there was no ghetto. That she'd invented it.'

Her eyes widened. 'Invented the ghetto?'

'And the attack, and how you escaped. He said she was inventing those things.'

'But inventing the ghetto? My *God*, we should be so lucky! Are you sure? You must have got it wrong.'

'"*We never went to any ghetto.*" Those were his exact words, Amit.'

372

Amit sank back in the chair, and spread her hands helplessly. She seemed about to speak again. Her mouth opened and closed. Cat and Ed waited.

'I shall never make that train.'

'You'll make the train,' said Ed firmly, 'if we have to talk all the way.'

'Well, why don't we?' Cat said eagerly, jumping up. 'Why don't we just go, and Amit can tell us on the way.'

She closed up the house, and they left. She gave Ed directions to the station. Amit sat in the front; she looked small and hunched, as if she was a prisoner. The sky was perfectly clear, full to brimming with a myriad of stars. The streets in the shopping centre were deserted, the shops shuttered against vandalism. Under the by-pass traffic lights flickered their changes to the empty road, their strident colours deeply discordant with the profound anguish emanating from Amit.

And hostility. 'May I just ask,' she said tightly, 'what you think gives you the right to ask these things you've asked? You weren't there...'

Cat felt a chill on her spine. 'She was my mother. I'm her daughter. I think that gives me the right. I'm sorry, but I was shattered by what Reuben said. He...

'You don't *know* Reuben!' said Amit roughly, twisting her head round to look at her. 'You don't know the first thing about him! You don't *begin* to understand him!' She glared at Cat angrily, her eyes huge, but Cat was determined that this time she wouldn't placate; she'd hold her gaze until she got an answer. It was Amit whose eyes fell first.

'Well,' she conceded. 'I suppose you do have a right... But to deny the ghetto? Reuben would never... Look,' she said, drawing breath, 'I want you to understand something about Reuben, why he might have said... what you say he said. I find it hard to believe... No, I don't believe it. My *God,*' she added,

373

putting a hand to her forehead, 'what *am* I to believe?'

They said nothing, and after a moment Amit started up again. 'Things aren't as simple as you think they are. Not so black and white...'

They still said nothing. They waited.

'Well, *everything's* changed,' she said. '*Nothing's* the same anymore. If they ever were. They've changed for us in Israel, radically changed. Well, I know they've changed everywhere. My God, the whole world has changed! Since we came to Palestine – Israel, I mean. Since the war.'

She hunched her shoulders to relax them.

'There's been a kind of – what do you call it? A back-lash. People now question everything. They question the immigration laws, whether they should be called up to the army, whether they should stay on the kibbutz.'

'Yes, you told me a bit about...'

Amit silenced her, gesturing impatiently, 'But one thing they don't question,' she said emphatically, 'is where they came from and why. But the *world* questions! They question whether or not six million Jews died in the Holocaust. You know that? This is not something that a Jew questions. But others? "Maybe," they say, "it was not quite so many, perhaps?"'

She twisted her head and glanced at Cat, her eyes glinting in the darkness of the car.

'So, Caterina, how many dead make a holocaust? Thirty thousand? Five thousand? Over thirty three thousand Jews died at Babi Yar, did you know that? *In one day*. Shot, all of them, and tossed into a gorge. Was that a holocaust?'

She paused, swallowed, and went on.

'Afterwards, after the war, they found records, you know, facts and figures, where, when, who. Names, the cities they came from, where they ended up. At first we thought it was only a selected few who had disappeared, like us. Then we thought, maybe just a region. That's what we hoped. Ach, *hope*, already! It wasn't until much later that the full horror of it hit us, when they began to seriously count. When they began the exhumations and the study of those records. I remember to this *day* when we heard the figures – I felt as I'd done in Cyprus; I wanted to wash; I couldn't get clean; Reuben and I, we spent the whole week in the shower. And even then it was only an estimate. At Theresienstadt *alone* the Germans imprisoned and then incinerated literally thousands of European Jews; many of them cultured, erudite people. When we heard about that... Well, it was the end, for us, for that's where we'd been. Yes, I admit it, we were there. I won't deny it, even if Reuben... From then on we stopped being German. We had no nation; we were Jews, and Israel was our nation.'

Ed glanced at her, the side of his face lit to orange chiaroscuro by the streetlamps. 'You're talking about complete denial.'

'*Yes!* she replied, wiping her mouth with her wrist. 'People like that man Irving – you know, David Irving, that British so-called historian? People listened to him. A couple of years ago, that was. And that man Zeuchter, posing as an engineer. His real job? Designing execution apparatus, my God! He tried to prove that the Nazis never used gas to kill us. He said he'd chipped bits off the walls at Auschwitz, and there was no trace of the cyanide gas they'd used there.'

She breathed heavily. Cat's hands were clenched hard against her face, and Ed's eyes were sombre.

'I heard something about Irving,' he said, 'but surely most people didn't believe him?'

'I never even heard the name,' said Cat. 'Was it in the papers?'

'So, Caterina, you don't read the papers,' snapped Amit angrily. 'So, you're not interested. Who is? Just tell me that. I'll tell you who's interested. *Jews* are interested. *Jews* read the papers. They need to, to stay alive. Never again...' Her lips closed against her teeth.

Never again... An echo of her mother's rage, almost a familial resemblance, and involuntarily Cat closed her eyes, warding off the memories.

'There was a court case. It was thrown out, but the damage was done, oh, years back. They saw it as a Jewish myth, a conspiracy. They said it hadn't happened, or not the way the Jews told it. That's how they *wanted* to see it. If it could be *proved* that it was a lie... If people could be *persuaded*... If a small seed of *doubt* could be sown...'

She gave a dry cough.

'And Reuben, you see. It did something to him. When people, not just anybody, not just the neo-Nazis, but respectable people, politicians, professors, dons of universities, professional people – when they said the Holocaust was a myth engineered by the perfidious Jew – and this happened not just in Germany, you know, but in France and Britain and America; yes, even America, Ed, where so many Jews had fled; it did something to him.'

They waited silently.

'So,' she went on, 'the Survivors. Survivors from what? And witnesses. Witnesses to what? Everywhere they sowed these seeds of doubt, while we listened and suffered all over again. Was it not enough to kill us once, that they had to try and kill us twice? *Ah*...'

Her breath rasped in her throat, and she raised her hand and massaged her neck slowly, her eyes closed. Tears oozed from her eyes and disappeared wetly into the wrinkles of her cheeks.

Cat touched her shoulder tentatively. 'Are you all right?'

Amit exhaled heavily. 'Ach, I shall never be all right.'

'My own uncle was a witness.' Ed's deep voice from the front of the car, looking straight ahead, accelerating as they joined the by-pass.

Amit's eyes snapped open and she looked at him

intently. 'He was? How?'

'He was at the liberation of Auschwitz. He was American, an observer with the Brits. They got there first. He saw what it was like and he told me about it. Piles of bodies,' he said tersely. 'Open graves, the death chambers... People wandering about, confused. Skin and bone. Walking skeletons, he said.'

'Ach,' muttered Amit, '*always* Walking skeletons'! These were *people*, Ed!' She was quiet for a moment, then she said, 'So that's good. 'It's good there are witnesses. But Reuben didn't know any witnesses. There was no one to say to him, "I was there; I saw with my own eyes what the Germans did." Plenty of people were there, Ed, but they weren't witnesses like your uncle was a witness. They were just Jews.'

They had arrived at the station. There was adequate time, so Ed pulled in and parked alongside dosing taxi drivers, leaving the engine running. Amit had paused and now she lit another cigarette, drawing in a great lungful of smoke with her head back and her eyes screwed up, and then stubbed it out violently in the ashtray.

'I was away visiting one of our schools in Gaza when it came on the television. Everyone was talking about it. One of the teachers there, an Arab Christian, he launched into a tirade against the Jews. Had they not been a source of trouble wherever they were? "Even in Germany," he said. I asked him when, in Germany. "Before Hitler was made king" – that was his reply!' She laughed contemptuously. '*King*, I ask you! So much history they know, already! I asked him why the textbooks were full of anti-Jewish propaganda, and there was no reference to the Holocaust. He said because everyone knew the Holocaust was exaggerated. "Your Holocaust was *nothing*," he said, "to our Catastrophe, what we Palestinians have suffered under the Zionists, not even one percent." He believed Irving. He said the death camps were propaganda, the Nuremberg trials just for show, staged by the Allies to cover up their own war crimes. He even said that Jews only testified to get compensation money. Quoting Irving at me, as if he knew anything, that some of us were living in Israel, happy and settled, under assumed names! Ridiculous! How could anyone believe that? But they did.'

She paused, catching her breath. 'Then, you know what he said? I'll tell you. It was those same Allies, he said, who'd sold their nation down the river, just to get a foothold in the Middle East. I was bewildered. I asked him, "What foothold? What nation?" And he almost screamed the answer at me. "Not Israel! That's *stolen* land," he said. He was banging his chest like he'd break his ribs. "*You* stole it from us," he said, and began to stammer. "And who... who lives there now? Turks and... and Poles and... and Russian terrorists. And *Germans*," he said. "German Jews who treat us as *they* were treated, as underdogs, as second class – no, *below* second class, as... garbage!"'

Amit looked up blindly at the windscreen. 'And yet, you know, there was something about what he said – oh, not so much his hatred, but the *way* he spoke, his passion... He thought he was speaking the truth. He wasn't lying to me, trying to provoke me; for him it was the truth. And something in me... well, I felt for him; I *felt* for him. No, I felt for what we'd done to him. Most of what he'd said was rubbish,' she muttered, 'but, *ja*... I felt for him.'

She went on, her voice harsh with emotion. 'I came back to the kibbutz that night. Reuben, he was in front of the television. My God, I thought he'd had a stroke! He could hardly speak. He just pointed at the television where Irving was being interviewed, and then he went to the bedroom and cried. He slept for two days. I couldn't wake him. Two days and I couldn't wake him! He refused to wake. When he came out his hair was completely white. He seemed smaller. He'd got himself a stoop. I'd never seen it before but I saw it then. *Ja*, I saw it then. He'd got old, suddenly. *Oy... oy...*'

For a moment she was lost in her own thoughts, her shoulders bowed; her arms coiled across her chest. A train must have arrived, for across the concourse taxis were starting up and pulling away, and a girl walked past, Deborah's age, her midriff bare.

'After that, he was never the same. Ask him something? He wouldn't reply. Tell him something? He would shrug, couldn't care less. Try and discuss it with him, and he'd deny having heard or seen. It was in all the papers, so we stopped getting papers. In the dining hall people talked about it, so he stopped going to the dining hall – I had to bring food to the house. If people mentioned it, he refused to listen. Ask him what we should do? Nilch. Nothing. He even stopped writing to Hannah. He had never written to your mother, Caterina, since she left the kibbutz, but he stopped writing letters altogether. All he cares about now is his garden.'

Her anger mounted.

'But tell him his plants aren't growing, that he should use the fertiliser? He flies into a rage and tells me they're OK; they're perfectly all right; we shall have avocados again and aubergines, but there are no avocados and there are no aubergines! Tell him about the Palestinians? My God, the *Palestinians...* Tell him what the Army's doing? He doesn't want to know. He says, "Incursions? What incursions? Fighting in Gaza? Why we want to fight in Gaza?" Tell him his friend, Pieter, who was in the kibbutz from the beginning, died in Haifa, in a café, in a suicide bomb attack, he says, "What suicide bomb attack, there was no suicide bomb attack. Pieter was old, he was tired, his body had had enough..."'

She stopped, exhausted.

'So it's not so surprising, Caterina, that he should say your mother had invented things, *hein?'*

'I understand,' said Cat quietly. 'I do understand and I'm sorry. But Amit,' she added painfully, 'why didn't you say something in the hotel? About my mother.'

'What could I say?' retorted Amit. 'What could I tell you? For God's sake, Caterina, I hardly know you! Your mother never saw fit to bring you to Israel, did she?'

'Reuben said...'

'What *is* this with your uncle all the time? I never knew he spoke to you! I went up, remember?'

'Well,' Cat said, with difficulty, 'why couldn't you have said something earlier? When I was asking you all those questions?'

'I had to think of *him*!' Her tone was bleak. 'Why go over it? He's an old man, Caterina, and your mother was his *twin*. When she left Israel, he felt she had abandoned him. She never came back. She was a *Jew*, my God, yet she was content to live away from Israel.'

'But what about... me?' Cat asked childishly.

'Oh yes, Caterina, you think about *'me'* if you like.' Her voice was scathing. 'But you wouldn't if you'd been through what we've been through. And you've forgotten about the necklace, what that meant to us. So what do Rute's children matter against that? The Diaspora, *pah!* An invention of hypocrites! Survivors? All those people at the house, all content to live away from Israel, while we struggle? You think they deserve some sort of ritual respect, because they survived the *Shoah*?' Her voice rattled with contempt. 'All of us in Israel have survived the Shoah and we don't go round saying we're Survivors – we just get on with life. No, Caterina, I had to think of Reuben. That's it!' She slapped her thigh. 'I had to think about *him*, what it would do to *him*, to go over all these... stories. The horror...'

The horror filled the car to silence. Cat thought Amit had finished, that there was no more to say, but she was wrong.

'It was the ghetto, you see. And the coal. It did something to him. In the ghetto, you'd expect people to help each other? Well, they didn't, or not much. The ones who were there before, they resented us. They resented everyone who came in later. They'd had music, concerts, theatre, God knows what. Heads in the sand. That all went with the overcrowding. We ate their food, drank their water. They hated us. *Ja*, they hated us.'

Her voice was husky now, no more than a faint whisper, and Cat had to lean forward to hear her.

'It was everyone for themselves; no one to look after us, tell us what to do and what not to do. *Me, me, me,* Caterina, that's what they thought. It's a *myth* to say that people hang together when they're in trouble! They weren't like that in the ghetto, I can tell you! Smash, grab, raid, lie, cheat, steal!' She choked on the words. 'That's what people did, some of them. Not everyone, and not us. They were *Jews,* for God's sake, a proud, cultured people! Hah! Even their own villages wouldn't have recognised them, but then the villages were gone. When I said it was the necklace... that was only half of it. The rest, it was the swindling, the cheating, the lying...'

She dropped her face into her hands. 'The bread from your hands and the clothes from your back. Women were *raped* for such things.'

She hesitated and then she said. 'Caterina, I'll tell you what happened. I wasn't going to, but I will.' Her voice was rough with weariness. 'When I said your mother was attacked...' She paused again and looked away. 'Caterina, when she was attacked... in that latrine... well, she wasn't just attacked. She was raped...'

Cat recoiled. She whispered, 'My mother was *raped?*'

She felt sick to the pit of her stomach. She could hardly breathe. The image of her mother as a young

381

girl, trapped in a filthy black hole – it was intolerable. It was not to be borne. Spots formed in front of her eyes and she lowered her head to her lap. The faintness passed quickly, but her ears were buzzing and her whole body was drenched in a cold sweat.

'She went out one morning and came back naked. Another Jew, for God's sake. *Animal!* A filthy madman. He probably *was* mad. People *became* mad, in the ghetto. He stuck her head in the hole and... did it. The shit was dripping down her face, in her eyes, in her mouth.

'Reuben had never been violent, but he was then. He couldn't take it in at first. "Where's your necklace?" he screamed at her, as if *that* mattered. But she'd got it safe. She gone to clean the lat, she said; she was afraid we'd all get ill. And she'd hidden the necklace before she went. So anyway, she got up – she looked old, bent – and went to a loose stone in the wall, and there it was. I remember her smiling through her tears. "My mother's necklace; it always protected me before. I'll never take it off again, never!" And that's why she'd never sell it...'

'Reuben blamed himself. Said *he* should have protected her. He'd *always* protected her, he said. So he went in search of him, the man, and when they were alone he... he killed him. He strangled him with his bare hands. He did it for Rute.'

'It broke him, what he did, and it nearly broke your mother when he did it. She was hysterical, hitting him, shouting at him, "What would Papa say? You've broken the sixth commandment! *Thou shalt not commit murder,* it says. *Thou shalt not commit murder!"* Then she cried out in a loud voice – I'll never forget it; she screamed it at him. 'Oh, Reuben," she cried, "Reuben, my dearest, dearest brother, what have you done to your *soul?"'

She swallowed, and the tears gushed from her eyes. 'He couldn't answer her,' she sobbed. 'He didn't even defend himself, just stood there, taking it. He knew it was wrong. But rape was wrong too, and he couldn't stop thinking about it. He *never* stopped thinking about it,' she wailed, 'ever, ever. All through our married life...' She mopped her face with her sleeve and subsided. 'If she kept silent about the ghetto,' she mourned, 'well, that's why.'

Cat had no words to comfort her.

Amit was speaking again, her voice muffled, strained, her energy spent.

'And the coal truck. The days in the train. The cold. The days on the sea. The cold. Being sick. Have you ever been sick, day after day, on an empty stomach? Nowhere to *be* sick? No privacy? And all the time, afraid we'd be discovered. No? Well, then you can't judge. But people who say all this, that it didn't happen, are lying.'

She coughed, and grasped her throat. 'Reuben is lying, too. That's how he *lives*, by lying. That's how he survives. If he admitted the truth he'd be dead already, so he lives by lying. Denying things ever happened. And denying God. That priest at the church,' she said contemptuously, 'that "search for meaning" – *hah*! How do you think it is for him, for Reuben – a man of courage and integrity, who fought against the British, who gave his life to the kibbutz, the son of a *Rabbi*, for God's sake! – to live his life by a lie? Is *that* meaning?'

PART 4

convergence point

And last, the rending pain of re-enactment
Of all that you have done and been;
The shame of motives late revealed, and the
Awareness of things ill done,
And done to others' harm,
Which once you took for exercise of virtue.

TS Eliot Four Quartets -- East Coker

1

Once they had said their farewells to Amit and were on the road, Cat was able to unwind. She didn't, at first, feel sleepy. She was just so glad to be out of it and alone with Ed. She pulled her coat close, for comfort, and he reached for a cushion and settled it behind her head. She didn't want to talk. Ed's face, lit by the dashboard, was calm, his eyes steady on the road; one hand warmly covering hers, the other loose on the wheel. The roads were empty and the car ate up the miles towards Lancaster, where the ground rose between the Cumbrian Fells and the Yorkshire Dales.

It was the darkest hour of the night. She could almost feel the hills, rearing up on both sides of the road, vast and mysterious, holding their secrets of springs and waterfalls, screes and slopes, loose stone walls, cattle and grazing sheep. She was reminded of the little Trahearne book in Ricci's shop and what he'd read out to her; here, everything seemed ancient, and yet, to her, new-made. Surely, now, the time of tears *was* past, the hateful family quarrels over, for her mother was innocent and at rest, and she was free.

Later, it came on to rain, a light, slanting rain, illuminated by their lights like miniscule shafts of lightning, and she could no longer sense the landscape. Always the road stretched before them, lit to radiant luminosity by the powerful headlights of the car, but it was the sound of the windscreen wipers that finally lulled her to sleep.

The rain stopped as they approached Carlisle, and the car slowed. Cat woke to the sight of long rows of high terraced houses with night-blind windows, and she gazed at them incredulously, wondering how people could live in such close proximity. Ahead, against the sky, was the Cathedral, and immediately afterwards, the high crenulations of the castle, and then shops, department stores, the anonymous concrete detritus of manufacturing; a hill, a country lane. A few miles on, they slowed completely.

'Cattle-grid ahead,' he warned, and then they were over it, on to a narrow, straight road between the marshes. Against the star-lit sky Cat could see the humped, black backs of grazing cattle, their limpid eyes caught by the headlights – almost she could hear them tearing at the grass. The sky, a dusky night-blue, was reflected in small pools and streams and rivulets, and beyond, in the distance, was the glistening strip of the Solway Firth. The road ran on the very edge of the estuary, through a village, then once more out into open country, towards a band of high trees. With no warning, she saw a gate, closed across the road, and Ed stopped the car to open it, drove through and stopped again to close it. Through the open door Cat could hear the sucking of the marsh and, nearby, something rustled in the hedgerow, and was still again.

The bothy was a little further on, an isolated, squat, white-washed house, the estuary visible as a close presence beneath the dark, silhouetted Galloway hills. Ed swung the wheel and manoeuvred the car on to the grass, its lights spilling across the water, sparkle against black. He switched off the engine and it ticked, settling.

'It'll be warm inside. I have a woman come in.'

Cat waited passively by the step, shivering slightly after the warmth of the car, while Ed shone his torch on the lock. The front door opened into a long room, and at one end of it, on a battered pine dresser, a lamp was lit, making her blink. The gas fire was on and a tupperware container stood on the table. She vaguely heard him say, 'You hungry, Catherine?' but whether she answered, or how she answered, she had no recollection. The narrow bed was icy, but when Ed pulled the duvet over her she went instantly to sleep.

Some time in the night, or what was left of it, she woke with wet eyes and his hand on her back: 'You're dreaming, Catherine, you spoke your mother's name...' and she turned over and slept again.

She woke, finally, to the sun streaming in through the thin curtains, to birdsong and a running tide, to the sound of cattle lowing. She lay there lazily, enjoying the sensation of waking to the first day of a holiday; the first of her life. It was a retreat in every sense of the word, especially as she felt she had come through battle. Here no demands would be made on her, no expectations thrust in her face. It would be a respite, only, but enough to take time out and breathe God's free air for a while.

The window was open and a soft breeze disturbed the curtains, translucent white gauze patterned with pale yellow squares, distorted to silvery diamonds and stripes by the movement of air. The room was tiny, with plain plastered walls and bare floorboards, on which stood a solid pine chair, a bachelor wardrobe and an old pine chest of drawers. On it stood an oriental figurine, twin to the one in Ed's house, and she saluted it gravely. A man's towelling dressing-gown hung on the door, which was unpainted, with an old-fashioned, gunmetal latch. On the windowsill were seashells and bits of driftwood. It was a man's room but, after the austerity of the studio, she found it pretty and attractive.

There had been no sound from downstairs, and she decided to get up and explore. She put on the dressing gown, knotting the belt tightly around her waist, and rolled up the sleeves. Then she made her way down the narrow flight of wooden stairs to the downstairs room.

At one end was the kitchen area, and a small sofa; at the other, two easy chairs in front of a wide inglenook fireplace containing an imitation gas fire, and on the wall above, a faded Constable print in a chipped gold frame of Salisbury Cathedral. On the kitchen table was a loaf of bread from which a couple of slices had been cut, and a cafetière. The coffee was tepid but she poured herself a cup and took it outside on to a grassy bank that sloped down towards the river. The tide was out, and black sandbanks, riddled with worm casts, gleamed in the bright sunlight. Seagulls were flying over the estuary, brilliant white.

Across the nearest stretch of water she could just discern the shape of a boat, and within it a figure standing upright, silhouetted against the light, an early fisherman, perhaps. She crossed the grass to a wide bank of shingle, where the mud-flats merged with the first shallow reaches of the sea. Nursing her mug, she turned and faced the cottage. It was not whitewashed here, but reddish, weathered brickwork below a steeply-sloping roof, glowing against the luxuriant green of the trees, eminently paintable. Each side of the door were two large square windows matching the dormer windows in the roof. Hers was on the right, where the thin curtains fluttered in the slight breeze.

She lifted her face to the sun, closing her eyes and inhaling deeply, hugging the dressing-gown around her, as the fresh, salty air was chill. Across the estuary the Galloway hills seemed closer than on the previous night and there were few dwellings, though when she looked back down the estuary she could distinguish the village they had passed, and in the other direction the estuary widened towards the long bar of the open sea. Apart from the occasional, raucous calling of the seagulls and the sibilant hiss of the in-coming tide, all was quiet.

She wondered where Ed was; the car was there, so perhaps he'd walked to the village for milk and eggs, or a nearby farm. That was good; she'd be quite content not to drive anywhere until it was time to go home.

She began to cross the shingle towards the

mudflats, thinking to dip her toes in the water, but as soon as she took a first step on to the black sand her foot sank up to the ankle, and she nearly lost her balance. She stepped back hastily, the sand sucking at her feet, and sat down clumsily on the shingle, dropping the mug. Her feet were filthy, the mud oozing black between the toes like wet coal dust. The smell was foul; a stinking paste redolent of decay, of a concentration of dead things on her flesh. She didn't like it. She didn't like it at all. She was repelled.

Over the water there was a shout, carried away by the breeze, and she looked up, startled. The man in the boat was gesticulating, calling, but she couldn't hear what he was saying. It frightened her somehow, in that lonely place, to have a complete stranger shouting at her, and she decided to ignore him. Some of the blackness had soiled the white towelling of the dressing gown, and she thought she might rinse it off before doing it properly in the house. Nearby was a shallow pool and she resolved to try her luck again.

The boat was shimmering so much in the bright light that at first she didn't realise that the man was rowing towards her. His whole body was moving rhythmically backwards and forwards as he plunged the oars into the water, wrestling with the cross-current. It was only when he began to shout again that she realised it was Ed.

A moment later, long drawn out, 'Keep still! Stay where you are!'

She stayed. He pulled towards her, the wide, brown boat surging through the deeper water in a long parabola against the shoreline. When he turned there was an expression of consternation on his face.

'Don't step on the sand again, Catherine!'

She called back crossly. 'I'm not! This bloody muddy...!'

She heard him laugh, and smiled ruefully.

The boat drew closer, into the nearest stretch of

water.

'Look, I've got a couple of planks here; I'll lower them over the side, then I'll throw you a line. You think you can catch it?'

'Well, I'll try, but I'm not a countrywoman, Ed.'

Ed turned the boat so that its prow slid on to the nearest bank, where it churned up the black sand with a grating sound. He tossed out the planks and then jumped out, breast-high in the water. For a moment she was alarmed for him, then noticed that he was wearing long rubber waders. He uncoiled the rope and, with a wide arm movement, hurled it towards her. It felt just short and she stepped forward to retrieve it.

'Leave it, Catherine. I'll have another go. Don't, for goodness sake, walk on the sand again.'

He recovered the rope, wound it up again, then threw the whole coil; it spun across the water and splashed on to the sand at her feet. It was wet, glutinous with mud and she picked it up gingerly. By now the dressing gown was covered with black smears.

'What do you want me to do? Pull you in?'

He chuckled. 'Hardly. But I don't want to lose the boat. Just leave the line as high as you can on the bank.'

Gripping the prow, he dragged the boat further up the sandbank, then, using the planks, he stepped across to where she was standing. He took her hands; his were icy and she pulled them away, bunching her fists in the pockets of the dressing gown.

She looked up at him, frowning. 'You were shouting at me, Ed.'

'I was calling, that's all. You've got to shout to make yourself heard. On the water the wind carries your voice away.'

'You frightened me,' she said peevishly. 'I didn't know who you were.'

He grinned. 'Well, you gave me a fright, too, stepping on to the sand like that.'

'You could see me? I couldn't see you.'

'You were looking into the sun. It could only be you, after all.'

He put his arms round her shoulders and turned her towards the water.

'Look at this...' His voice was grave.

'Yes, it's beautiful, Ed. I love it. I loved waking...'

'...it's quiet, it's secluded, and the views are fantastic, but, Catherine, these sands are treacherous. You must never, never try and walk on them again. I could see you from the boat plainly...'

'How could I know?' She felt slightly affronted.

'...There are holes in them, invisible from the surface, and in some places it's quicksand. You'll go in up to your neck if you're not careful. Promise me you'll never try and walk on the sands again?'

Cat felt rebuked, patronised. 'Why should I promise? You've told me now.'

She looked away miserably. She felt his eyes on her for a moment, then he half-picked her up as though he would carry her all the way to the cottage. She felt lumpish, awkward. He was treating her like a child. He could just as easily have taken her hand, walked up to the cottage together.

'Put me down, Ed. I can walk.'

'Let's get you in first. You're freezing.'

'No, put me *down*. You're all wet and muddy.'

In the cottage she stood clutching the dressing gown and watched him plug in the kettle.

'I'll just tie up the boat,' he said, making for the door. 'Fetch in my morning's work.'

'I dropped my mug...'

'I'll get it.'

By the time he returned she had washed and dressed. She left the dirty dressing gown in a ball by the bathroom door to wash later. She found him standing over the stone sink, cleaning his fish.

'Ed, did you have anything to eat yesterday?'

391

Attempting a cheerfulness she did not feel.

'Just a bit of cold meat and salad. And you?'

'Can't remember. Not much, I think.'

'You were crying on the beach, you know that?'

'I was upset, that's all. The sand...'

'And you cried in the night...'

'Did I?' She was surprised. 'I don't remember.'

'I heard you from my room.' He was quiet, then, appraising her. 'You know, Catherine, it's going to take a while for all this to sink in.' He grinned wryly. 'Sorry, bad pun. I meant, what Amit said, an' all.' He turned back to his fish.

She felt slightly exasperated with him.

'I know you find this funny, Ed,' she said to his back. 'But if I was upset just now, it was because I'd had a shock. I know I have issues to deal with. The sand, it got between my toes. It reminded me of ... of coal.'

'Coal. Well, that's what I mean.' He laid down his knife. It was slimy with blood and fish scales. 'Everything's going to remind you, Catherine. And I don't find it remotely funny. I'm quite aware that you can't expect to hear something like... like what Amit told you, and then dismiss it. Especially since you've been wondering if what your Ma told you was even true. I think you'll find your tears are very near the surface for a bit. You've gone through trauma, and not only with her. You're still recovering from your husband, though how... So, if there's something to smile about, well, let's smile.' He turned back to his task.

What he said was true enough, and she had to bear in mind that he had known his own grief. 'You're talking from experience, aren't you, Ed?'

'Yes. I've added quite a bit of salt to the Solway Firth in my time.' He put the fish on a plate, wrapped the debris in newspaper and washed his hands, drying them on a tea towel.

Cat sat down at the table. '...I'm sorry, Ed. For everything...'

He bent over her and took her face in his hands. 'OK, but you know who you are now,' he said softly. 'You know that your mother, when she refused to talk about those things, was protecting you. She loved you, Catherine.'

'I can't bear what happened to her. I can't bear it, Ed.'

'No.'

'Her own mother! To wake up and find you've smothered your own mother!'

'I know.'

'And the rape... face down in a filthy hole?'

'Yeah, that was horrific.'

'That black hole,' she murmured. 'I seem always to have known...'

She subsided, and again they were quiet. He knelt on the floor and held her very close, stroking her arms rhythmically.

'And the ghetto, Ed! Starving, like that, for months on end! Everything you had, gone. Her home, her family, her music... And I wore the necklace yesterday, not realising...'

'Yeah. You didn't know about Amit. It was a good thing to wear it.'

'And the things I *thought*, Ed! When I thought she'd lied to me. Horrible, angry thoughts...'

'Don't worry about that. It was natural. Water under the bridge, now.'

Cat felt suddenly drowsy, wrung out. She got up heavily and began to lay the table. She could feel the heat of the sun through the window. The estuary was slowly filling up and where she had been standing was already under water. She shivered with distaste.

'I thought you'd gone for milk. I didn't know you'd be out in the boat. Is it safe?'

He laughed. 'Oh, yes, it's quite safe at low tide, or

when it's coming in. I don't go out otherwise.'

She hesitated. 'Ed, about what happened to her... About the rape.' She took a deep breath. 'It all stacks up now. Why she'd never talk to me about the ghetto, why she got so angry when I asked about it, why she was so silent with me all those years. Why she was always so fussy about hygiene. She'd have *loathed* my father, my real father, that... that despicable old man. He was nothing but a paedophile, a filthy, filthy swine...! Aah...!' She burst into tears, long, heart-rending sobs that shook her chest.

Ed leapt to his feet and took her in his arms. 'Oh Catherine, you poor...'

'And what about Reuben?' she said into his shoulder. 'That Aaron Rosensweig, the man I *thought* was my father – Amit said he was proud of me – he looked after her, while *Reuben,*' she said scornfully, rearing her head back, 'Reuben just sent her away. OK, she was pregnant, and she could have had an abortion, couldn't she, but she didn't, did she? She didn't kill her child. But Reuben, who *had* killed, oh, he just got rid of her, didn't he? And which was worse, Ed? He was never punished for that... Not that I think he should have been, but...'

'Ah, but I think he punished himself...'

'It's not the same, Ed,' she mourned. 'It's not the same.'

Ed led her gently to the sofa and they sat down. Cat's sobs subsided, but the images would not leave her head and she started crying again, small pitiful wails of distress. Ed held her tightly and gradually she recovered herself. They sat quietly.

'Incidentally, have you no recollection of Israel?' he asked. 'What's your first memory?'

She roused herself. 'Oh, I don't know.' She frowned in concentration. 'Oranges. Lots of oranges. And a wasp came on my wrist and my mother slapped it away.' She gave a watery grin. 'I thought she was slapping *me* and I howled the roof down. I've never forgotten it.'

'Anything else?'

She puzzled over it, pinching her lips between her fingers. 'Noise. A great roaring sound. And clouds, and being squeezed tightly. I was about four, I suppose.'

'The plane.'

She looked at him, bewildered. 'What plane? Oh, you mean my dreams plane. I see...'

'No,' he said quietly, 'not the dream plane. The plane that brought you to England. And the seatbelt. That's where the dreams came from, I should think.'

'So all that 'bombs over Berlin' stuff was a chimera?'

'Probably.'

2

The cottage, in that blithe landscape, was a set-aside place, deeply satisfying, but it was also a place of severance, disconnected from everything she knew. *The Studio*, Gus, Ricci, even her children, seemed far away and in another time. Too much had happened too quickly, that was the trouble. Leaving Bill, her mother's illness and her death, the new friendship with Ed – into which she had plunged like a warm, healing stream. What Amit had revealed had been revealed suddenly, when she had totally abandoned the idea of finding out anything more about her mother.

Her mother. Rute. Who was innocent, vindicated. But what price her vindication, when she, herself, had been her sole accuser? She asked herself what it amounted to, the fact that she had doubted Rute for years, that she'd been prepared to believe Reuben, a bitter and sad old man, rather than a lifetime of love. That during this period Rute was gravely ill, dying, had died and been buried – without her feeling any genuine grief but almost antipathy – and it amounted to just that. A betrayal of the worst kind. It bordered, as Reuben might have said, on slander.

What would her mother have said to her, knowing that while she slept, she'd been looking at her with doubt in her heart, with resentment and suspicion, then with condemnation – how could she have borne it? *She* could not have borne it. She would have said, 'Go away, you. I don't need your judgement. How can you sit by me while I sleep, in that frame of mind? Just go away, will you, and don't ever come back!'

Rute hadn't known and she should have felt reprieved. Rute would not smother her with truths she didn't need to hear, anymore than she had deliberately smothered her own mother. Pity, shame, Ma, that so cleaving to your mother meant her death. How did you live with that? Reuben might be living a lie, but you lived the truth, and which is harder? Pity, shame, Ma, that so cleaving to your mother's necklace engendered such anger and hate. Did you finger it, loop it round in your hands, while all around you people died for want of bread? What were you holding on to? Your own mother, your roots, your insubstantial, hypothetical hope for a daughter? And oh, pity, shame; that so cleaving to your silence resulted in that daughter so utterly disregarding and doubting your whole integrity.

She talked to Ed, of course. She told him what was on her mind. He listened patiently enough, but he had little to say that helped. He spoke of Rute's early years in England, that she was probably completely overwhelmed; he didn't think she'd kept silence out of guile; she'd had no one else; this was how trauma emerged; and more of the same. He didn't say that she might not have bonded with a child of rape, so Cat said it for him.

'She must have hated me as a baby.'

'Ah, but it wasn't hate she showed, was it? It was reserve. What she *lived out* with you, that wasn't hate.'

By the afternoon of the next day they were still discussing it. They were strolling along the lane behind the house, and Cat had been completely silent for a while, almost morose, her head down and her hands stuffed in the pockets of her jeans. It had been sunny all day; on the other side of the hedge the river was a vivid blue, but inside her head were ghetto and cattle truck, emaciated children, blackened feet, the smell of damp coal, and her mother's green eyes on her from her white hospital bed.

'I don't see,' said Ed eventually, 'that you're going to throw this off immediately. We've been hammering away at it for quite a time.'

'I don't suppose I will. I'll have to learn to live with it, with the guilt and everything. I don't see how I can make amends.' Cat gave a wry laugh. 'I can't even confess to her.'

Ed hesitated. 'You could try giving it away.'

She glanced at him. 'Giving what away?'

'The burden of your guilt.'

'The burden of... You sound like a preacher-man, Ed! You're going to tell me next I should *pray* about it?' The idea revolted her.

'And why not, Catherine? It's been done before.'

'Huh! To which god, for heaven's sake?'

'Or... or you could give it to Deborah. She's old enough to...'

'*Deborah?* I thought the whole idea of nasty stories like this was not to burden your offspring with them. What possible good could it do?'

'It might help her to understand you better, act as a bridge. She loves you, you know.'

Now it was Cat's turn to hesitate. 'You're serious, aren't you? You seriously think I should tell her all this. But, which bit? About Reuben and what he said? About what Amit said? About the *rape*? Or just the bare bones,' she said sarcastically, 'what I've done to my mother.'

'Catherine,' he said patiently, 'you haven't done anything to your mother. She never knew you had doubts. Take space to rage, by all means, but don't let it poison your life. In the hospital you did good; you let her go. Now you have to let go of the guilt, otherwise you'll... you'll damage yourself. Guilt hurts, Catherine; it mounts up....' He stopped short and put a hand to his forehead. 'And don't I just know it!'

'I can't let go of it...' Cat said miserably.

'Can't – or won't?' he said under his breath.

She hardly heard him. '...until I've made some sort of amends.'

'For God's *sake*, what could you possibly do that would benefit her *now*?' He grasped her shoulders with both hands. 'You really mustn't go on thinking like this!

398

You really, really mustn't.'

He shook his head at her, sorrowfully, like a parent with a recalcitrant child, and then walked on again. Cat stood glaring at his back.

'"Really", Ed, "really?"' ' Well, *I* really wish you wouldn't tell me what to think all the time!'

He turned. He had paled slightly, and she regretted her outburst.

'I wouldn't dream of it,' he replied, a chill in his voice. 'But Catherine, just try, for a moment, to see things from where I stand, OK?'

'Go on, then,' Cat said mulishly, 'if you must.'

'*Catherine*!' He flung off her arm and turned away. Here the hedge had given way to gorse, the bright yellow flowers as vivid as butter, beautiful in the sun, but with a beauty that was illusory; the dark green stems were covered in long sharp spikes.

Ed walked straight at the hedge, pushed his way through, and the bushes closed up behind him. There was no sound, no indication that he'd ever been there at all. She was surrounded by silence. For a moment she stood stock-still. She looked up the lane frantically, searching for another way through. Ahead was a green hedge; beyond, more gorse. Hunching her shoulders, she closed her eyes, put her arms in the air and thrust herself at it. She felt a sharp pain in the tender flesh under her arm, like a wasp sting, vicious and deliberate.

'Get off!' she shouted stupidly. 'Let me through, damn it!'

Ed was standing down by the water, his arm across his forehead, and when he saw her he began to walk quickly away. She was appalled, and the tears spurted from her eyes.

'Ed, don't... Oh, God, *Ed*!'

He stopped, head down, and she caught up with him.

'What on earth are you doing?' she cried. 'Just *look*

at your arms!'

He was covered in bleeding scratches. This place, she thought furiously, it looks idyllic, but under the surface it's destructive. It has no soul.

'Ed, I'm so sorry. Come on, let's go back. Ed, take your hand down. Let me see your face. Have you scratched your face?'

She wrenched at his hand, and he let his arm drop. Except for a long, angry graze across one cheek his face was quite white. She put her arms round him and pulled his head down on to her shoulder. He didn't return her hug, but stood quiescent, as if utterly bone-weary, his hands, from which the red blood dripped, hanging slackly by his side.

3

Later, at the kitchen table, after she had dressed his cuts and he, hers, she asked him why he had disappeared like that through the hedge, why he had turned away from her, what he was feeling.

'Don't you know?' he asked coldly, raising his eyebrows. Then, seeing her expression, he relented. 'Oh, Catherine, I don't want to add to your problems...'

For a long time he sat with his head in his hands, refusing, or unable, to speak. Cat was desolate, and in the end her eyes welled up. He took his hands down and grasped hers. Blood was ingrained in his cuticles, like paint.

'Don't cry,' he said quietly. 'I... I can't bear it when you cry. I'm sorry. I just can't.'

His voice was thin, high-pitched, as though the heart had gone out of him; his face still ashen. Cat thought how much she had cried since coming to the cottage, of how moody she had been, and, by comparison, how resilient he always was, and how protective of her. She had come to depend on him, but how little had she allowed him to depend on her. She realised, then, what she should have realised all along. This could have been love, and she'd spoiled it.

'What have I done to us?' she said dully.

'No... nothing.'

Again it was he who was reassuring *her*, comforting *her*. Was there no way she could reciprocate? If the time was ever, she thought soberly, it was now.

'Ed, talk to me. Look, I'm sorry; I really am. Since we've come here I've been a... a moody, temperamental bitch.' She gestured outside. 'And it's not this, or anything. It's me. I really don't know how you've put up with me.'

He sighed heavily and leaned back in his chair. 'Oh... Let's have a cup of tea, shall we?'

Cat jumped up. 'I'll make it.'

He didn't say anything while she made the tea. She brought the teapot and the mugs to the table, poured out the tea and then waited. With an almost visible effort, he braced himself. When he spoke, it was measured and without emphasis.

'Catherine, you talk about living with guilt. Well, I *know* about guilt. I've lived with it for years – talk about the pot calling the kettle black! But I'm... I'm afraid of losing you, you see, and if I... if tell you why, I might.'

She leaned across the table and took his hand. 'No, you won't. I care about you too much for that...'

The words were said, a euphemism befitting her age, but her meaning was clear.

'I care about you, too.' He looked at her helplessly, almost smiling. 'I always have, right from the first... I'd have said something before, but for Anne.'

'Anne? Ah, I see. You're still grieving for her.' She felt deeply embarrassed. If Anne came between them there was no hope for them at all; she could never compete with the dead.

'No, not that! Oh, I do hope I've not given you that impression! No, Catherine,' he sighed, 'I'm not still grieving. Not in the way you mean. If I grieve, I grieve over what became of us. What you say you've done to your mother is nothing, compared to... No, not nothing, of course, but you didn't deprive her of anything, like I did Anne... And even when she died, I... I wasn't there...' A dying fall to his voice.

In spite of herself Cat was shocked. 'You weren't there?'

His head shot up, his face white. 'You see! Even you, tormenting yourself as you do, find that unforgivable, don't you? You find it inconceivable that a man should be... elsewhere, while his wife dies in a hospital bed. Oh, don't let's talk about it. Or let's at least finish this other thing first...'

'No,' said Cat steadily. 'I want to hear this. Other things can wait. So, tell me why you weren't there, Ed.'

He heard the implied accusation, and he bridled. 'Look, Catherine, I didn't know she was dying – not, I mean, at that moment. If I'd known I wouldn't have... left.' He closed his eyes, as if regretting the word, and there was a prolonged silence; a silence that, to her, seemed intensely secretive, a yawning into emptiness or horror.

'Where were you, Ed?'

He rubbed his face with his hands and then folded his arms almost defensively. 'I was never, never going to tell you this, but OK. I was simply trying to get... oh, I don't know, a bit of relief. Anne had said things, Catherine, in the hospital. It was natural; she was at the end of her life... but it just poured out of her, all her loneliness, all the resentment... She must have bottled it up for years. She was angry, bitter. She cried a lot. She got out of control.'

'And you found this so trying, you... what, took a break? And she died while you were away?'

'You don't understand.'

'Well, help me understand.'

A vein twitched in Ed's jaw and he flexed his fingers against his lap.

'Years ago, Anne had an affair. Very briefly, and it didn't come to anything. But when she told me about it, she wasn't exactly confessing it; more like attacking me.' He rubbed his chin, making the bristles rasp. 'Maybe she wanted to get her own back for my... neglect of her. But when it came to it, I made excuses for her. I just felt very, very sorry for her, even when she said that the strain between us, all those years, had caused her illness. And it may have done, for all I know. When I told her I still loved her; that I'd never stopped... she just went to pieces. She cried and cried. Then she apologised and I apologised, and we hugged. But she was exhausted, and so was I. That's when I went out, really to give her a bit of peace. And me, too, if I'm truthful. I just couldn't get my head round it so I went for a long walk, then I went home. I rang the hospital, and that's when they told me...' Briefly he wiped his hands over his eyes, and then looked at Cat, a grave, slightly distant, blue stare. 'She died while I was away.'

'But you intended to go back,' said Cat. 'You weren't 'leaving' her as such, but allowing a respite. It wasn't anger or heartlessness, was it? So you don't need to feel guilty about that. It was just bad timing, and – sorry, Ed, if this sounds callous to you – from what you told me in the car, you'd rather led parallel lives, hadn't you? That's no basis for marriage, Ed. I'm not surprised she had an affair.'

He seemed surprised, almost affronted. 'Did *you* have affairs?'

She laughed. 'Me? No, but I might have done, given the chance.'

'Catherine, to me, loyalty, keeping faith, means a great deal and Anne knew that.'

He seemed unable or unwilling to accept another point of view; too conditioned by his upbringing, she supposed, and the years of military discipline.

She said. 'Ed, it's complicated... but we need to unpack this. Do you mind?'

He had never seen her face so set, her mouth so determined. 'No, I don't mind.'

'You said you married late. Where did you and Anne meet?'

'In the Officer's Mess. She was advising about plants – she was a trained landscape gardener. I showed her round, and we went from there. She knew what marrying into the Army meant; that I wouldn't be working nine to five and that my presence was bound to be a bit erratic. She can't have felt unloved or anything. She knew what she was taking on.'

'Did she? I wonder. Do any of us know, in

marriage? But go on; you did your work, and she, hers. Parallel lives. But you also did things together as a family?

'Of course!' he said, bristling slightly. 'I gave her and Marie-Beth whatever time I could, whenever I was free.'

'So, for her, your work came first, and marriage second. And you think she didn't feel unloved?'

He was silent for a long time, wrestling with himself. 'I see what you mean.' He sighed heavily. 'I've never thought of it like that. It must have been very confusing for her.' He got up, stretched, and went to the window. The sun was setting, the sky a pale turquoise below pink clouds. He looked shattered, weary to the bone.

'I let her down, didn't I? I should have taken better care of her. I was just too preoccupied with my job, I suppose. She gave hers up for Marie-Beth. I told you someone needed to be there for her.' He sighed again. 'Ah well...'

'But when Marie-Beth started school, did she go back to work?'

'No, she stayed home, landscaping our garden. And she was never a... how do you call it? A nag. If something upset her she'd just go quiet, disappear into the garden or someplace. Sort it out on her own. But when she died Marie-Beth was furious with me, bitterly, bitterly hurt. She accused me of neglecting them both; said I'd done it for years. That's part of what made it so hard, when she went to the States.

'Yes, I expect it did.'

'I lost her for a time. But I don't want to start blaming Marie-Beth, Catherine. I love her. I just want her...'

'...to be happy. Yes. And perhaps to recognise you and forgive.'

'...Yes, I suppose so.'

Cat joined him by the window and took his hand. It

405

was pale, slightly liver-spotted, like her own. It reminded her that they were middle-aged, old enough to have learned a bit of wisdom. If that's how wisdom came, she thought bleakly.

'I'm glad you told me all this, Ed.'

'Well, it needed saying sometime,' he said quietly. 'Best say it now. I've had a hard time with it. It weighs on you, doesn't it, the guilt?' He smiled thinly. 'You OK with that, now; your mother an' all?'

'Yes.'

'What's changed?' he asked, smiling down at her.

'Listening to you.'

They were silent, then Cat said, 'Sorry, Ed, but there's more. Can you cope?' He nodded briefly, the exhaustion showing in his face.

Cautiously, not wanting to put words into Anne's mouth that she might not have chosen for herself, but yearning towards her – and realising, for the first time, what 'in deepest sympathy' meant, she said, 'Do you think that Anne knew she was dying, and she let you go, because you'd both said what needed saying and she really was at peace? Or perhaps she even chose to die at that point. People do that, I think; wait until the family is out of the room, then just go. There seems to be some choice in the matter, some effort of will. Not because of despair or loneliness, or in rejection of you,' she said swiftly, 'but as a positive act of relinquishment. And all that bitterness – maybe it needed saying, first. What do you think, Ed?'

He looked at her. 'That's generous of you...'

'No,' said Cat, 'not generous. But what do you think, Ed?'

'I think you're a very difficult woman and you'll give me a hard time.'

Cat didn't smile. 'No, Ed, we're talking about *Anne*. It's important, almost more important than... I expect she'd become a very private person over the years, and maybe dying privately was a way of setting you both free. Was that how it might have been? That she wanted you each to be free?'

He was quiet for a long time, distant, in another world, in his beginnings. She thought, then, how differently the people she knew had reacted to trauma, the whole crowd of them, her mother, Deborah, Ricci, Ed, herself and Anne. Her mother had been terrified, much of the time, but the spirited way in which she dealt with it Cat was only beginning to appreciate. She and Deborah had both fled. Little Welsh Ricci had hidden in his books. Anne had battled on, full of anger and resentment, had had an affair, had finally buried her hopes in the garden – where perhaps they had come up as flowers. As for Ed, he'd stayed silent. A silence like her mother's, heavy with the weight of guilt. Of all of them, her mother had shown the most courage. Yes, hers was a life well-lived.

Guilt deludes, she reflected bleakly, as does its twin, self-deception and the deception of others.

'The idea of it helps a little,' he said at last. 'You're not just making something up, to comfort me?'

'I have to be honest with you...' Cat said helplessly.

'You're always that! I could sometimes wish...'

'...I wasn't there. You're the only one who can tell yourself whether it might be true.'

'It might have been that way,' he said finally. 'At heart, she was completely selfless, was Anne. She'd never once complained. If she had, maybe things...'

'Well, then, perhaps it was her gift.'

'Her gift?'

'Yes. Setting you free. She probably never stopped loving you, Ed. So perhaps she did keep faith, after all. Perhaps setting you free was the last thing, the most real and the most honest thing, that she'd ever be able to do for you, so she did it.'

She put him to bed. They lay in each other's arms all night, and all night she hardly slept. She watched him as a mother watches over a sick child. Eventually he turned over and she knew he was really, deeply asleep. His face had lost that alarming whiteness and now looked ruddy again; his dark lashes, hiding those blue eyes, soft on his lined skin; his hair, longer than when she had first met him, tousled against the pillow. One arm was trapped under her neck, and she moved it gently so that it wouldn't cramp, and curled herself up into a ball, her hands under her chin. Later, it began to rain, a sudden end-of-summer storm, which thundered on the tiles, then diminished to a soft patter. At dawn, she slept.

In the morning they made love. He was gentle, sensitive. She had assumed all that was past, and fleetingly she wondered what Deborah would have said, but she knew the answer. Had they not been both father and mother to each other? Of such was love made and sealed.

4

Coming south from Leeds the rain made a river across the road, and oncoming headlights lashed the windscreen with bright shafts of white light. By evening they would be back in High Wycombe, by the next morning she would be on her way to *The Studio* and by the evening she'd have spoken to Deborah and James. She wouldn't tell them about Ed, not yet. But she would talk to them of *her.*

Above the noise of the engine and the blower and the swish of the windscreen wipers, and into the false twilight of the storm, Ed asked, tentatively, about her plans. She had to clear up the house, she said, and would probably meet her kids there.

'Awful job,' he said. 'Got to be done, though. And after that? You got commissions around at the moment?'

'One, a lady with Bell's Palsy.' She smiled. 'I seem to get stuck with lame ducks, don't I?'

'*I* wasn't a lame duck!' he protested. 'An odd fish, maybe, but not a lame duck.'

'Neither odd nor lame. Anyway, I've put it off. I need to sort the exhibition first. Post some things off to buyers, sort finances with Rudi.'

'And after that? Landscapes?'

'Yes, just the river, though, not trees or fields or anything.'

'Mmm...' he repeated. 'And after that, Catherine?' His face lit by the dashboard, his eyes on the road, a muscle flickering in his cheek.

'Ed! What *is* this? After that I don't know!'

'Then... will you marry me?'

She didn't need to hesitate. 'Yes. Yes, Ed, I will.'

'Then say it, Catherine, say it! Say: Ed, I love you and I want to make my life with you!'

She repeated his words back to him in such an

ironic monotone that he laughed out loud, but inside she was hugging herself, and it was all she could do not to wind down the window and shout her joy into the racing night.

'Y'know, Catherine,' he said lightly, 'I adore you,' his averted face and the calm way he said it almost belying the shocking, intensity of the words. 'Wonderful, isn't it, to have someone adore you and to know that there is nothing in the world you could do that'll make the slightest difference.'

'I don't think that I have ever been adored,' she said slowly, 'I associate it with... a less reciprocal kind of love.' Like plaster statues in churches, she thought, or that awful woman I painted. 'Just love, OK? Not... not adoration.'

'Can't promise.'

By the time they arrived at High Wycombe they were silent again, but content. Ed took the cases upstairs and when he came back he was carrying two glasses.

'I'm going to fix us a drink; I think we deserve it.'

They stood by the window together, their arms round each other, and sipped their drinks, the light from the room paling where it merged with the slope of the garden.

'We can put your studio there,' he said. 'You think the light'll be good enough, Catherine? It faces northeast.'

'In that case, it'll be swell.' And felt him smile.

'Swell,' he mocked. 'I ought to warn you, 'swell' went out in the fifties. I just sorta hung on to it...'

They turned together, away from the dark garden into the room. Then she said, 'So you hung the portrait as you said you would?' and he said, 'Oh yeah, come and look at it,' and switched on the lamps. There, in the shadowy darkness on the wall, was his portrait, and her eye was caught by something familiar hanging next to it, the Eastern European woman in her patterned scarf, looking vacant, vague, and in her eyes was the story of her years.

'Bought it at the Preview,' he said, sipping his drink. 'Got it couriered. I wanted the other one, actually, the portrait of the old lady, but it wasn't for sale, so I've gotten myself this one.'

'That not-for-sale one was a portrait of my mother – but you never met her, did you, Ed?'

'Was it? I *am* glad! I love this one, though, and I've told you, Catherine, you should keep your best things in the family.' He grinned down at her.

Next to the Eastern European woman was a tiny oil painting in a rustic frame, a little village scene; ancient, leaning houses, terra cotta tiles over terra cotta walls on the terra cotta earth.

'What's this one?' she asked.

'Oh, that,' he said, gesticulating with his glass. 'Had it ages. Thought it was a good twin to the refugee lady, the sort of place she might have come from. Thought, maybe she'll lose that distant look in her eyes, come alive again.' He took another sip from his drink. 'You know Goethe's play, Cat, *Torquato Tasso*?'

'No. No, I never learned German.'

'Oh, your mother never teach you? Well, there's a little poem in it, runs like this: *Es bildet ein Talent sich in der Stille.*' He quoted it softly, in a pure German accent. '*Sich ein Charakter in dem Strom der Welt.*'

'Ed, I never learned German,' she repeated faintly. She was warding off demons, here – the sound of that language on his lips!

'It means,' he said, '– and you'll like this, Catherine; it describes you, you see. It means, "talent develops in quiet places, character in the full glare" – no, *current* – "of human life."' He smiled at her, his blue eyes twinkling. 'Fits, doesn't it? The river an 'all?'

'You're fluent in German, are you? You studied it at school? Or you pick it up on one of your postings?'

'No, from Grandpa Henry,' he said lightly. 'My

411

grandpa was from Heidelberg, Catherine. Well, a village outside Heidelberg. Part of what your mother's Jewish friend called that ancient family of Christians. He was a professor at the university and a bit of a dissident. And during the Kaiser's purges he fled to America with his wife and son. My father. Just the other side of the river from Cincinnati. There's a German colony there to this day. I was born there. Marie-Beth has the old house. This village is something like his own village might have been. That's why I bought it originally. Only got it out the other day.'

Cat was not listening. Her mind was reeling. Ed, *German?*

She swayed inside, searched for somewhere to sit. Her whole body was trembling. She was about to faint. Sweat trickled down between her breasts.

Ma... help me now?

Run, Caterina! Run...

Not an adult voice, this; not the rounded, full tones of Rute's maturity, so lately mourned, nor a summoned echo from a darkened room somewhere in eternity. No, it came from further back than that, from out the murky depths of her ghetto solitude, and it startled Cat beyond imagining. It was a child's shrieked whisper, wide-eyed adolescent terror, panic-stricken and elemental.

It was then that the mist came down, dark, cold, chill, as though someone somewhere had let in the night, and when Ed turned to her, concerned, she could hardly hear what he was saying, so far away from her, and from anything she knew, had he become.

'Come on, you're dead tired. Let's get you to bed.'

Cat allowed herself to be led upstairs to his room. She had never slept there before; it was Anne's room; she had always slept in Marie-Beth's room... She made no protest, for then he'd surely know.

'Back in a minute. Just shut up shop.' He left the

door open.

At the basin she washed mechanically, brushed her teeth, looked in her bag for her tee shirt and climbed into bed. After a little while he came in. She supposed he had been switching off the lights, tidying up, perhaps unpacking. She lay with her eyes shut, feigning sleep. She felt the mattress shift as he got into bed, and then the heat of his back. Gradually his breathing steadied. She did not watch him sleep. She lay awake for hours, cold to her very soul, staring blindly up to the darkness of the ceiling.

The hours passed; they passed. It must have been well into the night before she realised, with that sinking feeling that came when sleep persistently eluded her, that there was no way she could continue to lie there rigidly, staring into the dark, her thoughts in tumult. Outside the trees muttered in the wind, the rough, slightly sinister, grinding sound of chafing branches, and once, the noise of a car going up from the Base.

This is Anne's bed, she thought; she slept here. From this window she looked down into her garden, speculating what to plant, whether to prune this bush or that, whether to grass it over or make borders. Her garden, which she had watered with her tears. On that soil, over those tears, he will build me a studio.

Oh, why hadn't he said before? But those blue eyes, that dark Teutonic gaze – why couldn't I tell? What colour was his hair before it silvered? What colour were the roots? Oh, my God, his roots... Germany, the culture which spawned *that man*.

Why did he not say before? Swing back a generation and there's his grandfather, Heinrich Buber – ah, so that was why, at the funeral, he was so interested in the name! But swing forward and it's Henry Barber, anglicised for anonymity, for ease of assimilation, just as her mother had tried to do. At the name Heinrich, she trembled.

She wanted to get up, get dressed, drive away. She wanted to break free... She wanted the familiarity of her studio and her friends... she wanted her little car. But the one time she really needed it her car wasn't there, and she felt all the impotent, pent-up rage of the dissembler, who, because she had not raged at him, or accused him, or struck out at him, but just hidden her feelings, was now prevented from leaving the house and just driving away.

She used to have a theory, a theory of drawing. It was to do with how you respond when you know you've made a mistake. Do you pretend it hasn't happened, and thereby condemn yourself to infinite wrestling, trying to transform it into something it was never meant to be – all the while losing the purity of the vision that had inspired you in the first place? Or do you get real and scrub it out?

Yet fear was less cerebral than that; fear burns; it creates demons where there were none, and how many times had she rejected the whole idea of sleep, whilst longing for oblivion, because fear made nightmares beyond imagining. The very thought of Ed's German ancestry was enough to trigger them. It was tantamount to inviting them in.

If you come this way... says Eliot airily – but his was an invitation to a carefree landscape, to May-time hedges white *with voluptuary sweetness*... not to a place of imperfections; say, to the mudflats or the sodden green marsh, where pools of water, supposedly reflecting the sky, turn out, instead, to be scummed with diesel fuel. Or a seabird, nestling quietly in the long reeds, its feathers tinged with sunlight, is revealed as a bundle of decomposing flesh. Yet none of these blots on the landscape detract from the ultimate beauty of the whole; all are exposed for what they are, merely part of that complex pattern of nature at both its best and its most crude. All is familiar, forgivable and ultimately acceptable; you don't reject the whole because part of it is flawed. You don't say, 'Right, I'm never coming here again!'

But come at night, or in the ghostly hours before the dawn; come fleeing your own fears, pursued by none other than yourself, then you can put away all notions of good sense and rational thinking, for what is flawed becomes demonic and what is only half-perceived, gargantuan.

Beside her Ed slept the sleep of the just, worn out, probably, with the emotional turmoil she had laid on him. She was all too conscious why he'd made that break through the hedge; she felt the same way now. She just wanted out of there.

Slowly she slid out of bed and, in the pitch darkness, moved warily to the door, and carefully let herself out of the room. The landing was bathed in a luminous orange glow from a streetlamp on the road. To her left was the bathroom, to her right, the stairs. Downstairs was the front door. No, not that way, for where then? She couldn't absolutely disappear, not after all they'd been through together, but neither could she lie beside him feeling as she did. Ahead was the door to Marie-Beth's room, yet so deep was her estrangement from him that she could not bring herself to enter it. She tried the other door and crept in, shutting it quietly behind her and found the light switch, blinking a little in the light. Hitting her eyes, Ed's uniform, hanging against the long mirror of the wardrobe, a double image with dual power to shock – ah, how right had been her first, instinctive unease! On a narrow single bed lay his half-open suitcase and a pile of neatly-folded blankets, and she took one and, with distaste, draped the uniform so that it was hidden from view. She hauled the suitcase on to the floor, and from it came the evocative, faintly acrid smell of fish and damp clothing. Leaving the curtains open and the light on, she wrapped herself in another blanket and lay down on the bed. At least she was alone and wouldn't have to lie immobile, listening to the sound of his breathing next to her in the bed.

She was assailed by images; tenuous, half-dreamt images from the past weeks; the officious, uniformed security man in the hospital garden; the uniformed Sister; the vicar in his fringed garment; the gabardined men dancing in her mother's house and on wet, cobbled streets; her portrait of Ed, his peaked uniform cap on his blue uniformed legs...

And rivers, the many rivers of her journey. The river running through the town, where Rute took her for picnics; the river outside the studio windows at Fiddler's Reach; Ricci's little *Troddi* and Ricci's huge *Kwai*; the Thames at Marlow and the Solway Firth. The wide black boat, running over shallows of salt and silt and blackened sand.

So many images, forged in so short a time. The rosemary bush, for remembrance. Gus's pot, a design of roots...

She blamed herself. All the time she had been questioning her mother's behaviour Ed had been just waiting for her to turn around. If she'd questioned him instead she'd have discovered he was German and she'd have run. She'd have done the portrait and run. No, as with Saul, she wouldn't even have done the portrait.

Oh, but why didn't he tell her before! He must have realised how significant it would be to her! She felt angry and immensely sad. In the morning, she thought grimly, I'll ask him why he took so long to tell me. I will not tolerate this despair; I refuse it!

She felt under the blanket for the necklace, only then remembering that she had left it on her bedside table. Anne's bedside table. She got out of bed and tiptoed back to the bedroom. The room was warm, fusty, as though they ought to have opened a window.

As she groped for the necklace in the darkness and curled it into her fist, it spoke its small sound, metal on metal. She returned to the study, closed the door gently and got into bed. She wound the necklace round her neck, clutched the end of it in her fist, and settled down again to watch the night.

She heard the traffic begin on the road, leaves rustling in the trees as the wind got up; later, the sound of birdsong, and later still, their silence. It was within this silence that she slept, but lightly. She heard Ed stir; heard him cross the landing to the bathroom; the flushing of the toilet; the sound of running water. It was still dark outside. A door opened and shut; Marie-Beth's door. She heard his feet on the stairs. She felt stiff, cold, and the skin on her eyelids felt puffy and tender. She waited.

He must have looked for her all over the ground floor, so it was some time before he came up again. Perhaps he'd gone outside, into the garden where in the past he might have looked for Anne – even at night? She watched the door; heard the brush of his fingers against it; saw the careful turn of the knob, and then he was looking in. He was wearing the shorts and singlet in which he slept. She met his eyes.

'Ah, you're in here!' He came forward and bent over her solicitously. 'Couldn't sleep?'

He sat down on the edge of the bed and she moved over for him, but kept the blanket bunched under her chin.

'You've been crying again, Catherine.' His voice was deep, concerned. 'You worried about something?'

She was mute.

'Oh, was it the bed? I'm sorry, I should have thought of that. Look,' he said decisively, smiling at her, 'you really mustn't worry. We can get rid of the bed – we can sell the whole bloody house if it disturbs you. Make a new start, just you and me. Oh, come here, Catherine! Let me put my arms round you!'

She let him take her in his arms. He felt warm, his wonderful hands on her back... but he held her tightly, almost too tightly, as though she was a child just woken from a nightmare. But she wasn't a child and she hadn't just woken, and the nightmare was still there. She felt the tears come.

'Let me go, Ed. Ed...' When he didn't stir, she added, almost crossly, pushing him from her, 'Ed, let me *breathe*!' She managed to smile to take the sting out of the words.

'Catherine, Catherine,' he said tenderly, 'you're worn out, that's all. Why didn't you wake me? Always wake me if you're feeling like this, OK? Never lie awake fretting on your own. Now, you want to sleep some more? I'll just leave you a bit, shall I? '

'I'm fine...' She covered her face with her arm. 'I'll get up in a minute.'

'You're not fine. Sleep some more and I'll wake you later with a cup of tea.'

'No, I'll get up. I need to get back. Oh, I just want to go *home*!' She burst out crying.

Perhaps it was the way she said 'home', rather than her tears, which told him something was terribly wrong. He didn't say anything, but took her in his arms again. Almost against her will, she felt some of the burden dissipate and she snuggled against him.

'Hiding again, Catherine, weren't you?' he said softly. 'What from? Not your mother, this time. Me? The thought of getting married again? Come on, my love... *talk* to me.'

How could she tell him? *What* could she tell him? 'Oh, Ed...' pulling away, 'I can't... It's... Oh, I wish...' she cried desperately, the tears spurting afresh. 'I *wish* I had my car!'

'No, Catherine,' he said quietly. 'You have to talk to me. You aren't going to run away from this, whatever it is. I love you, and I've asked you to marry me. We

418

belong together now. You can tell me anything.'

'Not this,' she mourned.

'Yes, you can. You can tell me anything.'

'I can't...' she said quietly. 'You see, I... I can't marry you. I'm sorry, but I can't.'

Ed was quiet. He didn't ask what had happened to change her mind so abruptly, but lay down full length with her, his warm hands running rhythmically over her forehead and across her arms. He held her for a long time, stroking her. She was so comfortable, so utterly soothed, and now she had spoken the words, so enormously relieved, that she could have fallen asleep. After a while he drew back.

'So you don't love me, after all?' Strange, but the thought didn't seem to upset him. Perhaps, as she had thought, he was relieved that he wouldn't be burdened with her.

'You've been such a good friend to me, Ed. I'll never forget...'

'My God, that sounds very final!' he exclaimed, sitting up. 'But it's not as simple as that, Catherine. You see, I don't believe you. I don't feel any different, and if you really had stopped loving me, I think I would. I love you and I want to marry you. Oh,' he went on, 'it's not that I don't believe you mean what you say. But I don't believe you've stopped loving me just because... well, because you've spent a night in Anne's bed – well, not the whole night – or that you've realised you can't live here. There's something else, but even so, I can't *feel* it, you see. I don't feel any less loved than at the cottage or when we arrived here last night. And I think I know myself well enough to trust my own feelings. I just don't *believe* it, Catherine. Something's spooked you. Now, why don't you simply tell me what it is and let me put it right.'

His voice was tender. It wasn't the alarming, high-pitched voice he had used when he'd been talking about Anne, but patient and firm.

419

She raised herself up so that they were face to face. 'Ed, this isn't about the house or Anne's bed. It's... it's just that...'

How could she tell him, if he didn't realise the significance of it for himself?

'Downstairs,' she said painfully, 'last night... you showed me a painting... Not the one you bought, the village painting.'

'Oh yes. And...?'

'You said you were... German.' The word was like wool in her mouth.

He looked at her blankly. 'Ah, it was that!' He closed his eyes for a moment and nodded. 'Now I understand!'

'Why didn't you tell me before, Ed?' she asked in a small voice.

'What's there to tell? *I'm* not German, Catherine.' He gripped her arms. 'I told you, it was my grandfather, not me. We were citizens of the US of A, all of us. Huh! Pity the man who gets judged for his ancestry!' He released her, and got up. He wrenched at the clothes in the open suitcase, found a sweater and put it on. 'You're as German as I am,' he said, straightening it over his shorts, 'and you don't even speak the language.'

'But my mother was *Jewish*,' she said to his back. 'After everything she went through – think of it, Ed, just *think* about it! Can't you see it makes a difference? It's impossible, don't you see? Oh, don't make me say it again...'

His lips tightened. 'You can keep saying it till you're blue in the face, Catherine, but you're not being rational.' He turned and gazed sightlessly out of the window. 'And remember, it wasn't a German who raped your mother. It was a Jew.'

She turned her face to the wall. 'Oh, just take me home, Ed,' she pleaded miserably. 'Please. Just take me home, will you?'

420

5

They dressed and Ed fetched the car. Dark shadows pooled under the trees, which rustled and swayed in a light wind, the leaves sending tiny droplets of moisture on to Cat's face as she waited with her case by the front door. They said little. Have you got your anorak? Yes. And your toilet bag? Yes. Did you remember to pick up your mother's necklace? Yes, of *course.* For once she had remembered everything. There would be no reason to come back.

It was still very early and the morning was overcast. Cat was glad of it. She could not have borne, just then, the beauty of a sunny day.

At first there was constraint between them while the road yawned past and the future receded; veiled, as though the dismal Cumbrian mists had come down out of the night. Occasionally she surfaced, conscious of his hands on the wheel, his fingers pale in the watery light, his tight jaw. There was little traffic. He drove fast as though wanting only for this journey to be over. She wanted it, too. Rewind the film, she thought desolately; retrace that last, lit up, exuberant journey from the cottage, unravel the pattern, and when we get back to the house let there be no late night drinking, and definitely no looking at paintings. The thought that she would have preferred not to have known, shamed her.

Once he reached out and took her hand and squeezed it, and she neither protested nor withdrew it, but let it rest in his for a moment, savouring the contact; yet, after he put his hand back on the wheel, hers felt cold as though life had gone from it.

With each mile the sense of unreality increased. I'm not here, she thought, I'm not doing this. It felt surreal, a Magritte composition come to life: if she looked in the mirror now, would she see only the back of her own head, retreating; and if she looked at him, would both their heads be sheathed in anonymity, as in *L'amant?* No, she thought, I am making my own Magritte; here, on these piled canvases, lies the landscape of my life, hidden but discernible, as though dense canvas was no more than gossamer web. Soon I shall have no right to take his hand, crawl into his arms or lie with him in his bed. He will turn from me, and he'd be justified, for I have negated him; tossed him away; sent him packing.

They drove in silence, but from the corner of her eye she could see his face, pale and tense, and there was a new cleft between his eyebrows. She wondered how she appeared to him, if he condemned her as a bitter, hard-hearted shrew, or whether any part of him could begin to understand what she, too, was going through; that this was necessary; that there was no other way.

Presently he flicked a switch. 'Getting light, Catherine.'

'Yes.'

'I'm driving you home at your request, but I still want you to trust me. I know what I'm doing, and I don't think you really do.'

She was mute. A little later he suggested they should stop, if she was hungry, as they had gone without breakfast. She shook her head, and he made no further offer of food.

Later he said, 'Let's just wait a bit; think things over...' but she could not comprehend what waiting, in his terms, might mean. Her mind was set against him. Yet when he said, 'I'll wait for you, you know, however long it takes. I love you, Catherine. I adore you' – she almost broke down.

'Don't wait, Ed. And don't... don't adore me. It's no good. It's impossible.'

After that, if he had anything more to say, he stifled it and they drove in silence again, but her eyes welled. She cared little whether he saw her tears; they were merely the outward sign of her inner grief and turmoil.

I'm losing him, she thought, handing him back, and to what purpose? In order to reconcile my memory of my mother with her memories? In order to embrace what I have never embraced, to dedicate myself, like a fanatic, to something I have never, in my whole life, espoused; to prove the veracity of my Jewish roots? And to what purpose, also, these marital allusions, when marriage was the one thing that was now out of the question?

His eyes were wet, too; he took out his handkerchief and wiped them; they must have clouded his vision. She wanted to reach across and comfort him, but she couldn't, for all this was her doing. One word from her would annul what she had said, yet she couldn't do it. In any case, she had been sitting so rigidly, her hands tight on her lap or gripping the sides of the seat or the window ledge, that to move now was impossible.

Tears enough to fill the tide.

The countryside was beginning to give way to high-rise flats and the long facades of untenanted terraces with boarded-up windows. People were queuing at bus stops, heads down in bleariness or sipping hot drinks out of cartons, or standing apart, reading the morning paper; people coming alongside them in full cars, their faces blank; in their eyes whatever happened last night colliding with the looming worries of the day. At the traffic lights a man in the rear seat of the next car caught Cat's eye and gave her a charming, rather whimsical smile; he was young, about the age of her twins. Perhaps she reminded him of his mother, yet it seemed that he could see into her heart, as though he knew full well what was going on inside this car. The queue moved and they caught up with him again and he turned his head to peer at her over his shoulder, his eyes sliding against hers again, frowning, perturbed.

More traffic lights; on the pavement a crowd of office-workers in dark suits waited to cross. Why did their heads turn as their car passed? Why did their eyes focus this way in particular – as though the car was somehow remarkable, painted with stripes or bright yellow dots, or as though from within it they could hear the deafening pulse of their silence, like a radio played loudly through open windows on a hot day. Cat took refuge in her lap, her fists balled – the backs of her hands had caught the sun; on the boat, perhaps – and with each breath she saw the glint of her mother's necklace through the gap between the buttons on her blouse.

'You're still wanting to make amends, aren't you?' Cat started; his voice familiar yet strangely loud. 'You think behaving like this will... propitiate your mother's memory, or something. And you really think that's the right thing to do? After... after everything I told you about Anne?'

An unpleasant suggestion, and she made no reply.

When he began to speak again it was a monologue – although she should be used to monologues, she thought dourly. Ed spoke quietly, almost to himself, as if he'd given up expecting any response from her. 'I was born in 1938,' he said. 'Work it out for yourself; that makes me fifty-five. America not yet in the war...'

Ricci, she thought inconsequentially, was seventy-eight or so, perhaps older. In 1943, when he was taken prisoner, he must have been younger than James... Mummy, I've had a dreadful, bad dream...

'My Pa was twenty five when I was born, about the age of young James,' he said. Once again their thoughts had collided, and she could hardly bear it... 'This was three years after he'd arrived in the States. They were destitute, Catherine, but the German Lutheran Church in Cinci found them somewhere to live. Does that preclude marriage, too,' he said relentlessly, glancing across, 'my forebears being

424

Christian? It ought to, if you're being at all logical.'

Just a hint, the merest hint of bitterness, and she didn't reply. His bitterness armed her; far from wanting to reach out to him, it made her more defiant. It strengthened her resolve, and the light thickened.

Again they stopped for traffic lights and Cat watched, in a desultory way, as a stream of traffic climbed the slip road on to the flyover and disappeared, like a stack of dominoes falling in slow motion, each one obliterating sight of the one before.

'It was years before my Grandpa was able to get a proper job,' he continued, as they set off again. 'Oh, he did some private teaching in people's homes, but not enough to make a living. Then he worked on the steamboats, in the engine room, mostly night shifts. Talk about *coal*, Catherine, I got to hate the very sight of it! People think steamboats are picturesque, but for me they represented years of hard graft for my grandfather, and a terrible downhill slide into Black Lung disease – inevitable in that environment. I watched him grow old before his time. He was gentle and kind; he never complained, and he never regretted leaving Germany, at least not in my hearing. My Pa was like that, too. He said that the difference between life and death was not whether you had enough to eat, but whether you were free to speak your mind. He also worked on the boats, but it was a dead-end job with no prospects; sheer, hard slog. I got so that I hated those boats and I hated the river too. Both of them died before they were sixty. First my Grandpa Henry, and then my Pa. The women were left taking in washing, things like that... Like your own mother did, I suppose.'

He pointed across the road to where a delivery van was being unloaded.

'See that, Catherine? That's a baker's van, and what time is it?' He glanced at his watch. 'Not quite forty after six. My Mom, she did that. Worked in a bakery, getting up each day at three in the morning to get the dough ready, and not going to bed until after her own chores were done. That's how you get fresh bread every day.'

His tone was slightly accusatory, as if those who came later were somehow to blame for his mother's sufferings, and again she resisted him. I don't need to hear this, she thought sourly; I've spent my whole life listening to other people's stories, and I'm full to brimming over. My mind can't take any more. It can't make room.

He was quiet for a bit, changing lanes and accelerating as they come to the dual carriageway.

'It wore her out; that, and not knowing where the next meal was coming from. She got a duodenal ulcer, and there was no money for an operation. She died at sixty three, just a year after she'd given up work because of it. She died of septicaemia, complicated by malnutrition. They never told me what was going on. I knew they were selling things; pieces of furniture, things like that, but I assumed they were just down-sizing and I didn't ask. And when I came home there always seemed enough to eat. I expect they'd hoarded it for me,' he said bitterly. 'Then I got a call. I set out right away but she died before I got back. It all happened quite suddenly in the end, just like Anne.... I wasn't there for them, either.' He paused. 'But I was there for you, wasn't I? And I'm here now.'

Again Cat didn't reply. She shook her head repressively and he tightened his lips.

'Well, I've said it, Catherine, like it or not.' He shook his head at her in quiet exasperation. 'So, anyway, I came home, and that's when I saw for myself how bad things really were. Most things that were worth selling had been sold by then. The house was an empty, rather shabby, shell, but I wouldn't have it pulled down or anything. Marie-Beth has it now, as I think I mentioned. I told her all this, Catherine; I passed it on. I thought she ought to know her roots. I told her after her Mom died, when we were out for a walk one day down by the river at Marlow. You remember the river at Marlow, Catherine? Anyway, she wanted the house, so I gave it to her as a wedding present. It's a brownstone house on the river,' he said, his voice pensive, 'by the bridge that goes over into Cincinnati, on the Kentucky side. It took me a long time before I could enjoy the river for itself, rather than for what it represented, the appalling suffering my family had endured.'

He glanced across at her. 'Doesn't that resonate with you, someplace, Catherine?'

She could hear in his voice what he meant; he was rehearsing his story, marking this place – this happened here, that happened then – but she was unforgiving stone. His words streamed over her like the traffic on the flyover, here and gone, of no significance.

They were off the motorway and into the suburbs. She saw signs for Sevenoaks and Gravesend, Swanscombe and Greenhithe, names of her home and her territory, the place of bridges, arches, cardboard dwellings, the little shopping centre, her studio, her river...

'You love the river, don't you?' His tone warmer now, less thin, and she realised he had been away from her in his memories. 'And what was it you told me Ricci said? About not being content with what's on the surface? You think about that a bit, Catherine,' he muttered, 'when you're on your own again. Maybe make some connections.'

Something in her woke a little, roused by the perpetual confluence of their thoughts, and she began to be very afraid. So afraid, that as they finally drove along the winding lane that led to the top of the slipway, she said, her voice thin and rusty, 'Ed, just stop here, can you?'

He raised his eyebrows. 'Ah, she's speaks – a miracle! Considering the miles I've chauffeured her...'

His sarcasm was deserved, but it hurt. 'Ed, don't! It's bad enough... Can we just... walk a bit?'

'Madam wants to walk *here*?' His eyes gleamed with disdain, and through them she saw the ugly, ramshackle buildings and the grimy, narrow alleyway between them. 'Madam needs her boots?'

'Ed, *please*! It's not like you. I know I've upset you, but... Can we go on down the river a bit? Can you drive us further down the river; just find somewhere to park, where we can talk?'

His expression was inscrutable. 'I can do that,' he said lightly, and turned the car.

6

There was only one place to go, Swanscombe Marshes, where she and Ricci had gone. The sound of her voice, giving him directions, seemed strange to her, tentative, less sure, as though she was expecting something, hoping for something, a reprieve of some sort. But if she could just retrace those footsteps everything might make some kind of sense.

It was beginning to drizzle and there was a lowering mist over the river; by the time they reached a place where they could stop, the whole surface was alive, churned up by the rain. No secret depths to give her clues; no indication of reflected light or hidden currents, but a maelstrom of choppy water; brown, forbidding, and cold. It was too wet to walk, so they stayed in the car and Ed switched off the engine.

'What do you want to talk about, Catherine?'

She knew she was clinging to him, that it was perverse, but just to keep him with her a moment longer; to hear his voice and feel the warmth of his body – to push away the dread future and the time when she would be alone again – that must be enough. The window was already steaming up, and she wound it down and looked out over the dark, sepia landscape, thankful for the air on her face. Immediately she heard the prolonged muffled call of a distant foghorn.

'Why, Ed...' she said in surprise, 'there must be fog out at sea!'

'*Catherine!*' he said sharply, 'I asked you if there were things you want to talk about. Else, why are we here? I've not come all this way to talk about the weather!' When she didn't answer he added, 'Well, then, let me ask you something,' and his tone more brittle than she'd ever heard it. He leaned his elbow on the steering wheel, making no attempt to touch her. 'Has anything like this ever happened before?'

She was taken aback, and the fog seemed to lift a little.

'Like what? You mean have I been in love?'

His mouth twisted. 'No,' he said, 'though maybe I'll hear about that some day. I mean an occasion in your life when you took fright, because someone you met was German?'

'I'm not taking fright,' she said mutinously. 'I know what I'm doing.'

'Do you?' He sounded dubious, sardonic. 'Well,' he persisted, 'was there?'

She didn't need to think very hard. The memory was as clear in her mind as though it had happened yesterday. 'Yes.'

'Or you had to go to Germany? You ever visited in Germany, Catherine?'

Cat gave a shudder of revulsion. 'No I couldn't. I couldn't possibly. It would scare me to death.'

'So...' he sighed. 'Well, this person you met...'

'He was just someone Bill invited to stay with us,' she said, the words like glue in her mouth. 'Something to do with a bank in Munich... Bill had to be at work so he couldn't meet him from the station. Actually,' she said, appalled at this resurgence of the old pattern of lies, and refusing, now, to dissimulate, 'he'd been disqualified from driving. So he gave me the time of the train and told me to pick him up.'

She felt cold, tremulous, as though an icy finger had laid its tip on her forehead.

'I didn't want to pick him up. I didn't want him to stay with us. I was terrified that he'd be, you know, square-headed, blond, crew-cutted, blue-eyed... I thought he'd know I was Jewish and that he'd, I don't know, treat me... Oh, how can I put it? It was as though he had some sort of power over me... to menace me or denounce me, or something. As if I'd been running away for years and now I'd been discovered. I was scared stiff.'

'But you *had* been running away for years. Your whole life with Bill was running away for years.'

Cat knew he was right, although she did not care to be reminded of her miserable relationship with Bill.

'And that's important, Catherine. It's actually very significant,' he said ironically. 'Running. That's what you do best. Well, go on.'

'Do you want to hear this or not? You asked; I'm answering.'

He didn't reply.

'His name was Karl,' she said. 'That terrified me all by itself... Those Germanic names make me tremble, Ed.'

'Yes, I realise that,' he said dryly. 'So how did you deal with it?'

'Well, as I say, I met him off the train. And he was all the things I'd imagined; blond, short hair; square head – the lot. And his eyes were blue. Not blue like yours, Ed, but a sort of cold, steely blue. And, to make things worse, he was wearing a black leather jacket...'

He chucked, and after a minute she smiled ruefully. She rubbed her palms together. They were sweating, clammy.

'Well,' she said, 'so there we were. I could hardly drive, I was trembling so much. He didn't seem to notice; just talked about his flight and how kind of us it was to put him up for a week. I thought, my God, a week! He's bound to find me out.'

'But there was nothing to find out.'

'No, I know... I can't explain... I don't know why I felt as I did...'

'You were identifying with your mother...? Amit got you mixed up with your mother,' he added casually. 'You notice that?'

'Did she?' Cat was bewildered. 'No, I didn't notice.'

'Well, she did. Anyway, this Karl. It was all right?'

'Oh, it was more than all right. He was the nicest possible man, mild and considerate, and I enjoyed the time he spent with us. It was all too apparent that most of the time Bill was the worse for wear and, although it was embarrassing, Karl was sympathetic – not that he said anything, but his expression, you know. A whole week without violence as well. I was sad to say goodbye, actually... I was all right in the daytime; he was just a very charming guest, but at night... I hardly slept. The children were quite small, and I was guarding them, I think; keeping watch. I found myself worrying that he'd take them away in the night. Oh, I know it sounds unreasonable, but I was always afraid of the children being taken away. I suppose I projected it on to him.'

'And afterwards?'

'Well, I began to think about it. I realised I'd been prejudiced and I felt ashamed. I couldn't talk to Bill because... well, Bill really *was* anti-Semitic. He'd known all along we weren't practising Jews but he hated my mother from the start.' The memory of those days forced itself into her mind, and unconsciously she put a hand on his arm. He laid his hand over hers and began to chafe her fingers.

'He used to bully her, as if she was some sort of foreign worker living in the house. If I hadn't been there I don't know what he'd have done. He loathed the way she used to go on about food, for instance. If there was a problem with one of the kids, it was always food she suggested.' She looked away, gazing at the runnels of water creeping down the window. 'It was absurd. She could see that there were deeper problems, behavioural problems, problems that couldn't be solved just by comfort eating, but she didn't know what else to suggest. It was outside her experience, that children could be rude to their parents... It wasn't the way she'd been brought up.'

She swallowed, her mouth dry, like Amit. 'Also, she'd known rationing – well, we know she'd known more than just rationing – we know that, now, don't we, Ed? She thought it was a scandal, that not only did we have the usual things, like a washing machine and a fridge, but a tumble drier and a freezer as well...' She smiled wistfully. 'Poor Ma. She was always thin, and she ate like a sparrow. Her comments... She drove Bill and the kids up the wall.'

'But about Karl...' Ed's voice seemed to come from a great distance. 'Knowing you'd been prejudiced against Karl – that was the word you used, wasn't it? How did that make you feel?'

'I told you,' she said stiffly. 'I felt ashamed.'

His tone was detached, cool, and she found herself resenting him again. He was behaving like a professional counsellor – let's stay with this for a while, shall we, Catherine? Pop up on this couch and tell me how you feel. Once more something inside her retreated, closed up.

'You know,' he said, 'CS Lewis once said shame was like a hot cup of tea. It's the sort of thing he said. You ever read any CS Lewis, Catherine?'

'No,' she said indifferently. 'Sounds prosaic.'

He ignored that. 'He said, shame, you have to sip it slowly. This is about *Karl*,' he said emphatically, 'not your mother, Catherine. There's something in what Lewis said, because as we get older the pattern becomes more complicated, and you have to unravel it. I'm talking about people who've been to war who then have to do business with their enemies. You learn to stop demonising people, or generalising. But it can't be done fast. It has to be done over time. You have to acknowledge that things change.'

She was bemused. What was he talking about?

'I'm talking about prejudice,' he said quietly, observing her. 'Look, stop thinking about your mother for a moment, would you, and let's just deal with that, OK?'

Let's explore this, shall we, Catherine?

She shrugged.

'Look,' he said, 'it's like this. Things which were important in wartime; crucial, even; like knowing who your enemies are, become kinda out of date when you start trading with them, like Bill was doing with your Karl. All those entrenched attitudes have to be un-trenched if you're not to ghettoise people or stay in one, yourself. You stop *noticing* difference, or you don't *mind* it so much, or you feel you can function within it – you might actually enjoy it, if you let yourself. Which you can only do, by the way, from a sure footing; if you've grown in confidence enough. And I'm not just talking about nations, here, but individuals.'

They had been sitting facing slightly towards each other, though her fists were once more balled tightly in her lap. He took her hand in his and slowly uncurled her fingers. They looked white, bloodless.

'That fridge you mentioned, or your freezer,' he suggested. 'You don't balk at having a Bosch fridge or a Toyota in the garage...'

Cat had been slightly hung up on the word 'ghettoise', but at this she relaxed slightly. 'Our kettle was a Bosch.'

He laughed. 'Well, there you are. "Dirty Boche", the French used to call them, but it didn't stop you buying it.'

'Bill chose the brand.' Surprising herself, Cat giggled. 'I wouldn't have had a 'Kraut' or 'Hun'. I never thought about Bosch being German. We bought it in High Wycombe.'

'Well, there's trade for you. But attitudes, prejudices, they take longer. They live to fight another day. Then something inconsequential happens,' he added, his voice measured and unequivocal, 'and they come up and hit you, don't they? Like there haven't been any intervening years.'

He does understand, she thought, and began to feel easier.

'*Yes*,' she said eagerly, 'that's how it was with Karl!

But I hadn't thought I *was* prejudiced. We had people of all races at school in High Wycombe. Prejudice wasn't something I felt capable of. And then this happened, with Karl, and it made me realise...'

'It made you realise that not all Germans were bad.'

'All *right!*' She was suddenly furious. 'But he was alive, wasn't he? *His* father survived the war! What am I? I'm the child of a Holocaust Survivor, and what's he? He was a child of, what, Hitler youth, the SS? So what did *his* father do when the Jews of Europe were dying in concentration camps? Or in the cattle trucks, or wherever, or on the long marches in the snow? I'll tell you what he did! He did nothing, otherwise he *wouldn't* have survived! *Nothing!* He was silent, like my mother's God was silent,' she said bitterly. 'Which is why so many of them lost their faith. She used to call God a false god, a god of broken promises – before she got religion,' she said scornfully. 'Before then, the whole *idea* of God made her angry – that he should rule over life and death, choose a people as his own and...' She slapped her knee, punctuating the words. 'And over hundreds of years teach them to serve *him* alone, and worship *only* him, and...and follow *his* Law above all local laws – and then, *then*...' She took a deep breath. 'Then what does he do? He *abandons* them!' She choked back her tears. 'Huh! If that's the quality of his presence, well, give me absence every time!'

Ed took a handkerchief out of his pocket and passed it to her, and, with a whispered 'Thank you...' she mopped her eyes.

'Catherine, I understand; lots of people feel like that about God. But we're not actually talking about God, are we? We're talking about *good* Germans. Those who hid Jews, looked after escapees or made some sort of stand. Like Bonhoeffer, shot in prison, and Pastor Ehrenberg, for another; he and Martin Niemöller died alongside your Jews, in a concentration camp. *Good* Germans, Catherine,' he added, taking her hand, and

435

warming it with his. 'Germans who paid the price.'

Cat frowned. 'How do you know all this?'

'Catherine, I told you I read. And not just poetry. What worries me is that, apparently, you don't. You just won't consider another point of view. Because there *is* another point of view. That God might have been *present* in Auschwitz, *present* in Bergen-Belsen, or those other places – present in people who made a stand, using their voices. Ever cross your mind?'

'I've never asked myself the question,' she muttered. 'I've never even thought about it. I didn't know you believed in God.'

'Whether I do or don't is irrelevant,' he said quietly. 'And maybe you *should* ask the question. And while you're at it, think about that sense of shame you had. You ever talk to anyone about it?'

Cat took a breath. 'I told my mother about Karl. She said she couldn't have had him in the house; she'd have run a mile. She'd never dream of going back to Germany, finding her old house, or anything like that.'

'So she just imprinted it, this fear...' he said neutrally, and made a gesture of resignation. 'Your prejudices were not addressed. Too deeply-rooted, I expect.'

Cat was stung. 'Ed! Your tone of voice!' She snatched her hand away.

'Well, it *was* prejudice, wasn't it? As it is with me. It's nothing but blatant racism, and you ought to be ashamed of yourself! It's me you're talking to, Catherine, *me, Ed.'* He thumped his chest. 'Change means moving on, girl, not slavishly adhering to old attitudes. Like your mother's groups; the Survivors, everyone gravitating towards each other. I almost feel the same way about it as Amit! All that huddling together, never really assimilating; those rituals, and that bloody Klesmer music! Do you really want to be part of all that? For God's sake, the world has moved on! By all means love them and respect them, but more than that would be unhealthy. It's not your story, Catherine. As you said to Ricci, you don't have to be the victim here.'

Cat stared at him in astonishment. 'How do you know I said that to Ricci?'

'He told me. It meant a great deal to him – not just that you'd said it, but the whole concept...'

'*Concept,*' she said in disgust. 'It's not that cerebral, Ed.' She looked out of the window. She felt completely estranged from him. How could she expect him to understand what he'd never suffered? Well, she would tell him!

'You don't have the right to pontificate, Ed. You weren't there...in the ghetto, in the camps...'

'Nor were you!' he shot back. 'That's my whole point. It was your mother, remember?'

'... and you aren't Jewish!'

'You think,' he snapped again, 'that the Jews have the monopoly on suffering?' He ran his hand through his hair. 'Why d'you think I told you about my family? Come *on*, girl! You've got to lay this to rest!'

'...And don't tell me what to *think* all the time!'

His jaw dropped and his eyes blazed. Cat looked away at the river, but the place suddenly seemed foreign to her, alien both her mother's experience and to hers, and she no longer knew why they'd come. Her whole world was falling apart; she was in a bubble of anonymity; she belonged nowhere.

Desperate to root herself again, she said to him, 'The least I can do is be loyal to my mother. At the funeral,' she said slowly, clinging to old truths, 'you spoke about her with affection, as if you'd known her. Now it seems, from the way you're speaking, that you don't like her very much after all. You couldn't be so... dispassionate, so disconnected from her, if you did. That's my fault, if so. I must have given you a false picture of her...'

'No, I don't think you did,' he said dryly. 'I reckon I

437

know what she was like, right enough.'

'She adored me, Ed – and I mean adored.'

'*Did* she?' His tone was sceptical, and she looked at him, astonished.

'What... what are you saying, Ed? That she didn't? How... how can you say that? What do you mean?' She slapped at his arm. 'Tell me what you *mean*!'

'Don't hit me, please. I thought you'd had a bellyful of hitting.'

Outraged, her mouth clamped shut, but he reached out to her. 'Sorry, shouldn't have said that.' He hesitated, as if he dared not speak the words. 'Oh, Catherine,' he said tiredly, 'have you never asked yourself *why* she told you all that stuff when you were so young? It just seems to me such a burden for a young child, much too much of a burden for it to have any right in it at all, whichever way you look at it. It was completely, utterly *wrong*. OK, she was traumatised, but *years* back. OK she was lonely; OK, she had no one else, but none of these is reason enough. And actually,' he said fiercely, 'if you want to know what I think, I think it was downright abusive...'

'*Abusive!*'

'Yes. Controlling, manipulative – take your pick! Not to show love to your only child? That was as traumatic for you as her own experience. There was no telling what effect it might have on you... All that trouble with your husband, with Deborah...' He shook his head in disgust. 'Her *silence*.'

'I might have exaggerated that,' said Cat painfully, striving for truth. 'It was how I remembered it, but... now I don't think her silence was... was as absolute as I thought. I don't feel too badly about that – I was a child when it all started. And everyone's memory gets warped over time, as I've said. Even Amit...'

'Yes, she sure was one hell of a mixed up woman...'

'You think that?' She looked at him in surprise. 'She's got a clearer mind than me! She's formidable!'

'Maybe. But some things didn't stack up. Like, she got very upset that Reuben denied the ghetto, but she wasn't nearly as concerned about the rape. And why let Reuben chuck your mother out of the kibbutz? OK, she was his wife, but she's a woman, with, presumably, a woman's sensitivity, and a very powerful woman to boot. So why didn't she intercede for her? She's got her own mind. So why didn't she use it?'

'Maybe she tried to,' she said bleakly, 'and Reuben overruled her. But there's another thing. Maybe, in his heart, he knew she'd got pregnant from the rape, and the thought of the child was too much for him – he had committed murder, Ed. Maybe he knew she was innocent – he made a great play about Hannah's virtue – but he couldn't live with the guilt. And the effect on her – well, maybe her silence was her way of supporting him.' She shrugged despondently. 'Oh well, this whole discussion is futile.'

'No, it isn't,' he said firmly. 'You've said, yourself, a number of times: "Look what it's done to me." That silence of your mother's was stamped on your memory, otherwise your life wouldn't have turned out the way it did. I'm not saying she wasn't sorely tested, but it was abuse, all right.'

'But at the funeral you said she was a person of integrity!'

Catherine,' he said patiently, 'she *was* a person of integrity. Look how she reacted to the murder. Amit told us she was concerned for Reuben's soul. Not for herself, that she'd just been raped. No, it was hidden, that's all. She'd had colossal problems, moving to a foreign country, struggling to make a home with you on very little money, or, I don't know, maybe a lack of bonding, after all. But when you grew up and started asking awkward questions, or maybe when she got some friends of her own – that's when she became a person of integrity. No, she had you on a string, I'm afraid. At least, early on.

Cat looked at him, stunned. 'I can't believe what I'm hearing.'

But she could. It rang all too true.

She felt, then, as though her mother had truly gone, finally, irrevocably, and that she had never understood her till now. Her love for her had been a constant membrane over her life, and she realised, then, with a great flood of recognition, that she would never slough off the old skin completely, that she would drag it around with her until she died. And even if it could be transfigured by a different truth, a truth without illusion and without prejudice, a more forgiving truth, that moment was not yet. She had tried so hard to search for her mother honourably, without her usual disquiet, but that search had taken on its own momentum, leading her on paths where she'd had no desire to travel and no right to trespass. To hidden, secret places; places of the mind and of the soul. To her own suppressed and enigmatic demons. To questions Rute would never have asked, even in her most troubled moments. It had led her to Ed, and now it had taken her away from him.

It was like the dark days of winter snow, leaden skies and no birdsong, when on the radio they'd say not to venture out 'unless your journey is really necessary.' A banal tune that rang in her head and mocked at her fragility, so that once again she was forced to rehearse the old enigma: had *her* questions been necessary? Had she really to go through all that turmoil just to learn the value of life, or to be taught again about human frailty? Or how it is that new growth emerges like a butterfly from its chrysalis, like green shoots from the darkness of the soil?

She asked herself what she could have done instead, a middle-aged woman afraid to open her Pandora box. To have considered herself old enough and formed enough to relinquish what Rute chose not to share, and been satisfied? But then she'd never have

440

discovered she was a child of rape, or that her father, for whom she'd yearned for so long, had been mad or bad, or both.

Or should she have taken those scattered remnants of her mother's past and imprisoned them in a place that, because of her own fear and suspicion, she would never visit again, like a cobweb full of dead flies too high to reach? Her own, self-betraying final solution?

She got out of the car.

7

'Where are you going? We haven't finished...'

Cat ignored him. She walked away across the mudflats, hugging her arms, immediately chilled by the wind off the sea. Her feet sank slightly, and she thought, my shoes will be a mess, but here the sand was coarse gravel and she didn't sink in, like on the Solway Firth. She stood at the very brink of the water, where it lapped smoothly over the stones, and gazed out over the river. She wished herself elsewhere, anywhere but there... I want Ricci, she thought. Then, absurdly, like a child, she said, 'I want Ed,' and she said it out loud.

Ed had followed her, and now he put her coat over her shoulders and held it there.

'You *have* me, Catherine,' he said softly, 'and I do understand. Oh, not as much as I would if I was Jewish. And I'm sorry if it sounded like I'm pontificating – I've no right. It's been a difficult time for you, and it's been brave, what you've done; most people would have swept things under the carpet. But, you see, I still think of us as belonging together. Can't you just be patient with me? Try to be a bit more... forgiving?'

She turned in his embrace, but looked down at her feet. His words were such a subtle reminder of what she was losing that she almost capitulated. Almost, but not quite; she could see no ultimate truth in them; they went over her head and disappeared into the mist. There had been a chink of light, that was all, and now it was dark again.

'I'm sorry, Ed. Take me home, would you?'

Sliding slightly on the mud she walked past him back to the car and got in, closing the door. For a moment he stood there, and she saw him lift his hand to his forehead. She looked away stonily.

Without a word, he got back into the car and

442

started the engine. They skidded a little, and Cat thought, oh no, not that as well, don't say we're going to be stuck here... but then they were on the concrete road, the mud flicking against the back wheels.

'Catherine,' he murmured. 'I'm not a complicated guy. Can't you set all this aside and see me as I really am? I don't espouse those values that condemned your mother. I love you, Catherine, but I'm not perfect. You know that. I failed Anne, and I failed Marie-Beth. But to fail you as well would break my heart.'

He paused, a groan in his throat. 'I love you, Cat,' he repeated, the strain in his voice almost palpable. 'Oh, so much, so very much. You've got such transparency, it puts me in the shade. But, my *God*,' he said, banging the steering wheel with frustration, 'you're sometimes so damn sure of yourself it makes me tremble! Don't you ever doubt yourself? For God's sake, give it up, Catherine...!'

'I don't know what you mean,' she said mulishly. 'Give what up?'

His temper flared. 'This whole story about your mother! It's become an obsession... a morbid and very selfish obsession! You and I,' he added more gently, 'we've shared so much over these few months. Can't you just trust me, Catherine? The past, it's *done* with! You really want to separate yourself from all that life can offer? From love?'

Cat couldn't answer. She was weary of it all. Enough, already!

The streets were deserted, except for a newspaper boy on his bike, whistling between the houses; on the corner a woman was putting away huge plastic toys, and there was a red and white banner on the gate, Play Group Starts Today. The summer's over, she thought bleakly, autumn term's beginning. The kids won't be out so much on the streets at night. They'll be inside doing homework, getting to bed at a decent time.

'I don't reckon much of ghettos, Catherine,' he said suddenly, 'especially a ghetto of one. Ricci's old; Gus'll move on... What then? More tenants? More stories? Listening, instead of doing? And if you can't see what I'm saying,' he said more heatedly, 'then I'm done pleading. You go your own way, and wallow in guilt if you must...'

'I'm *not* wallowing!'

'...and I wish you joy of it. But one thing I will say,' he added deliberately. 'You can't always run away when things get difficult. Sometime in your life, my love, you're gonna have to stop running. I'm just sorry I won't be around when you do.'

They had reached the slipway, and he stopped the car. There were no lights in the studio and she thought, good, no one's up; I shall be able to get in without being noticed. The idea of Gus's chatter, or even Ricci's ready sympathy, was anathema to her. She just wanted to climb into her bed and hide.

'Look at that,' he said, nodding up at *The Studio*. 'Doesn't it remind you of someplace? I paid it a compliment when I said it was a squat. Spell it out, shall I – your mother's ghetto? '

Cat looked at it, bewildered. No, she thought, he's wrong; this is my home, where I live. My friends are here, aren't they? Here I live out my creative life. Don't I?

She didn't cry. Finally, she had no tears left.

He carried her case up the steps. 'No goodbyes,' he said as he returned. Then, almost before she could take it in, he was back in the car, closing the door; his figure hidden as he reversed and drove back up the slipway.

Cat stared after him, aghast.

Behind her a window opened, and she heard Gus's voice.

'That you, Miss Cat?'

She hardly heard him. The car was reaching the

corner; it slowed, and she saw a puff of smoke from the exhaust as he changed gear. Then he was gone, disappearing round the side of the building as though into a Magritte painting. She could no longer even hear the sound of the engine.

'Cat? Whatcha doin'? Coffee's on. You gonna stand there all day?'

The rising tone of his question merged with the noise of the seagulls, their haunting, plaintive cries caught on the wind like cries of pain, wafting towards her above the more sonorous tone of a factory horn. The light was brighter now, yellowing the clouds, and away in the distance, clear as truth, was the long gleaming bar of the estuary.

If only my mother were here, she thought.

Caterina, what are you doing? Be careful you know what you're doing. This man is a Righteous Gentile among Righteous Gentiles. There is no violence in this man's mouth. This man has loved you, has held you dear, has cherished you and waited for you. What else matters?

The words Ed had uttered, in Coventry. Just to respond, he had said, was enough, and with this memory the sheer injustice of what she was doing gave the brick wall of her prejudice a small but very significant kick. It was as small as a pin-prick of light entering a heavily curtained room; you do not look at what it reveals, you only look at the source of the light, the light itself.

Cat could never explain what she did next. It was utterly illogical; a gut reaction that had no basis in rational thinking. It was as if the miasma which had lain on her mind for hours lifted suddenly, and the dream-like quality of what she was doing receded.

She began to walk up the slipway. She began to run up the slipway. Ed, wait. She didn't shout it; she thought it. Ed, wait... She knew everything was finished, that he'd finally gone, that she would never see him again, but Ed, wait. There was a constriction in her chest; her belly felt heavy as though she was about to give birth, her legs leaden. She reached the top of the slipway. Perhaps she would see his car as it went up the road, just one last glimpse.

She turned the corner. He was sitting in the car with the window down, his hands fixed to the steering wheel. He looked grim-faced and not remotely triumphant. He looked white, exhausted.

She came to a halt, looking at him uncertainly.

'I had a couple of bad moments there,' he growled. 'For some reason or other I couldn't just drive away. I think... I think I might be ill.'

She reached into the car and laid her hand over his wrist. 'I'm sorry,' she said, her grief and remorse so palpable on her face that he could have reached out and touched it. 'I'm not a good person, Ed. I've treated you very badly. How can I apologise? I'm not a good friend.'

His eyes were filled with pain. 'I... I just don't understand, Catherine. How can you do this to me, after all I've told you about Anne? Oh, God,' he groaned, his voice hoarse in his throat, '*how* am I going to spend the rest of my life?'

Her mouth opened and closed again, as if she was struggling to speak.

'With me?' she said hoarsely. 'Can you even consider it, after all I've said? If you'll still have me, that is.'

'Oh, get back in the car, will you,' he said wearily, 'and I'll drive us home.'

She glanced back at *The Studio*. 'Gus saw me. I'd better...'

'Oh, *bugger* Gus!'

epilogue

There are victories of the soul and spirit.
 Even if you lose, you win.

Elie Wiesel

The most significant conversation that she was ever to
have with Ricci took place just before she finally shut
up shop and moved in with Ed. They were sitting in
The Studio window, sipping coffee and watching a
dredger work its way upstream, seagulls mobbing it.

'Will you stay on, when I've gone?' she asked him.

He glanced at her. 'Actually, I thought no,' he said.
'Not just because you're going. Thanks to you I've got
some money saved, so I'll move back to the shop. I'll
go when Gus goes.'

'Gus is going? I didn't know.'

'Wants to shack up with Julia someplace.' He looked
at her, amused. 'He's not your problem, Cat. No need
to take on the troubles of the world, you know.'

She'd told Ricci everything; her own story, her
mother's history, Ed and Anne's story, everything
except that her mother was raped and that Reuben had
committed murder, and now she felt in her pocket for
the letter which had come that morning.

'Talking of which, this came from Amit. My uncle is
dead, Ricci. He committed suicide. Took a book and a
bottle of wine and went to sleep in his truck. He... he
suffocated, Ricci. Like his mother did, in the cattle
truck. Such a lonely death...'

'Yes. *Sans* hope, *sans* faith, *sans* family.

'He had Amit.'

'Maybe he couldn't see her anymore. Had they no
children?'

'I don't know. They'd be my cousins, wouldn't they, if they'd had any? She never mentioned them and I didn't take the trouble to find out.'

'No, well, don't blame yourself. But he was traumatised too, remember – the ghetto, and having to leave Germany like that. Maybe he'd been thinking of it for years.'

'Yes, that and other things.'

So, she thought, shall I sit *shiva*? No, she'd wept enough, thinking of the dead. But maybe that's what they were doing now, she and Ricci, sitting together and talking of the one who'd died, and mourning.

She looked up to find that Ricci was watching her.

'You know, Cat,' he said slowly, 'you ought to write down what happened to you – I mean to your mother. Might be cathartic, even.'

She was startled. 'But, Ricci, I'm a painter not a writer. And I've no evidence to show she's even lived.'

An inadequate, facile argument, born of panic and revulsion, cloaking her habitual anxiety about what she had inherited. Of genes, of character, of behaviour. A burden round her neck. But then she recalled her mother's sibilant, almost pleading, whisper... *Ask, Caterina, how a once broken body might be remembered...* and she thought of her passion, her frustration, her anger, her inarticulate scrabbling around in the dark for answers.

'Why would I want to do this?' she muttered.

'For two very important reasons, Cat. One, you're a natural healer. Your art heals and how you approach it heals; it's *healing* art. And the reason it heals is because you listen to people, and listening heals. It's costly for you, but you do it. Look at me – where would I be without you? Or Ed, for that matter? Or even your mother – no, especially your mother. The only reason we all came through was because you listened, willingly or otherwise. Yes, you're a healer, Cat. You're all the evidence you'll ever need that your mother lived.'

She was speechless with delight.

'My second reason: to bear witness, and to pass that witness on to your children. Especially your Deborah, so that she can come to know the ground of her being.'

Not so that Deborah could learn of her roots, but that she could come to know the ground of her being. She marvelled at his acumen.

So she would do it, and when it was finished she would give it to Deborah, its bare bones and its redemption, together with her mother's necklace, that lovely string of gold and silver bars which she wore close to her skin, as had Rute through ghetto and exile. But the turmoil and the agony and the sweet joy of that summer she would keep to herself. Her seventh veil.

Later they went out for a last walk together. On their return she looked up at *The Studio* as if seeing it for the last time. If she tried, she could imagine movement within its dim interior, though she couldn't make out whether it was Gus, wrestling with his clay, or Ricci, dreaming over his ancient books, or Cat, intent on her painting.

She thought: I am here, there, or elsewhere, and it's hardly relevant anymore. It's where I'm going that matters.

It struck her then how very similar were people's lives; everyone knew joy and laughter, tears and mourning, struggle and contemplation, memory and mystery. And mystery was not necessarily the shadow side, simply because it was unknown and unexplored. It had been too easy to be fearful of things she hadn't tried to understand.

As they stood there, watching the water, Ricci told her about his last dream.

'I'm on the path as usual... Oh, Cat,' he sighed, 'I

was so utterly sick and tired of it! So, anyway...
Suddenly, in the dream, I say, all right, that's enough,
and I turn and face the Jap who's threatening me. I
say piss off! Get lost! And this time he doesn't mock at
me, Cat, or beat me. Somehow he just fades away,
into the past – or into the future, I've no idea.'

He faced her, his eyes wide with disgust. '*Ych a fi* –
his *future*! What could it possibly have been? That's the
first time that question has struck me! You can't,
somehow, imagine them living beautiful lives, can you?
Pretending nothing ever happened, that it wouldn't
leave its mark on them.'

He looked away across the river, his eyes remote.

'Anyway, in the dream I'm alone on the path – and I
don't wake, Cat, even though I'm saying, 'I don't need
to be here.' I'm just standing there, looking out over
the paddy fields. The paddy fields never figured in my
dreams before. And coming towards me is a woman.'
He gestured over the river, as though she was walking
towards him on the water. 'She's Japanese, she's
dressed in white and she's carrying a bunch of red
poppies. Now, isn't that something? Since then I
haven't had any more nightmares. Not a single one. I
sleep like a baby. So what do you make of that?'

Cat did not want to interpret for him. She could not
pontificate who had not suffered.

He urged her, however, and by and by she grasped
the meaning of the dream and was awed. Maybe
there's a God after all, she thought, who speaks to us
as he spoke of old, in the language of poetry and
dreams. Even absence has presence, after all.

It seemed significant that it was a Japanese woman
who made the offering of red poppies and that she was
dressed in white. For although white, in Japanese
tradition, represented death, in Western culture it
meant absolute purity and innocence. Ricci was a man
of integrity and his innocence mattered to him.

When she tentatively shared with him her

interpretation of his dream, he looked at her in wonder. Then he threw back his head, an old man relieved of nightmares, his eyes alight; his face open and smooth, all lines washed away by joy.

'And poppies?' he asked.

'Well, I think poppies say you are allowed to remember, that it's not necessary, utterly, to forget. But once a year, only, Ricci, to make the walk to the memorial, and then get on with life, with choosing life. And, as the Jews say, with *tikkun olem*; repairing the broken world.'

Bibliography

Quotations within the text in alphabetical order:

James Bradley: *Towards the Setting Sun* 1982

TS Eliot: *East Coker* 1940 and *Little Gidding* 1942

Eric Lomax: *The Railway Man* 1995

Dylan Thomas: *Do not go gentle into that good night* 1951

RS Thomas: *Bright Field* and *The Kingdom* Collected Poems 1945-1990

Thomas Trahearne (1636-1674): *The Mystical Poetry of Thomas Trahearne* & *Third Century Meditations.*

William Wordsworth: *Lines Composed above Tintern Abbey* 1798

Chapter headings

T S Eliot: *Four Quartets* 1939 *Little Gidding* 1942

Elie Wiesel: *Night* 1960

Acknowledgements

Thanks are due to my friend, the late Eric Lomax, who gave permission for part of his story to be used in this novel, and to his loving wife, Patti.

Night Fires

A love story of mixed race and religion, featured at the
2010 Warwick Festival of Literature and Spoken Word
Raider Publishing International 2009
ISBN-10: 1935383965 / ISBN-13: 978-1935383963

What readers say about Night Fires

A gripping tale that vividly captures the sights, sounds
and smells of the African bush and the religious conflict
between Christians and Muslims.
Honest, brave and well-researched...

If you are expecting a simple love story then don't read
this book, but if you want to be challenged and delighted
then *do read this book!*

Not the usual black/white relationship of poverty and
dependence but an absorbing contemporary story of
tragedy and hope in modern Nigeria. Woven though the
narrative is a spiritual thread so delicate it does not
strangle the reader, but speaks of compassion for the
turmoil of life.

Restricted print, available from the author
k_priddis@hotmail.com

Angels in a Terracotta Landscape
Short stories of Nigeria and the Middle East
ASIN: B002840NKI

Fragments of War, Hope & Peace
Paintings & Poetry dedicated to Victims of War 1995.
Kathy Priddis & Margot Arthurton
ASIN: B001I5U4OI

The Hidden Passion
The last events of the life of Christ (full colour & text)
1989